STRAIGHT SILVER

The Ghosts rushed the step, joining Mkvenner and firing down into the smoke-thickened reaches of no-man's-land at the assault party that was trying to get in.

'Gak! There's too many of them!' Ponore yelled.

'Aim. Fire. Repeat,' Mkvenner urged.

Corbec looked up at the backs of his boys on the step and struggled to rise out of the warm layers of bodies. He got his left hand on a timber support and–

He froze. The grenade spoon tumbled from his clawing hand.

He'd dropped the fething bomb.

He looked down, looked down into twisted limbs and staring faces and spools of steaming guts. It was down there somewhere.

If he cried out a warning, he knew his squad would break and the assaulters would be all over them. If he didn't, he and most likely two or three of his team would be killed.

A WARHAMMER 40,000 NOVEL

Gaunt's Ghosts

STRAIGHT SILVER

Dan Abnett

For John Bergin and Gareth Branwyn
(for playing while I hammered)

A BLACK LIBRARY PUBLICATION

First published in Great Britain in 2002

This edition published in 2003 by
BL Publishing,
Games Workshop Ltd.,
Willow Road, Nottingham,
NG7 2WS, UK

10 9 8 7 6 5 4 3 2 1

Cover illustration by Adrian Smith
Map by Ralph Horsley

A CIP record for this book is available from the British Library

ISBN 1 84416 082 3

Distributed in the US by Simon & Schuster
1230 Avenue of the Americas, New York, NY 10020

Printed and bound in Great Britain by
Cox & Wyman Ltd, Reading, Berkshire, UK

See the Black Library on the Internet at
www.blacklibrary.com

Find out more about Games Workshop
and the world of Warhammer 40,000 at
www.games-workshop.com

It is the 41st millennium. For more than a hundred centuries the Emperor has sat immobile on the Golden Throne of Earth. He is the master of mankind by the will of the gods, and master of a million worlds by the might of his inexhaustible armies. He is a rotting carcass writhing invisibly with power from the Dark Age of Technology. He is the Carrion Lord of the Imperium for whom a thousand souls are sacrificed every day, so that he may never truly die.

Yet even in his deathless state, the Emperor continues his eternal vigilance. Mighty battlefleets cross the daemon-infested miasma of the warp, the only route between distant stars, their way lit by the Astronomican, the psychic manifestation of the Emperor's will. Vast armies give battle in his name on uncounted worlds. Greatest amongst his soldiers are the Adeptus Astartes, the Space Marines, bio-engineered super-warriors. Their comrades in arms are legion: the Imperial Guard and countless planetary defence forces, the ever-vigilant Inquisition and the tech-priests of the Adeptus Mechanicus to name only a few. But for all their multitudes, they are barely enough to hold off the ever-present threat from aliens, heretics, mutants – and worse.

To be a man in such times is to be one amongst untold billions. It is to live in the cruellest and most bloody regime imaginable. These are the tales of those times. Forget the power of technology and science, for so much has been forgotten, never to be re-learned. Forget the promise of progress and understanding, for in the grim dark future there is only war. There is no peace amongst the stars, only an eternity of carnage and slaughter, and the laughter of thirsting gods.

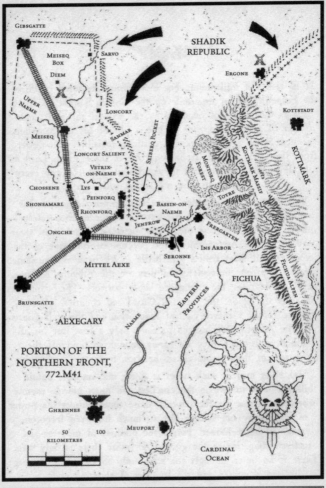

GIBSGATTE

MEISEQ
BOX

DIEM

SARVO

SHADIK
REPUBLIC

ERGONE

UPPER
NAEME

LONCORT

KOTTSTADT

MEISEQ

SANMAR

LONCORT SALIENT

VETRIX-
ON-NAEME

LYS

CHOSSENE

PEINFORQ

SHONSAMARL

RHONFORQ

ONGCHE

JENFROW

BASSIN-ON-
NAEME

INS ARBOR

SERONNE

MITTEL AEXE

FICHUA

BRUNSGATTE

AEXEGARY

NAEME

EASTERN
PROVINCES

MOTTOQ
FOREST

KOTTMARK MASSIF

TOYRE

FRERGARTEN

KOTTMARK

FICHUA ALPEN

PORTION OF THE
NORTHERN FRONT,
772.M41

N

GHRENNES

0   50   100
KILOMETRES

MEUPORT

CARDINAL
OCEAN

KEY   ✕ SITE OF NOTED
                  CONFLICT

🦅   ■   ⬛

CATHEDRAL CITY   VILLAGE   TOWN

✚✚✚✚   PEINFORQ
            LINE

✚✚✚✚   OSTLUND
            SHIELD LINE

------ EDGE OF
          MEISEQ BOX

//////// FRONT LINE

╫╫╫╫ RAILWAY LINE

-■-·-✱- SERONNE LINE

THROUGHOUT THE first six months of 772.M41, the seventeenth year of the Sabbat Worlds Campaign, the Imperial Crusade force under Warmaster Macaroth struggled to consolidate the wins it had achieved during the previous winter and turn them to its best advantage. Supremacy in the vital Cabal system now seemed possible, thanks to the lines of resource and supply – the so-called "victory veins" – opened up by the successful actions at Gigar, Aondrift Nova, Tanzina IV, Phantine and the mighty forge world Urdesh. But the infamous fortress world of Morlond still held out, and reports suggested that Urlock Gaur – who had, it seemed, become overlord of the arch-enemy forces since the death of Archon Nadzybar at Balhaut – was massing a renewed counter-attack in the Carcaradon Cluster. Furthermore, the Imperial Crusade was contesting hard along its coreward flank with Chaos hosts commanded by Anakwanar Sek, Shebol Red-hand and Enok Innokenti, three of Gaur's most capable warlords.

'With typically instinctive flair, and against all the advice of his staff chiefs, Macaroth divided the Crusade force between his most trusted generals. Crusade Ninth Army, under Lord Militant Humel, was sent to Enothis to break the grip of Sek's vile host. The Eighth and Sixth Armies, commanded by General Kelso and Chapter Master Veegum of the Silver Guard, was directed to the Khan Group to prosecute Innokenti, while the Seventh, under Marshal Blackwood, struck out deep to coreward, towards Belshiir Binary and Alpha Madrigo. Lord General Bulledin, in command of the Second, was charged with holding and protecting the spinward supply lines through to Urdesh. Macaroth himself pressed on with the First, Third and Fourth to lead the renewed push for Morlond and, as the Warmaster put it, "grapple with Gaur in his own backyard".

'Many voices were raised in objection. The Navy commanders in particular believed that Macaroth had only survived his gamble at Cabal by the thinnest of luck, and now saw him repeating the risk on an even greater scale. Other generals expressed unhappiness at being passed over for army command. Van Voytz had hoped to get charge of the Fifth Army, but that was given to Luscheim and tasked with rearguarding Macaroth's push. Instead, Van Voytz was given a brigade-strength taskforce, nominally attached to the Fifth, and sent to Aexe Cardinal, an Imperial world that had held out throughout the Chaos domination of the Sabbat Worlds. There, he faced the unenviable labour of breaking a deadlocked land war that had been raging for forty years...'

— from *A History of the Later Imperial Crusades*

PROLOGUE

'There are three things an Aexegarian may be trusted to do well: make love, make war, and worship the Emperor. Of these, warmaking is our finest skill. We have been doing it for years. I think you'll find we have the hang of it.'

– Leonid Fep Krefuel, High Sezar of Aexegary

BRUNSGATTE TOWERED AROUND him like a badly-ordered dream. He was weary from the long train journey and, as he had moved westward, the weather had become increasingly poor and wet, so now the pin in his femur ached rheumatically. He had tried to distract himself by reviewing the despatches once again, but it was too dark in the back of the limousine. Instead, he sat back, hands clasped across his belly, and watched the city as it passed.

Dusk was closing, and the lamps along the strasseways were beginning to glow amber under their frosted-glass hoods. In twenty minutes, they would be little stars of pearl-white light. The rain was coming down. To the south, it made dark, blurry sheets under the clouds that frothed above the commercial district and the Brunsgatte docks.

9

The limousine, shiny black like a dress uniform shoe, was an old Ampara Furioso Vitesse, as solidly built as a Leman Russ. On either side of the silver leaping-behj ornament above the car's snarling chrome grille, a pennant fluttered. The blue and gold state flag to the left; the gold, white and magenta colours of the Aexe Alliance to the right. He could barely hear the eight litre engine, such was the thickness of the bodywork and the upholstery, but the stroking wind-shield wipers squealed every ten seconds like fingernails down a blackboard.

The car crossed Congressplatz, passed under the shadow of Sezar's Gate, where slopes of red wreaths were piled up, and ran the length of the Colonnade of Fishers to Trimercy.

Squeak, squeak, squeak, stroked the wipers.

They stopped at the lights at Trimercy, and the southerly flow of traffic passed before them. The outriders each put a boot down to steady their bikes. The limousine's climate control seemed to be circulating nothing but warm exhaust fumes. He leaned forward and fiddled with the dial, to no appreciable effect.

'What's wrong with the heater?' he snapped.

The driver lowered the lacquered communicating screen.

'What did you say, sire?'

'The heater.'

'It's on, sire.'

'Could it be off?'

'Of course, sire.' The driver made an adjustment to the dashboard controls. 'Better?'

It wasn't. He thumbed down the reardoor window and let in the cool rain-scents of the city. He could smell damp tarmac and wet rockcrete. He could hear motor engines and distant horns. At the roadside, by the junction, he could see a flower stand closing up for the night. The seller, swathed in a transparent slicker, was hand-folding the fractal blooms into their metal cups. The glittering mathematical petals crackled as deft, expert hands collapsed them.

Some were a particular red. He felt his pulse rate rise. Not now… not now…

He closed his eyes and swallowed hard, trying to retard his breathing the way his physician had taught him. But the

Seiberq Pocket was only a heartbeat away. The lightning. The spraying mud. The dreadnoughts. The pools filling the shell craters. Red, red...

The lights changed and they pulled north, the outriders describing wide arcs as they roared away ahead, lamps flashing.

'Are you all right, sire?' the driver asked.

'Yes, I'm fine. Fine.' He closed the reardoor window to a thin slit.

Mons Sezari rose before them, dominating the skyline, dwarfing even the tallest of Brunsgatte's steeples and towers. They climbed the curling road and then pulled in under a glass awning behind the postern gate.

'Ready, sire?' asked the driver.

'Yes,' he said, and got out. A junior military aide held the limousine door for him.

In the days of the great sezars, generals had entered Brunsgatte from the Fortress Gate, carried in pomp on jewelled warcarts pulled by striding struthids.

Those times were long gone, but protocol demanded that he transferred from the car to a warcart for the final, formal approach.

A squadron of hussars had the warcart waiting. The struthids, some of the last of that dwindling species, were huge, proud beasts with massive, polished beaks and thick plumage, standing twenty hands high. He thought of the scabby, thin mounts the front-line cavalry were forced to make do with.

He stepped up onto the warcart's backplate, his attaché case tucked under his arm, and the hussar chief lashed the struthids forward. Their trimmed black claws drew sparks from the wet cobbles as they began to canter.

The fighting birds drew the warcart in under the entry arch of Mons Sezari and drew up at the west porch of the palace, a long aisle of electric lamps under a stained glass roof. Officers of the Bande Sezari were waiting in full dress uniform, struthid plumes in their shakos. They wore voluminous pantaloons of green silk, with gold chains linking the wide hips to their wrists, so that when they saluted, they seemed to spread wide green wings in his honour.

He dismounted, paid the driver his ritual scuto, and walked up the long blue carpet into the porch. The attaché case swung in his hand.

Sire Kido Fep Soten, the high sezar's chamberlain, was waiting for him under the glass portico. Soten parted the black velvet of his ermine-trimmed robes and made the aquila salute across his chest.

'My sire count, welcome. The sezar awaits you.'

He followed Soten down a long hallway decorated with heraldic motif wallpaper, through a chamber strung with stupendous chandeliers, and into the audience room. Halberdiers of the Bande Sezari opened the doors for them.

Soten bowed. 'My lord high sezar,' he proclaimed, 'Count Iaco Bousar Fep Golke, commander-in-chief of the Aexe Alliance forces, awaits your pleasure.'

The high sezar, Leonid Fep Krefuel, rose from his couch. He had been sitting near the fireplace, shielded from its direct heat by a fretwork screen. Through open doors on the far side of the room, the count could see a gathering of figures and hear the clink of glasses.

The sezar was clad in ceremonial gold battledress brocaded with silver wire and diamonds under a behj-skin mantle. He was a short, heavy-set man with a ruddy, colicky face, a wet, ample mouth and a thin, grey moustache.

'Count Golke, a pleasure as always,' he said.

'My high sezar, you do me an honour.'

'Welcome, welcome… take refreshment.'

A black metal-enhanced servitor whined up alongside them, carrying a tray of drinks. Golke took a small amasec and sipped it. He owned several estates, including a schloss in the eastern provinces, but still the sheer scale of the Mons Sezari architecture scared him. The ceilings were so high, the windows so sheer. Blue and gold silk banners, thirty metres long, hung down the walls, each one sporting the leaping-behj arms of Aexegary. Every month for four years he had come to the palace to deliver his war report, and still it humbled him.

'I could wait, lord, if you are with guests,' Golke said, gesturing to the figures in the adjacent room.

'No, no. We will join them directly. There are men I want you to meet.'

Golke wanted to ask who the men were, but he could tell the High Sezar of Aexegary was in one of his businesslike moods. He'd been the same when they'd met the week before the push on Jepel and Seiberq. He's preparing to give me instructions he knows I won't like, Golke thought. God help us, not another Seiberq.

Golke set down his drink. 'My report, lord?'

The sezar nodded. 'Let's have it,' he said, settling back onto his place on the couch.

Golke's fingers were shaking as he unbuckled the attaché case and slid the duplicate copies of the report out. Both were sleeved in blue covers and closed with gold ribbons. He passed one to his master, who took it and slit the ribbon with the behj-claw he wore on a signet ring.

Golke opened his own copy, stood before the high sezar and started to read.

'An account of the warfare between the forces of his glorious majesty the High Sezar of Aexegary and his allies, and the denounced oppressors of Shadik, in the period 181.772 and 212.772. Foremost, it must be seen that the concentration of artillery attacks along the Peinforq Line, and also in the Naeme Valley, has much harassed the progress of the enemy's infantry dispositions in that region. Observer estimates place a mortality figure of nine thousand on said enemy dispositions, with particular losses taken around Bassin-on-Naeme on the nights of 187-189. Munition expenditure in that period is given as forty-eight thousand nine hundred and eleven 0.12 medium explosive shells, nine thousand and forty-six 0.90 incendiary shells, two thousand three hundred and seventy-nine 0.50 heavy shells and–'

'Has the expenditure been costed?' asked the sezar.

'My lord, yes,' said Golke, skipping through the pages of his report. 'It is annotated in the fiscal appendix. Ahm... rounding up, two point two million scutos.'

'You say "harassed" the progress, count. Does that mean impeded? Halted? Denied?'

Golke cleared his throat. 'They suffered losses, as I said, and their advance was stalemated, though they retook the towns of Vilaq and Contae-Sanlur.'

'Move on.'

'My lord. Along the edge of the Meiseq Sector, I am pleased to report our line has held fast despite sequential attacks. On the afternoon of the 197th, a breakthrough was achieved by the Forty-First Brigade at Sarvo, and they managed to advance to hold the water mills at Selph.'

'How far is that?'

'Three… ah… three hundred and ten metres, lord.'

'Move on.'

'The north-western sector. At Gibsgatte, the Third Regiment of the Sezari Light held off a counter-push on the 199th. The regimental commander personally notes his gratitude to the high sezar for his foresight in disposing them to Gibsgatte so that they might achieve such glory.'

'Losses?'

'Twelve hundred and eighty-one, lord.'

The high sezar closed his copy of the report and put it down on the seat beside him.

'Should I continue, sire?' Golke asked.

'Will I hear anything new?' the high sezar asked. 'Will I hear anything apart from what is effectively a stalemate no matter how you dress it up? Will I hear anything apart from deadlock at the cost of thousands of men and millions of scutos?'

Golke lowered his report to his side. A loose page fell out and fluttered down onto the carpet.

'No, my lord.'

The sezar rose again. 'Forty years, count. Forty years of this. Forty years of waste and cost and stagnation. There are boy soldiers on the front these days whose grandfathers died in the first phases, when we stood against Shadik alone. Our allies are with us now, thank the Golden Throne, but…'

He looked into the fire for a moment. Golke thought how heavy the behj-skin mantle looked on his shoulders.

'Do you know what Soten told me the other morning?' the sezar asked quietly.

'No, sire.'

'He told me that since the Principality of Fichua added its strength to the Alliance back in… what was it? 764?'

'763, sire, with the Stromberg Pact.'

'Just so. Since 763, our Alliance armies have lost the equivalent of the entire population of Fichua nine times over.'

It was a stunning statistic. Golke blinked. He knew Fichua well, from vacations there in long-past days. The smallest country in Continental Aexe, to be sure, but still…

He felt his pulse rising again. Anger rose up in him like quicksilver in a thermometer that has been stuck in a furnace. He wanted to scream at the lord sezar.

It's because of you! You! You! You, and the staff chiefs who have gone before me, with your rules of war and your codes of battle! Damn you and your archaic strategies–

Instead, he bit his tongue and breathed deeply, the way his physician had taught him.

'The impasse is maddening, my lord,' he said. His voice sounded tiny and strained. 'But perhaps by the year's end, we might–'

The sezar turned to face him. 'Count Golke, please. I'm not blaming you for those forty years. I praise your efforts, the sterling work you have undertaken since you took over as commander-in-chief. I am not a stupid man, no matter what the popular press says–'

'Of course not, my lord!'

The sezar raised a hand. Firelight winked off the behj-claw ring. 'Let them blow off steam, I say. Let them rail in their editorials and goad me with their cartoons. I am beloved of the Aexegarian people.'

'You are high sezar, my lord.'

'And I will achieve my triumph, I have no doubt. I will break Shadik and drive its hosts out into the wilds.'

'I have no doubt, lord.'

'Neither have I. I never have doubted that, count. But as from tonight, I am assured of it.'

Golke glanced over at the room beyond where the visitors were talking and sipping drinks under the chandeliers.

'Why… tonight, my lord?'

'This day, Count Golke. It will be remembered in our history books. Our great-great-grandchildren will celebrate it.'

The sezar moved over to Golke and took him gently by the arm. 'It has not yet been publicly announced, count, nor will it be for some time. But you must be told. Five nights ago, Imperial starships arrived in orbit. The first of a liberation fleet.'

Golke swallowed and considered the words one by one. He felt a little giddy. The pin in his hip suddenly ached like a bastard.

'Imperial…?'

'The crusade has reached us, my dear friend. After all these years of fighting alone against Chaos in the dark. Warmaster Macaroth, praise be his name, has cut a swathe through the arch-enemy, putting them to flight. The Sabbat Worlds are his now, his for the taking. And, as is only right, he saw it as his first priority to despatch elite forces to relieve Aexe Cardinal. The first contingents are deploying as we speak. From next week, the war against Shadik will be bolstered by the Emperor's Imperial Guard. Our long struggle has not been in vain.'

'I am… overwhelmed, my lord.'

The sezar grinned. 'Take up your drink, Golke, and toast this redemption with me.'

Golke found his glass, and the sezar clinked his own against it.

'To victory, long pursued, rightfully ours.'

They threw their empty glasses into the grate.

'I have something for you, count,' said the sezar. 'Two things, actually.' He reached into his robes and produced a slim, oblong box covered in gold-flecked blue satin. The sezar opened it.

A Gold Aquila, pinned to a white silk ribbon, lay in the cushioned interior.

'My lord!'

'This is to acknowledge your devoted service to me, to the Alliance and to Aexegary. The Order of the Eagle. The greatest honour it is in my gift to bestow.'

The high sezar took the medal from the box and carefully fixed it to Golke's breast.

'You have done your country great service, Iaco Bousar Fep Golke, and you have acquitted yourself, in my name, with devotion, ability, obedience and humility. You have personally known the physical cost of war. I salute you.'

'High lord of all, it has been my duty and my duty only.'

The sezar clapped him gently on the arm. 'You've earned this, Golke. This – and my other gift.'

'Sir?'

'As of midnight tonight, you are honourably relieved of supreme command. Your toil is done.'

'Relieved of command...? My lord, why? Have I displeased you?'

The sezar laughed, loudly. It was forced, Golke could sense.

'Not one bit. But with the arrival of the Imperials, I am forced to make changes in the command structure. Radical changes. You understand, don't you, count? It's all tediously political.'

'My lord?'

'The Imperial general... Vonvoyze, I think he's called... he'll want authority, and space to cohere his forces. He and his senior staff need a liaison, someone who can help to acclimatize them and clasp them into our war effort efficiently. I trust you, Golke. I want you in that role.'

'Liaison?'

'Just so. Linking our forces with those of our liberators. You have the tact, I think. The objectivity. You are an educated man. And you deserve a rewarding job after the trials of supreme command.'

'I... I consider myself fortunate, my lord. So... who will take my place?'

'As commander-in-chief? I'm giving that to Lyntor-Sewq. He's all fired up and very much the coming man. He'll put a fire under our armies with that enthusiasm of his.'

Golke nodded, though it was just a mechanical gesture. 'This Imperial general... he will answer to Lyntor-Sewq?'

'Of course he will!' the sezar snorted. 'The Imperial Guard may have arrived at last to dig us out, but this is still *our* war. Aexegary will retain supreme command. Come...'

The high sezar put his hand on Count Golke's arm and steered him towards the cocktail party in the adjacent room.

'Come and meet these Imperial saviours we've been sent. Let them get the measure of you. You can congratulate Lyntor-Sewq while you're at it.'

'I can't wait, my lord.'

ONE
UP THE LINE TO THE NAEME

'It's all a matter of ratios.'

– Savil Fep Lyntor-Sewq, Supreme Commander,
Aexe Alliance Forces, on reviewing casualty lists

THE HULKING LIFT-CARRIERS had dispersed them onto lush green paddocks near a place they had been told was called Brunsgatte. They could see the city skyline in the distance, through leafy woodland and the low-rise roofs of outer boroughs. Some time that morning it had rained, but now the day was warm and clear and felt like spring.

Everything had come off in the paddocks: infantry, heavy support, munitions, supplies, even the disorderly, unofficial ranks of camp followers. Processions of big, dirty-sided trucks had begun to lurch onto the grass to gather them all up and transport them to the railhead. Two kilometres away, over the woodland, the drop-ships of the Krassian Sixth were visible in the air, gliding down onto their own assembly points.

Trooper Caffran of the Tanith First-and-Only wandered slowly away from the landing zone, where the grass was bent over by jetwash, and stood by a hedge, overlooking the belt of woods. He sort of liked this place already. There were trees. There was greenery.

Caffran, first name Dermon, was twenty-four standard years old. He was short but well-made, with a blue dragon tattooed on his temple. He had been born and bred on Tanith, a forest world that no longer existed. Caffran was an Imperial Guardsman – a highly effective one, according to his formal record.

He wore the standard issue kit of a Tanith soldier: cross-laced black boots, black fatigue trousers and blouse over standard issue vest and shorts, with webbing – which supported his field pouches and a plump musette bag – and lightweight, matt-grey cloth armour. A tight, black buckle-under helmet made of ceramite swung from his waist belt beside his warknife. On his collars he wore the skull and dagger crest of the Tanith First and around his shoulders was draped a camo cloak, the signature item of the Tanith regiment, the so-called 'Ghosts'.

A heavy pack was slung from his back. His standard pattern Mark III lasrifle, its stock and furniture made of nalwood, as were all Tanith-stamped lasguns, hung on a fylon sling over his shoulder.

Caffran could smell rain and beech-mast on the air, the wet odours of a woodland floor. Just for a second, the smell was unbearably evocative. His heart struggled to accommodate the feelings.

He glanced back to see if he was missed, but there already seemed some delay in loading the regiment onto the trucks. Engines idled and grumbled, and an occasional wheel spun in the muddy grass that the convoy was quickly chewing up. Local military had pegged out assembly points on the paddock with metal tent stakes and twine, but seeing the wait, few of the Tanith had stayed in their sections. Some sat on the grass. A few dropped their packs and started kicking a ball around. Stewards in long, tan greatcoats hurried about, shouting instructions, directing trucks and trying to gather guardsmen together as if they were escaped poultry.

At the end of the hedge, Caffran found a brick-paved path that ran away under an avenue of grey-barked trees. These paddocks were clearly a municipal park, he realised, turned into a makeshift landing zone.

There were benches facing the path, and he sat down on one in damp shade of the avenue trees. It was nice, he thought. Sure, the trees had none of the grandeur of Tanith trees, but still.

He wondered how Tona was doing. She was his girl, though she was a fellow trooper too. Tona had come in on a different carrier because they were in different squads now. Sergeant Criid. It still made him chuckle. Another first for the First-and-Only.

Between every other tree in the avenue, there was a large, smooth cube of white stone. Each had a faded oblong patch on the side facing the path. Caffran wondered what they were. Markers of some sort, maybe.

He heard someone coming up behind him and turned. It was Commissar Hark, the regiment's political officer. Caffran grabbed up his pack hurriedly and stood, but Hark waved him down with a relaxed hand. Sometimes Hark could be a bastard disciplinarian, but only when it mattered, and it clearly didn't matter now. He gave the bench a quick brush with his gloved hand and sat down next to Caffran, curtseying the tails of his stormcoat over his thighs so he could cross his legs.

'Some kind of general balls-up,' he said, indicating the dispersal area behind them with a sideways nod. 'I don't know. There's about twenty trucks packed with our people just sitting there, trying to leave the park. No wonder the war here's been going on for forty years. They can't even organise their way out of a field.'

Caffran smiled.

'Still,' said Hark, 'a chance to take the air. You had the right idea.'

'Thought I was about to get a reprimand,' said Caffran.

Hark glanced over at him and raised his eyebrows in a 'you never know' expression. Viktor Hark was a sturdy man, strong but fleshy from years of good living. His eyes were slightly hooded and his clean shaven cheeks slabby. He took off his commissariate cap and fiddled with the lining, revealing thick, cropped black hair on a skull that rose like the round tip of bullet from his broad neck.

'They've been at it forty years, sir?' Caffran asked.

'Oh, yes,' said Hark, gazing out through the trees at the rise and fall of lift-carriers at another dispersal field in the middle distance. 'Forty fething years. What do you think of that?'

'I'm afraid I don't know much about it at all, sir. I know this planet is called Aexe Cardinal, and that city over there is called Brunsgatte. Apart from that…'

'There'll be briefings, Caffran, don't worry. You're a guest of a nation called Aexegary, the chief amongst seven nation states that are at war with the Republic of Shadik. The brigade is here to bolster their forces and show Shadik how war really works.'

Caffran nodded. He didn't really care much, but it wasn't often he got to have a conversation with Hark.

'We're fighting a nation, then, sir?'

'No, we're fighting the same arch-enemy as ever. Chaos got its filthy claws into Shadik some time back, trying to use it as a foothold to conquer the entire planet.'

'I guess it's pretty impressive they've held them off so long,' Caffran ventured.

Hark shrugged. They were silent for a moment, then Hark said, 'How do you think that girl of yours will do?'

'Criid? I think she'll do fine, sir.'

'Bit of a gamble, giving a woman squad command, but Gaunt agrees it's worth it. Besides, we needed a Verghast to take the reins of Kolea's unit. You think she can take the pressure?'

'Easily. It's everyone else I'd worry about. Keeping up with her.'

Hark sniggered and put his cap back on. 'My appraisal precisely. Still, it's going to be interesting. Three new sergeants to test in the field.'

Criid wasn't the only trooper to have been promoted into dead men's boots after the tour on Phantine. A Verghast called Arcuda had been given charge of Indrimmo's platoon, and Raglon had been posted to lead Adare's. Best luck to all three, Caffran felt. Indrimmo had died at Cirenholm, and Adare had been killed during the penetration raid at Ouranberg. Kolea, one of the best loved Verghast troopers, wasn't dead, but a head wound during the final phase of fighting at

Ouranberg had robbed him of memory and identity. He could still function, physically, but Gol Kolea wasn't living in Gol Kolea's body any more. He was a trooper now, serving under Criid as part of his old squad.

Tragic is what it was.

'I see the old heroes and worthies of Aexegary have gone back to fight the war,' Hark said.

'Sir?'

The commissar pointed at the white stone blocks under the trees. 'Those plinths. The statues have been removed. Even the placards. Recycled. Melted down for the war effort. Whoever used to stand on top of those is probably shrieking towards the Shadik lines right now as part of a shell case. Aexegary is on its last legs, Caffran. Drained to the limit. We got here just in time.'

'Sir.'

'I hope,' Hark added. 'Maybe they're already dead, just still twitching. Guess we'll find out.'

His tone was flippant, but his words made Caffran uneasy. No one wants to get into a fight that's already lost.

Whistles started to blow up on the field. They looked round and saw things were beginning to move. Stewards were urging Ghost troops onto the trucks.

'Up and at 'em,' Hark said, rising. He dusted his coat down as Caffran hoisted up his bergen.

'Do me a favour,' Hark said. 'Loop back down this path and check there are no stragglers. I'll hold your transport for you.'

'Yes, sir.'

As Hark walked back up the grass to the LZ, Caffran went the opposite way down the path, covering the trees and the line of the hedge. He found Derin and Costin leaning against a vacant plinth smoking lho-sticks.

'Look sharp,' Caffran said. 'We're moving at last.'

Both of them cursed.

'And Hark's on the prowl.'

Derin and Costin finished their smokes and gathered up their kit.

'Coming, Caff?' Derin asked.

'Be there in a sec,' he replied, and continued down the pathway, leaving them to wander back to the assembly areas.

It all seemed clear. Caffran was about to turn back himself when he spotted a lone figure right down at the edge of the adjoining paddock, lurking under a small stand of trees.

As he jogged closer, he could see who it was: Larkin.

The regiment's master sniper was so lost in his own thoughts, he didn't hear Caffran approach. He seemed to be listening to the rustle of the breeze through the branches above him. His kit and his bagged long-las were piled up on the grass beside him.

Caffran slowed his pace to a walk. Larkin had never been the most stable of the Tanith, but he'd become particularly withdrawn and distant since Bragg's death.

Everyone had been fond of Try Again Bragg. It was hard not to be. Genial and good-natured, almost gentle, he'd used his famous size and strength to great effect as a heavy weapons specialist... never mind his terrible aim, which had earned him the nickname. Bragg had fallen to enemy fire at Ouranberg and everyone missed him. He'd seemed to be one of the regiment's permanent features, immovable, like bedrock. His death had robbed them all of something. Confidence perhaps. Even the most gung-ho Ghosts had stopped believing they would live forever.

Bragg had been Larkin's closest friend. They'd been a double act, the wiry sniper and the giant gunner, like Clarco and Clop, the clowns in the Imperial mystery plays. Larkin had taken the big man's death hardest of all, probably, Caffran guessed, because Larkin hadn't been there. The sniper had been part of the penetration mission, sent in ahead of the main force, and by the time he had been picked up and returned to the Ghost's ranks, Bragg was already dead.

'Larks?' Caffran began.

The knife was there in a blink. Larkin's Tanith warknife, its straight silver blade thirty centimetres long. It appeared as fast as one of Varl's barrack room sleight-of-hand tricks. Caffran saw the blade, and the fear in Larkin's eyes.

'Feth!' he said, backing off, his hands raised. 'Steady!'

It seemed to take a moment for Larkin to recognise Caffran. He blinked, swallowed, then shook his head and put the knife away with a hand Caffran could see was shaking.

'Sorry, Caff,' Larkin said. 'You made me jump.'

'I did that,' agreed Caffran, raising his eyebrows. 'You okay?'

Larkin had turned aside and was gazing away into nothing again.

'Larks?'

'I'm fine. Just thinking.'

'About what?'

'Nothing. You... on your own?'

Caffran looked about. 'Yeah. Hark sent me to gather everyone up. We're rousting out.'

Larkin nodded. He seemed a little more composed. It was often hard to tell with Mad Hlaine Larkin. He picked up his bergen and rested his sniper weapon over his shoulder.

'You sure you're okay?' Caffran asked.

'Jumpy. Always get jumpy before a show. Got me an ill feeling about...'

'The Emperor protects,' said Caffran.

Larkin murmured something that Caffran didn't catch and hooked the little silver aquila he wore round his neck out so he could kiss it.

'Sometimes,' he said, 'I don't think the Emperor's even watching.'

AT THE PARK gates, the reason for the convoy's slow departure became evident. The Aexegarian people had come out to greet the liberators. They thronged around the gates, filling nearby streets, blocking the route with a mass of cheering bodies, despite the best efforts of the local arbites to control them. From the back of the troop trucks, the crowd was a sea of waving blue and gold flags, with the odd Imperial crest pennant mixed in. At least three brass bands were vying for attention. Hab-wives held babies up to the sides of the creeping transports, calling to the guardsmen to touch them and make them lucky. Local hierachs in full regalia had come out to bless the off-worlders, and the district mayor had arrived with a delegation of selectmen. Blue and gold bunting threaded the rockcrete lampposts, chirring in the breeze. The mayor's aides cornered the first Tanith officer to emerge from the park, and dragged him off to be presented to the mayor, who granted him the freedom of the city, strung garlands round his neck and generally shook his hand off on the assumption that he was in charge. He wasn't. He was Sergeant Varl of nine platoon who had just happened to get his men onto a truck first. Varl was quite enjoying the attention until he was asked to address the crowd.

It took over three hours to get the Tanith from their LZ to the railhead. The massive convoy finally shook free of the crowds and moved off through an industrial suburb of Brunsgatte where long straight avenues of identical red-brick habitat blocks alternated with guild halls, labourers' welfare clubs and shabby grey manufactories. It started to rain along the way, a shower at first and then heavier and heavier until the downpour hid the receding towers of the city and obscured the great palace overlooking it all.

In the rain, the railhead was a blur of steam. Troop trains, converted from livestock wagons, were lined up in siding areas, their maroon locomotives panting wet heat and hissing out vapours of sooty fumes. Tractors with fat bowser tanks watered the boilers, and mechanised chutes fed gleaming floods of coke straight into the tenders.

The air smelled of coal-tar. Whistles shrilled. The Tanith exited the trucks and huddled under dripping temporary awnings as the local militia moved amongst them, issuing embarkation numbers. Heavy equipment and vehicles were loaded aboard freight trains with wide conflat wagons. From under the awnings, the Tanith waved and exchanged cat-calls with the Krassian troops mustering on the far side of the tracks. The regiments had fought together at Ouranberg. Old friendships – and rivalries – were renewed.

Ditching the military staff car that had brought him from the LZ, Colonel-Commissar Ibram Gaunt strode in through the steam and the bustle. The liaison officer appointed to him, a Major Nyls Fep Buzzel, scurried to keep up. Buzzel was a short, plump man who kept his right hand stiffly in the pocket of his green overcoat, and Gaunt presumed him to be an invalid veteran. As Gaunt understood the circumstances on Aexe Cardinal, all able-bodied men not in reserved occupations were at the front. The fronts, he corrected himself. This was a global war, with theatres to the north and west of Aexegary, along the sovereign states of the southern oceans, and in the east.

Buzzel was pleasant enough. He wore an officer's cap with cockade made from some sort of plumage. The feather was wilting in the rain. He'd said something about serving with the Bande Sezari, a name he mentioned with pride as if to suggest it was something special, but Gaunt had never heard of it.

'When do I see data-slates? Tacticals? Charts of disposition?' Gaunt asked as he strode along.

'There will be time, sir!' Buzzel replied, side-stepping a munition cart.

Gaunt stopped and looked at the Aexegarian. 'I'm moving my troops to the front line, major. I'd like to have a feel for that area at least before they get there.'

'We will be breaking the transit to Rhonforq, the allied staff headquarters, sir. Briefing dossiers have been forwarded there.'

'Are these cattle trucks?' Gaunt asked, banging the side of the nearest wagon.

'Yes, but–' Buzzel began before realising Gaunt was already moving again.

'Sergeant Bray! Secure those tent rolls!' Gaunt called.

'Sir!'

'Obel? Ewler? Which train are you supposed to be on? Look at the dockets, for feth's sake!'

'Yes sir!'

'Varl? Nice speech. You're missing a few of your mob. I saw them down past the gangers' huts, smoking and dicing.'

'Right on it, sir!'

Buzzel watched the colonel-commissar curiously. Apparently, he was quite a war hero, so they said. Tall, imposing in his black leather stormcoat and commissariate cap, with a face like… like his name. Narrow, sculptural, noble. Buzzel reflected sourly that he didn't know what a war hero was meant to look like. Sixteen years of front-line service and he'd never met one.

He liked Gaunt's manner. Authoritative, brisk, disciplined, and he still seemed to know every man by name.

'Daur!'

A handsome young Tanith captain rushing past stopped to salute Gaunt.

'You making any sense of this?'

Captain Daur nodded, producing a data-slate. 'I borrowed this from one of the local marshals,' he said. 'Makes more sense than a lot of whistle blowing and shouting.'

'Let me look,' said Gaunt and reviewed the slate.

'Managing all right?' he asked as he read.

'Yes sir. Trying to find Grell's platoon. They should be aboard C Train already, but they've been lost in the mix.'

Gaunt turned and pointed. 'I saw them over there, behind the signal gantries, helping to load munition crates from a stalled tractor.'

'Thank you, sir,' Daur said as he took back the slate and hurried off.

'A car has been prepared for you in Train A,' Buzzel said, but Gaunt wasn't listening.

'Surgeon Curth? What's the problem?'

A woman had appeared. She was young and wore a borrowed rain-slicker over her red medicae overalls. A stern expression gave her appealing, heart-shaped face a hard edge.

'All the regimental medical supplies have gone walkabout, Gaunt,' she said. Buzzel was surprised to hear her use the colonel-commissar's surname without the respect of rank.

'Have you looked around?'

'We've all looked around. Dorden's hopping mad.'

Buzzel stepped forward. 'If I may, sir… the medical supplies would have been loaded onto Train E along with consumables. That's already on its way.'

'There's your answer, Ana,' said Gaunt. 'Aexegarian efficiency is a step ahead of you.'

The woman smiled and disappeared into the mêlée of hurrying bodies.

Gaunt moved on, jumping down off the rockcrete platform so he could walk down the side of a troop train along the gravelly sleeper bed. Tanith troops pressed themselves eagerly against the wagon window slits and dangled like apes out of the doorways, clapping their hands and chanting his name. 'Gaunt! Gaunt! Gaunt!'

Gaunt made a mock bow, doffed his cap to them and then stood again, clapping back at them. There were cheers.

'Soric! Mkoll! Haller! Domor! My thanks to your men for that warm support! Are you ready to move?'

A chorus of 'Ayes!'

'We're ready, sir!' called a thickset, older sergeant with one eye.

'Good for you, Soric. Tell your boys to get as comfortable as they can. It's a six-hour ride.'

'Aye, sir!'

'It's only four hours to Rhonforq, sir,' whispered Buzzel.

'I know. But if they steel themselves for six, four will seem like nothing. It's called psychology,' Gaunt whispered back.

He turned to face the train again. 'Sergeant Domor?'

'Sir!' replied a soldier with bulky augmetic optical implants.

'Where's Milo?'

'Here, sir!'

A lad appeared in the crowded wagon doorway, the youngest Tanith Buzzel had yet seen.

'Milo… pipe us on our way,' Gaunt said. The boy nodded and, after a few moments, a wailing, haunting note rose up above the frenetic activity. Buzzel recognised the tune: The old Imperial hymn 'Behold! the Triumph of Terra'.

THREE TRACKS AWAY, Colm Corbec, colonel and second officer of the Tanith regiment, heard the pipes as he slammed the wagon's side-door shut and dropped the latch.

Corbec was an oak of a man, bearded and hairy limbed, with a fighting temper and a playful good humour that made him beloved of the men.

'Ah, the pipes,' he sighed. 'Magnifying the glory of Terra to the heavens in bitter-sweet lament.'

'You talk a lot of old feth sometimes, chief,' said Muril, the sniper in Corbec's squad, and the other troopers laughed. Muril was a Verghastite, one of a host of men and women recruited from the city of Vervunhive to bolster the original Tanith strength. The divided loyalties and cultural differences of the two sides – Tanith and Verghast – had taken a long time to gel, but now they seemed to be pulling together as one fluid unit and for that Corbec was grateful. They'd fought well together, mixed well, complemented each other's strengths, but as far as Corbec was concerned, the real breakthrough had come when they'd started using each other's curse words. Once he'd heard Verghastites saying 'Feth!' and Tanith saying 'Gak!' he'd known they were home and dry.

Muril was one of his favourite troopers. Like many of the female Verghast volunteers, she'd excelled at marksmanship and had specialised as a sniper. Her bagged long-las lay beside her on the straw-littered floor of the wagon and the grey silk marksman's lanyard was displayed between the third button of her field jacket and the stud of the left-hand breast pocket. Muril was tall and lean, with long dark hair that she kept pinned back in a bun, and a slender, sharp-nosed face framing knowing dark eyes and a refreshing smile. Corbec had seen her injured during the fight for Cirenholm. In fact, he'd almost got himself killed dragging her to safety. Despite the fact the surgeon had been required to rebuild her pelvis, she had recovered a fething sight quicker than he had.

He was still shaky, still weak, though he put a brave face on it. Several people had commented on how much weight he had lost. I'm old, Corbec told himself. Recovery takes longer for a man of my distinguished years.

Old in so many ways, he reflected. Sehra Muril was as lovely as any girl he had courted back in his oat-sowing days in County Pryze, but he appreciated she was quite out of his league now. He knew several young troopers were competing for her attention. Muril paid Corbec attention all right, but he was rather afraid he knew that look. The look a girl would give her father.

Mkoll, the regiment's chief scout, had told Corbec that Muril had put in for scout training. If she was successful, Corbec would lose her, but he didn't begrudge it. Stealth scouts were the Tanith First's forte, and so far no Verghastite had made the grade. Mkoll was doing his best to bring some of them up to scratch, and if one of those was going to be Sehra Muril, Corbec was determined to be nothing but fething proud.

The train lurched and then began to roll. Corbec shot out a hand to steady himself against the wagon's side.

He pulled his dog-eared tarot pack from his blouse pocket and grinned. 'Okay, lads and lasses. Who's for a game of Strip Solon Naked?'

TRAIN E PULLED OUT, rattling as it hunted over the multiple points and gained speed.

Major Elim Rawne, third officer of the regiment under Gaunt and Corbec, sat back in the first troop wagon and accepted a lho-stick from his adjutant, Feygor.

'What do you reckon to this one, major?' Feygor asked.

Feygor was a vicious whip of a man, tall and thin, who had allied himself to Rawne right from the off. Some said they had a murky history that went back to their days on Tanith. They were alike. Rawne was handsome, in the way that weapons and snakes are handsome. Slim but well-built, Rawne had a fine profile and eyes that, as Corbec put it, could charm the drawers off a Sororitas nun. When this comment had filtered back to Rawne, his only remark had been, 'Oh. Do they wear drawers?'

Rawne hated Gaunt. It was that simple. He hated him for a number of things, but foremost he hated him for letting the Tanith homeworld die. But it was an old hatred, and it had become feeble with neglect. These days, he tolerated Gaunt. Even so, most of the troops thought Rawne was the nastiest piece of work the Tanith First could offer.

They were wrong.

Murtan Feygor had got his throat shot away during the fight for Vervunhive, and his every word came flat and monotone through a speech enhancer sewn into his larynx. Since then, he'd sounded permanently sarcastic, though several Ghosts, Varl and Corbec in particular, had opined that it was no great disability because he always had anyway. Fierce as a cornered plague-rat, he was snide and cunning and trusted no one except Rawne.

But he wasn't the nastiest piece of work the Tanith First could offer either.

Rawne exhaled a long bar of blue smoke as he thought about Feygor's question. 'Dug-in war, isn't it, Murt? Drawn out, old. It'll be trenches, you mark my words. Fething field fortifications. We'll spend our time either labouring with nine seventies like common navvies or ducking for cover in some other bastard's latrine.'

'I hear you,' said Feygor with disgust. 'Fething trenches. Fething nine-seventies.'

A nine-seventy referred to the Imperial Guard's standard issue entrenching tool: a heavy, compact multi-purpose pick that could be stowed by detaching the helve from the head. Its official name was the 'Imperial Implement (General Field Fortification) Pattern 970'. Every Ghost wore one in a button-down leather sheath on the back of his webbing.

'Trenches,' Rawne muttered blackly. 'It'll be just like Fortis Binary again.'

'Fortis fething Binary,' Feygor echoed.

'Where was that?' Banda whispered to Caffran. They were sitting a little way down the wagon with their backs to the door, close enough to overhear their platoon commander's remarks.

'Before your time,' Caffran told her. Jessi Banda was Verghast, another grade one sniper like Muril. Fortis Binary was a piece of hell the Tanith had endured several years before the fight at Vervunhive had brought the new recruits in.

'It was a forge world,' Caffran explained. 'We were trench-bound for a long time. It was… unpleasant.'

'What happened?' Banda asked.

'We survived,' growled Rawne, listening in.

It was a straight put-down, but Banda just raised her eye-brows and grinned, letting it wash over her. Major Rawne had never been able to disguise his contempt for the female troopers. He didn't believe they had any business being in the Tanith First. Banda had often wondered why. She'd have to ask him sometime.

'Any advice?' she asked.

The boldness of the question floored Rawne for a second, but that was the way of these fething women. He tried to come up with something good, but 'Keep your head down' was all he could manage.

'Fair enough,' she nodded, and settled back.

'You hear that?' Feygor asked suddenly.

'What?' asked Rawne.

'Raised voices. In the next wagon.'

Rawne glowered. 'Sort it out, will you?' he said.

'I WON'T TELL you again,' said Tona Criid.

'So don't,' replied Lijah Cuu, not even looking at her. Every member of Criid's platoon, crowded into the wagon space, had fallen silent and was watching the confrontation warily.

'You will service your kit and field strip your weapon, trooper.' Criid's voice was firm.

'It's a waste of time,' Cuu replied.

'You got something better to do?' she asked.

Cuu looked at her for the first time, fixing her with his cold green eyes. 'Plenty,' he said.

No one had dared mess with Tona Criid before her promotion. Thin and tough, with cropped bleached hair, Criid was a ganger from the slums of Vervunhive, an environment that had schooled her wits, reflexes and fighting smarts. Though young, she could more than look after herself, and was reckoned to be one of the hardest of the female troopers. Unlike Verghastites such as Banda and Muril, she hadn't specialised. She was a regular trooper with front-line experience.

Her promotion to sergeant, and the squad command that went with it, was never going to be an easy ride. Gaunt had done it on Hark's advice. Hark believed it would send the right message to all the troopers in the regiment... take the Verghastites seriously. Take the women seriously.

Certainly ten platoon needed a Verghastite officer now Kolea was incapacitated. He'd commanded almost automatic respect because of his record as a guerrilla company leader during the hive war. But his squad was tight, and everyone knew they wouldn't take kindly to any replacement, no matter how qualified. There were some tough customers in ten platoon, and none tougher than Lijah Cuu.

Cuu was a bad ploin and no mistake. A competent trooper, with abilities that could probably take him into either sniper or scout speciality, but he had a mean streak as deep and obvious as the scar that split his face from top to bottom. At Cirenholm, he'd been accused of the brutal rape-murder of a civilian and had come within sniffing distance of a firing squad before Gaunt had got him off. Innocent of that, perhaps, but guilty of so many other things. The plain fact was that he liked killing things. You got troopers like that in the Guard sometimes.

Gaunt had considered transferring Cuu out of ten platoon but knew that would undermine Criid's authority. The Ghosts would read that as him giving Criid an easy ride. He'd told her she'd have to deal with him.

Criid took Cuu's gaze without blinking. 'Let's review,' she said, slowly and clearly. 'You're a member of ten platoon. I'm the squad officer. I've just given Ten a direct order to make use of this transit time to service kit and weapons, and everyone else is happy to do that. Aren't you? Lubba?'

'Yes, ma'am,' grunted the gang-tattooed flamer bearer.

'Nessa?'

The squad's sniper, permanently deaf from shell-damage at the hive, signed back 'yes'.

'Jajjo? Hwlan? Any problems with my order?'

Jajjo, a mixed-race Verghastite with dark brown skin and darker eyes shrugged and smiled. Ten platoon's Tanith scout Hwlan nodded with a brisk 'Yes, m-sarge!'

'Only you seem to have a problem, Cuu.'

'Seems so. Sure as sure.' He smiled. It was the most unsettling smile in the Imperium. The most evil servants of Chaos would have killed to have a smile that lethal.

Tona Criid was not smiling. Deep inside, she was trembling. Her greatest fear was not death or torture or grievous injury. It was failure. Failure to live up to the opportunity Gaunt had given her. She would make this platoon her own. Or die trying. And die trying, seemed more likely the case.

'Do it now,' she said.

Cuu deliberately dropped his pack and weapon onto the floor and took out a lho-stick, which he lit with a tinder box. 'You know what I hate,' he said, blowing smoke at her. 'What I hate is the fact that you talk to me like I was one of your gakking kids.'

'Oh feth me!' Trooper Vril whispered to Hwlan. 'There's gonna be a fight now.'

'Sure as sure,' Hwlan whispered back sarcastically.

Unless you were going to make nice, you didn't mention Criid's kids. Yoncy and Dalin. They weren't hers biologically,

just war-waifs she'd rescued from the killing grounds at
Vervunhive and looked after ever since. She and her man Caffran were parents to them, and when they were off in action,
the two kids were looked after by the regiment's camp followers. It was the Tanith First's one little happy-ending tale.
Criid and Caffran, true love, kids saved from death... you
couldn't make feth like that up.

'What did you say, trooper?' asked Criid.

'Here we go,' murmured Vril.

'Ah feth it,' whispered Hwlan. He slid the haft of his nine
seventy out to use as a baton. If it came to fists, he'd get in on
Criid's side. Cuu was a vicious worm. The scout saw that
DaFelbe and Skeen both looked ready to jump in, and Nessa
had got to her feet too.

But if it went off, Hwlan thought, would it help to get
involved? Would Criid thank them? Probably not. She'd
want to assert her command over Cuu alone, to make the
point. Hwlan could feel Vril's hand on his arm, pulling him
down. Vril clearly thought the same way too.

Cuu picked smoke-weed off his lip. 'I said I don't like it
when you talk to me like I was one of your kids. Why? Did
that upset you?'

'Not at all,' said Criid smoothly. 'But I notice you haven't
shown respect to my rank since this conversation began.
Would a "sergeant" or a "ma'am" really kill you?'

'Gakked if I'm gonna find out,' Cuu said, winking at the
troopers around them.

'Don' you talk that way,' said a voice from the back of the
wagon.

'What?' sneered Cuu.

'Don' talk that way. Don' be doin' that.' It was Kolea. He'd
risen, slowly, and was staring at Cuu. There was a vague ani-
mosity in his eyes, but his face was blank. The headwound
he'd taken at Ouranberg had made him very slow and direct.
His mouth slurred words.

'Sit down, you dimwit,' said Cuu archly. 'Go hunt for your
brain. I hear the loxatl have it in a little glass trophy box.'

Lubba, staunchly loyal to Kolea, threw himself at Cuu with
a snarl, but Criid blocked him and kicked him down on his
arse.

'Full marks for heart,' she told him. 'But I won't have brawling in this platoon.'

'Yes ma'am,' Lubba said.

'Why you bein' so bad?' Kolea asked Cuu. He shuffled forward, screwing up his eyes in confusion.

'It's all right, Gol. You sit down,' Criid said.

'Sit down, sarge?'

'Yeah, you go sit down and I'll deal with this.'

Kolea wavered. 'You sure, sarge? This... this man here was
being bad.'

Criid knew that Kolea had been struggling to remember
Cuu's name, and had failed. She also knew he only called her
'sarge' because he could see her pins.

'Sit down, Trooper Kolea.'

'Okay.'

Criid looked back at Cuu. 'Follow my order and service
your kit.'

'Or what?'

Criid pushed a hand out towards Cuu's face, and he
dodged back, but it was a ruse. The real sting was Criid's left
leg, sweeping round at knee height.

Cuu crashed over onto the straw-covered floor, hard.
Criid was on him in a heartbeat, one hand gripping his hair
and yanking his head back, one knee in the small of his
back.

'Or I exert my authority,' she said.

Cuu responded with a gender-related obscenity. In reply,
the base of her hand against the back of his head, she
smashed him nose-first into the decking. There was a crack
that made them all wince, and it wasn't wood.

'You gakking bitch!' Cuu coughed as she yanked his head
back again by the hair. Blood was running from his broken
nose.

'You wanna go again, Trooper Cuu?'

'Gakking b–OW!'

Another headslam.

'Oooh, that's gonna smart!' Vril gasped.

'I can keep going until we get to where we're headed and
then hand you off to Gaunt...' said Criid, digging her knee
into his spine and making him cry out, '...or you can service

your kit and your weapon and call me by rank. What do you say, Cuu? What do you gakking say?'

'I'll service my kit, sergeant!'

'…is the right answer. Get up.'

She got off him and he rolled over, his face dripping with blood.

'Off you go, Cuu.'

Cuu got up, and took his pack and lasgun off to the farthest corner of the wagon. The members of the platoon slow-handclapped and Criid performed a little bow.

'What don't you do?' she asked.

'Mess with you!' Lubba called out.

'Excellent. Carry on.'

'Everything okay in here?' Feygor called, pushing open the dividing shutter between the wagons.

'Just fine,' said Criid.

'What's wrong with Cuu?' Feygor asked.

'Nothing,' she said.

'Should he be bleeding like that?'

'Yes.'

Feygor shrugged. 'Rawne says keep it down.'

'We are.'

'Okay then,' said Feygor and left.

Criid walked down the rocking wagon and sat herself beside Kolea. 'That was nice what you did,' she said.

'What'd I do?' he asked, puzzled.

'Never mind,' she sighed.

GAUNT RODE THE A train. His carriage had once been a coach-class car, but its luxury days were long passed. Even so, he knew that the worn upholstery of the compartments was a fething sight sweeter than the transit arrangements of his Ghosts.

He sat in a compartment with Buzzel, Chief Medic Dorden, Hark and the regiment's chaplain, ayatani Zweil. Gaunt's adjutant, Corporal Beltayn, waited at the door.

Zweil and Hark were arguing about something, but Gaunt wasn't paying attention. He gazed out of the window, watching the vales and fields and woods and townships of Mittel Aexe flicker past.

Doc Dorden leaned over and tapped Gaunt's knee.

'Credit for them?'

Gaunt smiled at the grey-haired medicae. 'Not a lot of anything, to be honest. Just trying to focus.'

'An empty mind is like a pot for Chaos to piss in,' said Zweil. Buzzel looked shocked.

'Just kidding,' said the old priest, chortling into his long, wispy beard. He took out a clay pipe and began to stoke it with weed.

'This is a non-smoking area,' said Buzzel.

'I know that!' snapped Zweil testily, though he clearly didn't. He got up. 'I'm off to bless the poor bastards,' he announced, and stomped off down the connecting corridor.

'Your chaplain is an… unusual man,' said Buzzel.

'No kidding,' said Hark.

Gaunt returned his gaze to the landscape outside. Low, hilly country broken by stands of trees and small lakes. It would have been almost picturesque if not for the weather. Rain splashed along the windows of the speeding train.

'We're heading for Rhonforq, you say?' Dorden asked Buzzel.

'Yes, doctor.'

'Which is the gateway to the Naeme Valley?'

Buzzel nodded. 'The Naeme roughly demarcates the front line in the central sector.'

'It's dug-in?' Hark asked.

'Extensively,' said Buzzel, 'and has been for a long time.'

Hark scratched an earlobe. 'So the front's as stagnant as we've been told?'

'We make advances,' Buzzel said firmly.

'And so do they,' said Gaunt. 'As I understand it, there's a stretch of territory thirty kilometres wide and a thousand long that has remained disputed for forty years. That's one hell of a no-man's land.'

Buzzel shrugged. 'It's been a hard war.'

'An impasse,' said Hark. 'Which we're going to break. I take it you'll be using the Tanith to their strength as stealth infiltrators?'

Buzzel looked confused. 'I understood you were front-line troops. That's where you're being sent. The front line.'

Hark looked at Dorden and both men sighed. Gaunt beckoned Beltayn through the compartment window.

'Sir?'

'Can you patch me a link to the lord general?'

"Fraid not, sir. Something's awry. Vox is down.'

'When we get to Rhonforq, find Mkoll and tell him to move a recon team forward to the line. I want a detailed intelligence capture before we proceed.'

'Yes, sir!'

Gaunt looked at Buzzel. 'My Ghosts will fight to the last: harder, braver and stronger than any soldiers you have ever seen. But I will not see them wasted in the meatgrinder of a slow trench war. They have skills, and I'll have them use those skills.'

Buzzel smiled amiably. 'I'm sure the supreme commander understands that, sir,' he said.

The train slowed. Outside, Gaunt saw that the landscape had begun to change. The vegetation looked grey and sick, and acres of farmland had been rutted down to nothing but spongy brown waste. Stands of woodland had been felled leaving acres of dead stumps like badly planned cemeteries. They passed at least one team of timbermen denuding a hillside, their big, blacked-iron logging engine sheeting sparks and woodpulp up into the overcast sky. The roads were thick with drab motor transport and heavy carts drawn by oxen and hippines.

Towns and villages were scruffy and neglected, windows shuttered and boarded. Some had earthworks or pales raised around their eastern fringes, one in five had the steel mast of a shield generator rising from its midst. Apart from the masts and the motor vehicles, there was no other sign of metal in commonplace use.

They passed through one village where bells and horns were sounding. The westerly wind was bringing down not only rain but also a thin, yellowish smoke. Townsfolk in the street went about their business in canvas masks and rebreathers.

They clanked on through mercy stations – tent cities raised to cope with the exodus of injured, generated at the front. By Gaunt's estimation, they were still over a hundred kilometres from the real front. The war was so old, so chronic, it had spilled back this far.

He could smell it. War has its own smell. Not fyceline, not promethium, not water or mud or blood, not rank soil or ordure, not even the pungent decay of death itself. All of those scents were in the air.

War had a metallic tang. You could almost isolate it. A mineral smell quite subtracted from the diverse secondary odours it generated. A smell of steel and hate. Pure, repellent, universal.

Gaunt had smelled it on Balhaut, on Voltemand, on Caligula, Fortis Binary, Bucephalon, Monthax, Verghast, Hagia, Phantine and all the others. That diamond-tough scent of pure war, lurking behind the sweaty, more obvious perfumes that decorated human conflict.

This was going to be hard. Aexe Cardinal was going to cost them. It was in the air.

War. Waiting for them. Old and hard and cunning, like a wily, immortal beast, ready to pounce.

Ready to kill.

TWO
THE WOUNDED RIVER

*'From Bassin to Seronne, the rural valley commends itself
to the visitor, and in clement season there are many rewards
to be had: the old parish churches, the cafes and inns, and
the undemanding footpaths and bridle ways of the
tranquil riverbanks.'*

– Fweber's Touring Guide
to Mittel Aexe, 720th edition

THE GROUND WAS peppered with ancient, rain-filled shell
holes for as far as he could see. A pock-marked surface, like
the cratered plain of some dead moon. The wet soil was
greenish grey and the pools were dark emerald or black,
though some were skinned with frothy white scum. Nothing
seemed to stand taller than the height of a man's shoulder. A
few poles and staves jutted from the mud, the occasional
scourged remains of a tree, iron hoop-stakes and piquets and
coils of barbed wire.

The sky was leaden and bulging with creased blotches of
grey and yellow clouds. To the east, a dark haze of rain fuzzed
the horizon into a filthy smudge.

Mkoll lowered his field scope and spat on the ground. The air was heavy with a dusty, chalky smell that got into the back of the throat. He could feel the grit abrading his teeth. It was the smell of dead land, of earth that had been disturbed and pulverised and thrown over so many times that it leaked its powdered essence into the air.

'Well, this is fething lovely,' muttered Bonin sarcastically. Mkoll glanced round at him and nodded. It was disturbing, this place. Tanith scouts had an unerring sense of direction, but the sheer featureless morass around them made it feel like they were nowhere at all. All of his men seemed uneasy: the usually cheerful Bonin, Caober from Gaunt's own platoon, Hwlan from ten, Baen from Varl's mob. Even Mkvenner, Corbec's lean, taciturn scout from two platoon, normally the model of composed calm, seemed unsettled.

Caober had a small map that Gaunt had given him. He held it up, flicking his index finger against the paper in frustration. 'Sitwale Wood,' he said at last.

'Sitwale *Wood*?' Hwlan echoed, stressing the second word.

Caober shrugged. 'The levelling glories of field artillery,' he said, 'beneath which all things are rendered equal.'

There was a track of sorts, rutted and mired. The scout party moved off behind Mkoll, following it north-east. About a kilometre further on, and the track made a crossroads marked by a temporary sign. '55th/9th rg' pointed one arm. '916th/88/ac' read another. 'R'forq ASHQ & 42nd rg' announced the arm that pointed the way they had come. The last one, pointing west, read 'Real Life'.

'Company!' Baen called. There were lights on the track behind them, and the sound of labouring engines. Mkoll waved his men off the track.

A jolting field truck, smeared in mud, rumbled past, turning east. Behind it came a staggering file of artillery tractors towing 0.12 feldkannone pieces. Aexe Alliance infantry in filthy green greatcoats walked beside the column. Their heads were covered with canvas bag-hoods with rough-cut slits for eyes and mouths. Most carried metal pry-bars or coils of wire matting to free up wheels when they bogged in. The hooded men reminded Bonin of the scarecrows used on the fruit farms back home in County Cuhulic. No one paid any attention to the Tanith team.

Twenty tractors, thirty, thirty-five, then twelve high-sided haycarts piled with shells that had been jacketed for protection in wicker sleeves. The carts were drawn by hippine teams, ten to a cart. These beasts were thin and wild-eyed, and stank of disease as they whinneyed and snorted along, every step a struggle.

After the slow carts came infantry, trudging under the weight of full field kit, their heads wrapped up in their dirty scarves. Mkoll watched an officer step out of file and stand by the signpost waving his troops around in the right direction.

After a few minutes, the officer turned and walked over to the Tanith. His greatcoat was stiff with mud and when he pulled the scarf away from his dirty face, Mkoll was shocked to see how young he was.

'Lost?' he began. Then he noticed Mkoll's rank pins and made a more formal salute.

'No,' said Mkoll, stepping up. 'Sergeant Mkoll, Tanith First.'

'You're from the Imperial expedition?'

'That's right.'

'Lieutenant Fevrierson, 30th battalion, Genswick Foot.' His accent was tight and clipped. Aexegarian. 'It's a pleasure to see you. Where is your main force?'

'Moving into reserve,' replied Mkoll. 'Our commander's sent us up to scope the leading edge.'

'Scope the...?'

'Assess the disposition of the forward line,' Mkoll glossed. The young man nodded. It was partly the accent, Mkoll thought. Mine's as unfamiliar to him as his is to me. That and the fact that they're still using old terms. He reminded himself that this war – this world – had been isolated for a good time.

'We're moving up to the 55th sector,' said Fevrierson. 'You're welcome to tag along.'

Mkoll nodded his thanks and made a brief hand signal that the lieutenant didn't catch. Immediately, the five men in his patrol were at his side. They fell in with the still plodding stream of Alliance infantry.

Fevrierson made light conversation as they walked. He was a little wary of the newcomers. Their kit was very clean and in good order, apart from the splashes they'd picked up on the day's hike. The fabric of their uniforms was of a type he didn't recognise. It looked comfortable and strong, possibly synthetic. They carried powerful-looking rifles that didn't seem to have any sort of ejection ports for spent cartridges. Could they be energy weapons? Fevrierson had never seen a lasgun close up, and they made him feel ashamed of his long, heavy bolt-action autorifle. The off-worlders also had tech items like power scopes and ear-bead comm-links. Individual trooper comm-links! They were truly from another place, like the characters in the demiscuto science-romance digests his brother used to buy from the newsvendor.

'This a rotation?' Mkoll asked.

'Yah. It used to be a week up and then two in reserve, but it's alternate on and off now.'

'You and your men have been in billets for a week?'

'Yah.' Mkoll bit back a comment about the filthy state of the locals, but Fevrierson had seen the look.

'There are no washing facilities at Jen-Frow. The billets are poor. No water for laundry.'

Mkoll nodded. 'I meant no disrespect.'

'Yah, of course,' said the Aexegarian earnestly.

'You'll soon be dirty, soon enough,' muttered one of his file. Men around sniggered.

'That's enough, Herxer!' Fevrierson growled.

'It's okay,' said Bonin. 'We do dirty good. We've been in dirty scraps before.'

'Where's your commanding officer?' Mkoll asked Fevrierson.

'I *am* the commanding officer,' he said.

A WHISTLE BLEW from the rear echelon, then a second, then another coming up the file.

Fevrierson took out his own and blew. 'Off the road! Off the road!'

Mkoll wondered if it was an attack, though there was no sign of anything and the chilly, wet landscape was otherwise virtually silent.

They heard hooves. Cavalry was moving up the road at a canter, and the infantry were standing off to let them through.

The Aexegarians cheered and waved their scarves and gens-filly bonnets as the riders went past. The cavaliers were dressed in blue and gold coats with bright green sashes and white, bell-top shakos. They sat upright and haughty, eyes front, saddle-sabres clattering at their hips. Their mounts were gigantic flightless birds with grey feathers and vast hooked beaks, powering along on massive, blue-fleshed limbs.

'Feth me!' said Hwlan.

The front riders held lances with fluttering bannerols, but the rest carried short-action rifles. None of them seemed to be holding any sort of reins or bridles.

'Hussars. Carbine-hussars,' said Fevrierson proudly. 'A fine sight.'

'What are those bird things?' asked Caober.

'Struthids,' said Fevrierson. He frowned. 'You've never seen a struthid before?'

'I've seen plenty,' said Caober. 'And now I've seen everything.'

'They don't have reins,' said Mkoll. 'Do they control with their feet?'

'They're psicavalry,' said Fevrierson. 'They need both hands to operate the carbines in a charge, so each man has a puppeteer, linking him to his steed.'

'An implant? Augmetic?'

'I don't know those words. A puppeteer's a little machine. They put them in the men's heads surgically. The struthid has one grafted in to match. It creates a brain link and lets the man drive the bird.'

Over sixty hussars galloped past and then the infantry returned to the road. Mkoll saw some of the Aexegarian troopers retrieving the odd feather from the mud and fixing them to their coat collars.

'Lucky charms,' Fevrierson said.

AFTER ANOTHER FORTY-FIVE minutes, Mkoll realised the track was sloping down, though the landscape around remained spread out in its flat, pocked immensity. They were entering the rear portions of the trench network. The horizon had been clear earlier because everything vital had been sunk and dug in.

The workings were of immense size, some as wide as city streets and ten metres deep. Where they extended below the water table, duckboards had been laid down and teams of sappers were manning hand-pumped bilges. Strings of electrical lights ran down the carefully revetted walls and Mkoll could smell the ozone of shield generators. Armoured vehicles and trucks moved down the working line, and when one appeared, they had to stand to in lay-bys cut into the trench wall to allow them past. Troops hurried back and forth, some in greens, some in greys, a few in blues and golds or russets, all locals, all filthy. It was like entering a partially buried city. Some sections of trench were entirely roofed in with wired flakboard, with lighting hanging from the tunnel roofs.

'This is something,' said Baen to Mkoll. 'I expected trenches, but not like this.'

'They've had forty years to build it,' said Mkoll.

And they'd built it well. Massive, mainstreet-style reserve trenches, often shored up with rockcrete, off which ran barrack dugouts to the west and communication and support trenches to the east, towards the front. Running as they did from sap-heads and deep munition wells, the support trenches were shallower but zig-zagged, or were well provided with solid traverses to protect the vulnerable links and make them easier to defend compartmentally. To the east, about a kilometre away by Mkoll's estimation, lay the line of the fire trenches. To the west, rearwards, lay deeper pits accessed by communication trenches laid with narrow-gauge rails.

'The gun-pits,' Fevrierson said. Even the main artillery was dug in subsoil, Mkoll thought. The rails were for shell-carts. A few moments later they had to pause to allow barrows of massive wicker-wrapped shells to be heaved across the reserve trench and up the supply channels to the gun-pits. Fevrierson checked his watch. 'Readying for the night firing,' he said.

The Genswick Foot halted and stood easy in a firing trench as Fevrierson reported to the sector's staff blockhouse. He took Mkoll with him.

The blockhouse was a series of armoured rooms buried deep in the ground off the reserve mainway. It had folding shutters and gas curtains at the entrance.

Inside, it was warm and damp and busy. There was a chart room, and a vox-annex where a row of signallers chattered into bulky old-style field sets.

Sheafs of thick vox-line cables ran out along the entrance hall and away through loopholes. Inside the main entrance, sweating, ruddy-faced runners sat on a bench, waiting to be sent out again.

Mkoll waited at a reinforced door while Fevrierson signed in. From his vantage point, the Tanith could see a small command room filled with military aides grouped around a low map table. They were all in shabby but impressive number one uniforms: more blue and gold, more green, some yellow, some grey and some dark red.

Mkoll hadn't got the hang of the varied insignia or liveries yet. The men in grey tended to be quite dark skinned, and the few in red were pale and red or blond haired.

Fevrierson was reporting to a sallow-faced general whose green uniform seemed loose and ill-fitting. The man's face was drawn. He's lost weight since that kit was tailored for him, Mkoll thought.

The general talked to Fevrierson for a while, pointing to items on the map-table, and signed an order sheet. Then Fevrierson said something, and indicated Mkoll.

The general nodded and strode over to where the Tanith scout was waiting. Mkoll snapped a salute that the general gave back.

'We weren't expecting you for another two days,' said the general.

'We're not up in force, sir. My commanding officer ordered me forward in advance to assess the field.'

The general nodded and then surprised Mkoll by making the sign of the aquila across his chest and offering his hand.

'It's good to see you anyway and I thank the Throne you've come. I'm Hargunten, CoS, 55th region. Welcome to the Peinforq Line.'

'Sir. Mkoll, Tanith First.'

'What do you need, sergeant?'

'A look at the line and the chance to report back to Rhonforq,' said Mkoll. He produced the papers Gaunt had drawn up for him, countersigned by Buzzel.

General Hargunten looked them over. 'Wait here,' he said. 'The Genswick are moving forward to station 143, so you might as well go with them.'

He moved off to confer with other staff. As Mkoll waited he saw that one of the red-uniformed officers was looking him up and down. A colonel, by his pins. Mkoll didn't know the crossed-sabres and heraldic dragon of the man's insignia.

'Imperial?' he said after a while, his accent new to Mkoll. Thick, glottal, rich.

'Yes, sir.'

'Come to save us all.'

'Come to fight the arch-enemy, sir.'

The colonel snorted. His skin was very pale and slightly freckled and his side-shaved hair was red-gold.

'We can win this war,' he said.

'I have no doubt.'

'Without your help,' he finished.

'Not for me to say, sir.'

The colonel grunted and turned away. Fevrierson returned, with the general.

'Papers in order, sergeant,' Hargunten said, returning them to Mkoll. 'Go with the lieutenant here. See your way around. My compliments to your commander.'

Mkoll tucked the folded papers into his webbing pouch and saluted.

'See the front,' the colonel called out. 'See a war like you have never known.'

'I've known war, sir,' said Mkoll and, turning, strode out of the blockhouse.

'SCHLEIQ ME! I can't believe you did that!' Fevrierson exclaimed as they came out through the gas curtains into the damp evening air.

'Do what?'

'Smarted him like that!'

'Who was he?'

'Redjacq!'

'Who?'

Fevrierson blinked at Mkoll as if he was mad. 'Redjacq... Redjacq Ankre, of Kottmark?'

'Means nothing.'

'The Kottstadt Wyverns?'

'Really, I don't know. Kottmark is the neighbouring country, isn't it?'

'Yah... and the other senior partner in the Alliance. We'd be dead now if the Kottmarkers hadn't joined the war twenty years ago.'

'And this Redjacq... he's something special?'

'Their finest field commander. Leads the Wyverns. Furies, they are. We're lucky to have them in this sector.'

'I'm sure you are.'

IT WAS GETTING dark by then. Fevrierson got his infantry moving, and they went up through a series of zig-zagging communications trenches to the front-line position. There, things were more the way Mkoll had expected. No electrics, just the occasional promethium lamp or brazier. Dirty fire trenches dug in about three metres deep and heavily traversed with cross-spars and earth-filled gabions. A firestep made of stone lintels laid up against the base of the leading wall beneath the breastwork and iron loop holes. Despite the duckboards, the trenches were swilling with liquid mud and alive with vermin.

Wretched soldiers in blue coats stood down and began to retire in slow, weary lines as the Genswick Foot relieved them and took their places beneath the parapet.

The sky was clouding over and the light seemed to leak out of it. Thunder rumbled somewhere. The trenches stank. Mkoll turned to his men. 'Caober, Baen, Bonin... up that way. Mkvenner, Hwlan... back the other. Twenty minutes and back to me. See what you see.'

They moved away, but Mkoll caught Mkvenner's sleeve and held him back a moment. Unofficially, Mkvenner was Mkoll's number two in the scouts, totally dedicated and totally ruthless in a way that Mkoll, for all his reputation, could never hope to be. Some Tanith said Mkvenner had been trained in the old martial ways of cwlwhl, the fighting art of the Nalsheen, legendary warriors who had maintained law during Tanith's troubled feudal days. Mkoll always quashed those rumours, mainly because they were true and he knew how close Mkvenner guarded his background.

'Keep an eye on Hwlan,' Mkoll told him. 'Ten platoon is unsettled right now, with Criid taking over. Make sure he's together.'

Mkvenner nodded and made off. Mkoll watched the tall, lithe figure retreating down the busy trench.

Mkoll joined Fevrierson in the command dugout. It was little more than a shed built into the leading edge of the trench. There was a V-shaped binocular periscope on a tripod stand, and Mkoll took a lookout.

It was his first look at the battleground. In the twilight, it was a miserable place, though he was certain it would look even more miserable by day. Torn earth, incomprehensible wreckage, tall piquet fences of dangling wire. A kilometre away, the shattered land dipped a little and spread into a wide flood plain of poisoned water and stagnant pools interspersed with muddy islets and ridge-crests of shell-blown soil.

'A lot of water down there,' he said.

'That's the river.'

Mkoll looked again. 'It's no river...'

Fevrierson smiled at him. 'Oh yah! That's the beautiful Naeme, proud lifeflow of the borderlands!'

'But it's just pools and lakes and flooded flats...'

Mkoll's voice trailed off. He realised a river would look like that if it had been shelled for forty years. The banks, the environs, even the riverbed itself would have been ripped apart and pummelled into ruins. But the water still flowed. Where once it had been a proud, major river meandering through meadows and sleepy villages on its long journey to the sea, it was now cut loose, leaking out across the punished landscape like blood from a wound, its original form and structure lost to the war.

There was a soft 'pop' and the area below them was suddenly bathed in chilly white light. A few seconds more and other starshell flares burst, glowing, in the sky. Through the scope now, everything looked bleached and cold, hard shadows shivered as the flares slowly dropped.

'Corpse light,' said Fevrierson, putting on his steel helmet. 'Brace yourself,' he said.

'Why?'

'It's time for war.'

Distantly, a whistle blew. A bull-horn wound up and died again, its moan echoing across the front.

The gun-pits of the Peinforq Line woke up.

The sound and light split the darkness and eclipsed the tremulous glow of the starshells. The earth shook. In the deep pits and weapon-dens behind the line's spinal trenches, large calibre howitzers and mortars hurled munitions up into the gathering dusk. Elevated feldkannone and rocketshargen joined them.

Mkoll looked back at the Alliance lines and watched the thunderous light show. Two kilometres west of him and for twenty kilometres to north and south, the guns blazed and muzzle-fires strobed and danced. Massive, brilliant flashes flickered up and down the artillery line, some of them casting weird, momentary shadows from their pits. Mkoll heard the concussive screech of heavy shells lobbing overhead, the deeper, pneumatic twang of mortars, the huge crump of bombards. Rockets went up and over, squealing in the air and leaving trails of fire.

He'd never seen a bombardment on this scale before. Not even at Vervunhive.

Mkoll looked east, through the scope. A ragged strip of detonations and flame-storms was creeping across the ruined land on the far side of the wounded river. He could smell fyceline and iron in the wind, and then the stench of mud rendered into steam.

Fevrierson seemed content. He sat back and took a tin cup of caffeine from his subaltern.

'Want one?' he asked.

'No,' said Mkoll. The bombardment was shaking his marrow.

'They'll keep this up for a few hours, then they might signal us to advance.'

'Feth,' said Mkoll.

'You might as well have a cup,' said Fevrierson. 'We could be here for a w–'

There was a sudden roar and a shockwave of heat slammed across the front line from the west. Fevrierson stumbled to his feet. He stared back at the Aexe lines. A white hot cone of fire licked up from the direction of the allied artillery positions.

'Not a misfire, surely…' he began.

There was another colossal bang and a flash and this time it knocked them all over. Whistles were blowing.

'That's shellfire,' Mkoll said, getting up.

'But they've got nothing that–'

A third roar. Then a fourth. Then a dozen heavy impacts along the line to the north-west. Gargantuan fires blazed into the night.

'Schleiq!' Fevrierson cried. 'What the hell is that?'

'Something new?' Mkoll asked.

A runner almost fell into the dugout, dripping with perspiration. 'Order to repel!' he gasped.

'Repel?' Fevrierson said.

Mkoll grabbed the scope. Out in the no-man's land of the Naeme Valley, phantom shapes were advancing towards them.

'Get your men to stand ready,' he told the young lieutenant. 'We're being assaulted.'

MKOLL HURRIED OUT into the fire trench, unslinging his rifle. Men were shouting and running, knocking into each other. They'd panicked.

'Get them under control or we're dead,' the Tanith hissed at Fevrierson, who started blowing his whistle. Mkoll could hear the jangle of field phones and yelled exchanges begging for order confirmation.

He hadn't planned on this. He'd come for a little observation, not to get caught up in a storm assault.

He adjusted his micro-bead. 'Four! This is four! Sound off!'

'Thirty-two!' That was Bonin.

'Twenty-eight, four!' Caober.

'Thirteen. Moving up with sixty,' Mkvenner responded, accounting for Hwlan too.

'Forty-five, sir.' Baen.

'Four, got you. Close on me, at the dugout. Double time.'

'Thirty-two, I see contacts closing,' Bonin reported.

'Understood. Close on me. Permission granted to go active if you need to.'

More titanic impacts rocked the ground, and the sky to the west was underlit yellow with fire. The enemy's massive counter-bombardment had broken the discipline of the Allied barrage. Mkoll felt ultrasonic knocking and then smelled ozone as shields ignited along the Allied command line. In the semi-darkness, he could see the translucent white umbrellas of energy flickering over the main reserves. Still more enemy ordnance hammered down, splashing off the shields in great, deflected air blasts. In one place, a shield fizzled as it was struck and died out.

Mkoll was no artillery expert, but he knew the power and range of the enemy guns must be at least on a par with Imperial super-siege pieces. The front line, this 'Peinforq Line', had clearly been arranged to permit sustained artillery actions across ranges of five or six kilometres. The shells coming in had probably travelled more like fifteen or twenty. Fevrierson's astonished reaction alone was enough. He'd not seen anything like it. That wasn't a good sign.

Mkvenner and Hwlan rejoined Mkoll, as did Bonin a moment later. 'They're right on the parapet, less than thirty metres,' Bonin said.

'Why the feth aren't these idiots in place?' Hwlan said.

Fevrierson had got a few men onto the firestep and Mkoll heard the first dull bangs of trench mortars and the chatter of a machine cannon.

Almost immediately, as if in answer, the top of the trench's back wall started to take hits. Boards splintered and scads of earth flew out. Then one of the Genswick privates on the firestep flew backwards into the trench bottom as if he'd been clubbed in the face.

'Bayonets!' Fevrierson yelled. 'Stand by to repel!' The gathering mobs of Allied infantry slotted long, bill-tipped blades to their rifles.

'They've got to do more than repel,' Mkvenner said quietly. 'A few grenades or a well-timed push and the enemy'll be in the trench. They've got to go at them before they make the parapet…'

Mkoll looked round at Fevrierson. 'Well? While there's still time.'

'The order was to repel. Hold and repel...' Fevrierson's voice trailed off. His eyes were wide and wild in the gloom.

And then it was too late. Multiple explosions tore through the fire trench on the other side of the nearest traverse. Grenades. A second later, a stick bomb went over their heads, flung too hard. It landed on the top of the rear wall and covered them in dirt.

The infantry on the firestep started shooting. Their solid-ammo rifles made boxy, hollow bangs which overlapped with the clatter of the bolts as they were pulled back and forth. Enemy rounds whipped in low over the lip of the parapet. Two more men collapsed off the step, one spun right around by the impact.

'Hold to repel! Hold to repel!' Fevrierson was shouting.

Suddenly, a significant chunk of the facing parapet blew in, ripping panel-boards and brushwood revetting out of the wall and tossing men aside onto the duckboards. The first elements of the enemy wave scrambled down into the trench through the section their grenades had taken out. They wore khaki coats, brown corduroy breeches and slime-slick puttees, and dark green steel helmets over dirty woollen toques or chain-mail splinter masks. Most carried bulky autorifles with ugly saw-edged bayonets, but others had pistols and long-handled wire-cutters. Mkoll saw at least three who were wearing bulky grenadier waistcoats, the multiple canvas pockets stuffed with ball and stick bombs.

Spilling in through the breach, the trench raiders turned their guns and fired down the ditch line into the milling Genswick Foot. Other attackers breasted the parapet and started a rapid-fire enfilade into the heart of the section's defence.

There was a thick mob of Alliance men between Mkoll and the raiders, most of them trying to run or find cover. He could hear the whinnying smack of the enemy bullets thumping into the jostling bodies, punching through worsted and flannel, through canvas and leather, through flesh. Hit, some men convulsed but were held upright by the press. Others screamed because they were hit or because they were desperate not to be. One man was yanked up out of the mob by the force of an enfilading shot to the neck, his body cartwheeling over on top of the others. A ball bomb, round and black with a fizzing paper fuse, bounced off another man's shoulder and then blew the front of the command dugout into the air in a shower of planks.

There was general uproar from the Genswick troopers as they tried to flee from the breach and the crossfire. The bulk of them were penned in by their own confusion like animals in a slaughterhouse channel. Fevrierson and some of the men up on the firestep managed to return fire over the heads of the mob, and Mkoll counted at least two raiders go down. He thrust his way forward against the tide of panicking men.

'Feth this! Turn! Turn and fight! Come on!' he snapped.

Mkvenner and Hwlan got up onto the firestep and opened up sidelong down the trench. The sudden bursts of laser shots stunned the Genswick boys. Like they've never seen lasweapons before, Hwlan thought.

'Get down! Get down!' Mkoll yelled at the men in the trench and as they ducked and cowered, he and Bonin fired a storm of full auto-shots over their heads in support of the sideswiping fire of Mkvenner and Hwlan.

The raiders fell back under the hail of energy rounds. The front three or four were cut straight down, and fell onto the men behind them, tripping a few of them. Mkoll waded through the huddled Genswick soldiers in the trench base and opened up a field of fire on the raiders coming over the broken parapet, punishing their enfilade. He felt a rifle round thump into his chest armour, and others pass close by into the earthern wall, but he kept firing.

Fevrierson blew his whistle. 'Come on! Come on! The Imperials have got them on the turn!' Bolt-action rifles now began to volley at the intruding force. Bonin drew his lasrifle up to his shoulder and took a swift aim, snapping a single shot that dropped an enemy grenadier in the middle of the raider group. The ball bomb in his hand exploded and touched off the contents of his waistcoat. Channelled by the trench, the combined blast surged flame, shrapnel and broken pieces of duckboard in both directions.

'Go!' Mkoll yelled, storming forward with Bonin. The raided section had been effectively cleared by the blast. The air was full of soil dust, fine like flour, and it was settling across everything, making dark sticky patches where it mixed with spilled blood. The bodies of raiders, scorched black and twisted, lay across the firestep and the trench floor. One hung upside down from the parapet wire. Mkoll, Bonin and five of the Genswick Foot rushed the firestep at the broken section of the trench in time to intercept the next raiding party as it came over the parapet.

There was a savage flurry of point-blank shooting that knocked three of the raiders back out of the trench and one of the Genswickers off the step. Then it was hand-to-hand, brutal, blind. Mkoll used his rifle butt to deflect a bayonet that jabbed down at him, and then clubbed the attacker in the kneecap with it. One of the Genswick lads bayoneted an attacker through the belly and hoisted him up into the air like a labourer pitchforking a straw bale. Bonin, who'd had time to fix his silver Tanith warknife to his rifle's bayonet lug, killed one man outright and then slashed the thigh of another, cracking the man's head with his lasgun's butt as he fell. A pistol fired twice in Mkoll's ear and the Alliance private next to him screamed and fell, clutching his face. Mkoll fired his rifle and shot out the throat of the grenadier with the autopistol. The man slipped off the parapet where he had been standing, and ended up sitting, dead, on the firestep with his back to the trench wall.

Another few seconds of maniacal punching and clubbing, and the last of the raiders dropped back, denied.

Bonin and two Genswickers stood up at the parapet and started firing down into the dark to drive the raiders back out into the war-waste. Along the trench, Fevrierson and his men were now laying down a serious rifle fusillade from the step, the chatter of their solid round shots punctuated by the cracks of Mkvenner's and Hwlan's lasguns.

Mkoll crouched on the firestep and started to plunder the bombs from the dead grenadier's waistcoat. The balls had friction fuses that lit when a paper twist was yanked out. He fired them one by one, tossing them up and out over the parapet. The stick grenades had long wooden grips like brush

handles with loops of linen dangling from pins in their
bases. Mkoll realised you put your hand through the loops
before swinging the grenades out. As each one sailed off, its
pin was left hanging from his wrist on the loop. One of Fevrierson's men, wounded in the arm, came up and helped him
lob the bombs out into the night.

The Tanith sergeant switched round the moment he heard
las-fire from his left. Caober and Baen, along with three
Alliance soldiers, came around the next traverse, shooting
into the space behind. 'Flank attack!' yelled one of the
Alliance men. 'Raiders in the fire trench!'

'Hold this wall!' Mkoll yelled to Bonin, and jumped down
off the firestep, running along the trench to support Caober
and Baen. Mkvenner was running with him, along with a
handful of Fevrierson's men.

The traverse shielded them all from the raiders in the next
section, but also denied them aim. Baen hugged the end of
the traverse and snapped off shots round the corner as often
as he dared. A stick bomb came tumbling end over end across
the traverse. Almost too fast to see, Mkvenner caught it in
mid-air and slung it back. The blast curled smoke out round
the end of the traverse.

'They'll be reeling! Rush them!' one of the Genswickers
declared, and charged round the end of the defensive fortification with two of his comrades. All three were riddled with
rifle shots and slammed back against the revetment wall.
They hung there for a millisecond and then flopped onto
their faces.

Mkoll glanced at Mkvenner.

'Topside, flank and down,' said the tall, grim scout.

Mkoll nodded. He waved Caober with them and pointed
Baen to hold the corner of the traverse.

The three Ghosts threw out their camo-cloaks, and sheeted
them over their shoulders, draping them expertly so that one
hem-fold formed a hood over their heads.

Then they went up the back wall of the fire trench and over
the top.

The surface behind the fire trench was packed earth and
pools of mud. It was essentially dark, but the heavy barrage
continued to strobe the entire line with fierce flashes. In the

heat of the brutish trench fight, Mkoll had almost forgotten about the bombardment. It was still going on: the super-heavy long range shells plastering the command and supply trench areas of the entire Peinforq Line as far as he could see. Some shields still held, but only a half-hearted sporadic barrage answered the enemy thunder.

Mkoll, Caober and Mkvenner crawled forward, shrouded by their capes, hugging the mud. They'd sheathed their warknives and had slung their lasrifles over their shoulders under the capes so they wouldn't jar against stones or metal fragments on the ground. They slithered, feeling their way. Every time the light of a shell-blast lit the sky they froze.

Down in the trench to their right, they could hear Baen and the Genswick boys duelling patchily with the raiders, squeezing off shots around the traverse. Mkoll could hear the raiders shouting to each other in a language he didn't understand. But there was no mistaking the order 'Grenadze! Grenadze!'

They were just short of the rear lip now. Mkvenner undid a hoop of stiff but malleable wire from around his waist, straightened it, and pushed it out ahead of him until the tip just poked over the back edge of the fire trench. The wire had a strand of fibre optic cable wrapped around it. The tip was a tiny optical cell and at Mkvenner's end was a little pin-plug that he attached to his scope. Gently, he moved the wire around and studied the poor resolution images the cell was sending back down the cable to his scope's eyepiece.

He raised his hand just high enough for Mkoll and Caober to see. Five fingers, then three. Eight raiders. He moved his hand laterally, indicating four at the traverse corner, two below them and two more to the left.

Mkoll nodded, and reached back to slide a tube-charge from his webbing pouch. All three of them took off their lasrifles and laid them on the mud. This was going to be too tight, too constrained for rifle work. They drew out their pistols and warknives. Mkoll and Caober had standard pattern laspistols and Mkvenner had a .38 calibre auto with a twelve shot clip that he'd acquired on Nacedon. Caober and Mkvenner armed their pistols and lay face down with hand guns in their right hands and warknives in their left. Mkoll lay his laspistol on the mud beside his right hand and clamped his warknife between his teeth. Then he ripped the det-tape off the tube-charge and hurled it down into the corner of the traverse.

The blast threw the shredded form of one of the raiders right up out of the fire trench. His burning corpse bounced over the parapet and rolled into no-man's land.

By then, the three Ghosts had thrown off their cloaks and leapt down into the trench.

Mkoll landed awkwardly but squarely enough to coil into a firing crouch. He aimed right, and put las-rounds through the backs of two raiders stumbling blindly out of the blast smoke.

Mkvenner came down like a feline between the two raiders directly under their position. He headshot one point-blank, and as the man spasmed away, spun round and broke the neck of the other with a powerful sideways kick.

Caober's leap brought him down hard on top of the other two and all three collapsed in a writhing scrum on the floor of the trench. Fighting to rise, one of the raiders stood on Caober's ankle and wrenched it badly. The Tanith yowled and shot him through the pelvis. The raider went over again, screaming and hammering with his arms like a broken toy. The other raider rolled clear and slashed at Caober with his bayonet. Straight-armed, Caober blocked the spearing blade with his warknife and shot at the man, but missed. The raider drove on and Caober lost his pistol in his frantic effort to dodge.

The laspistol lay close by on the duckboards, but Caober didn't waste time trying for it. He grabbed the barrel of the raider's rifle with his now free hand and tugged it past him, stabbing the bayonet into the trench wall under his armpit and dragging the enemy's throat onto his extended knife blade. Blood squirted across Caober's chest. In his earbead, he heard Mkvenner say, 'drop,' and he did so, falling even as the corpse fell.

Five more raiders were hurtling down the trench onto them. Mkvenner ignored the rifle rounds whizzing past him and strode towards them, firing his pistol. The first and second raiders lurched backwards as if they'd been pole-axed. The third slumped on his face. The fourth was struggling with a jammed bolt when Mkvenner's shot snapped his head round and blew out his cheek. The fifth got off a shot that knocked Mkvenner sideways, blood gouting from his head.

'Ven!' Caober screamed, and threw himself at the raider, slamming him down hard. Caober pinned the soldier with his right forearm and expertly rotated his warknife in his left hand, switching the blade from tip up to tip down. Once it was down, Caober thumped the blade repeatedly into the raider's chest.

Mkoll had finished off the raiders half-killed by the tube-charge and came running back down the fire trench with Baen and the Genswick troopers on his heels. Still more raiders, including a grenadier, were behind the second five.

Mkoll's pistol toppled one, and then Baen was firing on full auto with his lasgun. The Alliance troopers beside him supported with fire from their rifles.

Mkoll moved forward over the crumpled bodies. 'You two! Ahead and secure the trench!' he ordered and a pair of infantry men ran ahead. 'You others, up on the firestep!' The rest clambered up onto the step and began shooting into the night.

'Trench secure!' one of the Genswickers shouted back. He'd linked up with members of his own platoon pushing out from behind the next traverse.

'Onto the step, then!' Mkoll urged. 'See them off!'

Caober struggled up and ran to where Baen was kneeling over Mkvenner. There was an appalling spill of blood.

'Sacred Feth!' Caober stammered. 'Ven!'

'Oh, shut up,' growled Mkvenner tersely. He had a nub of cloth jammed to his ear and when he took it away, blood squirted from his ear. 'It took my ear lobe off. That's all.'

'Feth!' Caober gasped with such relief Baen and Mkvenner both started to laugh.

THERE WERE NO more raids against station 143 that night, though Fevrierson's men stood to on the firestep at alert drill. Word filtered back that stations 129, 131, 146 and 147 had been intruded with serious losses, though by midnight only 146 was still the scene of fighting as Alliance troops doggedly drove the raiders out. Unconfirmed reports said that an entire section had been overrun between stations 287 and 311, and from the noise of combat washing down the line, Mkoll could believe it.

The enemy barrage ended, abruptly, at midnight, leaving just a dismal fog of ash vapour and fyceline smoke drifting down over the allied lines. At 01.00, the Alliance gun-dens commenced a counter-bombardment that mercilessly whipped the Shadik front-line positions across the Naeme until dawn.

At 02.15, with the punitive artillery searing the sky behind them, Mkoll assembled his team and bade farewell to Fevrierson. The young lieutenant saluted and shook Mkoll's hand, and many of his weary company clapped and cheered.

'You're going back?' Fevrierson asked.

'Should have been back long since. We've a reconnoitre to report.'

'Thanks,' said Fevrierson. 'Thank you. Emperor bless you.'

'These are good men,' said Mkoll, nodding to the mud-spattered infantry all around them. 'Keep them tight and you'll keep them alive.'

'I hope I never see you again.' said Fevrierson. 'I'd never wish this shit-hole on anybody, especially not for a second time.'

Mkoll nodded. Bonin grinned.

'What will you tell this commander of yours?' Fevrierson asked.

'The truth,' said Mkoll. 'The front's everything he was afraid it would be.'

THREE
A.S. HQ RHONFORQ

'…and to the general disposition of auxiliary support elements,
officers of said elements are to answer to (i) the primary
commander of their given area/sector, and (ii) the ranking
Alliance officer in their specific line subdivision.'
– Aexe Alliance *General Order Book*, 772th edition,
section 45f, paragraph iv, 'Command Protocol'

FROM RHONFORQ, you could see the massive smoke spume
rising from the Peinforq Line ten kilometres away to the east.
During the night, the old chafstone buildings of the town
had vibrated to the distant symphony of the guns.

Dawn was at 04.37 Imperial. The sun rose, dull and veiled,
over the woods towards Ongche, and mist fumed over the
strand meadows and market gardens west of the town. The
Tanith First had slept for about five hours in poor billets on
the southern edge of the town, but most of their motor pool
staff and armourers had been up all night. They'd laid off
from the trains at 21.00 the previous evening, along with two
companies of Krassians and a motorised battalion of
Seqgewehr coming up from Seronne.

Gaunt rose at 05.00, stiff and sour. All night, despatch riders and material transports had rattled by down the street under his window. He'd been billeted in a pension off the town square. Daur and Rawne occupied rooms there too, along with five of the Krassian officers and a number of Aexe Alliance staffers. Corbec had elected to billet with the Ghosts.

Gaunt's room was small and spare, with low, sloped ceilings and a window that wouldn't close properly. Beltayn knocked and brought him a canister of caffeine and a bowl of lukewarm water.

'Mkoll back yet?' Gaunt asked, attempting to shave using the tepid water. Beltayn was laying out Gaunt's service uniform on the bed.

'On his way, sir.'

'Delayed?'

'Something was awry.'

'For instance?'

'You heard the shelling, sir. The whole place is buzzing with it. New super-siege guns. The line took a pasting last night.'

'I thought as much,' said Gaunt . 'I wo–oow!'

Beltayn looked up. 'Sir?'

'Nicked myself,' said Gaunt, raising his chin to study the razor wound on his throat in the mirror. 'This water's almost cold, Beltayn.'

'That water's as warm as it gets unless it decides to be caffeine,' Beltayn said. He brushed the crown of Gaunt's cap and set it on the bed. Then he came over to Gaunt and peered at his cut. 'You've had worse,' he said.

Gaunt smiled. 'Thank you for that.'

'What you want is a needle,' said Beltayn.

'A needle?'

'Old family trick. A needle. Excellent when it comes to shaving nicks.'

'How does it work?'

'When you cut yourself with the razor, you take the needle and poke it into your gums.'

'That works?'

Beltayn winked. 'Sure as feth blots out the pain of the nick.'

* * *

DRESSED, AND WITH a tab of Beltayn's cigarette paper stuck to his shaving wound, Gaunt took his caffeine outside. The day was clear and promisingly warm, though the stink of fyceline was everywhere. He stopped on the pension's terrace to chat with a Krassian major and two officers from the Seqgewehr, and saw Rawne and Feygor demolishing a fried breakfast in the small dining room.

A column of tanks clanked past through the square. Gaunt finished his drink, put the empty cup on one of the terrace tables, and walked across the road to the Chapel St Avigns where the Allied staff headquarters was sited.

Rhonforq was one of the Octal Burgs – eight high church municipalities that sustained the authority of the See of Ghrennes through Mittel Aexe. Its church and cloister had been built in 502, ten years after the first colony footing at Samonparliane, and before the war its chief activities had been wool-carding, button manufacture and cheese making. Visitors were invited to throw a coin into the fountain of Beati Hagia or, if they were sound of limb, take in the hike to the Sheffurd Hills to view the birthplace of Governor-General Daner Fep Kvelsteen, whose autograph and seal were included in the famous four at the bottom of the Great Aexe Declaration of Sovereignty.

Gaunt knew that much from a dog-eared, obsolete touring guide he'd discovered under his bed the night before.

Allied staff headquarters was thronging with activity. In the inner cloister, a rank of despatch riders waited on humming motorcycles. Sheafs of telegraph and vox-cable trunked out of windows and noodled up into the dish arrays anchored to the rooves. A shield mast attached to a portable generator dominated the quadrangle, the grass beneath it brown and dead from radiation.

Gaunt hurried up the front steps of the main chapel, accepting the salutes of passing Alliance officers.

'Where's Van Voytz?' he asked an adjutant at the desk.

'You mean General Van Voytz?' the adjutant replied testily without looking up.

'If we're going to be formal, you say "Lord General Van Voytz, colonel-commissar", sir,' Gaunt growled, snapping his fingers so that the adjutant would look up. He did and gulped.

'Beg pardon, sir. The lord general has gone ahead to Meiseq, but he's expected back tomorrow night.'

'I want to vox him.'

'Vox-lines have been cut by last night's barrage, sir.'

Put another way, something's awry, Gaunt thought.

'What about Lyntor-Sewq?'

'The supreme commander has been called away, sir.'

'Feth it!' snarled Gaunt. 'I need to be briefed. I need to see charts! I need–'

'One moment, sir. I'll ring through.'

The adjutant hurriedly lifted the receiver of his field telephone and cranked the handle. 'Colonel-Commissar Gaunt, for briefing,' he said and paused.

'Wait one moment, sir,' he told Gaunt, replacing the handset.

'Colonel-Commissar!' the voice echoed around the hall. Gaunt looked round to see a tall, pale, ginger haired officer in a dark red uniform advancing towards him across the paved hallway.

Gaunt saluted him.

'Gaunt, Tanith First-and-Only.'

'Redjacq Ankre, Kottstadt Wyverns. I'm acting authority for the Alliance in Lyntor-Sewq's absence. Follow me.'

Gaunt fell into step with the taller man, and they walked down towards the doors of the main situations room. There was something about Ankre, something in his bearing and manner, that made Gaunt bristle. But he ignored the feeling. He'd been Guard long enough to know that you often didn't like the men you had to count as allies. Stifling personal opinion usually helped get the job done.

'I met some of your men last night,' Ankre said, apropos of nothing.

'Indeed?'

'A scout party.'

'Ah yes, I sent them ahead.'

'You didn't trust our intelligence reports?'

Gaunt stopped and made eye contact with the big redhead. 'I'm sure they're fine. I haven't actually seen one,' he said venomously. Ankre paused, not sure how best to deal with the criticism. Before he had time to make his mind up,

Gaunt smoothed past the remark by saying, 'So, you were at the front last night?'

'Yes, I was,' the colonel replied stiffly.

'It seemed like you took a bruising. New heavy siege weapons, I hear.'

'I didn't think you'd read a briefing,' Ankre said, enjoying the slyness of his retort.

'I have eyes and ears. So… new enemy tactics, then? New weapons?'

'Yes,' said Ankre. A sentry in green Alliance fatigues saluted and held the door for them.

The nave of the old chapel had been converted for military use. The windows were taped and blacked, though Gaunt could make out the lead ridges of the old stained glass. Flak-board baffles lined the room, banked with sandbags, and the air was dry and warm and smelled of electricity. Glow-globes floated beneath the rafters, illuminating a central area busy with technicians, aides and officers. Portable codifiers and high-gain vox-casters had been uncrated and set up on trestles. There was a constant murmur of voices, a chatter of machines, the occasional whistle of tuning vox-channels, background static. A pair of hooded acolytes from the Adeptus Mechanicus were blessing the servitors that were being installed at the new Imperial vox-units.

The situations room was a confidential area. Inside the door, Gaunt had to give his name and serial code to a clerk and was issued with a small green pin-badge. High Command wanted a thorough record of everyone who came and went.

Ankre led Gaunt across to a chart table, which Gaunt studied keenly. It was a complete mess of over-mapped gibberish. Ankre gave him a blurred, low-detail map showing only a small field section. It had been printed on flimsy paper.

'Your regiment is to move up to the 55th sector along communication line 2319 at dusk tonight and take position along the front to secure stations 287 to 295. Your chain of command is to Major Neillands at station 280 and then to General Hargunten at Area/Sector. Here are the day's challenge codes and vox frequencies.' Ankre handed Gaunt a data-slate. 'Familiarise yourself with them and then erase the slate.'

'My chain of command runs through a major?' asked Gaunt.

'Is there a problem?'

'This Neillands will relay orders from area/sector?'

'Of course, in the event that you can't receive them yourself… if, say, vox is down.'

'What if Neillands can't receive orders from area/sector… if, say, his vox is down? I answer to him?'

Ankre shrugged as if he still couldn't see what the problem was. 'Yes, as I have said–'

'I heard what you said, colonel. I just don't believe it. You are saying that, in certain circumstances, most likely the kind of circumstances when it really matters, I am supposed to answer to a junior officer? I am expected to put my command… my regiment… into his hands?'

Ankre frowned. 'Get me the *General Order Book*,' he told an aide. The man returned in a few seconds bearing a fat, red-sleeved folder stamped with the Alliance crest and the words 'Most Secret – Destroy in Case of Jeopardy'. Ankre leafed through it. Gaunt could see that most of the pages were type-written inserts, pasted or stapled in. 'The supreme commander has this arranged in black and white,' he said, unamused. 'His tactical staff working party drew it up once we'd been advised of your approach. Here… chain of command as I said.'

'Let me see that,' said Gaunt. Ankre seemed reluctant to let the book go, but handed it over after a pause. Gaunt read down the badly typed order docket. 'This says nothing about our position. No specifics. It simply says that we are to answer to the primary officer of whatever sector we are sent to–'

'That's General Hargunten.'

'And secondarily to the senior Alliance officer in our line area.'

'Exactly what I said. The senior Alliance officer in your line area is Major Neillands of the Feinster Highlanders.'

Gaunt shook his head. 'I don't think so. I think rather that Major Neillands should answer to me. In the event that we lose contact with area/sector, that would be the best protocol.'

'Well, that's unfortunate,' said Ankre. 'The word you seem to be ignoring is "Alliance". You are to answer to the Alliance chain of command. The supreme commander is merely following the will of the high sezar. He has made it clear that the Aexe Alliance forces are to remain in control of this war. If that means you have to swallow your pride and answer to a major, then deal with it. You have come here to fight for the Alliance.'

'I have come here to fight for the Emperor,' Gaunt hissed. 'We stand together against Shadik. We of the Guard are now part of the Alliance.'

'Not technically,' said Ankre, taking the folder out of Gaunt's hands and thumbing to another page. 'Here. It is quite specific. The Imperial expedition is termed "auxiliary support".'

He closed the folder and smiled as if to suggest he had won the short debate. Gaunt knew there was absolutely no point arguing with him. He'd met men like Ankre before. He'd go over his head.

Gaunt turned to the chart and found, with some difficulty, the station points Ankre had mentioned.

'This is the front line?'

'Yes.'

'My men are light infantry, specialising in covert action. It's a waste to put them there.'

'We do not have the luxury of being choosy. Stations 287 through to 311 were overrun last night by the enemy, the largest breach in the Peinforq Line. The enemy has been driven out, but reinforcement is essential in that area. Vital. A brigade of Krassians will move forward to fill stations 296 to 311, to the north of you.'

'I repeat my objection.'

'Are you afraid your men will be unable to hold a trench line?'

Gaunt took off his cap and his gloves and set them down on the edge of the chart table. This action gave him a few seconds to breathe deeply and still his rage.

'I am afraid of nothing except the stupidity of a blinkered high command system,' he replied.

Ankre stepped back a pace and lowered his head slightly, aggressively. 'The supreme commander selected the Tanith

for this position entirely on the basis of the good account
your scout party made of itself last night. The whole of 55th
sector is talking about it this morning. A handful of men, but
they turned the tide at station 143. That's the kind of expertise the commander wants at the line, especially at a stretch
that is weak and vulnerable.'

'Even if we are merely auxiliary support?'

Ankre handed the folder back to the waiting aide. 'I think
we're done here, colonel-commissar,' he said.

'I want a copy of the field charts,' said Gaunt.

'Why?' asked Ankre, now clearly beginning to lose his
patience.

Gaunt held up the flimsy field map. 'Because this shows
only my immediate position.'

'Your point?'

'How can I effect optimal command if I only get to see the
specific vicinity? How can I appreciate the battle as a whole?'

'You don't need to. You have a specific duty. That is what
you must perform. That is all you should be interested in.'

Gaunt slid the map and the data-slate into his coat and put
his gloves and cap back on. 'I can't believe that in this day
and age you're still fighting wars like this,' he said. 'Have you
never read Macharius? Solon? Slaydo?'

'None of those fine warriors are here on Aexe,' said Ankre.

'More's the pity,' snapped Gaunt. He strode away, then
turned and glared back at Ankre. 'I'll mobilise my troops. But
I will not move them up the line until I have met with an
Alliance commander – any Alliance commander – who can
verify these orders more satisfactorily than you. Make that
happen, colonel. Make that happen fast.'

Ankre's look was murderous. 'This is tantamount to insub-
ordination. I could have you–'

'Word of advice,' said Gaunt, cutting in sharply. 'You do not
ever want to mess with me. Bite your tongue, find me someone more useful than yourself, and never threaten me again.
Are we clear?'

Ankre said nothing. The whole situations room had fallen
silent. Gaunt turned his back on them all and marched out.

* * *

'Do me a favour,' sighed Dorden. 'Hold the feth still, eh?'

Trooper Caober shrugged. 'It's sore as a scalded shoggy, doc,' he moaned.

'You're a big boy. Shut up. Do you see Ven making a fuss? You do not. He's bleeding like a stuck hog, but do we hear a whimper? We do not at all. So shut up.'

Caober sighed and gritted his teeth. He was sitting up on a wooden table in the Ghosts' temporary medicae station, a derelict woollen mill on the southern fringe of Rhonforq. The mill was big and old, built from flinty, black stone, and straddled a gushing stream that the wool-workers had once used for washing excess lanolin from the fleeces. There was a damp, fatty smell, and every surface was sticky with grease. The orderlies had offered to scrub it down with bristle-brushes, but Dorden didn't suppose they would be there long enough for it to be worth the elbow. Midday sunlight, hard and yellow, stabbed down through ventilator panels in the high, tiled roof, and lit the hall with a sickly light. Most of the mill equipment had been shifted out long since. Tiny shreds of wool fibre still clung to nicks in beams and rough brick edges.

Mkoll's team had arrived back in Rhonforq at 11.30 that morning, and Mkoll, Caober and Mkvenner had reported immediately to the medicae station. Dorden was tending to Caober's wrenched ankle while Lesp dressed Mkvenner's ear-wound. Mkoll had said his own injuries could wait. An adjoining mill hall had been occupied by the Krassian medics, and many voices echoed through from the Krassian troops lining up for inoculator shots.

'How did this happen again?' asked Dorden, examining the scout's bared foot and ankle. The flesh was puffy and lilac with bruising.

'It – ow! – it got stood on. There was a fight.'

'So Mkoll says. A good one?'

'So-so. You know.'

Dorden glanced up at Caober. 'No, I don't. Tell me about it. Allow me to live the war vicariously through your bravado while I stay back here soaking bandages.'

'There was a fight. Ow! A fight. In the trench. Enemies came in, so we fought them. I – ow! – got my ankle stood on.'

Caober faltered and his voice tailed off. He was a fine scout, but his story-telling ability left everything to be desired.

Dorden continued to wind bandages tightly around Caober's ankle. 'Somebody fill me in. Ven?'

Mkvenner looked up, his ear packed with gauze. 'Pardon?'

Dorden laughed, and so did everyone else – Lesp, washing his hands in a tin bowl, Chayker and Foskin sorting surgical tools. Even Mkoll, sitting on a chair in the corner.

'What's funny? I can't hear,' growled Mkvenner. The laughter stopped. No one wanted Mkvenner to think they were taking the piss out of him. Mkvenner was one of those Ghosts you respected, every second of the day.

'When the barrage started, they tested the line with trench raiders,' Mkoll said as he got up. Dorden could tell at a glance he was holding himself stiffly as he moved. 'It got very messy. The locals weren't at all prepared.'

Dorden tied off the bandage and called over to Foskin. 'Get Caober's boot back on, loose, and find him a crutch. Stay off it for a few days and you'll be good to go.' He wiped his hands and moved over to Mkoll. 'Let's take a look,' he said.

Mkoll started to take off his webbing and jacket, but it clearly hurt him to lift his arms, so Dorden helped him strip down to the waist. The bruise across the pale flesh of his chest was ugly and black.

'Feth! You been playing smack-stick again?' asked Dorden.

'Rifle round. Took it last night. Didn't notice it at the time. Adrenalin, I suppose. Been hurting like a fether since dawn, though.'

Dorden tutted and sprayed Mkoll's wound with counterseptic. By his side, Foskin clucked in amazement. He'd been folding Mkoll's clothes and kit. He held up a mangled large calibre round. 'Your chest armour stopped this,' he said. 'It was buried in your breast-guard. You want me to throw it away?'

Mkoll took it and put in his trouser pocket. He had his own battlefield superstitions.

'I see the war's started without me,' said a voice from behind them. Gaunt had entered the mill. 'Carry on,' he added, before they all started throwing salutes. He peered at Mkoll's hefty bruise. 'First blood to them, I take it?'

'We gave a good account,' said Mkoll.

'So I hear. I met your fan club. A Colonel Ankre.'

'Who?' murmured Mkoll. 'Oh, him. The red-head. I didn't think he'd taken to us much.'

'You're the heroes of the line, my friend,' said Gaunt sarcastically. 'The locals are so impressed, they've given us a whole front trench to hold.'

'Feth,' Mkoll said.

'You told them–' Dorden began.

'Oh, I told them all right. I don't think they were listening.' Gaunt sighed. He handed the flimsy map to Mkoll. 'This is what we're taking on, if they have their way.'

Mkoll looked over the slip. 'Bad place. Took the worst of it last night. The very worst. The river comes in close here, you see? The parapet is low and waterlogged. Ideal for storming. I wasn't sure they'd even got it clear.'

'Tell me what you saw up front,' Gaunt said, sitting down as Dorden dressed Mkoll's nasty wound.

'The Alliance soldiers we saw were tired and over-stretched. Ill too, most of them. Low sanitation, low hygiene. What's worse, they have precious little discipline. They fight well enough when they're ordered up and controlled, but there's no sign of initiative.'

'They panicked when the raid started,' said Caober.

'To be fair,' said Mkvenner, 'they panicked when the shelling started. They'd never seen that before, not like that. I think they were fairly fit as front-line infantry, but when those new super-guns opened up, they were milling and broken and scared. And the enemy raiders punched right in through them.'

Gaunt nodded. 'The enemy?'

'Good, tight, professional. Solid ammo weapons, some body armour. The grenadiers are their strength. Simple explosives, but effective, and in large numbers.'

Gaunt listened to his chief scout and then said, 'So… what does Lord General Mkoll think?'

It was a private joke. Gaunt trusted Mkoll's tactical mind absolutely, and often voiced this hypothetical question. If Mkoll was supreme commander here, what would he do?

'This fight'll go on till doomsday,' said Mkoll, once he'd considered things. 'It's been going on forty years. A deadlock.

You might think that Guard reinforcements like us might overtip the balance in favour of the Alliance, but then so might these new super-guns, in favour of the enemy. What I'm saying is it'll take something new, something lateral, to break this. Can't say what with only this fething map to go by.'

'I'm working on that,' Gaunt assured him.

Mkoll shrugged, and then winced and wished he hadn't. 'I don't know. Something new. Something different or unexpected. Something from a new angle. We'd better find out what. Before they do.'

'I know something,' said Mkvenner quietly. 'These new super-guns they've got. They might have been developing them for years, but don't you think it's funny they first use them a day or two after we arrive? They must've seen our ships coming in. They must know the Guard is here and that the Alliance has off-world reinforcements at last. They're afraid the Alliance has got the edge. They want the edge back.'

'I'll give 'em the edge back,' Caober chuckled, testing the sharpness of his straight silver warknife.

'Hold that thought,' Gaunt told him with a smile. He looked at Mkoll. 'Write me up a full report. Everything and anything.'

'Will do, sir.'

Gaunt was about to say something else when angry voices broke into the mill hall. Ana Curth burst in. 'Dorden, where the feth are– Oh! My apologies, sir.'

Gaunt stood. 'As you were, Surgeon Curth. I believe you were about to cuss again.'

'Fething right,' she said. 'I can't find our fething supplies and the supplies should be there and the Krassians are blaming–'

'Whoa, whoa!' said Dorden. 'From the top and remember to breathe this time.'

Ana Curth took a deep breath. She'd been a well-respected and well-paid civilian medic on Verghast before the Zoican War and, to the amazement of Dorden and Gaunt, had elected to join the Tanith regiment at the Act of Consolation. No one had ever found out why she'd cast aside a comfortable, rewarding lifestyle in favour of the thankless miseries of an Imperial Guard medicae posting. Gaunt believed it was because she had a sense of duty that probably put them all to shame.

They were fething lucky to have her.

'Our supplies are missing,' she said. 'All of them. Everything we shipped in from the Munitorium vessels. I looked for them at embarkation and was told they had been trained ahead. But they're not here.'

'No, no,' said Chayker. 'I saw them. Piled up in the lean-to behind the mill.'

'Oh, there are plenty of gakking crates there, Chayks,' said Curth. 'And they're all marked with the Tanith and Krassian symbols. But they've got nothing in them except dirty cotton wool and straw. The Krassian medics are trying to give their men field shots, and there's nothing to use, and they're claiming we pinched them all–'

'All right, all right…' Gaunt said. 'What have we got?'

'About thirty cases of one-shot mire-fever doses and about the same in anti-toxin pills,' said Lesp. 'Everything we brought up the line ourselves, sir.'

'Give them to the Krassians.'

'Gaunt!' Curth started.

'Do it. I won't have bad feeling with good allies like the Krassians. I'll find our supplies, and the Krassians' supplies too. We'll make do until then.'

'Ever the diplomat, eh, Ibram?' smiled Dorden.

'They once invited me to join the Imperial diplomatic officium,' said Gaunt. 'I told them to feth off.'

THERE WAS LAUGHTER ringing from the old wool mill. His driver had told him this was the place set aside for the Imperial Guard medicae units. Laughter seemed a strange sound to hear. He walked in from the car, entering a large hall where eight men and a woman stood around, hooting and chuckling. It seemed like the officer had just told a really good joke. Four of the men and the woman were medics. The others, apart from the officer in his stern cap, were black-tunicked troopers, all of them injured.

He cleared his throat and the laughter stopped. They all looked round.

'I believe you were asking for me,' he said. 'I am Count Iaco Bousar Fep Golke.'

COUNT GOLKE WAS a quiet, silver-haired Aexegarian dressed in a dark green uniform that showed no decoration apart from the insignia of Aexegary on the collar and shoulder boards, and the golden aquila medal pinned at his throat. He walked with a slight limp, and Gaunt could see that his neatly trimmed silver beard had been grown, in part, to disguise old burns on his cheek and throat. He introduced himself as chief of staff/liaison.

They walked together across the yard outside the mill.

'We've met already,' Gaunt said. 'In passing. I was one of the Imperial officers presented to you that night at the high sezar's palace.'

'I thought so,' replied Golke. 'I confess that night I was rather distant. Forgive me if I was distracted. The surprise news of the Imperial arrival, my unexpected decoration...' He patted the gold eagle medal. Gaunt knew Golke wasn't mentioning the fact that he had just been stripped of rank too. That night had marked the end of Golke's four year tenure as supreme commander of the Aexe Alliance forces. A blow to his pride, Gaunt imagined. Another little puffed up aristo general, who'd made his rank by dint of noble blood rather than command merit, now drummed out of office to make way for the newcomers. Gaunt expected bitterness and resentment. He was surprised when he detected none. Golke seemed to be nothing except tired and disenchanted.

'My new role,' said Golke, leaning against a gatepost to ease his leg, 'as I understand it at least, is to facilitate communication between the Alliance and the Imperial expedition. It's all rather formless and vague, so I have to thank you.'

'How so?'

'Giving me something decent to do, colonel-commissar. Something other than the futile round of cocktail welcome parties and handshaking. You've quite rattled Redjacq Ankre.'

'If I may speak freely?'

Golke made an ushering sweep with his hand.

'Colonel Ankre displayed to me a real ignorance of modern warfare methods. He is blinkered, clinging to outmoded and

discredited principles and strategies. Indeed, this whole war–'
Gaunt stopped.

'Go on, colonel-commissar.'

'I should not, sir. I barely know you and I don't feel it is my place to deliver a critique of your nation's war-making.'

Golke smiled. It was quite a winning smile, even if one corner of his mouth, fused by scar tissue, refused to bend. 'Colonel-Commissar Gaunt, I was twenty-nine years old when this bloody war began. I served as a front-line infantry officer for twelve years, then joined the Office of Strategy for another fifteen, then some time in the east, then five years as area general in sector 59, then four as supreme commander. Never in that time was I one hundred per cent happy about the way Aexegary prosecuted this war. I criticised, objected, used my rank to try to make changes I thought would be beneficial. It was like pushing water uphill. So let's make a deal. Speak freely and speak your mind. If I am offended, we'll agree to disagree.'

Gaunt nodded. 'Then I'd say this war would have been over thirty years ago if the Alliance had for one moment overhauled their martial philosophies. You're fighting this like a pre-firearm campaign, like something from the days of antiquity. The use of infantry and cavalry, the dependence on cannon, the expenditure of manpower. And, forgive me, the reliance on the nobility for command personnel.'

Golke chuckled ruefully.

'There is a concept that we in the Guard hold true. Total war. The prosecution of an enemy that takes no account of national boundaries or political structure. War with a single, unswerving objective, to defeat the foe. War that never stays still but is constantly looking for new opportunities. True to such a concept, the Imperial Guard has triumphed over the enemies of the Emperor in all theatres. We advance, both physically and mentally. You have stagnated, intellectually, as truly and deeply as your front line.'

'You don't pull punches, do you, Gaunt?'

'Not when I'm invited to throw one for free. Look, sir, I know Aexegary has a long and illustrious history of military success, but you're still fighting wars the way your ancestors did. Shadik is not a bellicose neighbour state to be bested on the field and then invited over for diplomatic reparations. It is a cancer, a spreading evil of Chaos that will not, ever, play by the old rules. It will grind you down, invade you and consume you.'

'I know that.'

'Then you seem to be alone. Ankre doesn't know it. Not at all.'

'Ankre is old school. He's a Kottmarker. They're anxious to prove their worth in the Alliance. What am I saying? We're all old school.' Golke looked over at the roofscape of Rhonforq, squinting as if the afternoon light hurt his eyes. 'Enlighten me, then.'

'In the first place, the Tanith are stealth experts. They'll fight like bastards in a front line, but that'd be wasting them. They need to be used, not as cannon fodder, but as the incisive weapons they are.'

'That makes sense.'

'Second... dispersal of information. I know that it's vital to guard dispositional data from enemy eyes, but this is plainly ridiculous.'

Gaunt pulled out the scrappy map Ankre had given him. 'I think I speak for every Imperial officer when I say that we need an overall perspective. How can I press any advantages I might make if I have no clear idea of the bigger picture?'

'Ankre told me you were after general charts. The idea appalled him. Our way of warmaking revolves around individual commanders performing their appointed tasks and leaving the concerns of general strategy to the staff chiefs.'

'That's like fighting blindfold, or at least fighting with just a narrow view through a little slit.'

Golke put his hand in his jacket pocket and produced a data-slate. 'Copy everything on this,' he said. 'These are the full charts you wanted. But be circumspect. Ankre and the Alliance generals would have me shot if they thought I'd given these to you.'

'I'll be careful.'

'Give me time, and I'll get the idea accepted by the GSC. If we can prove the advantage, it'll make it easier for them to swallow. Your commander, Van Voytz, is working on them too. I don't believe he's terribly happy with the situation either.'

'I didn't expect he would be,' smiled Gaunt.

'Now do me a favour. Advance your regiment to the appointed stations. Show willing. I'll go back to the supreme commander and petition him to act on your advice. A day or two, perhaps three. Then we might see results.'

Gaunt nodded, and shook the count's hand. 'You have the chance to win this war, sir,' he said. 'Don't let the Alliance waste it.'

FOUR
287–311

*'Sergeant Tona Criid? Sergeant Tona Criid? I like
the sound of that. No other gak-face will, though.'*

– Tona Criid, sergeant

IT WAS THE Ghosts' third day on the line. They'd got used to the
routines: the patrol circuits, the wire-expeditions, the bilge-
pumping, the observations, the manhandling of latrine
buckets out up the communication trench, the man-handling
of food buckets back down from the cookhouse ('I swear they
get those fething buckets mixed up most times,' Rawne was
heard to say). They'd even got used to what Corbec called the
'trench walk' – stooped, head down, so nothing projected
above the parapet.

The tension remained. Since the night of Mkoll's advance
party, there'd been no bombardment. On day two, the enemy
had assaulted the line twenty-five kilometres north at station
317, but otherwise it had been quiet.

One-third of the regiment had advanced to the line, leaving the other two-thirds in reserve at Rhonforq. At the end of
the first week, they were to rotate, and begin a pattern that

meant no trooper stayed on the line for more than a week, and every trooper got two weeks' rest in reserve in every three. Gaunt, of course, hoped the Tanith wouldn't be staying at the front for anything like that long.

At the line, the Ghosts were caked in mud after the first few hours, and crawling with lice after the first day. They slept, as best they could, curled up under the lip of the parapet, or in hand-scooped dugouts.

Criid had become so muddy she'd decided not to fight it any more. She'd plastered mud across her face and matted it into her hair.

'What the feth are you doing, sarge?' Skeen had asked.

'Camouflage,' she said.

Fifteen minutes later, all but two of her platoon had followed suit and daubed themselves with mud. Kolea hadn't, because he hadn't understood what was going on.

Cuu hadn't, because, well, he was Cuu.

Still, Criid congratulated herself, I seem to have most of the platoon pulling together. Maybe I can do this.

Ten platoon occupied station 290, with eleven platoon, Obel's, to their north, and sixteen platoon, Maroy's, to their south.

Each station represented about a kilometre of fire trench, broken in twenty metre intervals by traverses. They had a dugout bunker with a field telephone and vox, but the Ghosts' personal vox-links had made that obsolete most of the time.

Three times a day, Criid did her tour, accompanied by Hwlan and DaFelbe. She checked trench integrity, she checked that food was getting through, she checked the obs stations. She individually inspected each trooper's kit, ammo supply, and feet for trench foot.

The third day was dismal. Rain blew in from the west, angled in such a manner that the trench sides offered absolutely no shelter. The rain also tasted of something, something faintly metallic, faintly chemical. Someone said that blister gas had been used the day before up north in the Meiseq Box, and some troopers put on their breather hoods or tied cloth over their mouths. The sky was low and oppressive, churning with fast-moving cloud that was almost black.

It sapped the colour from the day. Faces became pale, eye sockets shadowed.

Some of the trench's previous incumbents – the Seventy-seventh Lunsgatte Rifle Brigade – had stayed behind. A detachment of thirty had been remaindered to man the trench mortars in the pocket dugouts spaced behind the main fire trench. Their fire-officer, a sergeant called Hartwig, joined Criid when she toured the mortar dens. He was tall and humourless, huddled in a mud-flecked grey oilskin, toque and a green kepi with a metal badge that showed some sort of bear-like animal. His men didn't mix much with the Tanith. They seemed content to live in the cramped hollows of the dens. Criid got the impression Hartwig and his men didn't think much of a unit that included women, let alone one that was led by one.

The mortars were squat, blue-metal machines called feldwerfers, and used compressed gas to fire the three kilo shells pneumatically. The crews kept the weapons spotlessly clean, they were forever polishing and oiling them. In contrast, the men themselves were filthy and their uniforms piecemeal. Most wore toques or loose hoods, with sleeveless leather jackets or fleeces, and many had flat sheets of armour tied or strung across their chests. Dirt caked their hands and faces black.

Interspersed with the mortars were Favell-pattern spring guns, a heavy little catapult engine that looked to Criid like some kind of pipe organ. It took two men to operate the double windlass and crank back the long throwing arm to the cock-stop. When the trigger lanyard was pulled, the cluster of massive springs in the main body of the weapon slammed the arm up and lobbed grenades or ball bombs out over the fire trench and into the battlefield.

Hartwig assured Criid that the Favell could send a grenade over two hundred and fifty metres. The trick was to set the grenade's fuse so that it didn't detonate high in its arc. They needed to blow on the ground, or near it, but if the grenadiers left the fuse too long, there was a risk that the enemy would have time to gather them up and toss them back. One member of each spring gun team had a clay pipe on the go at all times, an ignition source ready and waiting to start fuses that was a lot less fiddly than matches or gun-string.

The Seventy-seventh Lunsgatte weren't the only prior inhabitants who had stayed in the fire trench. Shrunken, eroded body parts protruded from the trench floor and sometimes the wall, usually where the rain had exposed them. During a heavy period of action three years before, Criid learned, the troops at these stations had been obliged to bury their dead in the trench itself. Water damage was slowly raising them back into the daylight.

During her midday tour on the third day, Criid found Lubba and Vril trying to shore up a section of revetment that was falling in thanks to the rain. Part of the parapet overhang had become a gutter for the rainwater, which was now gushing into the trench in a thick stream. The task was made all the more unpleasant because where the timber had come away, ancient cadavers had been exposed, curled and almost mummified.

'Gak,' she said, viewing the scene.

'We need more planks,' said Lubba. 'Even if we get these back in place, they're rotten through.'

Criid looked at Hartwig. 'Planking? Flakboard?'

He laughed at her. 'You're joking.'

'Any suggestions, then?' she said. She was quickly becoming tired with Hartwig's dreary resignation.

'There's sometimes some brushwood at station 282. They bring it forward along the supply trench there when its available.'

'Brushwood?'

'Anything will do,' said Vril.

Criid turned to Hwlan. 'Go on down to 282 and see if you can get your hands on some.'

'Yes, sarge.'

'What about damming that stream?' DaFelbe suggested, pointing at the liquid mud gushing down over the lip.

'We'd have to get up over the parapet. So I'd rather be wet than dead,' said Vril.

'After dark, then?' Criid ventured.

'Sure, sarge. Once it's dark.'

There was a wet, loose gurgle and another section of the revet slumped into the trench where Lubba was trying to force it back in. Greasy mud slithered out, shedding another

vile body with it. The corpse was staring, its jaws open in a
scream, but its eyes and mouth were full of mud.

'Oh gak... Hwlan!' Criid called after the scout. He stopped
and looked back.

'See if you can find Zweil too.'

Hwlan nodded.

They moved on a little way. Criid checked the next two or
three troopers at the firestep: Vulli, Jajjo, Kenfeld, Subeno.
Kenfeld's boots were leaking and he needed foot-powder.

Then they reached Cuu, or at least Cuu's position. The
firestep was empty.

'Mkhef!' Criid called to the next man along. 'Where's Cuu?'

'Latrine, sarge!' the trooper called back.

They waited, and Cuu reappeared. As soon as he saw Criid,
he unslung his rifle and held it out for inspection, wordlessly.
There was no expression in his eyes. His face still bore the
bruise marks where she'd dented it.

'You left your post, Cuu.'

'Had to.'

'You wait until change-over.'

He shook his head. 'Couldn't wait. My belly's a mess.
Gakking food round here. An emergency, sure as sure.'

'How long have you been sick?'

'A day.' He did look pale and unwell, now she came to look.

'You keeping anything in?'

'Going right through me,' he said with unnecessary relish.

'Signal a man up to cover,' she told DaFelbe, then she
looked back at Cuu. 'Report to Dorden. Get him to fix you up
with salts or a shot. Then right back here, you understand
me? I want you back before 13.00, no excuses.'

'Okay,' said Cuu, picking up his kit. 'Back by one, sure as
sure.'

Criid watched Cuu walk away until he was out of sight
round the next traverse.

'He's trouble, that one,' said DaFelbe.

'Sure as sure,' she replied.

IN THE NEXT fire bay, Criid found Pozetine, Mosark and Nessa
Bourah huddled in scrapes hulled out under the dripping
parapet. They were playing dice, but she could tell their

hearts weren't in it. She ran a quick inspection, though the three were able troopers who didn't need much steering, and asked if there were any problems.

'Only the waiting,' said Pozetine. He was a short, square-set Vervunhiver with a boxer's splayed nose, ex-Vervun Primary, and a hell of a shot. A shoe-in for sniper specialisation in fact, had it not been for his grievous lack of patience. He worried, he fidgeted. A sniper he was not.

'Waiting's always the killer,' said Criid.

Pozetine nodded. 'S'why I hate digging in, sarge,' he said. His fingers were working the dice, making them move in and out between his knuckles. An edgy and all too practiced tick.

'Bide your time,' said Criid.

'What I keep telling him,' signed Nessa, a model of calm.

It was easy to say. No soldier liked the waiting hours. They had a habit of magnifying fears and gnawing at nerves. But they got to Pozetine worse than most.

'Do something,' Criid suggested. 'I could find you a job. Latrines–'

'Gak that,' growled Pozetine. Mosark laughed.

'Then take a turn on lookout.'

'I offered, but he's happy and set.' The 'he' Pozetine referred to was Kolea, down at the end of the bay. He was motionless, peering through a stereoscope rigged to peak out over the parapet.

Criid walked along the duckboards to him. 'Kolea?'

He didn't move. She put a hand gently on his arm and he looked up. She could tell it took a moment for him to work out who she was.

'You okay? You've been watching a long time.'

'Don' mind it. I can watch.'

He could at that. If Pozetine was the most impatient man in the platoon – gak, the entire regiment – then Kolea had become the most focused and tranquil.

She knew for a fact that he'd been manning the scope for at least two hours, slowly playing it back and forth through a one-eighty arc. He didn't get bored, he didn't get tired. She'd have pulled any other man off the duty ages before for fear that fatigue would make him sloppy. Not Kolea.

Criid didn't know precisely what the loxatl munition had done to Kolea's brain. Surgeon Curth had tried to explain it to her, but the technical terms had been beyond Criid. Something to do with memory and personality. All of it, ruined. Gol Kolea, the scratch company hero, wise, smart, strong... lost, and only this physical shell of him left with them. His dependability had survived, and expressed itself in an extraordinary attention span.

Or at least, Criid told herself, an ability not to get bored with the most mundane tasks. Kolea could watch the line vigilantly for hours. Pick up a conversation five minutes after it had lapsed and he wouldn't know what you were talking about.

Criid had admitted it to no one, but Kolea was the biggest problem in her command. Gaunt assumed it would be Cuu, but she knew she could handle that gak-pellet. No, it was Kolea. Ten was Kolea's platoon, for a start. He'd forged the unit. It was his still. If he'd died, that would have been a different ball game, but he was still here, a constant reminder of his mental absence, of the void where his inspired leadership had been.

Worse still, he'd only ended up this way because of her. She'd been wounded during the fight for Ouranberg. Kolea had carried her to safety and taken his headwound as a consequence. She'd never found out why, really. Varl had said that it was simply Kolea's way. He'd never leave a trooper down and in danger. Maybe so. But it felt like something else. Like Kolea had needed to save her for some reason, something more than simple loyalty.

Caffran reckoned it was because of the kids. Kolea had sometimes referred to the two orphans Criid had rescued from Vervunhive as a 'little piece of good', and Caffran believed Kolea had taken an almost patriarchal interest in looking after Criid and Caffran, the kids' ersatz parents.

Whatever. She'd never know. She'd never be able to ask Kolea, because Kolea couldn't even remember Ouranberg, let alone the motives that had once driven his life.

'You get tired, you sing out,' she said.

'Don' worry, sarge.'

'You see anything, you sing too.'

His big fingers reached into the neck of his field coat and held out the tin whistle. He beamed. 'Got my blower.'

'Good,' she said. 'Carry on, Trooper Kolea.'

She got up, but his next words stopped her in her tracks.

'The kids.'

'What?'

'What?' he echoed.

'What did you say, Gol? Just then?'

'Um…' he thought about it. 'The kids. They gonna be okay? They all right?'

'They're fine,' she said. Her heart was banging in her ribcage. It was almost like the old Gol Kolea was in arm's reach.

'They're young,' he said.

'Yes, they are.'

'But I guess they'll manage. If you say they're all right.'

'They will.'

He nodded. 'So young. S'pose war is all they've known. But so young, most of them. Boys. Not even shaving yet. Acting like soldiers.'

The Aexe Alliance troopers. That's what he was talking about. Everyone in the regiment had been shocked to see how terribly young most of the local soldiery was. 'Kids' Lubba had said.

Dear God-Emperor. Not her kids at all. She'd seen a spark, just for a second, but it had been false. 'Carry on,' she said.

'You OKAY THERE, sarge?' asked DaFelbe.

'Yeah. Grit in my eyes,' said Tona Criid.

THE CANTEEN BARROW had passed along the fire trench north of station 290 about fifteen minutes before, dishing out pieces of dry rye-bread and a watery gruel made of fish stock and tough root vegetables to the men of eleven platoon. Now Trooper Gutes was coming along through the rain with the wash bin, collecting up the troopers' mess tins to take them up the supply trench and rinse them at the standpipe tap at rear/290.

It was a rota task, and Gutes had drawn for the day. He didn't grumble, but it was a scummy job. By the time he'd collected all the mess tins, the wash bin would be slopping and full. Piet Gutes was one of the older Tanith troopers, drawn and tired. It wasn't physical fatigue he suffered from. It was the wearying attrition of Guard life. The hopeless struggle to get through each day, knowing there was no happy ending waiting for them. No homeworld. No family embrace to return to.

The day Tanith had died, Gutes's daughter Finra had been twenty-one, and her daughter Foona just four months old. It had been a wrench leaving them, but the Emperor called, and the Emperor was the Emperor.

Piet Gutes woke up some nights, sit-up-straight awake, with the last fire-flash of Tanith fading in his mind's eye. That final, shuddering cough of flame and light that signalled the death of the world that'd raised him. It had been just a little thing, a wink in the night. He'd witnessed it from the obs ports of the troop ship. Just a tiny, silent flash.

How could that have been Tanith dying, he often wondered. The mantle splitting. The oceans evaporating. The continents sliding into each other and disintegrating. The great nalwood forests licking into cinders in a wall of white heat. The core, cut loose, erupting and boiling out into the vacuum. Piet Gutes supposed that anything, even the most important and profound event in his life or anyone's life, would seem like nothing more than a tiny, silent flash if you saw it from far enough away.

He wondered about it, sometimes, washing grease off mess tins, sorting power clips, sewing buttons back onto his tunic. The galaxy was big and everything in it was small, and he was small too. The Emperor's dead! Really? Yeah... that tiny flash just then. Did you see it? The Imperium's fallen! Sacred feth, you kidding? No... just that little flash. You must've noticed.

Far away. That's where he'd like to be. 'Far away up in the mountains', like the old song. It was all he wanted these days. To be so far away that everything looked small and insignificant.

'Tins! Tins!' he called, plodding down the fire bay with both hands on the yoke of the big metal pail. Garond tipped his in, then Fenix and Tokar.

'Thank you kindly,' Gutes said to each, his voice so rich with sarcasm it made them laugh.

He struggled into the gun-nest, where Caill and Melyr were hunched down beside their support weapon. Caill tossed his tin in, half-finished, but Melyr was still chasing the last drips of gravy with a scrap of Caill's left over bread.

'Feth, you like that stuff?'

'Good eating, if you've a hunger,' said Melyr.

Gutes liked Melyr. Heavy-set, solid, an ace with a fat cannon or a rocket tube. But he hated seeing him there. Bragg had been eleven's cannon man. Hark had switched Melyr in from twenty-seven when Bragg was killed. It was almost unseemly. Caill, the best ammo humper in the regiment, in Gutes's opinion, had just about been wedded to Bragg. Now here he was running boxes and feeding belts for someone else.

Times change. Needs must. Get far enough away and none of it looks big enough to be important anyway.

Melyr finished up, smacked his lips appreciatively, and plonked his mess tin into Gutes's wash bin.

'My compliments to the chef,' he said.

'Melyr, man, you're a fething lunatic,' said Gutes.

'You wanna worry,' said Caill. 'I have to sit beside this feth-head.'

'Sit further back and it won't seem to matter so much,' Gutes suggested.

'What?'

Gutes shook his head. He was glad Caill was settling in with his new partner. That's what really counted. He knew Caill was still down on himself. He'd left Bragg to run for fresh ammo, and by the time he'd got back, Bragg was done. Three loxatl flechette rounds at close range, that's what Gutes had heard. Like he'd eaten a tube-charge. So much mess they'd been hard pushed to find enough to bury, and Bragg had been a big guy.

Feth happens, Gutes thought.

He stumbled on, under a reinforced arch, into the next fire bay, wishing he had a hand free to brush away the biter-flies that buzzed around his face. Loglas had told him about a trooper up the line who'd let those things settle and then woke up with his brain eaten out by hatching larvae.

Piet Gutes didn't fancy that. He did however wonder how someone with his brain eaten out by larvae had managed to wake up at all. An inconsistency in the story. Maybe Loglas had been pulling his leg.

'Everything all right, Piet?' called Sergeant Obel, coming the other way down the trench with his runner.

'Fine, sir.'

'You got mine already,' said Obel.

'I did so,' said Gutes. Every Ghost's mess tin was etched with his surname and pin code. The fun part of this job was getting the right tin back to the right body.

Fun part. Yeah, right. There was nothing about the collection, cleaning and redistribution of mess tins that could be considered fun.

'Carry on, Gutes,' Obel said.

Gutes stopped at the end of the bay and put his bucket down. Greasy slops rocked out over the lip.

'Hey, Larks?'

Mad Larkin slowly turned back from the loophole where his long-las was resting. He smiled slightly when he saw Gutes. They'd been good buddies since the Founding Fields. It was nice to see him smile. Larkin seemed edgier than ever these days. He and Bragg had been particularly close.

'Got your tin?' Gutes asked.

Larkin looked around and eventually produced his mess tin from a shelf in the revet side. It was full of gruel, the hunk of bread disintegrating into it.

'Ah, Larks, you gotta eat.'

'Not hungry, Piet.'

'You gotta eat, but.'

Larkin shrugged.

Gutes picked up the tin. 'You sure you don't want this?'

'Yeah. No appetite.'

'Okay, then.' Gutes left his slop bucket next to Larkin's firestep and went back down the trench. Melyr accepted the bonus rations with delight. 'You gotta wash that up yourself and get it back to Larks,' Gutes told him.

He went back to his wash bin.

'What you doing, Larks?' he asked.

Larkin had been working a screwdriver into the setting of his rifle scope.

'Calibrating,' he said.

Every sniper calibrated their scopes. It was a given. An adjustment to the milled ring on the back-sight, a moment to let the sighting scanner read your retina and set up the hairs, but Larkin played around more. He tweaked off the inspection cover and overrode the reader, calibrating his weapon to nuances of windspeed and shot-drop that were too subtle for the scope to set automatically. Gutes had heard him say sometimes that he saw the truth through his scope. The view through the scope was the one reality Larkin trusted.

'You wanna be careful no tech-priest catches you doing that,' Gutes admonished. 'They'd have you burned at the stake.'

'So don't tell 'em,' said Larkin.

'I won't,' said Gutes. Larkin was the best shot in the regiment, and Gutes wasn't about to tell him his job, even if tinkering with military tech was strictly forbidden. That was the province of the tech-priests, who guarded their secrets jealously. If Larkin had to be a heretic to shoot so well, that was fine with Gutes.

Gutes pulled up his sloshing bin and trotted on, picking up the last of the mess tins and then heading west up the supply trench.

'HEY, LARKS.'

Larkin looked up from his scope, thinking Piet Gutes had come back for some reason.

It wasn't Piet Gutes.

'How you doing?' said Lijah Cuu.

'What the feth?' Larkin cowered back into the corner of the firebay, his hand trying to find the hilt of his knife. 'What the feth are you doing here?'

'Oh, now, that's not nice.' Cuu crouched on the firestep, elbows resting on his knees. 'Just dropped by to say hello to a friend. And you're acting all unfriendly.'

'No,' mumbled Larkin.

'Yes, you are, sure as sure.'

'What do you want?'

Cuu straightened out his lean legs and sat down on the step with his back to the parapet.

'Like I said, just saying hello.'

'You shouldn't be here,' said Larkin.

'Who's gonna know, tell me that? I'm meant to be seeing the doc. Who's gonna miss me? Who's gonna worry about two buddies chatting together?'

'I'm not your buddy,' Larkin said bravely. His hand had found the knife now. He kept it behind his back.

Cuu thought about that. 'Maybe not. Maybe not.'

He leaned forward, pushing his scar-split face right up into Larkin's. 'Buddies ain't the right word, is it, Tanith? We got a score, you and me. You sold me out, sold me out to the commissars, back on Phantine. You and that big dumbo.'

'Don't call him that!'

'Big dumbo? Why the gak shouldn't I call that big dumbo a big dumbo? He was a big dumbo, sure as sure.'

'Shut up!'

'Hey, I'm just being nice and saying hello.' Cuu's voice dropped to a raw whisper. 'We got a score, Tanith. You know it, I know it. It's gonna get settled. Thanks to you, I got flog-scars on my back. I think about you, most nights. You and that holier-than-thou big dumbo. Sooner or later, you're gonna pay.'

Larkin pulled back even further. He knew he had no hope of getting his long-las free from the loop-hole. He wanted to shout out, but there was no one around.

'What do you mean, pay?'

'Sooner or later, sure as sure. War's a messy thing, Tanith. Confused and all shit like that. Middle of combat, all crap flying this way and that. Who's gonna notice if I get my payback? You'd just be another body in the count.'

'You wouldn't dare!'

'Oh, wouldn't I now? You'll get yours, just like big dumbo got his.'

Hlaine Larkin was petrified. Ever since Phantine, he'd been guarding his back, waiting for this moment. And now Lijah fething Cuu had just come up on him when he least expected it. But those last few words bit clean through his terror.

'What do you mean, he got his? What the feth does that mean?'

'Terrible shame. Big dumbo buying the farm like that.'

'No... no, that's not what you meant. Not at all! Feth... feth, you bastard... you killed him!'

'As if,' smiled Cuu.

'You bastard! I'll take this to Gaunt–'

Cuu snapped out a hand and closed it tightly around Larkin's throat. His eyes went dark, like a cloud had passed across the sun.

'Oh no you won't, you little gak. Who'd believe you, eh? Where's your gakking proof? This is just between you and me. You and me. Our little score. And it'll get settled, sure as sure. You'll know why. And I'll know why, and everyone else can take a gakking jump. You'll pay for the flog-scars I got. You'll pay with scars of your own.'

Larkin yanked out his knife. Straight silver, thirty centimetres. Tanith First-and-Only warblade. In simple desperation, he lunged at Cuu.

Cuu was ready. He blocked Larkin's wrist with his left fist, turning the knife aside, and tightened his choke hold. Larkin writhed away, but he was penned in and trapped, like an animal, like prey.

Cuu cuffed him around the temple and, as he swayed, dazed, threw him off the firestep. Larkin landed shoulders first on the duckboards, feeling them squelch underneath him.

His fingers groped for his warknife.

It was in Lijah Cuu's hand.

Cuu stood over him, raised Larkin's knife to his mouth and slowly licked the blade. The tiniest drop of blood welled up and fell onto Larkin's forehead.

'You're fething crazy!' Larkin gasped.

'Sure,' said Cuu, 'as sure. We've come this far. Let's do it.'

He flew at Larkin, blade extended. Larkin remembered the combat moves Corbec had told him, and rolled, kicking Cuu's legs away. Cuu crashed over, ripping the blade sideways and tearing a strip out of Larkin's trousers. Larkin squealed and kicked out again. But Cuu moved like a snake, wrapping himself over and under Larkin's jerking limbs.

The blade was at Larkin's throat. He felt its edge bite into his skin.

'What the feth is this?'

Loglas was coming down the trench bay towards them, his hands balled into fists. 'Cuu? What the feth are you doing?'

Fighting the pressure at his neck, Larkin screamed. Oddly, his scream sounded like a whistle.

A whistle. Two more blew. Then another.

Loglas halted and looked up. The shell hit the back wall of the firebay and went off, kicking mud and slime and pieces of flakboard fifty metres into the air. A twenty-pounder at the very least.

Larkin saw it, saw the actual shell. The flint-grey casing, the barbed fins, like it was a pict playing in slow motion. He saw the huge flash. He saw one of the fins, a broken chunk of metal twenty centimetres by ten, whizzing out from the impact, turning in the air like a kid's throw-toy.

Loglas was reeling back from the concussive force of the blast when the flying fin hit him in the face. In slow motion, Larkin saw the way it made Loglas frown, then grimace, then twist his features into an expression no human face could make while it was alive.

Loglas's face caved in nose first, and his forehead tore away from his scalp like a yanked curtain. His head convulsed with the whiplash, his neck shattering as it bowed back. His face vanished, sucked into the hole that was being driven into the front of his head, and then the whirling fin came out the back, strewing skull shards and bloody matter ahead of it.

'Nooo!' Larkin howled. Then he went deaf as the blast roar hammered him.

COLM CORBEC HAD emerged from his dugout at station 295 approximately sixty seconds before the first shell landed. He paused on the firestep, frowning, cupping his hands to shield his eyes from the rain.

'Chief?' asked Rerval, his vox-officer. 'Something up?'

Corbec had smelled ammonil wadding on the wind. Batteries loading up for barrage. Rerval watched with horrid fascination as Corbec slowly raised his whistle and blew.

Rerval grabbed up the vox-horn and started to yell. 'Incoming barrage!'

He repeated the cry three times before there was an ominous click which announced that the e-mag pulse of the enemy guns had killed the vox-signal.

Then the shells started to land.

THEY FELL IN the rain. They fell like rain. They scattered in and out of the leading fire trench of the Peinforq Line's 55th sector from station 251 right up to 315 and over into 56th sector as far as 349.

Ten shells a second, heavy gauge from the deep super-siege batteries, and smaller howitzer rounds from the Shadik front. In a space of two minutes, the air was full of mud fog and the atomised steam of debris over a stretch of fifteen kilometres. The ground was quaking.

Between 293 and 294, Rawne and Domor got their troopers into cover. Amongst three platoon, Wheln and Leclan took shrapnel hits, Torez lost an arm and Famoss was decapitated. Five metres of fire trench and a traverse simply vanished in a blizzard of spraying earth.

SERGEANT AGUN SORIC slept through the first thirty seconds of the onslaught. The roar and vibration didn't wake him. It took Trooper Vivvo, shaking him and yelling in his face.

Soric blinked open his single eye and looked up at Vivvo's pale face in the halflight of station 292's dugout.

'What?' he asked, tersely. But there was a background clamour of thunder and voices, and the little camp table was jarring.

'Gak!' Soric snorted, and scrambled up. How could he have slept through this?

Over the constant howl of shells, he could hear debris spattering off the dugout wall. Someone was screaming for a medic.

Short, stocky, grizzled, possessed of a mighty laugh and a temper corrosive as acid, Soric had been a smeltery boss back on Verghast. In the war there, he'd become a troop leader ad hoc, a resistance fighter. His exploits had left him with scar-tissue in place of one eye, a limp, and the eternal respect of Vervunhivers. Ibram Gaunt hadn't thought twice about making Soric a senior platoon leader.

His ability to sleep was a throwback to the old days, when he'd been able to catch a nap despite the tumult of the smeltery line. Now the knack seemed like a liability.

He bundled Vivvo outside, pressing a hand down on the younger man's shoulders to keep him low. The air was full of billowing, opaque fog that made them both choke and gasp violently. They couldn't see anything except the swirling vapour and fuzzy, bright flashes. The parapet at 292 was particularly low and waterlogged; a wide lake formed against its outside lip. The shells falling into it had raised the dense steam and coiling vapour.

'Gak! Back inside, son!' Soric coughed, and shoved Vivvo back into the dugout. He stood alone for a moment, though how alone he couldn't tell. There could be men just a few metres away, Soric thought, and I can't see them. He tried to shout out, but his mouth filled with mud droplets and he started choking again. Besides, the continuous noise of detonations totally drowned him out.

Soric staggered back into the dugout. Vivvo was on his hands and knees, his arms wrapped protectively over his head, retching up muddy liquid.

'We're going to die, boss!' he hacked.

'Did we die on Verghast?'

'N-no…'

'Then I'm sure as gak not going to die on this arse-wipe world.' Soric sat down on the canvas stool. Something jabbed into his hip and he discovered a message shell in the pocket of his breeches. He couldn't remember putting a message shell in his pocket.

He unscrewed the brass cap and shook out a small fold of blue tissue paper. A sheet from a Guard issue despatch pack. Every sergeant had one, though they were seldom needed because of the vox-link. They were for emergencies, and Soric was sure he hadn't used his pack since they'd arrived. But when he looked around, he saw it lying on the dugout's shelf, the paper seal torn off and the top sheet missing.

Soric unfolded the sheet. The brief message was hand written in pencil. 'Bombardment for sixteen minutes, then foot assault from the north-east, under cover of the drain outfall.'

He read it again. His fingers shook a little. There was no mistake about it.

It was his handwriting.

A WHOOPING SHELL struck the third traverse along from station 289, and threw clods of earth and pieces of wood and brick out along the fire trench. Gaunt threw himself flat, dragging Beltayn down with him. The troopers around them were hurled over by the concussion.

As debris and rain spattered down over them, Gaunt got up. He'd lost his cap. A man was wailing pitifully nearby.

'Beltayn?'

His adjutant rose slowly.

'You all right?'

'Feth,' Beltayn grumbled, fiddling with his left hand. His thumb was dislocated. 'Something's awry here…'

Beltayn's voice faded off as he saw the corpse of Trooper Sheric on the duckboards at his feet. The blast had mutilated the side of Sheric's head and jammed a broken plank through his upper torso. It made Beltayn's dislocated thumb suddenly seem quite insignificant.

Nearby, two other men from fifteen platoon were trying to field dress Trooper Kell's torn belly. It was Kell doing the wailing: a feeble, sick-animal sound. Yellowish loops of intestine were spilling from the bright red gashes in his black tunic.

Sergeant Theiss, the normally cheerful commander of fifteen platoon, ran up with one of his corpsmen. He said something to Gaunt that was inaudible over the shell fall. Gaunt waved him off and pointed to Kell.

Gaunt had been at station 289, reviewing muster, when the bombardment started. He cursed the sense of displacement. His own platoon, one, was at station 291, with Caober in charge. There was no way he'd be able to rejoin them in this.

He got up onto the firestep and viewed back down the line through the scope Beltayn handed up to him.

'Throne of Terra…' he murmured.

The valley was an inferno for as far as he could see. Banks of smoke, as vast and dense as thunderheads, hung over the fire trenches, obscuring the view. Shell blasts stippled through the smoke, catastrophic and murderous. An immense fire burned down in the vicinity of 256. At 260, it looked as if an entire section had been gutted. The barrage was creeping back into the supply and communication trenches. Shields had come on over the rearline and command sections, but they weren't the day's targets. Today, the Shadik guns were striking at the infantry lines. And that could mean only one thing.

It was the prelude to an offensive.

A WHISTLE BLEW. It was Kolea at his spotter scope.

'They're coming!' he cried.

Criid tumbled out of the scrape she'd been sheltering in. Steam and fyceline fumes clogged the trenchway. Station 290 had taken some hits in her post, but nothing like the punishment she'd seen fall on Maroy's section.

She blew her own whistle. 'Fix blades! Stand ready to repel!' She dearly wanted to check on Maroy's mob, but there was no time for that. Around her, the troops of nine platoon got up onto the firestep, warknives locked into the lugs of their lasrifles.

The shells were still falling. It seemed to her impossible that the enemy would advance into this.

But she trusted Gol Kolea. He'd never lied before and he wouldn't lie now.

Crouched on the rain-slick paving slabs of the step, she peered out through a loophole. Through the churning vapour, she saw figures, running forward at a halting pace, weapons swinging. Mkoll had briefed the First. Don't let them get close enough to deploy grenades. Hand bombs are their way into the line.

But a spring gun or a pneumatic mortar could throw a lot further than a man.

'Hartwig! Target the slopes, now!'

'Yes, ma'am!'

In the face of the bombardment, their little answering barrage seemed feeble as it began. Spring guns cracked and mortars drummed. There was a satisfying ripple of light munitions from beyond the parapet.

'Keep it up!' she yelled. She risked another look and saw the advancing line of Shadik troopers, just blurs in the fog.

Many staggered or were thrown up as ball bombs and mortar rounds fell amongst them.

She glanced down the line. Nine platoon was crouched, ready. She saw Vril spit and shake out his neck. She saw Jajjo drying the grip of his las on his cloak. She saw Nessa, still as a statue at her long-las. Nessa's hair was still boyishly short from the pre-mission buzz-cut she'd had on Phantine, and from some angles she could be mistaken for one of the younger men. One trooper – Criid thought it was Subeno – was vomiting with nerves, but still holding his place.

'Straight silver!' Criid bellowed. 'Step up and fire at will!' Her first battlefield order to the troops.

As one, nine platoon rose and rested their lasrifles on the parapet. They started shooting, dropping the nearest Shadik assaulters as support blasts from Hartwig's gun-dens lofted up over them.

Criid tried to find a target, but it was like aiming into murky water such was the density of the smoke boiling back off no-man's land. A raider in a chain-veil helmet suddenly loomed, winding up to hurl a stick bomb, and she squeezed the trigger. By her side, DaFelbe saw him too, and they killed the raider simultaneously. The stick grenade bounced away and blew up.

Now there were more, and they were running for the line. Some moved in groups, carrying makeshift storm-shields made of overlapped flakboard. Criid slammed off five shots at one shield, but it didn't slow down. It was just six metres from the parapet when a spray of fluid fire washed across it and turned it into a squealing mass of flames and thrashing human torches.

Lubba fired again, hosing the immediate vicinity with his flamer. Criid could distinctly hear his tanks knocking and spluttering despite the fury of the shells. Tracer shots began stitching across the muddy slope from the platoon's support weapon. Figures danced and jerked. Some hung in the wire.

Hand bombs started to bounce in at them. Criid had to duck fast as one went off right under the parapet. DaFelbe toppled off the step, clutching his right cheek where a hunk of shrapnel had punched into his jaw.

'Medic!' Criid yelled. She started firing again. They were so damn close now, and despite everything, there were so damn many.

BRIN MILO, THE youngest Ghost of all, was right beside his platoon sergeant when the raiders came leaping in. One went right over Milo's head and fell down as he landed awkwardly on the duckboards. Sergeant Domor turned and shot him dead where he lay.

They'd been swarmed. Sheer numbers had flung themselves at 293 and 294 and made it over the parapet. Now three and twelve platoon faced the very worst that trench warfare had to offer. Hand-to-hand in the narrow trench gully.

The raiders wore khaki and brown, and most had gashoods and heavy helmets clamped over their heads. They carried old-pattern autorifles, pistols and curved hangers.

The world became very, very small. Just a tight space between earthen walls, deafened by shells, full of jostling bodies. Milo slashed and jabbed with his bayonet, staggering back a step as blood gouted over him, and then fired pointblank at a khaki figure clawing at him.

For a while – longer than most of the Ghosts had been comfortable about, to be truthful – Milo had been the only civilian to escape the fall of Tanith. Gaunt had rescued him, though sometimes Milo liked to explain it had been the other way around. Because of that, he'd been seen by all as one part mascot, one part lucky charm… and his skill with the Tanith pipes had come in handy.

Milo had made trooper as soon as he was old enough. According to Corbec, Varl, Larkin, Bragg – God-Emperor rest him – Milo had received more combat experience by the time he sewed on his first cap badge than many Guardsmen did in five years.

That was how it went when you were one of Gaunt's chosen. At his own request, Milo had been placed in Domor's platoon. He knew a spot in one, Gaunt's own, was likely, but he wanted to distance himself a little from his 'saviour'. And from the notion that he was Gaunt's lucky mascot.

Brin Milo was no mascot. He was twenty-one years old standard, tall and strong, and he'd take no feth from anyone

now. Despite his age, the Ghosts – especially the Tanith –
took him quite seriously. Though Milo only suspected it,
both Gaunt and Corbec considered him squad leader material.

Brin Milo had something to prove. It would be his destiny
to have something to prove until the day he died.

BARELY TWENTY METRES north of Milo, Rawne's platoon was
fending off an assault too. The trench was packed with
wrestling, stinking, sweaty bodies. Rawne couldn't see more
than a few metres in any direction. He fired his laspistol, and
slashed out with his warknife.

Feygor, soaked in blood, appeared alongside him, and
together they smashed a little way into the khaki bodies bot-
tled in the trench. They were treading over the wounded and
the dead of both sides alike. Melwid was with them, and,
briefly, Caffran and Leyr.

'Crush them against the traverse!' Rawne shouted. 'Where's
Neskon? Where the feth is Neskon?'

The squad's flame trooper was nowhere to be seen. Nothing was anywhere to be seen, except the churning, stabbing
figures of the enemy.

Then a pistol banged, its noise muffled by the close-packed
bodies. Rawne saw Melwid fall, clutching his belly. He felt a
dull ache in his own midriff. Feygor yelled something and
impaled the owner of the pistol on his bayonet.

Rawne fell over. He didn't mean to, but his legs had gone
numb. He slumped sideways and hit his head on the revetment. Sounds had become dull and distant.

What a fething stupid way to fight a war, Rawne thought.

'A fething stupid what?' said a voice behind him.

He struggled over and looked up. He dearly wished his legs
would work. Jessi Banda, the platoon sniper, was curled into
a scrape in the trench wall behind him.

'What?' said Rawne.

'A fething stupid what did you say?' she asked, her voice
hoarse.

'Way to fight a war,' he replied. 'Did I say that out loud
then?'

'More kinda screamed it,' she said.

Someone stood on his legs and he yelped. Banda reached down and dragged him up into her scrape, holding him tightly so he wouldn't slip back into the base of the trench.

'You'll be okay,' Banda said.

'Of course!' Rawne snapped. He paused. 'Why?'

She didn't reply. He looked down and saw the blood soaking his lower tunic and his breeches. He saw how limp and lifeless his legs were.

'Oh feth!' he barked. That wasn't right. Not right at all.

He turned his head, angry now, and looked at Banda. 'Why the feth aren't you fighting, woman? I thought you females were meant to be tough!'

'Oh, I'd love to,' she said. A shell went off overhead, and Rawne flinched into her. When he did, it made her cough. She aspirated blood out over her chin.

'Not today though, I think,' she said.

'Feth! Where are you hit?'

'Worry about yourself, not me,' she answered.

'Banda! Trooper Banda! Where are you hit?'

She didn't reply. She'd passed out. Rawne found the broken chunk of Shadik bayonet still sticking out of her rib cage.

Banda was so limp, she nearly toppled into the fire trench. Rawne clawed onto her and held her in place, helpless himself, trying to stop the both of them getting trampled in the vicious, endless welter of close combat seething along the trench.

'Medic! Medic!' he cried. No one was listening.

Her head nodded down. Rawne tried to support her.

'You'll be okay,' he told her. 'I fething order you to be okay...'

HEAD LOW, COLM Corbec scurried down the zig-zag defence trench that joined his dugout to the main front facing of 295. The fury of the long range Shadik artillery was still smashing up the day, but it seemed eerily still in his part of the line. There was nobody coming at them.

He came up along the step, patting Surch, Orrin, Irvinn and Cown reassuringly on their shoulders as he came by. Each one was crouched at the parapet with his gun slotted into a loophole or bracket.

Corbec dropped in beside Muril. She was training her long-las back and forth, her eye pressed to the rubber gusset of her scope.

'Care to guess where the feth the enemy is today?' he asked.

She chuckled. That dirty laugh he liked so much.

'They don't seem to be interested in us, chief.'

'You making anything?' he wondered.

Muril shook her head. 'I thought I saw a wire-cutting party out there at the fifty-metre mark a few minutes ago. But it wasn't. Just bodies on the wire, stirred by the blasts. Nothing else.'

'May I?' he asked. She slid her long-las out of the loop and passed it to him. He set it to his shoulder and rose slowly to the top of the parapet.

'Chief!' she hissed.

He knew he was taking a risk, but this total lack of activity was driving him spare. Corbec peered into the scope, adjusting the setting ring, waiting a second as the optic scanner read his retina and automatically recalibrated for his eyesight.

There was nothing out front but mud, wire tangles, twisted piquets, craters and streams of white and grey smoke driven almost horizontal by the crosswind.

He looked to his right. Just five hundred metres south, at 294 and 293, he could see a hellish trenchfight tearing through the positions occupied by Rawne and Domor. Swarms of khaki-clad troopers were pushing up from the mire and assaulting the main line. To his left, again no more than half a kilometre away, the defences held by their Krassian allies were swamped with raiders. Corbec could hear the frantic crackle of small-arms and the bang of grenades.

He dropped back down. 'This is fething… peculiar,' he said, passing the sniper weapon back to Muril with a grateful nod. 'Why the feth aren't they coming at us?'

'They know the great Colonel Corbec is here and they don't want to risk it?' Muril suggested.

'You're a sweet girl, and obviously correct, but there has to be more than that.'

Muril deftly calibrated her gunsight back to her own requirements and sat back on the step, straightening her right leg and flexing it. Maintaining the firing crouch clearly caused her discomfort in her freshly rebuilt pelvis.

'Maybe put yourself in their place?' she said.

'Like what?'

'If you were ordered to take this line, what would you do?'

'I'd attack under the barrage,' he said simply.

'And go for the weakest point,' said Cown from his place behind Muril.

'Well, feth… yes!' Corbec said.

He jumped off the step and planted a kiss on Muril's dirty brow. 'Thank you for your suggestion!' he declared. She was nonplussed. Then he put a smacker on Cown's forehead too. 'And thank you for your insight!'

'What, chief?'

'Imagine! You're going for a line. Frontal assault. But before you get there, the units either side of you break through into their areas. Why lose men pressing home at an unbroken line? Any field commander worth his water would divert towards one of the holes already kicked in. You can bet the bastards intended for us are in support at 294 or 296 right now. Text book. Secure and hold and then hit us from the sides, along the trench. Vox-man!'

Rerval ran up. 'Sir?'

'We got links again yet?'

'No sir.'

'Okay… here's what we do. Every second man, stand down from the step. Those still on station, hold and stay vigilant. Irvinn, you've got fire command here on the step. First sign of action, set up will-fire response and blow your fething whistle.'

'Yes, chief.'

'The rest split into two groups. Where's Bewl?'

'Chief?'

'Take half. Move south. Support Domor's mob. Hold the trench lengthways.'

Bewl nodded, and moved off to communicate the instruction to the troops along the south end of the line section.

'The rest with me,' Corbec said.

* * *

THE REST WERE Rerval, Cown, Mkvenner, Sillo, Veddekin and Ponore. Detowine, two platoon's new flamer man made the cut too, but Corbec sent him back to the step. If an assault did come late, he'd need the flamer on the line, along with Surch and Loell's .30 support.

Corbec double-timed the six men up along the trench, moving north. Every Ghost still on the firestep wished them the God-Emperor's grace as they went by.

The attack had been going on for seventeen minutes according to Corbec's timepiece. The smoke and steam kicked up by the immense barrage had now become so chronic, someone, presumably in the support lines, had started to fire off starshells to light the field. The flares served no good purpose except to turn everything into a white haze.

Corbec's team ran on, pausing and flinching every few metres as yet another shell went in over them, shook the ground, and anointed them with a rain of loose earth. By the time they reached the armoured traverse that marked the edge of station 295, Corbec realised he was out of breath.

'You okay, chief?' Mkvenner asked him quietly, so the others couldn't hear.

'My bones are too fething old, son, and they've seen too much war.' Corbec paused a moment and coughed. He'd always led from the front, and that had cost him. He'd lost the little finger of his left hand at Voltis City. That had been the start of it. The start of the tally. Menazoid had hurt him hard. Hagia worse. On Phantine, he'd been lucky to come out alive. Deep wounds to the body and leg, taken during the Cirenholm feth-for-all, followed up with a nosocomial dose of blood-poisoning.

It was a wonder he wasn't made up of augmetic prosthetics.

It was a wonder his luck had lasted this long.

A VERGHASTITE TROOPER named Androby occupied the last slot before the traverse.

'Lot of noise, these last few minutes,' he reported. 'Not much to see.' He'd been using a battered artillery scope borrowed from the mortar teams to keep a watch round the blind end of the traverse.

'Hold here, and stand ready to relay an alarm shout back down the line,' Corbec told him.

They moved around the traverse. For the second time in a week, Mkvenner was advancing around a defence-divide into what could well be an enemy-stormed trench. Corbec knew that. He'd heard Mkoll's debrief about the fight at station 143.

Mkvenner didn't show any nerves at all. He was quiet, expressionless, his camo-cape draped over him. He led the way with his lasrifle up against his shoulder so that everywhere he looked, his gun pointed. He was so silent, Corbec couldn't tell he was there unless he could see him.

Corbec followed him, laspistol in one hand and a grenade in the other. The pin was already out and Corbec was holding the spoon tightly in place with his big, hairy fist.

Behind Corbec were Sillo and Cown. Both had rifles with warknives fixed. Sillo had been a dye-cutter on Verghast, and he was quick and dependable. Cown, good old Cown, was one of the Tanith die-hards, who'd been at the front of just about everything since the awful day they'd first shipped out. He was still getting used to the augmetic bicep and collarbone he'd won at Cirenholm.

To their rear came Ponore and Veddekin, both Verghastites. Ponore was a young, lank prematurely bald fellow who complained incessantly, and Corbec didn't like him much. Veddekin was taller, buck-toothed and younger. Both of them knew how to use a lasgun, and both had seen action, most particularly on Phantine. Corbec wondered if either of them had killed yet. He didn't know, and it was too late to ask.

Rerval brought up the back. He'd left his vox-set with Androby, and carried an extra bag of field dressings. Corbec knew Rerval was a solid fighter. It was easy to forget the warskills of the vox-troopers. Corbec hoped Raglon would change that conception now he'd been promoted from vox ops to platoon leader. Besides his rifle, Rerval carried a Pharos-pattern flare pistol so they could signal back if things started to cook.

The trench seemed empty. The light was bad and the air was misty with ordnance fumes. Corbec could smell wet soil, promethium, the raw stink of the untreated timber used for the duckboards.

This section of fire trench ran for ten metres, curving slightly north-west, and ended in another solid traverse. There was an opening in the back wall four metres in that went through to a gun-den. Mkvenner checked it, and reported it was empty. A pneumo-mortar and shells, but no gunners.

'This is gakking w–' Ponore began.

Mkvenner put a finger to his lips and the Verghastite shut up.

They crocodiled along, squad members hugging alternate walls.

Here was a discarded lasrifle. Here, the broken haft of an entrenching tool. Items of personal kit were visible in the scrapes. Musette bags, picts of loved ones, igniters and smokes, respirator masks, vacuum-packed ration bricks, bed rolls, balled-up woollen vests.

Like they'd left in a hurry, Corbec thought.

They reached the second traverse. Mkvenner held up a hand. He pointed to the flakboarded back wall of the trench. There was a clotted splatter of blood, matted with strands of hair.

Mkvenner made a signal, one hand over the other, and dropped onto his belly. Corbec stepped aside and let Cown through. Cown and Mkvenner edged round the end of the sturdy earthwork divide, Mkvenner on his front, Cown crouched over him so that two lasguns, stacked, would greet whatever was round there.

'Ahead,' Cown whispered.

Corbec led the others around.

The next fire-bay was empty too, of the living at least.

Fresh corpses virtually filled the trench bottom. Slaughtered Krassian troopers, dead Shadik raiders, all twisted and wrapped under and over each other in an orgiastic celebration of feral murder. Smoke plumes drifted out from some las-punctures where uniform fabric had started to burn. Fountains of blood had splashed up the wall and step in some places. In others, grenades had rendered bodies down into abattoir chunks, and scorched the earth walls black with soot. Where they stepped, the duckboards sank and bright pools of blood welled up through the slats.

The smell was truly nauseating. Blood, cordite, offal, sweat, fyceline, faeces.

All the Ghosts had seen war before, to a greater or lesser extent, but this sight stung them. So many bodies, packed in so tight, into such a little space.

'Gak…' said Ponore.

'Shut up,' Corbec told him. He tried to walk forward, but there was nowhere except bodies to step on. Corpses groaned and sighed, burped and farted as he put his weight on them, squeezing lungs and guts. He was trying to make his way to the mouth of the communications trench that opened into this strand of fire trench halfway along.

It was hard balancing on the dead. Corbec reached his hands out to brace himself against the sides of the trenchway. He spat a disgusted curse as his weight caused a little geyser of blood to squirt from a Krassian's chest wound.

Veddekin suddenly swivelled, and the movement startled Corbec. Veddekin's lasrifle banged and a bright bolt of energy whickered across the width of the trench and punched through the face of a Shadik raider who had just appeared at the parapet.

The raider jerked with whiplash and then toppled head first onto the firestep before falling over, back and feet first, into the bottom of the defence. Corbec had jumped so much at the shot he'd lost his footing and fallen over amongst the heaped dead.

'Sharp eyes,' Mkvenner growled in approval to Veddekin. The scout leapt onto the step, and swung his weapon up, shooting dead the next two Shadik who loomed up at the parapet.

The Ghosts rushed the step then, joining Mkvenner and firing down into the smoke-thickened reaches of no-man's land at the assault party that was trying to get in.

'Gak! There's too many of them!' Ponore yelled.

'Aim. Fire. Repeat,' Mkvenner urged.

Corbec looked up at the backs of his boys on the step and struggled to rise out of the warm layers of bodies. He got his left hand on a timber support and–

He froze. The grenade spoon tumbled from his clawing hand.

He'd dropped the fething bomb.

He looked down, looked down into twisted limbs and staring faces and spools of steaming guts. It was down there somewhere.

If he cried out a warning, he knew his squad would break and the assaulters would be all over them. If he didn't, he and most likely two or three of his team would be killed.

'Sacred feth!' Corbec howled, lunging his hand down into the sticky mess of burst viscera, exposed bone and burnt fabric beneath him. He groped for the grenade. Of all the stupid fething ways of dying. How long had the fuse been set to? Ten seconds? Fifteen?

How long had he been scrabbling for it?

His fingers closed on the bomb. It felt red-hot, toxic, and he wanted to let it go.

But he daren't. He yanked it up and threw it. Threw it as hard as his big, tired, old arm could manage. Threw it up and out, hoping it would fly all the way to the Republic of Shadik and never come back. Threw it as desperately as he'd thrown the sewn-leather batter-balls that had come his way across the rec-field at Pryze County Ground when he'd been just eleven and detesting his forced participation in the County Scholam Tournament.

He'd hated batter-ball. He'd never been able to catch. Never been able to field. He'd been doomed, as a kid, to be the last boy picked for teams.

'Feth!' he screamed, and threw. Threw hard. The best throw of his life.

The hurtling bomb went off in the air, three metres up, as it spun into no-man's land. Shrapnel from the airburst caught five of the raiders at the heart of the attacking platoon.

They broke and fell back, shots from Mkvenner, Cown, Veddekin and Rerval punishing them further. Veddekin hit one in the back as he ran away and ignited the poor bastard's ammo web. The retreating figure caught fire in a flash and carried on running, burning, jolting erratically over shell holes and mud-ridges until he dropped out of sight.

'Are we clear?' Corbec asked, on his feet again. His voice was hoarse with stress. He prayed to every pantheon imaginable that no one had noticed how fething close he'd come to screwing up. Especially Mkvenner. Corbec was meant to be top dog. Mkvenner would never have screwed up like that, not in a million years. And Mkvenner would most certainly have picked Corbec last for his ball team. Old and tired and slow, Colm Corbec, old and tired and slow.

'We're clear,' said Cown.

'Should we stay here?' asked Rerval.

'They won't come back any time soon if they think the line's secure,' said Mkvenner, wisely.

Corbec beckoned them after him and advanced up the jink-cut communications trench. He led the way now, his officer's pistol holstered and his rifle pulled off his back. He'd fixed his bayonet.

There were more bodies up the communications cut, Krassians most of them, distinguished by their copper-coloured coats and grey helmets. Rerval recognised a face or two from Ouranberg. Poor fething bastards. They'd fought to hold every miserable centimetre of this arbitrary hole in the ground. The way some of them had died beggared belief. The suffering, the indignity…

They were four zags down when Corbec stopped them. Small-arms fire was whizzing back and forth along the next angled stretch.

'Way I see it,' Corbec told them quietly, 'the enemy got in and overran the line, killing the Krassys or driving them back up the communications. Probably lost a lot themselves on the way. So we're coming in behind them. Let's make it count.'

The Ghosts nodded and checked weapons.

'Three abreast,' Corbec instructed. 'Me, Ven and Veddey. There's no more room than that. Sillo, Cown, get some tube bombs ready and lob them over the divide as we go. Lob them far – you hear me, you fethers?'

They did.

'And get in behind us,' Corbec said to Ponore and Rerval. 'If we go down, fill our spots. Cown, Sillo, you too, after them. Let's show them how it's done.'

On Corbec's signal, they came round the zag-end and onto the backs of a pack of Shadik raiders clustered in at the next turn. Some of the enemy troopers began to turn as the first las-rounds sliced into them.

'First-and-Only!' Corbec yelled, firing on full auto, smacking las-shots into khaki backs.

Veddekin fell back, his weapon jammed.

Rerval pushed past him, and maintained the tight line. Tube-charges wobbled through the air above them, hurled by Sillo and Cown from behind the trench turn. The blasts filled the narrow defile.

'Straight silver!' Corbec shouted, and, without further warning, charged the enemy. He'd charged because he'd spotted that their angle wasn't secure. Not by a long way. A secondary trench, probably a munitions track, intersected with their stretch from the right on a dog-leg. If there were more Shadik up there...

There were.

Corbec crunched his bayonet into the ribs of one of the Shadik, then kicked the man off the blade as he turned to shoot another raider behind the first. Somehow the first Shadik managed to wrench Corbec's blade off his gun as he went down. As a third came in, swinging a trench club with an iron head, Corbec speared him with his lasrifle anyway. For all he bemoaned his age and diminishing strength, Corbec was still one of the biggest, strongest men in the First. Bayonet or no bayonet, you didn't get up again if Colm Corbec put his weight behind the steel muzzle of a lasgun and rammed it into your sternum.

Now Corbec had an angle into the secondary trench. It was narrow and well-boarded, and sloped away from him downhill in a slight incline. He dropped to his knees and fired down it. His shots hit two of the enemy bunched up fifteen metres away, then a third. A fourth returned fire with a compact sub-autogun, a little bull-nosed slugger with a hooked magazine obviously designed with trench-war in mind.

The burst of small-calibre bullets ripped into the support palings of the trench gabion behind Corbec, showering out splinters. Corbec fired twice, unruffled, and knocked the shooter off his feet and sideways into the revetment. The man slithered down and rolled over.

There were other figures deeper in the secondary trench, veiled by the shadows and the smoke. Corbec fired on them a couple more times, and then ducked back into cover as a ball bomb landed near the mouth of the secondary and threw mud and broken duckboards into the air.

Corbec took stock. He, Mkvenner and Rerval were on one side of the secondary's opening, the rest still back at the start of the zag. Cown tried to dart across to them, but jerked back when rifle rounds and what seemed to be buckshot came stinging up the munitions track.

Corbec looked up the zag. His squad had cleared out the raiders right up to the next turn, about ten metres away.

'Check ahead,' he told Mkvenner. 'I'm hoping there's Krassians round that bend. Don't let 'em shoot you.'

Mkvenner nodded and grinned. He got to the end and peered round. Serious las-fire made him dip back at once.

'Guard! We're Guard!' he hollered. More las-shots. The Krassians, a new outfit with comparatively little battlefield experience, had taken a pounding in the last forty-five minutes. They were spooked and angry and shooting at anything.

Rerval joined Mkvenner.

'They're not taking the chance we're not Shadik,' Mkvenner said.

'We better get their attention,' Rerval said. He pulled out his flare pistol, broke it open, and began sorting through his satchel of smoke and colour pellets. 'What's today's recognition colour?' he asked.

'Blue,' said Mkvenner. He knew full well Rerval knew that. Rerval was vox-ops, up there with Beltayn and Rafflan as one of the best signals specialists in the regiment. The question had been Rerval's way of stress management. A coping strategy. A chance to find out what Mkvenner thought of the idea without actually asking it.

'Blue. Right,' said Rerval. He slid a colour-coded cartridge into the flare pistol, snapped it shut, cocked it, and said, 'Look away.'

They both averted their eyes. Rerval fired the signal gun round the corner of the zag so that the flare embedded itself in the muddy wall beyond. It began to burn with phospho-rescent white light, tinged blue by the smoke it was spilling out. The light was fierce and harsh. It threw off long, inky shadows and made everything look cold.

The las-fire stopped.

'Guard! We're Guard here!' Mkvenner tried again. 'You Krassian up there?'

A pause. An answering shout.

'Krassian?' Mkvenner called again.

'Aye! What's the day code?'

'Alpha blue pentacost!' Rerval called.

'Blue eleven salutant!' came the correct answer.

'I'm coming out,' called Mkvenner. 'Hold fire!'

He walked slowly into a trench still lit by the brilliant glare of the fizzling signal round. Blue smoke wafted around him. It was a theatrical entrance, and Rerval was rather proud of it.

Krassian troopers came down the trench to meet them. Their weapons were still raised, and they all looked edgy and scared. Young, a lot of them. Faces white against the copper worsted of their coats.

'Where the hell did you come from?' asked the officer in charge.

'The nalwoods west of Attica,' replied Mkvenner with typi-cal inscrutability. The officer looked puzzled.

'We're Tanith First-and-Only,' said Rerval. 'We pushed in from the south.'

'Tanith?' echoed the officer. Two or three of his younger men had tears in their eyes. Relief, Mkvenner presumed.

'They hit us bad, so bad,' said the officer. 'Are they gone? Did you get them?'

'Not yet,' said Mkvenner.

FIFTEEN METRES BACK around the zag, Corbec was negotiating the clearance of the secondary trench. Along with Cown, Ved-dekin and Ponore, he'd been squirting off shots down the length of it on a regular basis, but the response was firm. The worst part of it was that at least one of the raiders had a shot-gun, probably a sawn-off, an ideal weapon for trench fights. Ducking in and risking a bullet was one thing, and Murten

Feygor would probably give you odds on it. But a shotgun blanketed the space.

Sillo had found that out. Ponore had dragged him back from the junction and dressed his wound, but Corbec knew a scatter-shot hit like that was gangrene waiting to happen, even if the enemy hadn't treated their lead with bacterials as he'd known to be the tactics amongst the arch-enemy.

Sillo had been hit in the left thigh with such force it had shredded his trouser-leg off, broken his belt, and gouged the flesh so deeply Corbec had seen yellow fat and bone. Sillo had screamed, passed out, then woken again screaming. He shut up when Ponore stuck him in the buttock with a one-shot disposable full of morphosia.

'Might be another way round,' Veddekin suggested, his back to the wall by the junction.

'Might be. Who knows?' Corbec grumbled. 'If we had a fething map…'

He did have a fething map. All XOs had been given one when they checked in at 55th sector HQ on their way up the line. The map was deficient in three particulars. First, it showed only the immediate locale of the XO's posting, which meant Corbec's finished at station 295. Second, it showed no minor detail of supply trenches, communication lines, munition tracks or ops centres, because Aexe Alliance Command feared that a map showing such detail would be too sensitive to risk it being captured. So even if Corbec had possessed a map of 296 and northwards, it wouldn't have shown him this track anyway.

Third, perhaps most importantly, it looked like it had been made by a hallucinating, ink-dipped cockroach that had been allowed to run across a piece of used latrine paper.

'We could go over the top,' Cown said, thinking aloud. 'That's what the scouts did at 143 the other night.'

Well, they were fething scouts, the best of our best, half a century younger than me and tough enough to crack nalnuts in their armpits, Corbec wanted to say. But he bit it back. Cown was only trying to help.

'I'd wager they're expecting that, pal,' Corbec said. He picked up a Shadik helmet, hung it on the nose of his las and hefted it up above the revet.

He only had to wiggle it for a second before a rifle round cracked it and sent it spinning away into the air.

Cown smiled at Corbec feebly, and shrugged.

Ponore was looking around. 'Holy gak!' he began. 'We're lucky we didn't go up like bonfires when we started fire-fighting down this!'

More complaints. Corbec wasn't really interested in what Ponore had to say any more. He'd march over and slap him quiet if it wasn't for fact he'd have to get in line of shot to do it.

Ponore wouldn't shut up. He'd crossed to the other side of the zag and yanked up a tarpaulin. As was the case with many supply trenches, funk-holes had been dug out of the sides to make space for storage and then veiled with canvas curtains. Ponore was revealing stacked bags of dressings, tins of veg-etable soup, muslin bags of candles, and three or four drums of lamp oil.

'If a shot had hit this,' Ponore moaned, 'whoomff! That'd been us.'

Corbec suddenly grinned. 'Ponore?'

'Yes sir, chief?'

'I could kiss you.'

'He does that,' Cown warned earnestly.

'Get those drums out. Careful, mind.'

Veddekin and Ponore manhandled the first one up to the junction.

Corbec peered around the corner again. He saw what he'd seen the first time he'd looked down the munitions track. Back then, he'd been too busy killing Shadik to pay attention.

The secondary trench sloped away from them. Not much, barely, in fact. But enough. That's why the duckboarding was good. Water drained away down this side trench.

'What now?' asked Veddekin.

'We need a tube or something,' Corbec improvised. 'Cown? There must be a syphon or a funnel or something in there.'

Cown searched the funk hole store, cursing every time the curtain fell back, blocking him in darkness. Ponore went over and held the tarp back for him. Cown emerged with a tin jug.

'What about this?'

'Toss it over.'

Cown threw the jug across the junction and Corbec caught it by the handle. Four or five shots whined up the secondary at the movement.

Corbec recovered his warknife from the ribs of the raider who'd somehow managed to rip it off. He mumbled an apology to the knife for what he was about to do.

It took him about a minute of chopping and levering to bend out the base of the jug and cut it lengthways. He ended up bracing it against a trench post and ripping the curled-away half off by hand.

He'd made a little trough. Not the best trough in the world, but a little trough all the same, with a spout end and everything. His machinesmith father would have been proud.

He flipped it back to Cown. More shots.

'Dig it into the earth there,' he instructed. 'No, at the corner so the spout hangs over the edge. That's it. Keep the back end in cover. That's the lad. Dig it in if you have to. Make it stable.'

Cown raked the earth away with the head of his nine seventy and made the trough stable.

'Fine and lovely,' approved Corbec. 'Now start pouring the oil down it.'

Ponore unplugged the first drum and then tipped it over with Veddekin's help. Clear, sweet-smelling lamp oil glugged out, swirling down the makeshift trough. It began to run down the secondary, gurgling under the duckboards.

'And the rest,' urged Corbec, as Cown and Ponore rolled the first drum away, empty, and Veddekin tipped the second. Corbec realised he was fidgeting from foot to foot. He so wanted to be on the other side of the junction, mucking in with the work, but he could only stand and issue instructions.

A sudden thought hit him. An epiphany. That's what it was called. He'd heard Captain Daur talk about epiphanies. Daur was an educated lad. He understood these fine, subtle things.

A moment of unexpected clarity. That's what Corbec believed it to mean. A sudden revelatory instant of comprehension.

He should never have become an officer. Never. Not even a sergeant, let alone XO of the Tanith regiment. Sure, he had the presence and the charisma, so he was told. He was a personality, and the men rallied round him. That was what Gaunt had seen in him, first time they'd met. Must've been. And Corbec was happy to serve.

But there it was. Gaunt had made him colonel. He'd not asked for it. He'd not chased for it. He wasn't a career man, like Daur or, Emperor protect them all, Rawne. He had no ambition.

What was it they all said about him? That compliment? He led from the front. Just so. He was never happier than when he was at the very workface of fighting, confronting the practicals.

He was the big, strong son of a machinesmith from County Pryze. He should have been a trooper, a dog-grunt, fething well mucking in. Mucking in over there, in fact. Not standing this side of the junction, yakking out orders.

Corbec thought about that for a moment, watching the oil swirl away down the secondary.

'Third drum going in now!' Cown hissed. 'Is this going to work?'

'Let's find out,' Corbec grinned. He looked up-zag to the turn where Mkvenner and Rerval were talking with a bunch of bewildered-looking Krassians.

'Rerval! Over here, son!'

The vox trooper hurried down to Corbec.

'Gimme your flare gun. What burns best?'

'Sir?' Rerval said, handing over the fat-nosed signal gun. Corbec cracked it open.

'Your flares, Rerval. Which one burns best?'

Rerval searched in his bag. 'Red, I guess, chief. It's got the biggest powder charge. But we're only supposed to thump one of them out in predicaments. It's the emergency signal.'

'Give me one. If this works, I'm sure as fething certain our Shadik friends yonder will consider this a predicament, and no mistake.'

Rerval shrugged and handed Corbec a red-tabbed cartridge.

Corbec slotted it into the gun and closed the spring-loaded mechanism.

'Clear?' he asked Cown.

The Ghosts on the other side had rolled the last drum away. Cown nodded.

'Duck and cover,' Corbec told them. 'Fire in the hole!'

He pointed the flare pistol down the secondary and squeezed the trigger.

Nothing happened.

'What the feth is wrong with this piece of crap?' he snarled, bringing his hand back in.

'There's a safety lock,' said Rerval, fussing and trying to be helpful. 'Just there. No, the lever there by your thumb. Uh huh.'

'Well, I knew that,' said Corbec and fired the flare down the munitions track.

Superheated, glowing like a laser torpedo, it ricocheted off the right-hand wall, tumbled left, bounced off a timber post and went spinning away towards the cowering Shadik raiders, kicking off streams of bright red smoke.

Corbec pulled Rerval back against the side wall of the zag.

There was a distant yell. A crump of ignition. Then forty metres of the secondary trench went off like a flamer's kiss. Fire leapt up into the sky, clearing the tops of the walls. Thick, intense, sweet-smelling like the wick-burn of the little lamps they'd given them.

Then there was another smell. A terrible smell. Cooking fat and meat.

'Good job,' Corbec told his boys, wincing into the bright flame light. 'Good fething job.'

THE FOOT ASSAULT on 292 came at precisely sixteen minutes after the start of the bombardment. It came from the north-east, the Shadik using the big, rusting tube of the drain outfall as cover.

Just like the note had said.

Not a single raider made it closer to the parapet than fifteen metres. Agun Soric had clustered his rifles around the outfall, and they blazed at the advancing khaki.

Trooper Kazel reckoned they slaughtered at least fifty, maybe sixty even. It was hard to tell. Five platoon had certainly blown them back to wherever they'd come from.

Soric missed Doyl. Doyl had been his platoon's scout. He'd died on the special mission at Ouranberg. Doyl would have been counting. Doyl would have known.

Soric stood on the step and closed his good eye. He'd always refused a patch or an implant for the eye he'd lost at Vervunhive. He wore the rouched scar with some defiance. It made him look as if he was perpetually winking.

He closed his eye and waited. He saw they'd killed at least seventy-six raiders, a multi-platoon force. Kazel had been underestimating.

Sometimes, Soric saw better with his good eye closed. It was just one of those things. He didn't think much of it. His eye was dead, and so he reckoned it saw things only the dead could see. It had a vantage his good eye didn't.

That had been particularly the case since Cirenholm. He'd been badly wounded there. Recovering, he'd had such strange dreams.

Soric knew he should've kept quiet about them, but secrecy wasn't his way. He'd talked about the dreams, and now Gaunt and Dorden and that sweet girl Ana Curth regarded him with mistrust. He should never have told them about his great-grandmother.

Grandam had possessed the sight. Some called her a witch. So what? It wasn't like she was a psyker, for gak's sake! Grandam had just been able to… to see stuff others didn't. Now Agun could, being the seventh son of a seventh son, as Grandam had always assured him.

It hadn't always been that way. Not until Cirenholm. Passage so close under death's black wing and out the other side, that marked a man. That woke him up. That opened his senses.

Opened his eyes.

The handwritten note though, that was another thing altogether. Soric felt his heart skip as he thought about that.

How had he known that? How had he written it to himself?

'Stand down,' he told his men, and the word was passed along. There'd be no more Shadik at 292 today.

Soric realised he knew that for a fact. Why was that?

He felt scared, really scared suddenly. He limped back to his dugout, ignoring the calls and questions of his men.

'Vivvo?'

'Boss?'

'Get them settled,' he said and dropped the gas curtain after himself.

In the dim lamp-light, he sat down at the little raw-wood table. The brass message shell was sitting there, on end, casting a little blunt shadow. There was no sign of the scrap of blue paper.

Soric breathed slowly, clutching the edge of the table tightly with his gnarled hands. A drink. That might help.

He got up, and waddled his stiff leg over to the shelf. Scope, ammo clips, candles... 'spare water bottle'.

Gaunt had said he'd have men shot for drinking on duty. Except in special cases.

This was a special case.

Soric unstoppered the flask with hands that were quaking more than he'd have liked them to. He took a slug of sacra. Good old Bragg had supplied him with the stuff. Soric had developed a taste for the Tanith liquor. Who'd get him sacra now Bragg was gone?

The blue-paper despatch pad lay on the shelf beside the flask. Soric thought about picking it up, then took another swig instead. The grain alcohol burned in his belly. He felt better. He looked at the pad again.

The first two sheets were missing.

Soric glanced over at the table. The brass message shell sat there, ominous.

'Go away!' he said.

'Uh, I did knock,' said the shell.

But it wasn't the shell. It was Commissar Hark.

The commissar peered in at Soric, holding the gas curtain back.

'Sergeant?'

'Oh, oh! Come in.'

Hark entered.

Soric felt hugely exposed. He tried to keep his mouth clamped shut so he wouldn't exude the smell of liquor. Gaunt might have forgiven him. Hark was a different matter. Hark was a commissar, unqualified, unalloyed.

'Everything all right?' Hark asked. He seemed suspicious.

'Fine, fine,' said Soric, breathing through his nose.

Hark looked at him. 'You could relax, sergeant.'

Mouth clamped shut, Soric grinned and shrugged.

Hark sat down on the stool, removing his cap. 'Good work today, sergeant. Excellent, in fact. How did you guess the Shadik's approach route?'

Soric shrugged again.

'Lucky, huh?' Hark nodded. 'Shrewd is a better word. You're very shrewd. You know your stuff, Agun. Can I call you Agun? It doesn't offend your sense of rank?'

'Not at all, sir,' Soric muttered, trying not breathe as he spoke.

'The bombardment's stopped,' Hark said. Soric realised he hadn't noticed.

'We've held them off for the most part,' Hark added. 'Tough stuff around 293 and 294, and also with Criid, Obel and Theiss. And Maroy's dead.'

'Shit, no!' said Soric, despite himself.

'Yeah, it's too bad. Good soldier. But his section took seventy per cent losses. Shells caught them hard. Lasko, Fewtin, Bisroya, Mkdil. All gone. Not you, though, eh?'

'Sir.'

Hark gestured expansively. 'I don't have the full picture yet, but I'm pretty sure your platoon gave the best today, unit for unit. A hell of a job, Agun. Good work. Smart to pick up on their route of attack. I'm impressed.'

'Thank you, sir.'

'I'll be commending your unit to Gaunt. Any one you want to pick out?'

'Uh… Vivvo and Kazel.'

Hark nodded. 'I tell you what you could do now.'

'Sir?'

'I don't know about you, Agun, but I'm shaking fit to drop. Man like you must have some hard stuff hereabouts.'

'Oh,' said Soric. He rattled round on the shelf. 'Forgive my inhospitality, commissar.'

He poured sacra into two of the least chipped shot glasses cluttering his shelf and handed one to Hark.

'Excellent. Knew I could count on a trusty Vervunhiver like you.'

Hark knocked back the shot. Soric sipped his own. He refilled Hark's glass and breathed more naturally.

Hark finished the second shot. 'Takes a while, but that Tanith stuff is good, isn't it?'

'Becoming a favourite, sir,' said Soric.

'You'll have to tell me how you did it, some time,' said Hark.

'Did what, sir?'

'Outguessed the Shadik. Good work, though. Excellent. The regiment is proud of you.'

Hark got up.

'I have to get down the line now. Rawne's been hit. His section is a mess.'

'Hit bad?'

'I'm going to find out. Again, good work, Agun. My compliments to your boys.'

Hark pulled back the gas curtain to leave.

'Thanks for the drink,' he added, and disappeared.

Soric sat down hard as soon as the commissar had gone. He played with his shot glass, and then finished the dregs.

Vivvo stuck his head through the curtain.

'Boss? Do you w–'

'Go away,' said Soric.

'Yes, boss.'

Alone, Soric picked up the message shell and unscrewed the top. He had to thump the base of the canister twice to get the fold of blue paper out.

The message was written in his own handwriting, just like before. It said: 'Don't drink. Commissar Hark is coming.'

FIVE
SILVER, RED AND BLACK

'Waiting is crap. It's crap for a hungry man in a canteen line, it's shit for a groom at his wedding supper, and it's double triple quadrilateral crap for a soldier boy like yours truly.'

– Colm Corbec, colonel

IT HAD BEEN a bad day at the front. The Tanith First reserves at Rhonforq could tell that just from the false dusk caused by the wall of black smoke rising in the distance. They waited for news, hoping for good, steeled for bad.

Gaunt had left Captain Ban Daur in command of the First's reserve section, a full two-thirds of the regiment's strength, and Daur fretted miserably throughout the afternoon. Every ten, twenty minutes he wandered outside and watched the flickering lights and puffing smogs of the distant battle. At first, the thump of the shells had been like the thunder of a distant storm; muffled, remote, lagging behind the flashes. Then the sound had become continuous, without break or breath or pause. A constant rumble, as if the earth was slowly faulting and tearing.

Sometimes, the ground shook, even this far away.

Once in a while, there came a blast roar so loud and plan-
gent that it rose out of the rumble. Daur couldn't work out if
these noises came from shells that had landed closer to his
position, or bigger shells landing with the rest. They'd been
told the enemy had brought up some big-reach, huge calibre
weapons. All the men were talking about 'super-siege' guns.

Daur tried to occupy himself, but the rumble was too distracting. At around 14.00, he went to eat at one of the
pensions, and got a curious look from the matronly owner
when he ordered scrambled eggs. Only when it arrived did he
remember that he'd already taken lunch – scrambled eggs –
just an hour before.

He thought of visiting Zweil. The unit's chaplain was
refreshing company sometimes, and good at distracting a
man's mind with provocative conversation. But he was told
that Zweil had gone to the front that morning with Gaunt, as
if he'd known he'd be needed today.

Daur toured the billets instead. The Ghosts had occupied
the stableblocks and barns of a pair of farmsteads in the
south of the town, their overspill camped out in a sea of tents
pitched in the paddocks behind. The paddocks adjoined an
old tannery occupied by a company of Krassians, and a little
vee of derelict shops and outbuildings at the junction of the
two southern roads, which was the billet of a local brigade,
the Twelfth Ostlund 'Shielders'.

Daur wandered into the muddy yard of one of the stableblocks. Burone, Bray and Ewler had taken the long, left-hand
barn for their platoons. The men mostly lurked around,
dejected in the light rain, like prisoners of war in a blockhouse
pen. Daur saw the coals of burning lho-sticks in the shadows
of the high-loft hatches. Under the slope of a lean-to roof,
Pollo from seven platoon was trying to teach card tricks to a
crowd of onlookers. Pollo had been bodyguard for a noble
house back on Verghast, and his nerves were augmented by
extravagantly expensive neural enhancers, so his fingers split
and spread the cards faster than the eye could follow. It was a
little piece of magic to watch, and the men around him were
captivated. Daur watched for a little while, until Pollo had
exhausted his repertoire of tricks and produced three cups and
a shell case instead. The audience groaned.

'Who wants a try?' Pollo asked, his hands circling the up-turned cups in a blur. He caught Daur's eye and winked. 'You, sir?'

Daur smiled. 'You see my rank pins, Trooper Pollo? I get those for being smart. No thanks.'

Pollo grinned. 'Your loss.'

'I don't think so,' said Daur and wandered on. At the back end of the yard, Haller's men were kicking a ball around with some of the Krassians. It was a lively, muddy game. Noa Vadim was running circles around the Krassians, his squad mates urging him on. Daur was sure they were really shouting and whooping to shut out the distant growl of the battle.

Daur heard low-level gunfire coming from one of the stable pens and went to investigate. He found Trooper Merrt practising his aim against old bottles ranged on the cross-beams of the end wall.

Merrt looked up as Daur appeared. 'Sorry, sir.' he said. 'Just gn… gn… practising. I've set it to gn… gn… low-charge.' He looked a little shame-faced, though it was hard to tell. Merrt's jaw and one side of his face were crude metal implants, poorly disguised by a flesh-coloured mask. Daur knew why he was practising. Merrt practised every chance he got. A Tanith, he'd been one of the regiment's original snipers, with a hit rate lower than Larkin's or Rilke's but still impressive. Then, on Monthax, he'd taken a horrific head wound and his aim had gone to hell. Gaunt had kept him as sniper for a time – too generous a time, according to Hark – but Merrt's lack of success on Phantine had finally obliged Gaunt, reluctantly, to reassign him back to a standard trooper role.

Daur knew Merrt hated his loss of status even more than he hated the loss of his face. Merrt practised and practised, striving to regain his prowess and win back his marksman's lanyard.

'How's it going?' Daur asked.

Merrt shrugged. 'I'd like to be working with a gn… gn… long-las, but they took it off me and gn… gn… gave it to some girl,' he said bleakly, indicating the standard-pattern lasrifle he was holding. His speech was distorted by the rebuilt portions of his head. Merrt seemed to gnaw the words out. He stammered a lot, thanks to that ugly replacement jaw.

'Some of those girls are good shots,' said Daur smoothly. He knew too well a lot of the Tanith resented the Verghastite volunteers, particularly the females, and especially the females like Banda, Muril and Nessa who excelled at shooting.

Daur wouldn't hear them bad-mouthed. They were the Verghastites' one claim to excellence in the regiment.

Merrt stammered particularly badly, realising he'd spoken out of turn to the senior Verghastite officer. 'I didn't mean anything gn... gn... by that, sir.'

'I know,' said Daur. There was no real anti-Verghast or misogynistic rancour in Merrt. He was just a damaged man struggling with his own failure.

'Gn... gn... sorry.'

Daur nodded. 'You carry on,' he said.

Daur felt wretched as he walked away from the stall. There had been plenty of scorch marks on the end wall, but precious few broken bottles.

DAUR CROSSED THE end of the back paddock, passing the time with a few soldiers there. Then he followed a quaggy path up onto a bank that ran down through what had once been an orchard, before the men in the billets had felled most of it for firewood. Arcuda and Raglon were sheltering from the rain by a low wall, their capes pulled up around them.

Daur knew they were both nervous. Both had been promoted, along with Criid, to platoon command just prior to Aexe. Both were anticipating their first taste of field command.

But both had reason to be proud, in Daur's book. Arcuda, a Verghastite with a long, thin doleful face, had proved himself in the ranks and won his pins. Raglon had made his way to squad command through distinguished service in company signals. It was odd not to see Raglon with his vox-set. Daur was pleased to find them together; Verghastite and Tanith, on equal footing, counting on each other.

They greeted him and he squatted down beside them.

'Action at the front,' Daur said.

'We noticed,' said Raglon.

'Chances are, we may move forward early,' Daur added.

Arcuda nodded. 'I want to get up there, sir,' he said. 'I just want to get in it. Sort of… get it over with. Did you feel that way on your first command?'

Daur smiled. 'My first command was a sentry detail at Hass West, Vervunhive. Very pedestrian,' he said. 'I was nineteen. I didn't see action for four years. Not until… the War.'

Someone sniggered. Daur looked up and saw Sergeant Meryn leaning over the wall and listening in.

'Something funny, Meryn?'

Meryn shook his head. 'No, captain. I'm just always amused the way you Verghasts refer to Vervunhive as "The War", capital emphasis and all. It was a big do, certainly, and hard as fething bastardy for everyone involved. But it wasn't "The War". The War's what we're fighting now. We were fighting it before Verghast and we'll be fighting it still in years to come.'

Daur got up and faced Meryn. The man was young, one of the youngest Tanith-born officers, several years junior to Daur. He was trim, compact, good-looking, and had recently taken to cultivating a moustache that made him look sinister in Daur's opinion. Meryn had charm, and a fine record, and his brevet-ranking to sergeant as part of Operation Larisel on Phantine had become a permanent thing. His pins were as new as Arcuda's and Raglon's.

'I know there's war and there's war, sergeant,' Daur said. 'You'll have to excuse a Verghast his memories.' Daur deliberately used the word Meryn had used. 'Verghast' not 'Verghastite'. All the Tanith did that. To them, it was a contraction. To Verghastites, it was insulting slang. 'We know we're fighting The War now. But you'll forgive us if we tend to focus on the fight that saw our home-hive ransacked.'

Meryn shrugged. 'And Tanith died. We all have our memories. We all have our wars.'

Daur frowned and looked away, the drizzle splashing off his face. He didn't like Meryn much. He'd been an obvious choice for platoon command, some said an overdue choice, but he'd become unpleasantly hard-edged and cocky. Sometimes, he reminded Daur of Caffran. Both Tanith were of a similar age, a similar build even. But where Caffran was young and eager and good-natured, Meryn was young and ruthless and arrogant.

Colm Corbec had a private theory about that. The theory was called Major Rawne. According to Corbec, Meryn had been 'a fine, honest lad' for some time until he'd made corporal and, thanks to the vagaries of regimental structure, fallen under Rawne's wing. Rawne was Meryn's mentor now, and Meryn was learning well. The fresh-faced attitude had vanished, and been replaced by a bitter, hostile air. The stain of Rawne's corrosive influence, Daur believed. Rawne was grooming Meryn. Unofficially, the rumour was that Meryn had ordered, or performed, some excessively brutal actions during Operation Larisel. Certainly Larkin and Mkvenner were tight-lipped about him. Meryn had been zealous to achieve his Larisel mission targets and prove himself for promotion.

Too zealous, maybe.

'So, any word from the line yet?' Meryn asked. Daur wished Meryn would go away so he could spend some time bolstering Arcuda and Raglon without an audience.

'No,' said Daur. 'Not yet.'

'If there are casualties, you can figure we'll be moving up before tonight,' Meryn said.

'If there are casualties…' Daur admitted.

Meryn made a sarcastic gesture at the smoke rising from the front. 'There'll be casualties,' he said.

'You'd wish that, would you?' snapped Daur.

'Not for a moment,' said Meryn, his face turning stony. 'But I'm a realist. That's bad feth up there. "The War", you know? Someone's going to get hurt.'

Daur wanted to tell Meryn to go away, but Raglon and Arcuda had got to their feet, shaking the water off their capes.

'We're going to check on our units, sir,' said Raglon.

'Get them ready, if and when,' Arcuda added.

'Good idea,' said Daur.

The two novice sergeants walked away down the bank towards the village and the tower of the Chapel St Avigns. As soon as they were out of earshot, Daur turned on Meryn.

'Do you understand the concept of morale, Meryn?'

Meryn shrugged.

'Those two are on the verge of their first field command. They're scared. They need building up, not knocking down.'

'It's a crime to be realistic now, is it, captain?' Meryn asked, insolently. 'This is my first action as sergeant too, if you'll recall.'

'You've had command, Meryn. At Ouranberg. You did all right there. Too well, maybe.'

'What does that mean?'

'Whatever you like,' said Daur, walking away. He uttered a silent prayer of thanks that within a week or so, Meryn would be Rawne's responsibility again.

THERE WAS A lot of noise coming from the end sheds of the tannery. Daur pushed his way into a barn space that stank of sweat and bodies. The place was full of Ghosts and Krassians and a good number of the red-tunicked Ostlunders.

The Ostlunders were from Kottmark, the country that bordered Aexegary to the east. They were a fair-skinned, hardy breed, generally much taller than the Imperials.

Daur peered through the crowd, trying to establish the source of the commotion.

'Varl,' he sighed to himself. 'Why am I surprised?'

Sergeant Varl, head of nine platoon, had found himself a new game to bet on. Varl, a likeable, handsome rogue, had come up through the ranks and earned his sergeant pins with sweat and blood. His own, for a start. On Fortis Binary, he'd taken an upper torso wound that had resulted in serious augmetic work to his shoulder, collarbone and upper arm. Not long after that, Gaunt had made him sergeant. He'd done it to prove there was no pecking order in the Tanith. Varl was one of the boys, common as grox muck, but he had attitude and charisma in bucket loads, and that made him an ideal leader of men.

You couldn't help but like Varl. All the men did. He was a joker, a prankster, a troublemaker. He also proved that a dog-grunt could have the mettle to lead.

Gaunt had hoped he'd bring a common touch to the command echelon of the First. Varl had brought it in spades.

Daur knew that Varl had made sergeant long before the more upstanding and clean-cut Meryn. Maybe that was why Meryn was such an insufferable feth-head.

Ceglan Varl was playing ringmaster here. His men had made a pit from straw bales, and they appeared to be orchestrating fights between chickens.

Daur moved his way to the front of the press. No, not chickens...

'Struthids! Lovely young struthids, fit to fight and tough as hell!' Varl was declaiming from the wooden loading dock above the pit. He lofted one of the birds by the scruff of its neck, expertly avoiding its clacking blade of a beak and its windmilling, clawed feet. Expertly, that was the word. Daur chuckled. They'd only been on this world five minutes, and Varl was suddenly an expert handler of the local wildlife.

'Look at this jolly fellow! Look at him, eh?' Varl bantered. 'We call him the Major, because he's nasty as all feth!'

The Ghosts in the crowd laughed at this.

'Look at his foot-claws! Look here!' Varl grabbed one of the bird's pistoning feet and splayed the vicious claws for the crowd to admire. 'Three centimetres long, sharp as straight silver! What more do you want?'

A Krassian shouted something.

'Beak? Beak?' Varl replied, looking over and swinging the squirming struthid round. 'I'll give you beak! Mr Brostin, if you'd be so kind?'

Brostin, the heavy-set flame-trooper from Varl's platoon, strode out into the straw-strewn ring and held out a spent brass case from a .30. The bird lunged and cracked the case in two with its scissoring beak.

The crowd roared. Brostin retrieved the broken parts and threw them into the press. Men huddled and fought for them.

'He's tough, all right! Yes, sir! The Major is a tough old bird! We all saw what he did to the Captain just now, didn't we?'

More shouting.

'The Captain?' called Daur.

Varl saw Daur and balked. 'Ah... hello there, sir! How are you? The Captain I refer to... rest his poor soul... was named after another captain who in no way was meant to resemble you... uh...'

'I'm sure. How much on the Major?'

Varl's smile returned. 'Perhaps you'd care to place your wager with one of my friendly assistants, sir?' Daur saw Baen, Mkfeyd, Ifvan and Rafflan moving through the crowd, collecting cash and quoting odds.

'What's he up against, this Major?' Daur shouted.

'Three rounds, no holding, first bleeds, first pays...' said Varl, '...against Mighty Ibram here!'

There was a throaty bellow of approval. Trooper Etron appeared on the other side of the stage, clutching a white-plumed struthid juvenile with a silvery beak. He was having trouble holding on to it. Feather fibres drifted in the warm air.

'No, thanks,' smiled Daur. 'My money's on Mighty Ibram every time.'

'This is fixed! You fix this!' some of the Kottmarkers were yelling.

'Calm yourselves, friends,' said Varl.

'We have our own fighter!' called the tallest of the Ostlund Shielders.

Varl addressed the crowd. 'A new contender, gents and gents, trained by our worthy Kottland allies here... what's the bird's name?'

The clique of Kottmakers had brought a snapping, scarred struthid fledgling forward. 'Redjacq!' their leader hollered.

'Redjacq indeed! He's a fine looking beak-brain, and no mistake!' Varl yelled. 'Place your bets, folks... next round is the Major, Tanith-reared and hard as feth, facing off against Redjacq, trained and maintained by our delightful Kottmark allies there! Ante up! Who's for the Major?'

'Ten!' shouted a Verghastite.

'Twenty on Redjacq!' howled a Krassian.

'My warknife says the Major guts him.'

Daur peered through the crowd to identify the source of the voice. It was Mkoll. The chief scout was standing, arms folded, in the middle of the frenzy.

'We spit on your knife!' cried one of the Kottmarkers.

'I... uh... wouldn't do that if I were you,' said Daur, but the Kottmarkers weren't listening.

'Gentlemen! All bets now stand!' Varl said, taking a nod from Baen. 'Round one! Release your fighters!'

The juvenile struthids exploded into the ring from either side to a cacophony of jeers and taunts. Feathers fluttered up from them. Redjacq sliced and chopped at the Major and more plumage flew. Then the Major lunged in and broke Redjacq's neck with a clean bite of its formidable beak.

The tannery's roof tiles rattled with the uproar that followed. Tanith – and some Krassians – were shouting and dancing. Wagers were paid out, back and forth: local currency, Imperial coin, trophies, badges, mementos…

Up on the loading dock, Varl did a strutting chicken walk, back and forth, his head bobbing in and out, his elbows beating chicken wings.

Caught up in the middle of it all, Daur laughed. For a moment, he almost managed to forget how bad things were.

A firm hand gripped his arm. It was Mkoll.

'Stay sharp, sir,' the chief scout said softly. He nodded towards the door. 'Over there.'

Daur looked. Varl's lackey Ifvan was trying to get a group of Kottmarkers to pay out. Daur couldn't hear the exchange, but he could read the body language. More Kottmarkers were closing in through the oblivious, dancing Tanith.

'Back me up,' Daur said.

'I will,' said Mkoll.

Daur pushed through the dancing men. Nine or ten Kottmarkers were gathered around Ifvan now, and others looked like they were bang out of sportsmanship.

One of the Ostlund troops started shoving Ifvan in the chest. They were all a lot taller than him. They were all a lot taller than Daur.

Daur cleared his throat and prepared to intervene. At that moment, the Kottmarker behind Ifvan suddenly produced a trench club. It was a thick cylinder of hardwood with a metal boss, the size of a stick grenade.

Daur lunged forward. The club came down–

–and stopped. There was a solid, meaty thunk that shut the room up suddenly.

The Kottmarker had dropped the club. His sleeve was pinned to the doorpost by a Tanith warknife. There was a terrible, pregnant silence.

Daur glanced back at Mkoll, but the scout chief simply shrugged in bemusement.

'I hate a bad loser,' said Varl, from the stage ten metres away. He was staring at the Kottmarkers surrounding Ifvan. 'This is an entertainment. Sport. It isn't war. We come in here in the spirit of friendly competition and leave the killing at the door. You're pissed off. Well, tough. In the spirit of this place, I say take your money. We don't want it. Your bets are wiped. Take your money and get out.'

Some of the Kottmarkers took a step towards the stage.

'Or,' said Varl, sharply, 'I start chucking a few more warknives. Someone give me some straight silver.'

Daur blinked. An extraordinary thing happened. There was a ripple of thuds, and a semi-circle of Tanith blades appeared around Varl's feet, tips buried in the wood, thrown without hesitation and with complete accuracy from the crowd.

Varl bent down and plucked out one of the still vibrating blades.

He tossed it up in the air without even looking at it, and caught it again by the grip.

'Well?'

The Kottmarkers fled. So did some of the Krassians. The owner of the club left part of his sleeve pinned to the doorpost.

The men of the First began to cheer and clap. Varl did a little bow and then balanced the knife on his nose, tip down.

'That's enough!' Daur raised his voice. 'Let's clear out and get ready for kit inspection!'

The Ghosts filed out, chattering and laughing. One by one, the knives were retrieved from the stage planks. Brostin recovered Varl's blade from the doorpost and tossed it back to the sergeant. Varl returned Brostin's. The knives passed in mid-air. Neither man was looking as he deftly caught his weapon.

The shed was almost empty. Mkoll lingered. Daur climbed up onto the loading dock next to Varl.

'I'm impressed,' said Daur. 'You kept control.'

'You don't start something like this if you can't police it,' Varl said. 'First rule of showmanship.'

'Still, it was magnanimous of you to let them go without paying.'

Varl smiled. 'All part of the show. Besides, Ifvan and Baen picked their pockets on the way out.'

'Captain?'

Daur looked down into the body of the shed. Mkoll stood in the doorway.

'Signal's come through,' Mkoll said. 'They're moving the wounded back up the line.'

THE FIRST WOUNDED had begun to filter back during the late afternoon, and by the time the bombardment ended and the assault had subsided, they were streaming into the field stations. Some came walking, others carried by stretcher bearers or supported by their comrades, some were borne on barrows or on shellcarts.

Dorden, the First's chief medic, had moved his team up to a triage station just after lunch. The station, designated 4077, was just four kilometres to the rear of the front line. They endured the later stages of the bombardment while they prepped the area. The ground shook. Tent canvas flapped. Surgical tools rattled on their trays.

'There's no mains water supply,' reported Mtane, one of the regiment's three qualified medics.

'None at all?' asked Curth, laying out clean blades on a cloth-covered tray.

Mtane shook his head. 'There's a bowser. About half-full. The Alliance orderlies can't promise it's clean.'

'Lesp!' Dorden called. The lean orderly ran up. 'Set up some stoves and start boiling water. Wait!' Lesp paused as he prepared to dash off again. Dorden handed him a small paper packet. 'Sterilising tablets. Do your best.'

Curth broke open a box of anti-bacterial gel packed in fat metal tubes and passed them around. 'Use them sparingly,' she admonished. 'It's the only carton we've got.'

The triage station was a collection of dirty, long-frame tents pitched to the west of a dead woodland. The access ramps into the first dugouts of the 55th sector workings began just fifty metres east of them. They were terribly exposed, the first above-ground features this side of the Peinforq Line. The wood – Hambley Wood, apparently – was proof of their vulnerability. It was a sea of soft mud and old craters, stubbled with the burnt stumps of thousands of trees. The whole area smelled of wet-rot and mulch.

The First's medicae team shared the station with a Krassian detail and a gang of Alliance corpsmen. When Curth went outside the Ghosts' tent for a final lho-stick before the real work began, she was surprised and disgusted at the filthy state of the locals. Their scrubs and – worse – their hands, were soiled. Many were ill. Some were intoxicated, probably from drinking neat rubbing alcohol.

Foskin, the most junior orderly, joined her for a smoke.

'How many are they going to kill by transmitting infection?' she asked.

'Let's just make sure all the Ghosts come to us,' he said.

It was nothing like that simple. The bodies and the walking wounded that began to pass back to the triage station were so drenched in mud it was impossible to distinguish rank or regiment or even gender.

Curth spent five minutes sewing up a thigh wound before she realised it was Flame-Trooper Lubba she was treating.

One of Kolea's old mob, from nine platoon.

She rinsed his face and smiled when the tattoos were revealed. 'How's Gol?' she asked.

'He's okay, ma'am. Came through it, last I saw.'

'And how's Tona shaping up?'

'The sarge? She was fine.'

Curth was pleased. They were calling Tona Criid 'the sarge' already. Ana Curth was the only person in the First who knew the secret. Kolea had known, but it had been lost along with his identity. There was a madam called Aleksa who knew too, but Curth hadn't seen her since Phantine. The two children Criid and Caffran had 'adopted', two kids who now waited with the camp followers at Rhonforq, were, in truth, Kolea's. He'd presumed them lost. When he'd found out they were alive after all, it was too late. Orphans, they'd bonded with Criid. It was too late to wreck their world again.

That's what Kolea had believed anyway, before injury had robbed them of his character.

Curth felt it was her responsibility to watch over them all.

* * *

THE ANONYMOUS WOUNDED plodded in, through the late afternoon. Dorden found cases of shrapnel wounding, concussive damage and several chronic examples of harm done by gas, both caustic and lachrymatory. He extracted a five centimetre piece of hand-bomb casing from DaFelbe's jaw, twenty-two nails from the foot and leg of Trooper Charel, and a broken length of bayonet from the ribcage of Jessi Banda.

She came round on the table as he was cleaning the wound prior to excising the foreign body.

'Rawne!' she gasped. 'Rawne!'

'Easy there,' he scolded. He looked at Lesp. 'Any morphosia?'

Lesp shook his head.

'How's Major Rawne?' Banda called out, convulsing.

'Easy,' said Dorden. 'You'll be okay.'

'Rawne…' she murmured.

'Was he hurt?' Dorden asked.

Banda had passed out.

'No breath sounds on the left,' Lesp reported. 'We're losing her.'

'Her lung's collapsed,' said Dorden matter-of-factly, and set to work.

SOME OF THE most terribly wounded came from sixteen platoon, though there weren't many of them. One of the Krassians told Curth that sixteen had been virtually wiped out by shellfire.

Trooper Kuren, who'd made it through the horrors of Operation Larisel on Phantine unscathed, had lost part of his leg. 'They're all dead,' he told Curth. 'Maroy's dead.'

She shivered. 'Dead?'

'Almost all of us. The fething shells, like murder…'

She looked across the station. Mtane was trying to pull together a Krassian's gaping chest. Foskin and Chayker were holding down a man who was going into a grand mal seizure and vomiting blood. Dorden was fighting to save Banda's life.

'Sergeant Maroy's dead,' said Curth.

Dorden nodded sadly. 'Rawne may be too,' he said.

* * *

AROUND 17.00 HOURS, the tide of wounded ebbed. Dorden's triage station alone had dealt with nearly five hundred bodies.

The light was bad, choked by the shell-smoke. Drizzle pattered in. The ground inside and outside of the tents was awash with blood, and pieces of discarded uniform and equipment were scattered everywhere.

Light wounded had been sent along the road to Rhonforq and the other reserve stations. The really sick and injured were being ferried by cart and stretcher to the main field hospitals. Dorden made sure that all the seriously wounded Ghosts were labelled so they would be conveyed to his mill infirmary at Rhonforq.

Curth and Dorden exited their triage tent during the lull, complaining to each other about their parlous lack of supplies. Curth smoked another lho-stick, which Dorden shared briefly, though it made him cough. She was afraid she was teaching him bad habits.

'Hey,' she said, nudging him. 'Over there.' Across the churned mud of the station, Alliance orderlies were conveying medical supplies to their tents on sack-barrows.

Curth ran over, tossing her stick-butt into the mud. 'Hey!'

Dorden tried to stop her. 'No, Ana! Don't!'

It was too late. Curth had reached the sack-barrows. She grabbed a box off the nearest and ripped open the lid, the Alliance orderlies objecting angrily.

'Imperial supplies! This stuff is stamped for use by the First-and-Only! You bastards! You stole this!'

'Be off!' growled an Aexegarian.

'I will not! Our supplies went missing, and we've been fighting to survive without them! You had them diverted, didn't you? You fething well stole our med supplies!'

'Ana! Please! It's not worth it!' Dorden cried as he came over. He'd seen this kind of despair-induced corruption too many times before. The Alliance was running painfully short of essential supplies. A big shipment of fresh medical goods must have seemed too choice a treasure to ignore. He'd get some more, he'd get some more shipped in from the Munitorium vessels. It wasn't worth confronting these miserable, desperate wretches.

'Hell, no!' Curth exclaimed, and tried to gather up some of the cartons.

A thuggish Alliance trooper with a dirty bandage around his head struck out at her, and knocked her over into the mud. The cartons went flying.

'No, oh no... no you don't!' Dorden yelled and leapt at the Alliance orderlies, pulling them back off the fallen Curth, who was hunched in a foetal position in the mud to protect herself from their toecaps.

They turned on him. One punched him in the mouth, another kicked him in the hip. Dorden yelped, and then threw a jab that laid one of the Aexegarians out. Then they really started to pound on him. Curth got up and threw herself back into the fray, clawing and punching and kicking.

A bolt-round went off, very loud in the close air.

The brawling figures broke away from Curth and Dorden at the sound. Ibram Gaunt walked across the muck, white smoke escaping through the vents of his bolt pistol's flash retarder. He was splashed from head to toe in mud and blood, and powder burns marked his cheeks.

'I am Imperial Commissar Gaunt,' he said. 'I am known to be a fair man, until I am pushed. You've just pushed me.'

Gaunt lowered his weapon and shot two of the Aexegarians dead where they stood. The rest fled. For good measure, Gaunt sighted and shot down one of the escapees too. Guardsmen, medics and Aexe personnel all around the field station stood and gawped in shock.

Gaunt helped Dorden and Curth to their feet.

'No one does that to my medicae core,' he said.

Curth looked at him in frank fear. She'd never seen him like this.

'I'm a commissar,' he said to her. 'I don't think you realise what a commissar is, Ana. Get used to it.'

Gaunt looked away. 'You men!' he shouted at a group of stunned onlookers. 'Gather up these supplies and distribute them evenly between the Guard and Alliance medical teams at this station. Surgeon Curth here will supervise.'

She nodded.

'Dorden?' Gaunt turned to the old medicae. He had a swollen eye and his lip was split.

'All right?'

'I'll survive,' said Dorden. Gaunt could tell he was more angry than hurt. Angry that the fight had started at all, angry that he'd been stupid enough to get involved. And more than anything else, angry at the way Gaunt had just demonstrated the bleak side of Imperial Guard discipline. Dorden had vowed never to kill. He'd broken that vow once, on Menazoid Epsilon, in order to save Gaunt's life. Now he saw Gaunt take life wantonly, in the name of iron discipline.

'Doctor?' Gaunt said.

'Sir?'

'See to Rawne, please.'

GAUNT'S ARRIVAL HAD marked a fresh influx of casualties, the majority of them Krassians and Alliance, but also a good number from at least seven Ghost platoons, including those of Rawne, Domor, Theiss and Obel. The injuries in Theiss's and Obels's units were mainly from shells. Some of these wounds, like Trooper Kell's, were devastating. Others were insidious.

Trooper Tokar would be the first Tanith man to have to learn as a necessity the sign language used by previously blast-deafened Verghastites.

In Domor's platoon, and in Rawne's, the injuries were from close-quarters fighting. Milo, unharmed himself apart from a few bruises, carried in Trooper Nehn, who'd had his skull cracked by a trench club. Trooper Osket had lost an eye, and then had suffered the misfortune of grabbing a bayonet thrust at him. The blade had chopped in between his middle and third finger, right down through the palm to the base of the thumb. Corporal Chiria, one of the Verghastite girls in Domor's outfit, had massive lacerations that would scar her plain but cheerful face forever.

Rawne was unconscious. Feygor and Leclan carried him in on an improvised stretcher made of duckboards.

'What do you know?' asked Dorden briskly as he started to cut away the major's tunic and undershirt.

'Solid round to the gut,' said Leclan, three platoon's corpsman. 'Close range.'

'How long ago?'

'Two, maybe two and a half hours. It was mayhem in the trench. Bloody mayhem. I found him in a funkhole. Banda was holding on to him, but he'd passed out long before that.'

'Banda was brought in earlier,' said Dorden, washing the filth from Rawne's stomach.

'I sent her up,' said Leclan. 'In the first wave. I didn't want to move Rawne. I called for a surgeon to come to him at the front, but the vox was down and the runners I sent never came back.'

'Feth!' Dorden said, examining the gunshot. 'He's lost a lot of blood. A feth of a lot.' He leaned over and grabbed Rawne's dog-tags, calling out the blood type printed on them to a waiting orderly.

'Is Banda all right?' Leclan asked.

Dorden stopped his relentless work, and looked at Leclan. The man was frightened and worried. Corpsmen like Leclan were standard troopers trained to administer only the most basic first aid. They weren't medics. They were just there to do the fundamentals until medics came. 'Jessi Banda's going to live. It was touch and go. But she'll be fine.'

Leclan sagged visibly with relief.

'You did all right,' Dorden said, returning to his work.

'He's not going to die, is he?' Feygor asked. The involuntary sarcasm injected into his voice by his augmetic throat made Dorden snort.

'We'll see.'

'How's the thumb?'

Beltayn looked up and saw Gaunt. He scrambled up from the ammo hopper he'd been sitting on and showed the colonel-commissar his bandaged hand.

'Hurt a bit when they reset it, but it's fine. Doc Mtane says no heavy lifting, and absolutely no complicated vox work. In fact, he recommends a vacation somewhere where there's no gunfire.'

'Nice try,' said Gaunt.

They were alone at the edge of the triage station, by the side of the trackway where long grass bushed out from broken fence posts. The sun had begun to come out, its light turned sooty by the vapour of war.

A train of stretcher bearers went past, heading west.

Gaunt sat down on the grass bank, and Beltayn resumed his seat on the old hopper.

'You have the casualty lists?' Gaunt asked.

Beltayn produced a data-slate.

Rawne had once joked, bleakly, that the Tanith spared Gaunt that one grim responsibility of commanding officers everywhere, the letter home. In truth, few Guard COs bothered to inform next of kin, though a handful of regiments were famous for the scrupulous way they did it. Gaunt had no one to write to, even if he'd felt the inclination. Tanith was gone, and most of the Verghastites who'd joined the Ghosts had done so because they were leaving no one behind.

Gaunt remembered the old days, when Oktar had charged him with composing the LIA notices for the families of the Hyrkan dead. After Balhaut, it had taken him the best part of a week.

Gaunt studied the data-slate.

'Sixteen platoon pretty much doesn't exist any more,' said Beltayn. 'I suppose we fold the survivors into squads that need making up.'

Gaunt nodded. From the list, he realised that the Ghosts' strength had dropped to less than one hundred platoons for the first time since Verghast. He felt his anger returning. War consumed manpower. That was one of the first things they drummed into you at the commissariate.

But this war… this war consumed manpower like a glutton. It fed on death, even though it was bloated and full.

'Can you get me a link to Van Voytz?' Gaunt asked.

'I can try,' said Beltayn.

As his adjutant began to set up his vox-caster, Gaunt got to his feet, and wandered a little way down the track. Columns of Aexe Alliance foot soldiers were moving towards him from the reserves, weary and dirty. More bodies for the war machine.

Gaunt saw a lone figure trudging his way, overtaking the toiling infantry ranks.

'Captain Daur?'

'Sir,' Daur saluted. He was out of breath. He'd been jogging all the way from Rhonforq.

'The reserves are in safe hands, I trust?'

'Mkoll, sir,' Daur panted.

'And you're here?'

'It looked bad. The vox was down. I wanted to... to know.'

'It was bad. Over a hundred casualties. Thirty-six dead that I know of, including Maroy. Rawne may not make it, either.'

Daur looked away, gazing across the neglected fields and the withered woodlands.

'It's going to chew us all up, isn't it, sir?' he said.

'Not if I have anything to say about it,' Gaunt replied. 'Be advised, Ban... with Rawne out, you have third ranking as of now.'

'Understood.'

'I want you to bring up five platoons early to replace two, three, eleven, twelve and sixteen. You call it. We'd best forget the standing rota. Any platoon that sees hard action gets rotated for fresh from now on.'

Daur nodded. 'You want me at the front now?'

'I understand Colm saw some feth today too. I'll drop him back in favour of you.'

'He's all right?'

'Far as I know. But I want to go easier on him. He's had a rough time these past eighteen months. He's still not... not his old self.'

'That's fine, sir,' Daur said.

'Colm will take the reserve, and you and I will lead at the front.'

'Yes sir.' Daur registered a certain pride. For the first time it would be Gaunt and a Verghastite in command at the sharp end. It felt like a coming of age. But his feelings were mixed. Rawne wounded, Corbec pulled back... would the Ghosts still be Ghosts without them?

When he first signed up, at the Act of Consolation, Daur had imagined a time when he'd be Gaunt's XO. He'd all but willed death on Rawne and Corbec so that he could bring the Verghast strength to the fore.

Now it was happening, and he felt nothing but keen loss.

'Sir?' Beltayn called out. Gaunt strode over to his adjutant, who was listening intently to the phones of his vox-set.

'No luck with the general, sir,' Beltayn explained, 'but I've spoken to his aide. You're invited to dinner with the staff chiefs at Meiseq tomorrow night. Sixteen hundred hours. Dress uniform.'

LARKIN WANDERED DOWN the fire trench between stations 290 and 291, his long-las hanging from one hand and his Tanith blade hanging from the other. Troopers got out of his way. Mad Larkin was mad again.

'Larks?' Corbec called out, approaching him. 'How you doing?'

Corbec had been shipping Sillo off to a triage station when word had reached him that Larkin was on the prowl. 'He looks like he's gone right over!' Trooper Bewl had said excitedly.

Larkin blinked and slowly recognised Corbec. He glanced down at the weapons he was carrying as if he'd only just become aware of them, and carefully set them down on the firestep. Then he sat down next to them.

Corbec shooed the gawking troopers around him back to their duties and went down to Larkin's side.

'Bad day, Larks?'

'Horrible.'

'It's been tough all round. Anything you want to talk about?'

'Yes.' Larkin paused. He opened his mouth to speak the name 'Lijah Cuu', but stopped himself. So badly, he wanted to tell Corbec about Cuu. Cuu the maniac. Cuu the psycho. Cuu, who would have killed him but for the sudden shelling.

Cuu, who had killed Bragg.

But now it seemed pointless. Loglas, the only witness, was very dead. If Larkin brought a charge, it would be Cuu's word against his. And Cuu had proved to be bulletproof up till now.

Larkin knew Colm would take him seriously. But he also knew that Colm was hidebound by the rules.

As soon as the shells started to fall, Cuu had fled, leaving Larkin alone. Larkin had been so terrified, arms up over his head, eyes closed, it had taken him a moment to realise Cuu had actually gone and only Larkin's fear of Cuu was left behind.

No, there was no point, Larkin decided. The only way to be free from his fear was to face it. Corbec couldn't help him. Gaunt couldn't. The system couldn't.

Lijah Cuu had to die. It was that simple. Cuu wanted the score settled, didn't he? So it would be settled. Fething straight, sure as sure, one way or another.

'Larks?' Corbec said. 'What did you want to tell me about? You look like you're all upset.'

'I am,' said Hlaine Larkin. 'Loglas died,' he confessed.

That was true, but it was also a lie. That wasn't why Larkin was most upset.

But it was all Corbec needed to know.

SIX

ONE HAND GIVES, ONE HAND TAKES

*'I say, if they want to skulk, let them. I'd be interested
to see great skulkers at work.'*

– Colonel Ankre

THAT NIGHT, AND the morning that followed, it was mercifully quiet in 55th sector. It was as if the tide of war had drawn out from that part of the line, slack, low.

It was flood tide elsewhere. Further south down the Naeme Valley, the 47th and 46th sectors were brutalised by twelve straight hours of heavy bombardment. A considerable stretch of the so-called Seronne Line, which ran east from the end of the Peinforq Sectors right across country to the Kottmark Massif, came under shellfire, and then armoured assault. The worst clashes were just south of the Vostl Delta.

To the north, there were intermittent light attacks and raids all through the night at Loncort and the Salient. Unconfirmed reports were circulating that sectors north of Gibsgatte had endured the biggest offensive of the year, and that battle still raged there.

The morning was damp and fog-bound. With Beltayn his only companion, Gaunt travelled north for Meiseq. Beltayn said little. He could tell Gaunt was in a foul temper, and didn't want to provoke anything.

A staff car conveyed them as far as Ongche, where they boarded a despatch train bound for the north. The train was half-empty, and rattled along through misty farmland and rain-swept heath.

Prior to departure, just after dawn, Gaunt had made a final inspection of the First's positions. Daur's relief squads were at the front by then, though Corbec was to remain as line XO until Gaunt's return.

At the end of his tour, Gaunt had made a call at the military hospital in Rhonforq, spending time with the injured and looking in on the critical cases. Rawne had survived the night, though he'd required secondary surgery in the small hours to staunch internal bleeding.

Dorden was so fatigued by then he seemed almost asleep on his feet, and the bruises he'd taken in the beating were starting to nag at him. Gaunt had been intending to ask the chief medic to accompany him to Meiseq, but one look at Dorden stifled the idea. Dorden was needed at Rhonforq, if only to get some rest.

Gaunt knew that Dorden was still angry with him about the discipline killings. He had a right to be, in Gaunt's opinion. Gaunt had been in a dazed rage the afternoon before, weary with the pointless losses he'd witnessed at station 289. He'd just snapped.

As an Imperial commissar, Gaunt was unusual, quite apart from the fact that he held command rank. Commissars were universally feared. They were the Guard's instruments of discipline and control, the lash that kept the soldiery in line and drove them forward. They were there to drum the tenets of the Imperial creed into the minds of the enlisted men, and then give them stark, regular reminders of that truth. Summary execution, even for minor violations, was acceptable stock-in-trade for a commissar. The great Yarrick himself had once said that it was a commissar's job to be a figure of greater fear and threat to an Imperial Guardsman than any enemy.

That was not Gaunt's way. Experience had shown him that morale was better served by encouragement and trust than by an unpredictable temper and a pistol. He'd had a good example in the form of his mentor, the late Delane Oktar. Oktar's philosophy of morale had been based on trust and tolerance too. There had been times when a firm hand had been called for, a few more when action had worked better than words.

But Gaunt prided himself on his fairness, and knew that he was able to count men like Dorden as friends because of it. At the field hospital, he'd acted just like a typical commissar. Dorden hadn't said anything, but Gaunt had seen the disappointment in his eyes.

As the train rattled north, he turned the incident over in his mind. There was no point setting the blame on fatigue. Fatigue implied weakness, and a commissar could never be weak. He realised it was more a matter of futility. He'd come into the Aexe war with reservations, and each step of the way to the front had confirmed his fears. War was not senseless of itself. Faced with the immortal obscenity of Chaos, humankind had a true cause to rally around and fight for. There was a greater good, a purpose, even here on Aexe.

It was the manner of this war that was senseless. The dismissive contempt with which the Alliance threw men and materiel at the enemy. The antique thinking that believed brute strength was the main determining factor behind victory. It made Gaunt angry to see this, angrier still to have the First caught up in it. The afternoon before, he'd been smothered by the futility, and it had worked its ministry on him.

Outside, the world went by. One world, just one of thousands, hundreds of thousands, that combined to form the greatest achievement in human history. The Imperium of Mankind. Many believed that the Imperium was so vast in scale, so huge in scope, that the actions of one man could not affect it. That wasn't true. If everyone thought that way, the Imperium would simply collapse in upon itself overnight. Each and every human soul determined their part of Imperial culture. That was the only thing the Emperor asked of a man. Be true to yourself, and all those myriad tiny contributions would combine to build a culture that could endure until the stars went out.

Beltayn was asleep, his head nodding onto his chest, his bandaged hand cradled in the other. Beyond the window pane, broken woodland flickered by, cut by hillsides dark with rain. A stream flashed like a drawn sword. Meadows lay invisible beneath cloaks of white mist. Uplands broke through fog like the tips of grey reefs. A lone, lightning-scarred tree stood vigil on a bare hill. A village slumbered, derelict. Clouds as thick as ruffled taffeta chased each other across the sky.

GAUNT WOKE FROM a recurring dream about Balhaut, and realised the train had stopped. The rain drummed down and gloomy woodlands surrounded the carriage windows. He checked his timepiece: an hour past noon. They should be in Chossene by now.

He got up and walked down the empty carriage to the door. Opening the window, he smelt the damp undergrowth and soil of the wood, and heard birdcalls and the batter of rain on the leaves. Other passengers were peering out. Down at the locomotive, engineers had dismounted.

Gaunt opened the door and jumped down onto the over-grown track side.

The locomotive had broken down, one of the engineers told him. Repairs were beyond them. They were going to have to wait until a relief tender could come out from Chossene.

'How long will that be?' Gaunt asked.

'Three or four hours, sir.'

GAUNT SHOOK BELTAYN to wake him up.

'Come on,' he said. 'We've some walking to do.'

'What's wrong, sir?' asked Beltayn sleepily.

Gaunt smiled. 'Something's awry.'

THE MISTS WERE beginning to clear as they trudged up through the woods, heading west on a little-used path. Pale sunlight shone down through the branches of the wood. The rain had stopped, but still rainwater fell, dripping down from the canopy. The air smelled of wet, and the scent of some wild-flower.

The engineer had given them directions. A village, Veniq, lay half an hour's walk to the west. Someone there could provide the Imperial officer with transport, the engineer supposed. In his opinion, it was better to stay with the train. Help was coming. Eventually.

Beltayn had been in favour of waiting too. 'We might walk for hours. Or get lost. Or–'

'If we wait for the relief tender, we'll miss my appointment for sure. Meiseq's still a good way away. We walk.'

The track was muddy and it was slow going. Beltayn insisted on carrying Gaunt's overnight pack but, with his own kit and his damaged hand, he was over-encumbered and kept stopping to put something down and resettle his load.

The cool air was bracing. Gaunt realised he was raising a sweat, and took off his stormcoat, flopping it over his left shoulder. Behind them, back down through the woods, they heard a train whistle. If that was the relief tender, then they really had made a bad choice and wasted a lot of effort.

'You want to go back, sir?' asked Beltayn when he heard the whistle note.

Gaunt shook his head. This brisk walk through the empty calm of the wood was like a balm. His lungs were full of cool, smoke-free air and his nostrils full of flower scent. It was amazingly strong now. He didn't know what it was. Little bright-blue flowers with odd-shaped petals covered the ground between the trees, showing over the wet moss and ivy. He wondered if it was them.

He turned to Beltayn and took his overnight bag from him. Then he took Beltayn's pack too.

'That's not necessary,' said Beltayn.

'Ah, let me carry them a while,' said Gaunt.

THE TRACK WOUND through the wood, but there was no sign of farmland or the village. They crossed a rushing brook by way of an ancient stone bridge, black with mould. Bird calls and the burr of insects floated eerily through the trees. In one dense thicket, the beythorne was strung with spider webs that glinted with beads of rainwater like quartz.

'What did the engineer mean about brigands?' Beltayn asked, pausing to get a stone out of his boot.

'Deserters, I believe,' said Gaunt. 'Over the years, bands of them have run to ground out here in the wooded country. They live by pilfering from farms, poaching…'

'Brigandry?' Beltayn added. 'Being, as it seems, brigands.'

Gaunt shrugged.

'Well, maybe this was a bad id–' Beltayn began, but shut up as Gaunt raised a hand.

Across the next clearing, a stand of white birch with gleaming bark, a deer had emerged from the smoke of mist. It stood for a moment, regarding them with its head cocked. Then it turned and darted away.

A heartbeat later, and they saw others, distantly, chasing soundlessly through the woods.

Like ghosts.

A FULL HOUR after they had begun their hike, they emerged from the edge of the wood at a point where the land became planted fields. Swaying heads of young, green wheat covered the slopes down the waist of a hill towards a fresh line of woodland in the valley.

It was a decent vantage point, but there was no sign of any village.

'I'm hungry,' said Beltayn.

Gaunt looked at him.

'Just saying,' he said.

Gaunt put the bags down and mopped his brow. The walk had reinvigorated him, but he was beginning to agree with Beltayn. This had been a bad idea.

He checked the position of the sun, and read his timepiece. He wished he'd brought his compass, or his locator, or even his auspex, but there had seemed no need that morning. His bag contained nothing but his shaving kit, his number one uniform, and his copy of *The Spheres of Longing*.

He wanted to ask Beltayn which way he favoured, but to do so would be to admit he was lost. He decided they should follow the track down the edge of the field where it curved into the bottom of the valley. Perhaps there'd be a road down there.

They'd gone about a hundred paces, when he stopped again. 'You see that?' he asked.

Beltayn squinted. Down in the valley, hidden in the woodland there, was a building. Grey chafstone, the roof made of slate. Some sort of tower poked up through the canopy.

'You've got sharp eyes, sir,' said Beltayn. 'I'd never have seen that in a thousand years.'

'Come on,' said Gaunt.

IT WAS A chapel, old and rundown, buried in the green twilight of the wood. Trailing ivy and fleece-flower clung to its walls. Bright green lichens gnawed the chafstone. They walked around the partially-collapsed wall, in through the old gate, and up the path to the door. The scent was back, that flower scent. It was so strong, it made Gaunt feel like sneezing. He could see no flowers.

Gaunt pushed open the door and walked into the cold gloom of the chapel. The interior was plain, but well-kept. At the end of the rows of hardwood pews, a taper burned at the Imperial altar. Both men made the sign of the aquila, and Gaunt walked down the aisle towards the graven image of the Emperor. In the stained glass of the lancet windows, he saw the image of Saint Sabbat amongst the worthies.

'Well,' murmured a voice from the darkness. 'There you are at last.'

SHE WAS VERY old, and blind. A strip of black silk was wound around her head across her eyes. Her silver hair had been plaited tightly against the back of her skull. Age had hunched her, but stood erect she would have towered over Gaunt.

There was no mistaking her red and black robes.

'Sister,' Gaunt said, and bowed.

'Welcome here. There is no need for obeisance.'

Gaunt looked up. How had she known he was bowing? For a scant second, he wondered if she was some gifted seer, but then he caught himself. Stupid. Her senses were sharp, and attuned to her blindness. She'd simply noted the direction of his voice. 'I am Colonel-Commissar Ibram Gaunt,' he said.

She nodded, as if she didn't especially care. Or, Gaunt thought, as if she already knew. 'Welcome to the Chapel of the Holy Light Abundant, Veniq.'

'We're near the village then?'

'Well, the name is a little misleading. Veniq is about four kilometres south of here.'

Beltayn groaned quietly.

'Your boy is disheartened to hear that,' she said.

'My boy? My adjutant?'

'I hear two of you. Am I mistaken?'

'No. We're trying to reach Veniq, to find transport. Our train... well, it doesn't matter. I need to be in Meiseq tonight.'

She sat down on one of the pews, feeling her way with one hand, leaning on her staff with the other. 'That's a long way,' she said.

'I know,' said Gaunt. 'Can you perhaps set us on the right road?'

'You're on the right road already, Ibram, but you won't reach your destination for a while.'

'Meiseq?'

'Oh, you'll be there tonight. I meant...'

'What?'

She settled herself against the stiff back of the pew. 'My name is Elinor Zaker, once of the Adepta Sororitas Militant, the order of Our Martyred Lady. Now warden and keeper of this chapel.'

'I am honoured to meet you, sister. What... what did you mean about my destination?'

She turned her head towards him. It was the fluid neck-swivel of a human who had been habituated to helmet-display target sensors. For a moment, Gaunt felt like she was aiming at him.

'I should speak less. There are things that mustn't be said, not yet. You'll have to excuse me. I get so few visitors, I feel the urge to gabble.'

'What things mustn't be said?' Gaunt started to say, but Beltayn spoke over him.

'How long have you been here, lady?' he asked.

'Years and years,' she said. 'So many, now. I tend the place, as well as I am able. Does it look trim and clean?'

'Yes,' said Gaunt, glancing around.

She smiled a little. 'I can't tell. I do my best. Some things I see clearly, but not my environment. He doesn't sound very young.'

Gaunt realised this last comment had been made about Beltayn. 'My adjutant? He's... what, thirty-two?'

'Thirty-one last birthday, sir,' said Beltayn from the far end of the aisle.

'Well, he's no boy, then.'

'No,' said Gaunt.

'I understood it would be a boy. No disrespect, Ibram. You're important too. But the boy, he's the crux.'

'You seem to be speaking in riddles, sister.'

'I know. It must be very distressing. There are so many things I can't say. It would ruin everything if I did. And it's really too important, so that mustn't happen. Was there a boy? Very young? The youngest of all?'

'My previous adjutant was a boy,' said Gaunt, suddenly very unsettled. 'His name was Milo. He's a trooper now.'

'Ah,' she said, nodding. 'It gets it wrong sometimes.'

'What does?' asked Gaunt.

'The tarot.'

'How can you read cards when you can't see?' Beltayn asked warily.

She turned her head towards the sound of his voice. Another careful aim. Beltayn stepped back slightly as if he had been target-acquired. 'I don't,' she said. 'It reads me.'

With her head turned, Gaunt could see the long, pink line of the scar that ran over the top of her skull, seaming her white hair like a plough-furrow through corn, down to the left side base of her neck. He sighed inwardly. He'd almost been taken in by her talk. He'd been on the verge of believing they had stumbled upon – or been fatefully drawn to – a prophetic being. But now everything, even her peculiarly apt references to Milo, took on another meaning.

She was mad. Brain-damaged in some long-ago action. Rambling, talking at shadows, deprived of contact by her lonely vigil.

Gaunt needed to get on. 'Look, sister... we are heading for Meiseq. I believe lives depend on us getting there. Is there any way you can help us?'

'Not really. Not in the grand scheme of things. You're going to have to help yourselves. You and the boy, I mean. As far as Meiseq goes... I wouldn't want to go there. Ugly place. An affront to the eyes. But you can borrow my car, if you like.'

'Your car?'

'No use to me any more. It's garaged in one of the barns across the lane. You might have to clear undergrowth from the doors, but the car runs. I turn it over every day. The keys are on the doorpost hook.'

Gaunt nodded to Beltayn, and the adjutant hurried out of the chapel.

'Has he gone?' she asked.

'Gone to find the car,' Gaunt said.

'Sit with me,' she whispered.

Gaunt sat beside her on the pew. Rambling though she was, Sister Zaker was doing him a favour, so he could at least humour her for a minute or two.

He could smell the flower-scent again. Where had he smelled that before?

'It will be hard,' she confided.

'What will?'

'Herodor,' she replied.

'Herodor?' The only Herodor Gaunt knew of was a tactically insignificant colony world some distance to coreward. He shrugged.

'I've been allowed to pass on a few things,' she said. 'There is harm throughout. But the greatest harm, ultimately, is within. Within your body.'

'My body?' Gaunt echoed. He didn't really want to get drawn into this. But she deserved civility.

'Figuratively, Ibram. Your body, as DeMarchese describes the body. Have you read DeMarchese?'

'No, sister.' Gaunt wasn't even sure who DeMarchese was.

'Well, do so. The harm is in two parts. Two dangers, one truly evil, one misunderstood. The latter holds the key. It's important you remember that, because you commissars are terribly trigger happy. I think that's it. Oh, there is something else. Let your sharpest eye show you the truth. That's it. Your sharpest eye. Well, that about does it. I hope I've made myself clear.'

'I–' Gaunt began.

'I have to sweep the floor now,' she said.

She paused and turned her head towards him. 'I really shouldn't say this. I'm stepping way beyond my role... but when you see her, commend me to her. Please. I miss her.'

From outside, the cough and snarl of a motor engine racing into life broke the stillness.

'Of course,' said Gaunt. He gently took her hand and kissed it.

'The Emperor protect you, sister.'

'He'll have his hands full protecting you, Ibram,' she replied. 'You, and that boy.'

Gaunt retreated down the aisle. 'We'll return the car.'

'Ah, keep it,' she said with a dismissive wave of her hand.

OUTSIDE, IN THE damp trackway, Beltayn sat behind the wheel of a massive old limousine. Its night-blue body was chipped with rust and lichen caked its running boards. Weeds had sprouted from the grille and fender. Beltayn had turned on the headlamps, which burned like the eyes of a nocturnal predator.

Gaunt walked up to the car and ran his hand along the grey hide of the retractable roof.

'This come down?' he called.

Beltayn fiddled with the dashboard controls. With a creak, the hood retracted on concertinaing iron hoops so that the car was open-topped.

Gaunt got into the back. Beltayn looked back at him and raised his bandaged hand in a rather pathetic gesture.

'I... uh... don't think I can handle the transmission, sir,' he said.

Gaunt shook his head, amused. 'Change places,' he said.

THEY ROARED AWAY down the woodland lane, leaving the chapel behind. Sunlight dappled and flickered all over them.

'So...' shouted Beltayn from the back over the roar of the eight cylinder engine, '...how strange was that?'

'Forget it!' yelled Gaunt into the slipstream, changing down as he took the massive, elderly automobile around a hard bend. 'She was just hankering for company.'

'But she knew about Brin–'

'No, she didn't. A few enigmatic remarks. That's all. Hive-market preachers use that kind of routine all the time. It works on the gullible.'

'Okay. So she was trying to fool us?'

'Nothing so calculating. She was just... not altogether there.'

A DROVE ROAD brought them through Veniq, and then on across open arable tracts to Shonsamarl where they joined the Northern Highway. Southbound, the highway was thick with munition trains and troop carriers. Northbound, they caught the end of a convoy of Guard Thunderers and light armour moving up to Gibsgatte. They played leapfrog up the line of heavy tanks as well as the passing traffic would allow, until the convoy turned off at Chossene, and then they raced on over the Naeme viaduct and into the cornfield flats of Loncort County.

Fitful light rain and patchy sun followed them through the afternoon along metalled roads that lay like ribbons over the salty-green fields. They saw slow formations of Alliance tri-planes buzzing east towards the front, and once or twice the glint of Imperial air support banging in supersonically, taking a new kind of war to this lingering, old-fashioned theatre.

Shortly before 18.00, Gaunt saw the skyline of Meiseq rising over the fields.

MEISEQ WAS A new town built on old roots. It had been almost entirely razed in the early years of the Aexe War, when the initial Shadik advance had sliced mercilessly right across country to the Upper Naeme. Five years of counter-fighting, focused especially on the Battle of Diem, had eventually ousted the enemy from a portion of territory marked in the north-west corner by the city of Gibsgatte and in the south-east by Loncort. This, the so-called 'Meiseq Box', was now perhaps the most sturdy of the Alliance's line defences, forming as it did the middle section of the Northern Front. To the south, from Loncort, ran the Peinforq Line that held the Naeme Valley. To the north ran the hotly contested sectors beyond Gibsgatte. The Alliance considered the Box so sound it had turned the areas around Diem into a Memorial Park for the fallen. An eternal flame burned at the site of Diem's cathedral, and the oceans of grass around it were lined with row upon row of white, obcordate grave markers.

Meiseq had been rebuilt. Its buildings were made from pressure treated wood-pulp, coated with an emulsion of rock cement. It perched on an escarpment above a bend in the Upper Naeme, encircled by pales of timber and flakboard. At its centre rose the wooden cathedral of San Jeval.

It was getting dark by the time they drove up through the fortress gate in the south face of the walls and entered the town. The cathedral bells were ringing, and lamplighters were igniting the caged chemical torches that lined the streets.

Meiseq reminded Gaunt of a frontier city. Its prefabricated bulk smelled new and entirely at odds with the old, stone-built population centres he'd experienced so far on Aexe. It was strategically important, and wanted visitors to know that, but it seemed little more than a camp, an earthwork. The air smelled of roofing pitch and sweating wood. He remembered moving in to occupy Rakerville, years ago, with the Hyrkans. That had smelled the same. An outpost. A brief statement of Imperial activity. A gesture made without confidence at a frontier.

They parked near to the cathedral in a yard surrounded by trees. The trees were old and withered, but the Aexegarians who had remade Meiseq had remade the trees too, grafting new boughs onto the old trunks shattered by war. Late blossom and fresh green growth formed a roof over the gnarled, grey trunks.

Gaunt and Beltayn walked down the neighbouring streets, through the light crowds, and found the military hall, a grim, twin-towered edifice with a walled precinct of its own.

It was nearly 20.00 hours.

WASHED AND CHANGED, Gaunt left Beltayn in the officio suite appointed to him, and went down to dinner. His guides were two subalterns of the Bande Sezari, dignified in their plumed head-dresses and green silks. Night had fallen, and the narrow passages of the military hall were caves of fluttering rushlights.

The dinner had just begun in a terrace room overlooking the river to the west. The last scraps of day-fade smudged the sky outside, and drum-fires flickered along the low river bend.

There were nineteen officers present, and all stood briefly as Gaunt took his place at the empty twentieth place. He sat, and the mumble of conversation resumed. The long table was dressed in white cloth, and lit by four large candelabra. Gaunt's place setting twinkled with nine separate pieces of cutlery. A steward brought him an oval white bowl and filled it with chilled, blush-red soup.

'Imperial?' asked the man to his right, a short thin-faced Aexegarian who had clearly drunk too much already.

'Yes, sir,' said Gaunt, careful to acknowledge the man's rank boards. A general.

The man stuck out his hand. 'Siquem Fep Ortern, C-in-C. 60th sector.'

'Gaunt, Tanith First.'

'Ah,' said the drunk. 'You're the one they've been talking about.'

Gaunt looked down the table. He saw Golke nearby, and Lord General Van Voytz at the head of the table. He didn't recognise any other faces, except for Van Voytz's chief tactician, Biota. Like Ortern, all the others were senior Alliance officers, either Aexegarians or Kottmarkers. Gaunt began to feel like he'd walked into a lion's den. He'd assumed Van Voytz had summoned him to attend a private dinner where he could voice his disquiet at Alliance tactics in the company of chosen staff chiefs. He hadn't expected this, a full, high brass banquet. Though Van Voytz, imposing in his dark green dress uniform, dominated the head of the table, the presiding influence seemed to come from the man to Van Voytz's left, a bullish Kottmark general with a disturbingly bland, pale face, half-moon clerk's spectacles and white-blond hair.

Gaunt said little, and ate quietly, catching the conversation strands as they cut back and forth along the table. There were a lot of thinly veiled, disrespectful remarks about Imperial soldiery, which Gaunt felt were entirely for his benefit. The Alliance staff were goading him, seeing what they could get away with, seeing what would make him comment.

Three courses came and went, including the main course of braised game, and were followed by a sticky, over-sweet pudding called sonso that the Alliance officers greeted with much approval. It was a local speciality. Ortern, and some of the others nearby, extolled its virtues. To Gaunt, it was almost unbearably sugared. He left a good deal of it.

The stewards cleared the tables, brushed off the cloth, and served sweet black caffeine and amasec in large, green-glass balloons. The locals, who had all dined with their pressed white napkins tucked into the buttons of their dress frocks like bibs, now tossed the loose ends over their left shoulders, apparently a custom that showed they were finished. Gaunt folded his own loosely and left it on his setting.

A tiny servitor drone circled the table, clipping and lighting cigars. One of the Kottmarkers pushed his chair back and started to smoke a long-stemmed flute-pipe with a water bowl. Ortern offered Gaunt a fat, loose-rolled cigar, which he declined.

Ortern chuckled. 'Your customs, sir, are rather alien. On Aexe Cardinal, a gentleman never leaves his sonso unfinished. And he never declines the offer of another man's smokes, for when can he be sure he'll sample such delights again?'

'I mean no offence,' said Gaunt. 'Is it protocol to accept a cigar and save it for a later time?'

'Of course.'

Gaunt nodded, and took one of the proffered cigars. He knew Corbec would appreciate it.

The conversation now opened up more freely across the table.

'Ibram,' Van Voytz greeted Gaunt from the table-head with a toast of his amasec, 'you joined us late.'

'My apologies, lord. I encountered transit problems on my way from Rhonforq.'

'I was afraid you wouldn't make it,' said the bespectacled Kottmark general. 'I was looking forward to meeting you.'

'Sir,' Gaunt acknowledged.

'Ibram, this is Vice General Carn Martane, commander in chief of the Kottmark Forces West, and deputy supreme commander of the Alliance.'

Lyntor-Sewq's right hand man, then.

Martane smiled blandly at Gaunt and sipped his amasec delicately. 'I have been intrigued by certain reports,' he began.

'Come now, Martane!' Van Voytz cut in, good humouredly. 'This is a social event. We can leave the war room talk for the morning.'

'But of course, lord general,' said Martane deftly, sitting back in his seat. 'The war consumes our every waking moment in ways I forget must seem strange to visitors.'

Van Voytz's face darkened. It was a tremendous but subtle slight. Martane was deferring to Van Voytz, but doing so in such a way that suggested the Imperials took the Aexe struggle far less seriously than the locals.

'Actually, my lord,' said Gaunt brightly, 'I'd be interested to hear the vice general's comments.'

The conversation stilled. It was a duel, no more or less, verbal but still vicious. Imperials versus Alliance. Martane's remark had been cutting and poised, allowing Van Voytz two options: pass over it and take the put-down, or trigger a more obvious clash by marking it.

Either way, Van Voytz would lose grace. Now Gaunt had stepped up and deflected the slur as deftly as Martane had made it.

Martane chose his words carefully. 'Colonel Ankre, that worthy son of Kottmark, has suggested to me in despatches that you have been… less than impressed with our military organisations.'

'Colonel Ankre and I enjoyed a robust exchange of views, sir,' said Gaunt. 'I imagine that is what you are referring to. I admit I'm surprised he took them so to heart he needed to bother you with them.'

Gaunt saw Van Voytz disguise a smile. There was a word that usually followed a remark like Gaunt's latest. The word was 'touché'.

'I was not bothered by them, colonel-commissar. I was glad Redjacq took the time to instruct me. I would hate to think that our new Imperial allies are fighting against us. Administratively, I mean.'

Martane was a skilled political operator. There was another comment that seemed light and warm yet had sharp steel running through it.

'Why would you think that?' Gaunt asked, parrying directly.

'Ankre said you took issue with the workings of chain of command and field etiquette. That you remonstrated with him over a lack of intelligence.' Martane was more direct now. He clearly felt he had Gaunt on the back foot and was about to force him into damning himself.

Gaunt saw Golke across the table. The man was impassive. Gaunt recalled clearly how direct and brutal he'd been with Golke at Rhonforq, Ankre too. He could tell Golke was willing him not to be similarly forthright now.

As if I'd be that stupid, Gaunt thought to himself. 'I did, sir,' he said.

'You admit it?' Martane caught the eyes of some of his fellow officers slyly. Gaunt saw Van Voytz ever so slightly shake his head.

'The Imperial Expedition has come here to be your comrade in arms, vice general. To be, as it were, part of your determined Alliance against the Shadik Republic. Surely it is right we enmesh ourselves properly into the Alliance forces? Elements of field etiquette and intelligence were particular to this war, and I needed clarification. I've fought many battles, sir, but I can't pretend to understand the nuances of this one yet. My question came, vice general, simply from a desire to best serve the high sezar and the free people of Aexe.'

Martane's pale cheeks flushed briefly as red as the first course soup. Behind a guard of honesty, Gaunt had just outstepped him. Martane fumbled. 'Ankre also suggested you believed your men too good for front-line combat,' he began, but it was the blunt move both Gaunt and Van Voytz had been waiting for. Unable to force Gaunt to condemn himself with his own words, Martane had stumbled and voiced an actual insult.

'For shame, vice general,' growled Van Voytz.

'I am affronted, sir,' Gaunt said.

'Come now, Martane,' Golke said, speaking for the first time. 'That is hardly the courtesy we of Aexe extend to voluntary allies.'

Voices rumbled round the table. Many of the officers were embarrassed by their commander's comment.

Gaunt smiled to himself. As with war, so with decorum, Aexe was so old-fashioned. He remembered some of the staff dinners when Imperial commanders had hurled abuse at each other across the table and then sat laughing over the port. There was no such frankness here. There was simply a culture of martial formality that stifled any hope of victory.

'My apologies, colonel-commissar,' Martane said. He made his excuses, and left the table.

'NICELY DONE, IBRAM,' said Van Voytz. 'I see the old political skills of the commissar haven't left you.'

Gaunt had retired with Van Voytz, Golke and Biota to a small library room. Servitors adjusted the lamps, refreshed drinks and then left them alone.

'Did you summon me here to make a fool of Martane, sir?' Gaunt asked.

'Maybe,' smiled Van Voytz, as if the idea was delicious.

'Vice General Martane needs no help making a fool of himself,' Golke said.

'I was hoping I would come away with more than that satisfaction tonight,' Gaunt said.

'Just so,' said Van Voytz. 'I've studied your despatches, and listened to the comments our friend Count Golke here has passed along... unofficially, of course. You could have caused trouble with Ankre, Ibram. He speaks as he finds, and he speaks ill of you.'

'Quite obviously. But I won't stand by and see Guard units hammered for no reason.'

Van Voytz sat down in a large padded armchair by the fireplace, and took a book at random off the nearest shelf. 'This is a difficult theatre, Ibram. One that requires tact. If we had supreme command here, I'd gladly take the Alliance and shake it by the scruff until it worked properly. Worked like a modern army. God-Emperor, a full Guard army employed here purposefully could turn Shadik back in a month.' He looked up at Gaunt. 'But we don't have that luxury. Albeit nominally, the Alliance leaders – Lyntor-Sewq, who I'll confess I cannot stand, and the high sezar himself – have battlefield command. My Lord Warmaster Macaroth himself made it clear we were here to support the Alliance, not take command from them. Our hands are tied.'

'Then men will die, sir,' said Gaunt.

'They will. We are obliged to fight this war at the Alliance's pace, to the Alliance's rules, and following the Alliance's traditions. Aexegary and its allies are desperate to retain control of the fight. No offence, count.'

Golke shrugged. 'I'm with you on that, lord general. I tried to change things for years. Tried to modernise tactics and strategy. The simple fact is that Aexegary has a long and illustrious martial history. They will not admit, not ever, that they are capable of losing a war. Aexegary never has, you see. And especially against an old foe like the Shadik.'

'The Alliance won't admit they are fighting a modern foe,' said Biota quietly. 'They will not accept that the Shadik Republic has changed, been corrupted, that it is no longer the neighbouring power Aexegary has bested in five wars.'

'And the Alliance members don't see it either?' asked Gaunt.

'No,' said Golke. 'Kottmark especially. They see their entry into the war as an opportunity to prove their worth on the world stage.'

'Pride,' said Gaunt. 'That's what we're fighting. Not Shadik. Not the arch-enemy. We're fighting the pride of the Alliance.'

'I think so,' said Van Voytz.

'Undoubtedly,' said Biota.

'Then I am ashamed of my country,' Golke said sadly. 'When the high sezar told me the Guard was coming to assist us, my heart leapt. Until I saw the look in his eyes.'

'What look?' asked Van Voytz.

'The look that told me he saw you Imperials as brand new toys... toys that he would use in just the same way as the old ones. I had hoped that the Alliance might learn things from the Guard... new ways of fighting... things like fluid field orders and unit-level decision making...'

'You've been reading your Slaydo,' said Gaunt with a smile.

Golke nodded. 'I have. I think I'm the only man on Aexe Cardinal who has. To no avail. The Alliance is still living in the glory days of the great sezars. They will not change.'

'A dutiful father,' said Biota softly, 'is distressed to find his son mourning the death of the family pet, a feline. The boy complains that he looked after it, groomed it, fed it, and yet it passed away despite his care. Anxious to please, the father purchases a new pet for his son, a hound. He is horrified when he catches his son pushing the hound off the balcony of the family house to its death. The son is distressed once more. "That pet wouldn't fly either," he tells his father.'

Biota looked around at them. 'We are the hound,' he said.

DAWN FOG FROM the Upper Naeme shrouded Meiseq the next morning when Gaunt rose. He had made sure Beltayn woke him early for the return trip to Rhonforq. While he was shaving in the cold, new light, a messenger arrived and asked him to attend Lord General Van Voytz.

Van Voytz was taking breakfast in his staff apartments, along with Biota and a small group of aides. At Van Voytz's instruction, a steward brought caffeine and fried fish and egg mash for Gaunt, so he could eat with them.

'You're starting back to Rhonforq today, Ibram?' Van Voytz said, eating heartily. He was dressed in an embroidered cape and a linen field suit of dark red.

'I've been away too long as it is, sir. And you?'

'North. Lyntor-Sewq awaits me at Gibsgatte to address the Northern generals. It's a mess up there. We're deploying our Urdeshi units there tomorrow. I've good news for you, however.'

'Sir?'

Van Voytz dabbed his mouth with his napkin and munched, taking a sip of fruit juice. 'Well, it was good news until five-thirty this morning. Then it simply became interesting.'

'Go on.'

'Our friend Count Golke has been working his influence on the Alliance GSC planners for the last few days, and after last night's dinner it paid off. The First is to be reassigned, in keeping with their scouting abilities. Right over to the west, an area called... what is it, Biota?'

'The Montorq Forest, sir.'

'That's it. Orders will follow. But you've got your way. The Tanith will be used to its strength at last. Don't let me down.'

'I won't, sir.'

'Me or Golke. It was the devil's effort to convince them.'

'What's the interesting part, sir?' Gaunt asked.

Van Voytz paused, chewing, and emptied his mouth. Then he picked up his glass. 'Come with me, Ibram.'

Van Voytz led Gaunt out onto a verandah overlooking the river. The landscape below them was barred with chalky mist.

'There's a rider,' Van Voytz said. 'Golke talked your mob up, emphasising how terrific they were as stealth scouts so the GSC would agree to reassign them. Trouble is, he may have talked them up too well. They've taken the idea to heart. Suddenly, they like the idea of scouts. They see uses of their own.'

'Right, and what does that mean?'

'It's a give and take thing, Ibram. Fifty per cent of your force gets to scout the Montorq Woods. In return for that, the other half gets deployed into the Pocket.'

'The Pocket?'

'The Seiberq Pocket. Front line. Their job is to penetrate the Shadik defences and locate... and maybe disable... these new super-siege guns. They reckon if you're so good at recon...'

'Feth!' said Gaunt. 'There's a word for a deal like that.'

'I know. "Ironic", I think it is. I'm pretty sure Martane and Ankre had something to do with it. Give and take. You get to play to your strengths in the west... provided you show the same skills at the blunt end. I'm sorry, Ibram.'

'Sorry? I play the odds, my lord. All of my men on the front or half of them.'

'Good lad. One hand gives, one hand takes, as Solon used to say.'

OVERNIGHT BAG IN hand and his mind full of troubles, Gaunt walked out of the military hall into the Meiseq sunlight. It was 08.30. Imperial personnel threaded between the Alliance sentries as they loaded Van Voytz's transports.

Gaunt looked around for Beltayn and the car. He found only Beltayn.

'What's up? Where's the car?'

'It's really weird, sir. Something's awry. I think the car's been stolen.'

'Stolen?'

'It's not where we parked it.'

Gaunt put his bag down. 'Give me the keys, then. I'll find it.'

Beltayn grimaced. 'That's the other weird part, sir. I can't find the keys either.'

'Feth! What'll I tell her?'

'The old woman?'

'Yes, the old wo–'

Gaunt sighed. 'Don't bother, let's not waste any more time. Scare us up some transport… or at least get us tickets on the next southbound train.'

Beltayn nodded and hurried away.

'A problem, colonel-commissar?'

Gaunt turned and found Biota behind him.

'Nothing much, nothing I can't deal with.'

Biota did up the neck clasps of his red, tactical division body-glove and nodded.

'That story last night. About the feline and the hound. Very pertinent. Very sharp,' said Gaunt.

'I can't presume credit,' Biota said, off-hand. 'One of DeMarchese's fables.'

Biota walked away towards the waiting vehicles.

'Tactician Biota! A moment!'

'Gaunt?'

'DeMarchese? You said DeMarchese. Who is that?'

Biota paused. 'A minor philosopher. Very minor. You know the name?'

'I've heard it.'

'DeMarchese served as an advisor to Kiodrus, who in turn stood at the right hand of the beati during the First Crusade. His contribution is rather eclipsed by Faltornus, who was the real architect of Saint Sabbat's strategy, but still his homely fables have some merit. Gaunt? What is it?'

'Nothing,' said Gaunt. 'Nothing.' He looked up at the pale sun and then said, 'Elinor Zaker. Does that name mean anything to you?'

'Elinor Zaker?'

'Of the Adepta Sororitas Militant, the order of Our Martyred Lady?'

Biota shook his head.

'All right. Never mind. Good luck at Gibsgatte. May the Emperor protect.'

Gaunt walked off to find Beltayn. He had seldom felt so uneasy. He had finally identified the pervasive flower-scent from the previous day.

Islumbine. The sacred flower of Hagia.

SEVEN
POACHING

'And this, my friends, is what they call sweet.'
– Murtan Feygor

THE FOREST BECKONED.

They could smell it. From Ins Arbor, coming off the transports, they could see it. Rolled like green fur around the uplands east of them. Big. Silent. Inscrutable.

It wasn't as if the Tanith hadn't seen forest since the Founding. There'd been plenty. The thick rainwoods north of Bhavnager, the tropical groves of Monthax, the Voltemand Mirewoods. But there was something about this forest, something temperate, old and cool, that reminded them all achingly of the lost nalwoods.

Ins Arbor was a shabby dump of a town, ill-supplied and stinking in the summer heat. There were no proper billets, virtually no water, and the worst rations they'd yet experienced.

But morale had improved overnight.

* * *

THE FOREST BECKONED.

Corbec could see the renewed spirit in the faces of the men around the camp. He sat back on the fender of a half-track, and made a last few adjustments to squad lists he was drawing up. Each ten-man detail needed a good mix of scouts and fireteam, and Hark had requested Corbec spread the scout-trainees evenly.

Corbec sucked on the big cigar smouldering between his teeth. A gift from Gaunt. He'd been going to save it for a special occasion, but the smoke was doing a fine job of screening out the odour of the Ins Arbor latrines.

Gaunt's real gift had been this mission. Half of the First taken out of the Naeme meatgrinder and given something useful to do. That was what had lifted morale, despite the grim facilities of the staging town. Anything was better than the line, and the prospect of forest work was better than anything. Tanith were smiling. Verghastites, who had no special affinity with woodland, were smiling too, simply lifted by the mood and the last minute reprieve from trench postings.

He called Varl over and sent him to round up the troops for the first details.

THE FOREST BECKONED.

Brostin kept going on about it. Thuggish, brutal, tattooed, one of the most barbarian of all the enlisted Tanith, he would not shut up about the wonder of it all.

'Smell that!' he said. He paused, cocking his head, wistful. 'Not the leaves. The smell of wet earth beneath trees. Hmm-mmm.'

'All I smell is your gakking p-tanks, Tanith,' Cuu said mildly.

'You've got no soul, Cuu. No soul at all.'

'So they say, sure as sure.'

'Here's an idea,' said Feygor, his voice a quiet hiss through his throat-box. 'Why don't the two of you shut up?'

Brostin shrugged and smiled, and picked up his sloshing fuel tanks again. Cuu melted away into the bracken.

Feygor raised his right hand and swept the fingers round twice in a paddling motion. The members of nineteen detail fanned forward through the underbrush.

It was late afternoon. The sun was a yellow dapple to the west behind the leaf cover. The glades of the forest were misty hollows pillared by black trunks. Wild birds called aloud through the wood spaces, and the air smelled of damp bark, wood-poppy and beythorn.

Nineteen detail had been out now for three hours, having left the company command at Ins Arbor with the other details after Corbec's briefing. On the hike up through the villages, the details had separated, one by one, each striking off towards their own designated patrol. Nineteen had been ordered to sweep the Bascuol Valley as far as the pass road down to Frergarten. Two, maybe three days, out and back. They'd made decent time, moving in country. A gentle stroll into the woods.

'I thought Brostin was born and raised in the slums of Tanith Magna,' whispered Caffran.

Gutes shrugged. 'Me too. I guess even the city-boys amongst us get sentimental once in a while.'

Caffran nodded. He didn't begrudge Brostin's enthusiasm. These were dark pine woods, the nearest thing to Tanith they'd experienced since the loss. The spark of recognition he himself had felt at the landing zones was magnified here. Forest. Trees. Aexe Cardinal felt enough like home to please him.

The Verghastites in the detail were less settled. Muril and Jajjo, children of the hive, were jumping at shadows, moving their weapons to cover every last mysterious creak and crack the forest made.

'Cool it down,' Caffran whispered to Muril as she snapped round, her lasrifle aimed.

'Easy for you to say, tree-boy,' she said. 'This is spooky.'

Feygor raised his hand to signal a stop and turned back to face his scout-team.

'Feth!' he said, 'I've heard quieter beer-dances! Could we act professionally? Could we?'

They nodded.

'And tell me… ' Feygor added, 'isn't this better than slogging it at the front?'

'Yes, Mister Feygor,' they all agreed.

'Good. Excellent. Now come on.'

Feygor turned and walked smack into Mkvenner.

'Feth me backwards! Ven! Damn!'

Mkvenner looked at Feygor dourly. He had no love for Rawne's adjutant. A speck of feth, if you pressed him for an opinion, and few dared.

'Way's clear,' Mkvenner said. 'Through to the big oak at the dip. Want me to spread forward?'

'Yeah, why don't you do that?' Feygor said, recovering his composure. 'And take one of the fething wannabes. That's the idea of this, isn't it?'

'So I'm told,' said Mkvenner. He glanced back at the spread out members of the detail. 'Trooper Jajjo! Front to me!'

Jajjo tumbled forward to join the lean, scary Tanith scout. Jajjo was one of the few Verghasts to show potential as a scout.

'Ahead and low, fan south. Calls are standard,' Mkvenner said to the eager Jajjo. 'Go!'

Mkvenner and Jajjo forked away ahead of the detail. Feygor kept his eyes on them. He could still see Jajjo's creeping, hunched shape after two minutes. Mkvenner had vanished almost immediately.

Rerval made a vox-check to make sure they were still in range. He looked up and saw Muril with a grim expression on her face.

'What's up, Verghast?' he said.

'Nothing. Nothing…' she answered. Rerval shrugged. He knew what was bothering her. Muril and Jajjo had both signed up for scout training, and this tour in the woods was meant to be their proving ground. So far, only Jajjo had benefited from Mkvenner's expertise and tutoring.

It's a female thing, Rerval thought. Just like Rawne, though I'd never have expected that kind of prejudice from Ven.

'Let's pick it up!' Feygor called back down the line. 'Moving on!'

They advanced, spread out, through the dim forest space: Feygor, Gutes, Brostin, Muril, Caffran, Cuu.

Cuu paused to look back at the tenth and final member of the detail.

'You with us?'

'Sure,' said Hlaine Larkin. 'Sure as sure.'

* * *

FEYGOR WAS PRETTY pleased with himself. He'd made the cut into what had become known as the 'lucky half' of the First, and now here he was with command of a foot patrol. Minimal effort, a little walk-and-look job, and open ended. And if they found somewhere nice, maybe an old farm or something, then a two-day patrol might turn itself into three or four days of R and R.

He'd have preferred to pick his own detail. Nineteen was a mixed bag, but Brostin, Rerval and Gutes were okay, Cuu had his moments, and Caff was all right in his way. Larks was a nut, but what else was new? He could shoot. Maybe he'd bag them something for supper. Feygor acknowledged to himself that he had no idea what sort of wildlife lived out here, but he was pretty sure there would be something with a mouth at one end, an arse at the other, and decent eating in between.

The Verghasts he could do without. Jajjo was a stiff, and in Feygor's opinion, no Verghast was ever going to cut it as a scout. It wasn't in the genes. The girl was better. Decorative. Maybe he'd get really lucky and bag another kind of game out here in the wild woods.

The real pain was Ven. Sure, Feygor respected the scout, everyone did. But everyone was afraid of Mkvenner too. He was straight as a die. Feygor knew he'd have to plan very carefully if they were going to have any fun without Ven getting in the way.

Of course, there was meant to be a job to do, too. The Montorq Forest covered upwards of three thousand square kilometres and ran down from the Toyre, bearding the western flanks of the Kottmark Massif, a wall of mountains that split the eastern provinces of Aexegary from Kottmark. Most of the Montorq terrain was steep, thick woodland slopes, pretty much impassible unless you were on foot or had time to scout out a decent track.

The Shadik Republic lay to the north. The nominal border was about eighty kilometres away, beyond the headwaters of the Toyre. During the long years of the war, Shadik had pressed Aexegary and Kottmark along all viable routes, gradually establishing the pattern of the front line. Seen on a tactical map, the forest uplands were the one break in that line. West of them lay the Seronne Line, the Naeme Sectors

and Meiseq, tight as a drum. North and east, the so-called
Ostlund Shield Line that blocked the Shadik thrusts into
Kottmark. Shadik had never touched Montorq. It had been
spared the war because of geography. Just a few hours' walking in the skirts of the forest showed how hard the going
would be. Only a fool would try and push an army through
the forest. Feygor had heard the Republican commanders
called a lot of things, but fool wasn't one of them.

However, times change. The Alliance had become concerned with the idea that Shadik was about to change
tactics in an attempt to throw the deadlock. Instead of
directly assaulting Frergarten, the Alliance's great eastern
bastion, they might push elite infantry with light support
down through the Montorq, and encircle Frergarten,
achieving by stealth where three previous assaults had
failed. They could take Frergarten, Ins Arbor, snap the
Seronne Line and be marching into the Eastern Provinces
in under six weeks.

It was unlikely, but it was possible. The Ghosts' orders were
to assess enemy disposition and communication routes in
the Montorq area. To bring early warning, if necessary. And,
Corbec had suggested during the briefing, work out the feasi-
bility of the Alliance pulling the trick in reverse. By the
autumn, maybe an Alliance force would be heading through
the forest, marching north...

Feygor didn't care. He didn't actually care who won, who
lost. He wouldn't give a feth if the Shadik President came
along and took a dump in the high sezar's ear. Just as long as
Feygor was left alone. He was tired. It had been a long fething
road from Tanith, and they'd been through plenty.

Rawne always said that Gaunt led them like he had something to prove. Well, they'd fething well proved it enough,
hadn't they? It was some other bastard's turn. Maybe when
they were done with this feth-hole, the First would get
rotated back to regimental reserve for a few months. Six,
maybe. A year. Feygor had seen other companies get the call
back out. The fething Vitrians, for instance. They'd gone
back into crusade reserve about eighteen months earlier and
as far as Feygor knew they were still there, sitting with their
fething glass boots up on a table, smoking someone else's

lhos, playing at garrison. The Bluebloods too, those bastards had been pulled to the rear after Vervunhive.

There was no fething justice.

Feygor reached the next crest, a slope of loose rocks and ferns that bounded a deep dell where a thin stream splashed down its course under the dark trees. The trees, mountain ash, link-alder and some kind of spruce, creaked and moved their heads gently. A slight rise in the wind. Westerly. The scent of rain.

On one of the rocks lay a leaf, fresh, curled into a loop with the stalk stabbed through the blade of the leaf. Feygor picked it up. One of Ven's waymarkers. All the scouts left marks like this to show the squad behind them they'd cleared and passed ahead. You wouldn't notice them unless you knew to look. Ven and Jajjo would be half a kilometre ahead of them by now.

As the detail made their way up the fern trail behind him, Feygor pushed on, clambering up the tumble of rocks on the crest into a break in the trees where the sunlight could fall on him. The sky was tinged yellow, what he could see of it. Clouds chased, gathering. Rain definitely. Maybe even a summer storm.

Feygor knew the signs. Like Brostin – and like his mentor Rawne – Feygor was a city boy. But even if you grew up in a place like Tanith Attica, you were never far from forest. Feygor had got to know woodcraft and how to read the weather as a teenager, making the early morning runs out of Attica's mercantile district into the Attican woods. You'd needed the skills in his trade. Skills to find a particular clearing at a particular time, skills to get home the long way round without getting lost. Skills to avoid the arbites and the excise men. The movers and shakers in Attica's black market didn't go much on excuses like 'I got lost' or 'There was a sudden downpour and I ran late'.

Feygor sat down and waited as the members of the detail came up over the crest. Cuu, then Caff, then Gutes and Rerval. Brostin came back in the line, so that the betraying smell of his flamer's fuel tanks would be minimised. Muril next, quiet as a feline. Feygor watched her move by, his gaze lingering once she'd gone past and afforded him a rear view.

Larkin was right in the tail. According to Brostin, Larkin had specifically requested this detail, which seemed odd to Feygor. Everyone knew that Larkin and Cuu were not exactly best buddies. Larks usually did his level best to find occupation as far away from Lijah Cuu as possible. Indeed, Cuu had seemed puzzled by Larkin's inclusion. Puzzled. Almost annoyed.

But Larkin seemed strangely relaxed. That was good, in Murtan Feygor's book. The last kind of crap he needed out here was Larks in one of his manic phases. He'd keep an eye on the sniper. He'd asked Piet Gutes to do the same.

Feygor got up and slithered back down the crest to join Larkin as he made the top.

'Gonna be looking for shelter soon,' Feygor said. 'Wind's up. Would be good to eat. Fancy your eye?'

Larkin shrugged. 'Why not?'

'Don't go far.' Feygor looked back down the trail. 'Muril!'

She turned and made her way back to them.

'Larks is on dinner duty. Buddy him up. Don't get lost.'

'Okay,' she said. The order clearly pleased her. Half an hour poaching with Larkin wasn't scout training with Ven, but it was better than nothing. Feygor knew she was itching to show her ability. Anything to get in her good books.

'I saw some spoor down on the path,' Larkin said. 'Let's try that way.'

The pair of them began to descend the slope the way they'd come.

Feygor moved ahead, catching up with the rest of the detail. Brostin had stopped to take a swig from his billy. Right at the front, coming up the next rise in the shadow of the trees, Cuu had paused too. He was staring back down the dell at the departing figure of Larkin.

LARKIN KNELT AND checked the spoor. It was fresh. Some small animal, probably a grazer. He sat on a rock for a moment, exchanging his hot-shot ammunition clip for a low-volt pack.

'What's that?' Muril asked.

'You hunted before?'

She shook her head.

'A hot-shot'll mince anything smaller than a deer. We wanna eat. We don't wanna paint the scenery with liquid animal.'

She smiled. She sat down and put her lasrifle on the earth beside her. Larkin had got used to seeing her with a long-las. It seemed odd for her to be carrying a standard Mark III carbine.

'Miss it?' he asked.

'Sort of,' she admitted. 'But I want to be a scout. I really want to make that grade. And that means packing in my beloved long-las for a standard Mark III. Besides, I get the hat as compensation.'

She was referring to the soft, black wool cap she was wearing. Standard kit order for troopers was the ceramite helmet for line duties, and a choice of black beret or forage cap otherwise. Unless you were a scout, or a trainee scout like Muril. Then you got to wear the wool cap for all duties. It didn't obstruct movement or vision like a helmet, and there was no danger of it clinking against your weapon during a crawl. The caps were the mark of the First's elite, one of those subtle but crucial uniform differences that lent prestige. If she made scout, she'd get to wear the matt-black speciality badge on the brim. No Verghast had done that. No woman, either.

Larkin smiled. Whatever standard kit order said about headwear, the First was extraordinarily lax about it. Many went bare-headed. Berets were common under fire. He'd once heard Corbec tell Hark that more Ghosts had used their hard-bowls as buckets than had worn them in combat. Here was this girl keen to win the right to wear a hat she'd probably never use anyway.

Except, of course, on parade. That's where it would matter. That's where Sehra Muril in a scout cap would be a fething big deal.

'What's funny?' she asked.

'Nothing,' he said.

He got up and practised sighting his long-las into the trees.

'You don't think I'll make it?' she said.

He shrugged. 'You made marksman. I know this. If any of you hivers ever make scout, it'll be one of you girls.'

'Mkvenner doesn't seem keen on the idea,' she muttered. 'When the colonel told me he'd put me in this detail to shadow Ven, I got really excited. I mean, Ven's the real deal. Him or Mkoll. The very best. I thought this was it. The big step forward. But he only seems interested in Jajjo.'

'Jajjo's okay.'

'Sure. But Jajjo's getting all the attention. Who did Ven call up just now? Me? I don't think so. Did I do something wrong? Or am I fooling myself? Or does Ven have a thing?'

'A thing?'

'About girls.'

Larkin lowered his weapon and squinted over at her. 'We all have a thing about girls.'

Muril laughed. 'But really…'

Larkin raised his weapon again. Distantly, through the trees, he could see the members of nineteen detail skirting up the next slope under a bank of spruce.

'It ever occur to you,' he said softly, 'that Ven's taking time with Jajjo because Jajjo's the one who needs the work?'

'Gak!' she said. A broad smile spread across her slender face. 'That's a way of looking at it that hadn't occurred to me.'

'You gotta see all the angles…' Larkin said. His voice had dropped to a hush. He let the las float in his hands, the aim fluid. He coasted the muzzle around. He wasn't blinking. Through the sight, he saw the distant figures, crossing in and out of the leaf-cover. He waited for the scope to lock. The read-out lit up in his eye. Target-fix. Four hundred and seventy two metres. The back of Feygor's head. Coast. Target-fix. Four seventy-nine and half. Brostin's promethium tanks. Coast.

Four eighty-one. Target-fix. Lijah Cuu. Side of the skull. Adjusted for cross-wind. Tracking.

'What are you doing?' Muril asked.

Larkin had stopped breathing. The long-las felt weightless. The target-fix rune was flashing steady now. His right index finger slowly tightened on the trigger. Lijah Cuu stopped and turned to speak to Gutes. The horizontal of Larkin's cross hairs made a bar across Cuu's eyes. The vertical almost followed the line of the trademark scar. Right there. Right now. Kill-shot.

Larkin lowered the gun, breathed out and snapped the safety.

'Just getting my eye in,' he said.

HEQTA JAJJO COULDN'T get the gakking leaf to bend. Every time he looped it, it sprang back, and when he'd finally got the stalk pushed through the leaf, it tore.

'Problem?' said a voice.

Jajjo looked up. Mkvenner was standing over him.

'Gak, you made me jump.'

'That's a good thing because I'm a scout. And it's a bad thing because that's what you want to be too.'

'Sorry.'

'Don't be sorry. Be better. What's the problem?'

'You told me to leave a sign here. I can't get it to make the shape.'

Ven hunkered down and plucked a fresh leaf from a nearby clump of beythorn. 'You're trying too hard. It's just a twist. It has to look casual.'

Mkvenner made a perfect loop and set it on a crop of white stone.

Jajjo sighed.

'You'll get it,' said Mkvenner, almost encouragingly.

'You think we're wasting our time, don't you?' said Jajjo.

'Why?'

'Because we're not fit. Not fit for scouting.' Jajjo didn't have to qualify the 'we're'. They both knew he meant 'Verghastites'.

'If that's what you think, then the only thing I'm wasting is my effort. Take the point.'

'Only if–'

'Take the point, Jajjo. Show me you can work terrain.'

Jajjo picked up his Mark III, and advanced, head low. They'd reached a long, curved valley of pine wood with a steeply tilted rake that was thick with last year's needles. The wind was up now, and the trees swayed and shushed over him.

The air was cold. The sunlight had died off and plunged the forest floor into twilight. Jajjo tried to make as little sound as possible. His foot cracked a piece of dead bark, and he looked back guiltily towards the place where he'd left Mkvenner.

The scout had gone. How the gak did he do that?

Jajjo worked the cover all the way down to a thick copse of link-alder. Halfway down, he knocked his rifle-stock against a sapling. Then he realised he hadn't draped himself with his camo-cape properly. Gak on a flakboard, was there anything else he could get wrong?

The sound of the wind in the trees was mesmeric now. Like a sea, Jajjo thought. His family had come from Imjahive originally, down in the archipelago, one of Verghast's tropical cities. He knew what the sea sounded like. He'd missed it when his family had moved to Vervunhive, the year he turned six.

Jajjo stole past the copse, and crossed a spread of swishing ferns. The first spots of rain started to come down, smacking hard impacts into the leaves of the ground cover. Jajjo tried to stick to the shadows. Through the stand of pines ahead, there seemed to be something, he couldn't tell what. He switched cover, making short runs between trees, the way he'd been taught in scout preparation. Now the sounds he made were being masked by the gathering rainstorm and wind. He kept his Mark III tucked up under his right armpit, barrel down, so it wouldn't catch on anything.

The rain got heavier. The drops beat down like a non-stop drum roll on the leaves. The temperature immediately rose by a few degrees, lifting skeins of mist from the ground and choking his nose with a damp, mulchy reek.

Jajjo reached the pine stand, and slid through the trees. What the hell was that up there? There was definitely some sort of clearing. A break in the trees. He could tell that simply from the light.

He got down in the ferns and crawled for the last twenty metres to the edge of the clearing, pushing his weapon in front of him. He raised his head, and saw, through the rain, what lay beyond.

'Gak!' he stammered. He turned to rise and work back, but Mkvenner was crouched right behind him.

'Good work,' said Mkvenner quietly. 'Look what you found...'

* * *

It wasn't on any of the maps. Mainly because it was old, and the maps were new. Ven and Jajjo back-tracked to meet the detail, and led them forward.

It was a house. A big house. A retreat. Rerval described it as a manse, and the name stuck. Derelict and overgrown, it occupied a cleared stretch of hillside within the forest, facing west. Lime-washed grey stone, black slate. Two storeys and maybe an attic. Blind windows looked out across an unkempt garden from the front. There was a weed-choked path leading to the front porch, and the signs of an old wall and gate in the overgrown hedges. Gutes and Caffran circled round the rear and found a single-storey wing extending from the back, and a clutch of outbuildings clogged against the back garden wall around a paved yard. Beyond that, a wild garden and lawn stretched up hill to the edge of the pine woods. There was an old wall at the top of the lawn, against which sat several more dilapidated outhouses.

The rain was torrential now.

'Let's check it,' Feygor said.

They split. Feygor, Gutes, Cuu and Brostin to the front door; Caffran, Rerval, Jajjo and Mkvenner to the back.

'Armed,' Feygor said on the front steps. The dripping Ghosts with him nodded. Gutes and Cuu dropped in either side of the big, old doors. Paint was flaking off the panels. Feygor peeked in through ground floor windows, but saw nothing except dust and shadows.

'Going in,' he said over his micro-bead.

'Read you,' crackled Caffran.

Feygor nodded. Brostin stepped up and put his shoulder into the doors. It took two shoves, but the wood splintered and the doors swung open.

Gutes and Cuu, lasrifles aimed, screwed in behind him.

The hallway was dark and the air was stale. Mildew. Old carpets. Damp. They edged into the gloom, making out a staircase and several doors off the hall on the ground floor. Water dripped from the ceiling and the stairwell. Feygor crept inside, his rifle at a hunting tilt.

He snapped his fingers and he, Gutes and Cuu turned on lamp-packs. They slung them from the bayonet lugs of their weapons and played them around the hall. The spots of light revealed a lacquered sideboard with cobweb-strung candle stands, a massive gilt-edged mirror that threw their inquisitive lights back at them. A coatstand, hung with a single, lonely raincoat. An embroidered rug. Dried flowers in a dedemican vase. A console table with a brass letter rack.

Cuu tried the wall switch. The big chandelier remained dark. 'No power,' he said.

'Yeah,' Feygor smiled, 'but it's a roof.'

The rain pelted down. Thunder rolled. Feygor worked his way over to the left hand door off the hall.

Brostin hand-cranked the feeder reservoir of his flamer's broom, and clicked the lighter flint. There was a wet cough, and then a hiss as the flamer came to life. Brostin had it turned right down, so that just a cone of blue-heat sizzled around the nozzle. The hiss of the burner filled the air. They could all smell promethium.

Brostin edged his way over to Feygor, using the barely-lit flamer like a lamp. 'After you,' he said.

Feygor opened the inner door and pushed it wide, keeping his back to the doorpost. Brostin went in, revving the flamer up into little, quick flares of hot yellow flame.

'Dining room,' he said. Feygor prowled in, sliding his lamp beam off the walls. Old oil paintings, grim faces. Vases and porcelain. A long, dark-varnished table lined by twenty chairs. A single plate at one setting, decorated with a pair of fruit stones, and a small paring knife.

Feygor went back out into the hall. Gutes and Cuu had opened the room on the other side. Some kind of sitting room, with armchairs and sofas covered in dust sheets. A big fireplace with a basket of logs. More cobwebs.

Feygor moved through the space to another door at the end. He pushed it open, aiming his lamp and gun through the slit. A small room, lined with empty shelves. Dust. A library? A study? He edged inside, covered by Gutes. There was a desk and a captain's chair on brass castors. Racks and hooks on the walls that had once held something. He swung his beam right.

Framed by his light-beam, the monster loomed out of the darkness, its lips pulled back from its huge teeth, its clawed paws raised to strike.

'Holy feth!' squeaked Feygor and shot it.

He hit it in the belly and there was a loud burst of fur and dust. Gutes, startled by the sudden shot, rolled round through the doorway and blasted off a burst himself.

'Stop! Stop!' Feygor shouted over Gute's fire. The monster continued to snarl at them. The micro-bead link went wild.

'Who's shooting?' That was Caffran.

'Confirm contact! Confirm contact!' Jajjo.

'Feygor? Sign back.' Ven.

Feygor was laughing, his giggles rolling flat and dry from his voice box. 'Relax. No contact.'

Gutes was sniggering with relief too.

'What the feth?' said Brostin, shouldering in through the door and raising his flamer. He gunned the torch and the flare lit up the room. The huge beast in the corner was starkly lit, poised on its plinth, paws raised to strike. Sawdust dribbled from its shot-open gut, and the flames reflected in its glass eyes.

'Feth!' said Brostin. 'Are you trigger-happy or what?'

'I thought it was a real fething thing!' Feygor protested and chortled. 'Took me by surprise.'

'Well,' said Brostin, 'you pair sure killed it.'

Feygor walked over to the stuffed trophy. It was quite a beast. Raised on its hind legs, three metres tall, covered in black fur and sporting teeth the length of his fingers.

'What the feth is it?' asked Piet Gutes.

'Some kind of ursa,' said Feygor, truculently punching it in the chest. It was hollow.

'It's a behj,' said Cuu, from the doorway. 'Big deal here on Aexe. The totem animal, the king predator. I heard the sezar wears a pelt, and the locals barter the claws as lucky charms.'

'How the feth d'you know that, Lijah?' asked Brostin.

Cuu smiled. 'I made a cred or two playing the trench markets. It always helps to have local knowledge. A struthid feather is lucky, but a behj-claw–'

'Always got your eye on the main chance, eh, Cuu?' admired Feygor.

'Sure as sure,' said Lijah Cuu.

* * *

CAFFRAN HAD LED his team into the back kitchen.

'Odd,' Mkvenner said.

'What is?'

'Everything's clean and put away… except that cup and dish by the sink.'

'Someone left in a hurry,' said Rerval. 'This whole region is supposed to have been evacuated.'

'Then why do I smell garlic?' Ven asked.

Aiming his lamp into the shadows, Caffran edged through the scullery and an empty, damp-smelling washroom. Jajjo followed him.

Jajjo found a door off the kitchen that came free with a kick. It was a walk-in pantry, the shelves lined with fruit pickles and jars of preserved vegetables. Four haunches of salted meat hung from the beam hooks.

'Gak me, my mouth is watering,' said Jajjo. They'd been on lousy rations since landfall.

The vox chimed.

'Come see what I've found, boys,' said Feygor.

CAFFRAN'S TEAM FOUND Feygor's in the cellar of the house. A short run of stone steps let down into it via a door in the hall. Labelled by vintage, the wine racks were arranged in five rows of shelves.

Feygor took a bottle off one of the racks, cracked its neck off against the cellar wall, and splashed a large measure into his upturned mouth.

'Gutes, Cuu,' he said, belching and licking his lips. 'Go light the fire. Stoke it up, mind. We've found our billet.'

'We should secure it,' said Mkvenner.

'Okay, so secure it,' Feygor snapped. They could all hear the wind and rain beating down outside. 'Do what you want.'

Mkvenner glared at Feygor for a moment. Then he turned to Jajjo. 'Come on.'

The pair of them left the cellar.

Feygor took another knock from the bottle and glanced over at Caffran. 'It ain't sacra,' he said, 'but I think I'm gonna like it here.'

EIGHT
THE POCKET

*'The worst day of my life. The worst part of the line.
I wouldn't wish it on any bastard. I don't ever want
to go back there.'*

– Count Golke, on the Seiberq Pocket

IN SILENCE, THEY waited until the guns had stopped. Then they went out. Up over scaling ladders, up over the parapet. Into the blackness and the mud. Into little, individual worlds of suffocating gas-hoods.

It was just before 03.30 in the morning, and day seemed a whole lifetime away.

'Keep it tight,' Criid grunted into her micro-bead, the sound of her own breathing resonating inside her canvas gas-mask. Her platoon was straggled out. Somewhere to their left was five platoon, Soric's band. Somewhere to their right was seventeen, Raglon's. Somewhere around her was her own gakking platoon, not that she could see them. The damn hoods: blindfolds, gags, earmuffs all rolled into one.

There was a kind of light. It twinkled through the imperfect plastic lenses of her hood. Amber, dull. Just enough to pick out the landscape of no-man's land. Smoggy vapour fumed from the craters. It hid the wires. Pools of chemical water in deep shell holes gave off a leery phosphorescent glow.

This was a game. Not a fun one. Nobody had been looking forward to it. Not since they'd been transferred to 58th sector.

Criid missed having DaFelbe with her. Word was he was recovering from the face wound. She'd had to move Mkhef up as her adjutant, and she didn't get on with the lanky Tanith as well.

The ground was wet and sticky. It was like striding through caramel. All she could hear was the muffled pant of her own lungs inside the hood.

'Wire!' said a muffled voice. She turned her head. It was Mkhef, waiting while Kenfeld and Vulli came up with the cutters.

Criid crouched down. All around her, anonymous, hooded ghosts were slipping in, just shadows in the bad light. Everyone was cloaked up, shrouded in their camouflage capes.

'Breached!' Kenfeld reported, his voice sounding like it came from a box. He stood up, pulling the broken strands of wire aside with his gloved hands.

'Move up, with me,' Criid whispered.

BARELY FIFTY METRES to Criid's left, Soric guided his platoon ahead. Despite the proximity, he couldn't see any of Criid's bunch, or Obel's, which was allegedly running to his left flank.

Agun Soric was sweating inside his hood. He hated hood work. He was blind and stifled, his already reduced vision cut down to a pathetic scrap.

The mud was hell. Wet-soft and deep. It sucked at boots, pulled feet down at every stride, like the earth was hungry. Soric had to pause to cover Trooper Hefron, who hadn't secured his boots well enough and had therefore lost one to the grab of the ground.

'Get your gakking boot back on!' Soric barked, panting in the humid darkness of his hood.

'I'm sorry, sarge, I'm sorry...' Hefron was repeating.

'Shut up and get it tied!' Soric stood back, trying to let his lungs fill. All he could taste was damp, hot air. Perspiration was running into his one good eye. He couldn't wipe it.

'Gak!'

Hefron got back up and Soric sent him on his way with a cuff to the back of the head. He'd gone a pace or two himself when he tripped on something hard buried in the muck and went down.

Liquid mud drowned his hood's visor. He couldn't see. He could taste filthy water pouring in through the gauze filter.

Hands grabbed him and pulled him up.

'Sarge? You okay?'

It was Vivvo, his voice crackling over the link.

'Yeah.'

'You hit?'

'No. I fell.'

'Gak, I thought you were hit.'

'Wipe me gakking eye slits, for god's sake,' Soric said.

There was a squeak and vision returned. Vivvo was scooping the mud from Soric's hood-lenses with his fingers.

'You hurt?' he asked.

'No. Yes, bruised my leg. Fell on something.' It was even harder to breathe now. Soric had never felt so stifled. The infernal hood…

'Give me a moment, Vivvo. Step on. Get the platoon focused before they run too far ahead.'

Soric trudged forward, feeling his leg for the bruise. Something had smacked into it hard when he fell.

There was something in his pocket. Blindly, he took it out and held it up. It was the brass message shell.

Soric's heart began to race even harder. He was sure he'd left that fething thing in his dugout.

Fumbling with muddy, gloved fists, he unscrewed the cap. There was the folded sheet of blue tissue paper he'd been expecting.

It was hard to read through the smeared hood visor.

It said. 'Air's clean. No need for hoods. Warn ten about mill house.'

Something else was written underneath that he couldn't make out.

Soric tore open the buckles and pulled off his hood. He took big lungfuls of the cold exterior air, air thick with the taste of fuel and mud and water.

But not gas.

He pulled off his gloves and wiped his good eye, shoving the sweat back into his hair.

'Signals! Signals!' he called.

Mohr, his vox-man, came stumbling over the mud-plain towards him and started visibly when he saw Soric bareheaded.

'Feth, sarge! Orders was hoods!'

'Air's clean,' Soric told him. 'Vox it out. Air's clean and you have my word on that.'

Mohr knelt down in a shell hole and adjusted his set, removing his gas-hood as he did so. His young face was flushed and beaded.

'Give me the mic,' said Soric. 'This is twenty, twenty to all. The air is clean, repeat, clean. Ditch the hoods.'

Soric sat down, still holding the vox-horn to his mouth. He twisted the paper scrap until the feeble light caught it so he could read.

'Twenty, ninety-one.'

'Ninety-one, twenty. You certain about the hoods?'

'Certain. Trust me, Tona.'

'Read that, twenty.'

'Twenty, ninety-one. I think you're coming up on some kind of mill house. A building.'

'Ninety-one, twenty. Not on the maps.'

'There's nothing on the maps, Tona. Just watch it, okay. You see a structure, be wary.'

'You got inside information, Soric?'

'Just be careful.'

'Ninety-one, twenty. Careful. Confirmed.'

Soric clicked off the mic and sat back for a moment, gazing up. The sky was dark, fumed with a haze of yellow. There were no stars. He wished there could be stars.

'Finished, sir?' asked Mohr. He was getting anxious. The platoon was leaving them behind.

'Not quite,' said Soric, looking down at the piece of paper clenched in his dirty fist. That line under the first. His wet fingers had blurred the ink. It was just a smudge. He peered at it. What the gak did it say? He ought to know. He'd gakking written it.

Or something with handwriting just like his had, anyway.

Something, Soric knew, even if it scared the living gak out of him, he had to trust.

Something something don't let something… what was that? It looked like 'Raglon'. Was it? Shit, what had this said? The first part had been a warning to Tona. Was Raglon going to get into a mess too? God-Emperor, what did it say?

'Next time write it in gakking pencil!' he said.

'Sarge?' Mohr asked nervously.

I said that out loud, thought Soric. He lifted the vox-mic. 'Twenty, two-oh-three?'

'Two-oh-three, twenty.' Raglon's voice came back swiftly, as prompt on the link as any ex-vox man.

'Twenty, two-oh-three… uh, just watch yourself, okay?'

'Say again, Soric?'

'I said watch yourself. Don't know why, don't know what. Just… be extra careful, okay?'

'Understood. Two-oh-three out.'

Soric tossed the mic back to Mohr. 'Let's go,' he said, and levered his squat frame up. The mud and darkness closed in on all sides. There was no sign of Vivvo or the rest of five platoon.

Soric grabbed Mohr by the arm and started to trudge forward.

THERE WAS NO landscape out here to read in any proper sense. Just burst earth and wreckage. For all Criid knew, they could be heading back to their own lines. But somehow Hwlan saw the way.

The Tanith scout had the lead, nudging the extended line of ten platoon across the wasteland. At least they had the relief of losing the hoods. How'd Soric known it was clear? A message from the atmos-sniffers at the line, Criid presumed.

The darkness seemed solid, vicing them in. The odour of death and soiled water was almost suffocating. Criid ducked into a shallow crater with Nessa and Vril, and they found themselves swimming alongside bloated, swollen corpses.

Mkhef splashed in with them a moment later and recoiled in disgust.

'Feth!'

'Shut up, for gak's sake!' Criid whispered. 'We must be getting close to the Shadik lines.'

Nessa crawled up the forward edge of the crater and scoped with her long-las.

'Wire, about twenty metres up. No movement.'

'Feth this,' murmured Mkhef, trying to shoo away a gas-distended corpse that kept bobbing towards him.

The link chimed. Criid heard Hwlan's voice.

'Got some sort of structure, sarge. Nine points west. Looks like... I dunno...'

'Stay put,' said Criid into her micro-bead.

She hand-signalled over to Nessa, Vril and Mkhef. 'With me.'

The four of them scrambled up out of the wet slick of the crater and ran west over the pock-marked mud, ducking under an old stretch of rusted wire. They came in behind the jagged, partial boarding of a stretch of fence where Hwlan was hiding in a scrape.

The building beyond was backlit by a yellowish fog rising off the enemy lines. It was a ruin, a shell, one wall gone, the remains of a chimney stack rising like a tombstone. The structure lay in a hollow, swimming with creek water, festooned with wire. It looked like some kind of... mill. Some kind of water mill.

Criid had an unpleasant nagging feeling left over from Soric's last transmission.

She glanced up again at the ruin, a blankness against the yellowy dark. Caffran had a great rep for building assaults. What would he do?

The thought stopped her. Caff. Criid felt a terrible ache. Where was he? What was he doing, right now? Was he even alive?

How fething stupid was this, scampering through darkness and mud with a gun in your hand, when some things really mattered?

Caff...

'You okay, sarge?' Mkhef whispered.

'Yeah, why?'

'You looked kind of funny–'

'I'm fine,' she said. She was. She was fine. She was Sergeant Tona Criid, Tanith First-and-fething-Only, the only fem who'd ever made that grade. She wasn't going to gak it up now. It didn't matter what she felt about Caff, or Yoncy or Dalin.

She'd chosen to be a soldier, and worked to get the pins. Love was just an anchor she didn't need.

Not right now.

'Kenfeld?' she said quietly into her bead.

'Sarge?' the vox link crackled.

'Report?'

'I'm east of you, round the front with Mosark, Pozetine and Lubba.'

'See anything?'

'Just a ruin.'

'Okay, send Lubba forward with Pozetine. Cover space. But wait for my word. We're going to stealth assault from this side.'

'Read you, sarge.'

'Stealth assault,' Criid repeated to her companions, removing her blade from her bayonet lug and slinging her rifle over her shoulder. The others did the same.

'Why the caution, sarge?' Vril asked.

'I've got a hunch,' she said. 'This could be nasty, but I want it quiet.'

The four of them advanced over the black mud towards the shattered ruin. It was bigger than Criid had first thought. Tall. Thick walls, what was left of them. She snuggled in behind a fallen section of roof, and waved Hwlan through. Vril followed him. Criid dropped in behind them, Mkhef at her heels. Nessa hung back, scope raised.

Inside the mill, it was like a cave. Water dripped in through the open roof, and through the punctured second floor above. The ground was a mess of fractured rockcrete and tumbled girders.

Criid moved forward almost blind through the mess of debris. She climbed up over a slumped girder, tossing her knife into her left hand to brace herself with her right. To her west, Hwlan crawled forward under a slumped beam, and then folded himself through a blast hole in what remained of one of the interior walls.

She waited, then heard two, quick taps click through her micro-bead. It was a standard First non-verbal signal made by gently flicking the mic of your intercom. Two taps… clear.

She edged forward again, trying to fit herself through a narrow gap between rockcrete slabs, but her cape kept getting hung up on some of the twisted reinforcement bars jutting from one of the slabs. She had to back off, and go round.

A single tap. Not clear. She froze.

Two taps. She resumed her crawl, moving through a stagnant pool on her hands and knees and then making her way slowly up a mound of rubble that climbed out of the water, trying hard not to dislodge any loose chunks.

Hwlan was waiting for her at the top in what remained of an old doorway. There was a nondescript dark lump lying in the shadows near his feet. Criid realised it was the corpse of a Shadik sentry.

They waited until Vril and Mkhef caught up with them, and then went through the doorway into the next portion of the ruined mill. It was very dark here too, but down at the far end, there was a flickering light, like shadows cast by flames. Then they saw movement. Larger shadows moving against the meagre firelight.

There was a Shadik forward observation post in the far end of the mill. Three, maybe four men in hoods and long, grey coats moved about the end room. They had a fire, for warmth, in an oil can, its light shielded from the outside. Hwlan caught at Criid's arm and directed her attention upwards. Through missing floorboards, they could see another Shadik up in the remains of the second floor, crouching at a tripod-mounted spotter scope and gazing out over the wasteland to the west.

They'd never get near him without him noticing them.

Criid signalled the other three to move up, ready to take the Shadik on the ground floor level with their blades. She unslid her rifle, and took careful aim on the dim figure overhead. She'd have to risk one shot. But it had to be a good one.

She waited for Hwlan's signal. She had a good angle. One shot was worth the risk.

HALF A KILOMETRE south of the mill, Sergeant Raglon's platoon had reached the water-logged remains of an old field trench. There was no sure way of telling which side had constructed it, and certainly no way of knowing why it had been dug east-west. Once upon a time, its orientation had made some kind of tactical sense.

Raglon was sweating hard, more nervous than he dared admit. He'd seen plenty of combat before, and had brevet-led a unit on Phantine, but this was his first formal command in an active operation.

Raglon was a serious, thoughtful man, determined, just like Criid and Arcuda, the other neophyte sergeants, to prove to Gaunt and Hark that they'd made a good choice of promotions. He envied Criid the fact that she'd had a chance to blood her platoon in combat at the line. Then again, he envied Arcuda, who was still waiting in reserve back at the fire trench. Gaunt had made no bones about the hazards of these scouting raids into the waste. And Raglon had learned from the Alliance soldiery he'd met that the Seiberq Pocket had a particularly bad reputation as one of the hardest contested regions of the Peinforq Line.

He signalled his men down into the abandoned trench. At the very least, it offered his platoon a means of pushing east out of sight.

The trench was littered with dead. Old dead. The unidentifiable remains of men who had fallen out here perhaps years before, their bodies never recovered. Brown bones stippled the mud like broken twigs.

Seventeen moved single file, heads down, occasionally having to crawl on their bellies to pass sections where the trench walls had caved and filled the ditch.

Raglon had ordered Lukas, his vox-operator, to rig his set for headphones only, so that the caster wouldn't suddenly blare into life and give them away. It was a smart move, the sort of thing that another novice team leader might have overlooked. But Raglon had come from signals and knew about these things.

Where Raglon lacked experience, it was in character judgement. Since taking command of seventeen, his primary efforts had been to establish authority. Seventeen had been Lhurn Adare's platoon, and Raglon was all too aware of the fact he had nothing of the mourned sergeant's charisma. He'd just never be popular the way Adare had been.

So he'd decided the best way to run seventeen was to let them function the way they had under Adare. He didn't want to mess around with habits and established routines. If seventeen had evolved field practices they were happy with, who liked to buddy who in fire-teams for instance, he didn't see the point in changing things. He thought arbitrary changes would make the platoon resent him, and that was true, up to a point. But some habits stemmed from sloppiness.

When they reached the dead trench, the men formed a file automatically, as they saw fit, and Raglon didn't question it. So it was that they advanced now with Suth, the scout, in the lead, and Costin right behind him. Raglon fell into place about four men back.

It was his first command error.

Suth was a good scout. Costin, his buddy, was a drunk.

Adare had known that Costin drank too much. He'd tried to keep a lid on it. Costin was a nice guy, despite his carousing, and a decent trooper if kept away from the sacra. In a situation like this, Costin would inevitably want to get in beside his friend Suth. Adare would have stopped him, pushed him back down the file, just to be safe.

When Costin moved up eagerly with Suth, Raglon hadn't thought to object. Everyone knew Costin liked the drink. Raglon didn't realise how much Costin had been knocking back since Adare's death.

The abandoned trench had actually been constructed by the Alliance during an early phase of fighting, before the full bulk of the Peinforq Line had been built. The Shadik, to whose lines it was now closest, had never filled it in, because it afforded them excellent cover for raid-teams and wire-cutting parties. Indeed, they had extended its eastern end into the verges of their own fire trench system.

As Raglon's platoon advanced along it, a raiding squad was coming the other way.

Suth stopped, and signalled back down the line for a halt.
He'd heard something, and wanted to check it.

'I'm coming with,' hissed Costin.

Suth shook his head. He could smell the liquor on Costin's
breath. *Stay put*, he mouthed. Costin was making too much
damn noise.

'Fine!' said Costin, and sat down, glancing back at Azayda,
the next man in line with a 'what can you do?' shrug.

Angry, Suth took hold of Costin by the jaw and gave him a
sharp slap on the cheek. *Be quiet!* he mouthed, urgently.

Glowering, Costin sat back.

Suth turned, and began to edge forward along the watery
swill of the trench pit, then levered himself out of the trench
on his belly and started to crawl.

Costin stared after Suth for a moment, his pride wounded.
He wiped his hand across his mouth, and then spat the slime
he'd inadvertently deposited there. It tasted foul.

He leaned up to see how far Suth had got, but the scout
was out of sight.

Costin sniffed, and then took a flask bottle out of his
fatigue pocket. He took a swig, but it was virtually empty and
he tasted only fumes. So he tipped it back. Tipped it right
back to get at the dregs.

The glass bottle flashed as the background light caught it.

Costin wailed as a rifle round exploded his hand and the
bottle it was holding. A second later, and another shot tore
open his tunic across the right shoulder.

Costin began to whimper as he fell into the bottom of the
trench.

Azayda leapt forward, desperate to quieten Costin, and a
third round burst the Verghastite's head like a ripe fruit.

Back down the line, Raglon heard the cries and the sudden
shots, and cursed aloud. He tried to push forward, but his
men were being driven back by furious sniper fire and quick
bursts of semi-automatic shooting. Zemel dropped, killed
outright. Tyne took a hit in the knee and another through the
arm. Lukas lurched over with a yell as a shot smashed his vox-
caster.

Suth was down, alone, out in the open. He could see the
glitter of shots cutting up the trench towards his platoon.

He could see the shapes of the raiders as they hurried forward.

He felt the worst possible feeling a Tanith scout can ever feel: that he had led his comrades into danger.

He didn't hesitate. He got up, and ran the trench from the side, his lasgun blazing, assaulting the stormers from the flank.

He made several kills before their massed firepower cut him down.

To THE NORTH, Soric's platoon froze and dropped as they heard the gunfire start up. Agun Soric heard solid fire, and then las-rounds.

'Gak,' he said, 'Some poor bastard's engaged.'

And though he hated to admit it, he knew for certain who that poor bastard was.

Raglon.

THE ABRUPT GUNFIRE just a half kilometre south startled Criid and made her lower her aim for an instant. She'd been about to take the gakking shot.

She saw the spotter on the second floor of the mill get up and hurry over to the other side of the building, stepping expertly over gaps in the planks. She heard voices in the rear room of the obs post.

Do I wait or do I go for it, she asked herself?

She took aim again.

'Bets are off,' she said into her link and fired.

Her shot punched through a floorboard from below and severed the right shin of the spotter. He screamed out, fell, and came crashing through the rotten planks, bouncing off a jut of girder-post on his way down.

Vril, Mkhef and Hwlan ploughed in, killing the others below with quick, merciless shots.

Criid ran in to join them, ordering the rest of her group to hold position. The sounds of a serious firefight was rolling in from the south. Vril and Hwlan stood cover as Criid and Mkhef searched the obs post area. Cooking pots, boxes of ammo for a .45 cannon set up in a broken window, cans of processed meat, a field telephone. A strange, ugly statuette made of painted clay that Criid smashed against the wall the moment she saw it.

'Check around!' she said.

'Here!' Mkhef called.

At the back end of the chamber, corrugated metal sheets roofed in the entrance to a tunnel. They peered in. It was dark, but well shored up with flakboard.

Chances were it ran directly back to the Shadik lines.

'What do we do?' asked Vril.

Criid ignored him. She was looking at the field telephone. The light on top of it was blinking.

Feth.

'We can't stay here. They'll either close this tunnel when they don't get an answer or they'll start coming through in force.'

Away across the no-man's land they could hear cannons and mortars opening up from the Shadik front.

She looked back at the tunnel mouth. Such a great chance to reach into the enemy lines. But not tonight.

'Fall back!' she ordered, her micro-bead set on the platoon channel. She was last out of the mill. Pausing as she left, she tossed a tube-charge into the mouth of the communications tunnel, closing it off in a flurry of mud and earth spoil. If they couldn't use it, neither would the Shadik.

DAYLIGHT CAME EARLY over the Peinforq Line, dirty and hazy. It had begun to rain again, and an early bombardment was thumping to the north.

Gaunt waited in his dugout station, toying with an almost empty cup of caffeine.

The gas curtain was pushed back and Daur came in.

'What's the story?' Gaunt asked him curtly.

'Five, ten and eleven came back in. Ten just a few minutes ago.'

'Losses?'

Daur shook his head. 'They didn't make much contact, they just dropped back when things got lively.'

'Anything useful?'

'Criid did well. Her gang reconnoitred some old mill structure that isn't on the maps. Obs post. They picked off the troopers manning it. It had a dugout run back to the enemy line. Criid sealed it.'

'How?'

'Tube-charge. She's annoyed. I think she'd have taken a team down it to see what was what if things hadn't woken up.'

'She did the right thing.'

Daur nodded.

'Seventeen?' asked Gaunt.

'Nothing yet. No sign. Zero on the vox. Soric and Criid both confirm the commotion came from Raglon's area.'

Gaunt put the porcelain cup down on the table carefully because he was aware he'd been about to throw it. He'd sent four platoons out on this first night to play the Alliance's new game, and he'd only got three back. Raglon. He'd been Gaunt's vox-officer for several years. He'd been so proud to get his pins and his command.

'What do we do, sir?' asked Daur.

'We do it by the book,' Gaunt replied. 'Stand everyone down. Tomorrow night, four more platoons, four new areas. Haller, Bray, Domor, Arcuda. Get them ready. Tell them–'

'What, sir?'

'Tomorrow night, I'm going with them.'

Daur paused. 'As your XO, sir, I have to recommend you don't.'

'Noted.'

'Just for the record, you understand, sir.'

'I do. Thank you for observing your duty, Ban.'

'I'd like to go too, sir.'

Gaunt managed a thin smile. 'You know I can't allow that. Not both of us.'

'Then let me go in your place.'

'Not this time, Ban. I won a decent operation for half the Ghosts. I'm damn well going to stand by the ones who got the lousy half of the deal. Maybe you go the night after. Deal?'

'Deal, sir.'

DAUR HAD BEEN gone for some minutes when the gas curtain was pulled back again. It was Zweil.

'I hear we're missing some people,' said the old Hagian cleric, setting down without being invited.

'Raglon's platoon.'

'I want to go out tonight. If there's a chance we find them, I'd like to be there.'

'We won't even be covering that area again, father. There's no point.'

Zweil frowned. 'You won't even go back to look?'

'We are obliged to try other areas, father. Not the zones where the Shadik are expecting us. Standard field policy.'

'Whose?'

'Mine.'

'Hmmmm,' said Zweil. He sat down facing Gaunt. 'Tough job you've got here.'

'It's always a tough job.'

'Yes, but sending your platoons out into that... wasteland... hoping you'll find a gap in their lines. Why would that be again?'

'You know damn well, Zweil. Don't pretend Daur hasn't told you.'

Zweil grinned. Gaunt had always liked that grin, from the moment he'd first met the old priest on Hagia. It was confident, wise.

'Very well, Ibram. Pretend I'm Daur. Confide in me your plans.'

'I don't think so. You haven't got the clearance.'

'I could have the clearance, if you allowed it.'

'No, Zweil.'

The old man held out his hand, knuckles bunched, palm down. 'Play you for it. Knuckles.'

'Oh, for goodness' sake...'

'Unless you're afraid an old priest'll beat you?'

Gaunt turned round smartly and put his bent knuckles against Zweil's. 'Never taunt a Guard officer,' he said.

Zweil nodded. In a flash, he'd cracked Gaunt's knuckles with a blow from the right.

'Ow!' cried Gaunt. 'I didn't think we'd started!'

'Now you do. Best of three?'

Gaunt paused, then rapped down, missing as Zweil's hand pulled away.

In reply, Zweil snapped his hand round in a feint, and then smacked Gaunt's knuckles again from the right.

'Best of five?' asked Zweil, grinning.

'No. Enough.'

'So you'll grant me clearance?'

'No.'

Zweil sighed and sat back. 'Got you twice.'

'Yes, yes—'

'Both from the same angle.'

'What?'

'The same angle.'

'Do you have a point?'

Zweil nodded. 'I caught you because you didn't think I'd try the same thing twice. What if the Shadik think the same way?'

'Very clever. Now get out.'

Zweil got to his feet. 'Promise me something. I think that's the least you can do seeing as how I won.'

'Go on.'

'If you decide to go out into the same zones again tonight, take me with you.'

Gaunt hesitated. 'Yes, father.'

'Bless you,' said Zweil.

GAUNT HAD CALLED Criid to his dugout. He wanted to know more about this mill she'd found. But when the knock came, it wasn't Criid. It was Count Golke.

He was wearing battledress.

'Going somewhere?' Gaunt asked.

'When you head out again tonight, I'll be with you.'

'Why would you do that, sir? You're liaison. Front-line work is behind you.'

'I know the Pocket, Gaunt. I served here. I got you into this mess, though it wasn't my intention. I think I can help you.'

'Really?'

Golke nodded.

'So… what about the mill.'

'I'm guessing it's the old Santrebar watermill. I didn't know any of it was still standing.'

'Well,' said Gaunt. 'You've given it a name. But I don't think—'

'I was a soldier, Gaunt, before I was anything else. Before I got drawn into the political nonsense running this war. I think I've outlived my usefulness as a staff officer. Let me be a soldier again.'

There was a knock.

Criid entered. 'Reporting as ordered, sir,' she said.

'Sit down, sergeant, and tell me and the count about this mill...'

NINE
THE MANSE

'Haunted? Well, there are ghosts here, that's for certain.'

– Trooper Brostin

THE STORM THAT had begun the previous evening showed no sign of easing up. Rain drummed the roof of the manse and pattered against the windows all night. Past midnight, peals of thunder and brilliant flashes of lightning had made it seem like they were still back at the line, enduring shelling.

By dawn, the electrical tumult had stopped, but the rain had got harder. It was as if the vast, black thunderheads were too heavy to clear the peaks of the Massif and had hooked there, deluging the forest like dirigibles trying to shed ballast.

From the streaming porch windows of the manse, Caffran could see out onto the gloomy garden at the front. Already overgrown by the time they'd pitched up the night before, it was now littered with torn leaves and broken boughs brought down in the night. Swirling rivers of rainwater gushed from the higher slopes of the rear gardens, via a hedged ditch on the east side of the manse, to the gate. A lower part of the lawn was actually underwater.

He went back down the hall to the kitchen. It was early still. From the drawing room, he could hear loud, bellicose snoring. No point disturbing those sleepers, he decided. Various pots and pans from the kitchen shelves stood on the floor of the hall and up some of the stairs, pinging and beating as they caught steady drips coming in from above. Caffran nudged one around with his foot, so it was more completely under a particularly busy trickle.

Mkvenner, Jajjo and Muril were in the kitchen. Ven was sitting at the table, studying the map and chewing on a C-bar ration. Muril was occupying the window bench, sipping a can of caffeine. Jajjo greeted Caffran and offered him a cup from the pot on the stove. He was munching on some leftovers from the previous night's meal.

Muril and Larkin had caught up with them about an hour after they'd entered the manse. Soaked through, they were carrying a knife-trimmed branch from which hung a plump buck. Nineteen detail had eaten well. Some of them had drunk well too.

'What's the plan?' Caffran asked, sitting down opposite Mkvenner.

'Don't ask me,' Mkvenner replied tersely, without looking up.

Caffran held up his hands in a gesture of surrender. 'Only asking,' he said.

Mkvenner sighed and sat back. 'Sorry, Caff. Didn't mean to snap.' He folded up his map, got up, and pulled his camo cape around him. 'I'll be outside, checking the perimeter.'

He stepped out into the torrential downpour and closed the door after him. The old latch fell with a clack.

'Feth!' said Caffran. 'What bit him on the arse?'

'He seems pretty normal to me,' muttered Muril. Her tone was as dreary as the daylight.

'Come on, that's grim, even by Ven's standards,' said Caffran.

'I think he's pretty gakked off with Feygor's attitude,' Jajjo said. 'He wanted to get an early start, move on into the woods, but they're all still sleeping it off. And... no one stood watch last night.'

'I did,' said Caffran.

Jajjo nodded. 'Yeah, all three of us did. But Brostin and Cuu were meant to do the small hours, and they didn't bother. They were too busy being unconscious.'

'Feth…' Caffran said. The idea alarmed him. He couldn't remember the last time he'd spent a night in the field without someone on perimeter. Anyone could have snuck up in the dark. The whole fething Shadik Republic could have snuck up in the dark.

'I'm gonna go wake Feygor up,' Caffran announced.

'Is that really a good idea?' asked Muril.

'No, maybe not.' Caffran reconsidered, sitting back down. 'The amount he was putting away last night, it's not going to be pretty this morning.'

'Him and Brostin and Gutes and Cuu,' said Jajjo, the level of his disapproval obvious. 'Like they were off duty.'

Caffran smiled. He liked Jajjo, but the man could be a real stuff-shirt sometimes. Though only Feygor and his drinking buddies had got wasted the night before, everyone had enjoyed the luxury of a glass or two, even Ven. But not Jajjo. Come to think of it, Caffran had never seen Jajjo drink.

'You got to cut them some slack,' Caffran told the Verghastite. 'I know we're on a tour here, but this is easy-hive compared to the line we were in. They're gonna blow off steam a little, given these opportunities.'

Jajjo sniffed. 'Whatever.'

They heard voices in the hall, and Larkin and Rerval entered the kitchen. Neither one of them had disgraced themselves the night before either, though Rerval had become a little tipsy. Larkin had disappeared early.

'Could be the weather,' Larkin was saying.

'It doesn't feel right,' replied Rerval. 'I'm not getting a signal at all.'

'What's the problem?' asked Caffran.

'Vox is down,' said Larkin, helping himself to caffeine.

'Vox isn't down,' Rerval insisted. 'There's something up with the caster set.'

'You sure?' said Muril. 'Could be the weather.'

'Don't you start,' Rerval said, shaking his head. 'I'm gonna have to strip it down. Once I've got some brew inside me.'

'Heavy head?' Jajjo asked, without sympathy.

'No,' replied Rerval. The intended rebuke had annoyed him. 'I slept badly. Kept waking up. This place is full of the strangest noises.'

'Yeah, I know what you mean,' said Caffran. 'How'd you sleep, Larks?'

'Like a baby,' said Larkin quietly. Caffran wondered where. The heavy drinkers had spent the night in the drawing room by the fire. The rest of them had occupied bedrooms on the first floor: Jajjo and Mkvenner in one, Rerval, Muril and Caffran in another.

'Well, I'm going to do something useful,' Jajjo announced. 'Cleaning up, maybe.'

'You're kidding!' said Muril.

'We left a mess in that dining room last night. This is somebody's house.'

'Somebody who left years ago,' said Rerval. 'This whole sector has been evacuated. Corbec told us so.'

'I still think it's polite. We're not looters. Well, I'm not anyway. Someday maybe, someone will come home here again.'

They were all looking at him.

'Oh, all right. If we stay here another day, we're going to need clean plates ourselves.'

Caffran sighed. 'I'll help,' he said.

THE PAIR OF them left the kitchen and walked back down the hall towards the dining room. The hall was dark, and they easily saw the little flash that briefly lit the windows. A short delay, and thunder growled distantly.

'Feth,' said Caffran. 'Is it ever going to let up?'

Jajjo paused in the doorway of the dining room. He was staring at something.

'What's up?' asked Caffran.

'That raincoat. It was on the coatstand last night when we came in.'

'Yeah, and it's still there.'

'Right. But now it's wet.'

A little puddle had collected on the tiles under the wooden stand.

Caffran glanced round and saw the look on Jajjo's face.

'Don't start. Someone used it last night, that's all.'

'Who?'

Caffran shrugged. 'I don't know! Someone very drunk, maybe? There are several candidates.'

Jajjo smiled, reassured. They went into the dining room and stopped dead.

The table was clean and wiped. The chairs set back in place. All the crockery was gone.

'What the feth–?' Caffran began.

'I thought we were supposed to be the ghosts,' Jajjo muttered.

'I said don't start–' Caffran snapped. His words were cut off by a sudden yelling from the drawing room.

And by a blast of las-fire.

'YOU FETHERS! You fethers!' Feygor was howling. Naked except for his undershorts, he was sitting up on his crumpled bedroll, his rifle in his hands. Caffran and Jajjo rushed in, blades drawn. A second later, Rerval, Larkin and Muril burst in from the kitchen.

The stuffed behj was lying on its back in front of Feygor, its head shot off. Sawdust drifted down in the air. On their own bedrolls around the room, Brostin, Gutes and Cuu were blinking awake.

'What the feth's going on?' asked Caffran.

'Those fethers!' Feygor squawked. 'I woke up and that fething thing was standing over me! Ha ha… very fething funny, you bastards! Who put it there?'

'You killed it for sure this time,' said Cuu and slumped back onto his mat.

'Who put it there?' demanded Feygor again.

Gutes shook his head.

'Bastards!' cried Feygor and kicked out at the stuffed beast.

'Did anyone put it there?' asked Caffran. There was a chorus of 'no' and 'not me'. He glanced at Jajjo before the dark-skinned trooper could speak. 'Don't even think about it,' he warned.

'I think this place is haunted,' Jajjo said anyway.

'Feth off!'

'You dumb gak!'

'I said don't go there,' Caffran admonished.

'Well, who washed up then, eh?' asked Jajjo.

There was a pause.

'I did,' said Gutes. Rerval and Caffran groaned.

'Feth you! Old habits die hard.' Gutes got to his feet and wandered off to find the can.

'Good old wash-bin Gutes,' smiled Larkin.

'I heard that, you fether,' Gutes's voice trailed back from the hall.

'And the stuffed animal?' snapped Caffran. 'Brostin? Had to be someone with a bit of muscle to move that thing.'

Brostin turned over in his bedroll, and put his hands behind his head. The pose emphasised the huge girth of his arms and pecs. He stared at Caffran. 'You accusing me, Caff?'

'Seems like your style, yeah.'

'Yeah, well… it was. Funny as feth, eh?' He closed his eyes and rolled over again.

'Bastard!' Feygor snarled, and threw a boot at him.

Caffran turned and ushered Larkin, Rerval, Muril and Jajjo out. 'Leave them to it,' he said.

Gutes was in the kitchen, drinking the last of the brewed caffeine.

'Thanks for putting the stuff away, though,' he said.

'What?' asked Caffran.

'The plates and stuff. I washed it all up, but I didn't know where it went, so I left it by the sink.'

He looked at their faces. 'What? What?'

By noon, everybody was up. Brostin, Feygor and Cuu were still in their underwear, grim and hungover. The rest of nineteen were kitted up, filling time.

Muril had found a regicide set from somewhere, and was playing a game with Larkin.

Rerval came into the kitchen. 'Which of you fethers took it?' he asked.

'Took what?' Feygor asked.

'The caster's down because someone took out the main transmission circuit. I don't carry a spare for that. Who's got it?'

There was a general shrugging and shaking of heads.

'Come on–'

'We're not tech-heads, Rerval. We don't feth around with tech-kit,' said Brostin. 'Do I look like an adept of the Mechanicus?'

'Someone did it. Clean job too. Mister Feygor?'

'Why are you looking at me, trooper?'

'Maybe you thought we'd get to stay here an extra night or two and enjoy the facilities if we unexpectedly lost contact.'

Feygor set down his mug. 'You know what, Rerval? I wish I'd thought of that. I really do. It's neat, it's sneaky. It serves my purpose. But I was planning on staying here a while anyway, vox-link or no vox-link. I didn't feth with your beloved caster.'

He leaned forward, staring Rerval in the face. 'Don't ever fething accuse me of crap again, you little bastard.'

Rerval blinked and looked away suddenly.

'Sorry,' he said.

'Sorry what?' snapped Feygor. Everyone looked on, stony-faced. Caffran didn't like what he was seeing. Feygor was a bully, with a mean-streak as wide as the Kottmark Massif.

'Sorry, "Mister Feygor".'

'Better,' said Feygor, leaning back.

'Sure as sure,' murmured Cuu from the rear of the room.

Feygor yawned. 'Anyone want to tell me about this circuit? While we're on the topic? Like I said, it suits me fine, the vox being down, but I'd like to know who sabotaged it. Anyone?'

No one spoke.

'Okay–' said Feygor with a wicked smile. 'If our culprit would like to fit it back into the little whining bastard's caster-set in… oh, three days? That'd be fine and I won't mention it to Corbec. Understood?'

The troopers shifted awkwardly. Thunder was still grumbling around the forest and the rain was lashing down. Feygor looked over at Brostin. 'Go and get some wine,' he said.

Brostin got up and shambled out.

'Are we not moving today?' asked Caffran.

'Do I look like I'm moving, Caff? Do I?'

'No, Mister Feygor.'

'Then I'm probably not moving.'

'We should–' Jajjo began.

'And not a word from you, Verghast. Okay?' Feygor rocked his chair onto its back legs. 'Look,' he said, slightly more softly. 'Have you seen this weather? It isn't letting up. The way I call it, we stay put until it breaks. We'd be mad to try and push on in this. No offence, Larks.'

'None taken,' said Larkin.

'Anybody else got a problem with that? Anybody else got a problem with me being in charge? Because I seem to remember that's the way Colonel Corbec wanted it.'

The back door opened, and Mkvenner came in, water streaming off the folds of his cape. He looked around at the silent assembly of figures.

'I take it we're not going anywhere,' he said darkly.

'Any contacts?' Feygor asked him.

Mkvenner shook his head. 'Nothing. Perimeter's secure. The area's quiet. Though someone or something's disturbed one of the outhouses. Like someone's been sleeping out there.'

'Recently?' Feygor asked.

'Couldn't tell,' Mkvenner said.

'We won't worry about it, then.'

'Your call,' said Mkvenner.

'Why, yes it is,' said Feygor.

Mkvenner paused. 'Mission requirements call for us to scope this valley,' he said.

'And we will,' said Feygor.

'When?'

'When I'm ready,' Feygor said, looking round at Mkvenner. 'You ought to relax, Ven.'

'There're many things I ought to do, Mister Feygor. But I won't.'

Feth, thought Caffran. This could turn really ugly.

'Tell you what, Ven,' said Feygor. 'You want to scope so badly, you go ahead. You'll move faster without us. Head out, get the lie of the land, and swing back. By then, the weather may have cleared.'

'Is that an order?'

'Yeah, why not? Run a deep patrol, check things out, come back here. Once the storm's gone, we'll move out and finish the sweep with you. Think of us as base camp. As HQ. We'll hold things here.'

Mkvenner had an icy look in his eyes. 'Should we check that with Ins Arbor base?' he asked.

'Ah, sadly, vox is down,' Feygor said, with a contented smile.

Mkvenner looked around the kitchen. 'Okay. I'll be gone a day, tops.'

'The Emperor protects,' said Feygor.

Brostin came back in, his arms full of wine bottles. 'These do?' he asked.

'They most certainly will,' said Feygor.

Mkvenner took one last contemptuous look at Brostin, Feygor and the bottles, and left.

'VEN! VEN!' CAFFRAN called out as he ran through the rain, up the back plot of the manse, after the retreating scout.

Mkvenner stopped and waited for him. Thunder clashed above them.

'This isn't right,' said Caffran.

'Yeah, but it's what's happening.'

'Feygor's out of line.'

Mkvenner nodded. 'He is. But he's got command of this detail. What are you going to do? Mutiny?'

'Corbec would understand.'

'Yes, he would. But if you or I get into a clash with Feygor, it could get nasty long before Corbec arrives to intervene. It's crap, but it's better just left.'

Caffran shrugged. 'We could just go with you.'

'We?'

'Me, Muril, Rerval… probably Larks. Jajjo definitely. Maybe even Gutes.'

Thunder rolled again.

'I'll take Jajjo. Send him on up.'

'That's it?'

Mkvenner fixed Caffran with a fierce stare. 'Think about it this way. I'd be happy to sit out a few days in that place, getting plastered and telling old stories. But there's a job to do. There's a chance… just a chance… that there's enemy activity in this forest. And while that chance exists, I'm going to look for it.'

'Yeah and–'

Ven held up a finger to silence Caffran. 'In an ideal galaxy, we'd all go. The way we were meant to. But thanks to Murtan Feygor, this isn't an ideal galaxy. So we improvise. That's what we're good at, after all. If I find something out there, Emperor protect me, I'd like to have a patrol fire-team at my back. Failing that, I'd like to know there's a secure, well-defended strongpoint position not too far away at my heels. Stay here, Caff. Right here. Get Muril, Rerval, Larkin – maybe even Gutes, like you said – and lock this place up ready. Just in case.'

'Okay. If that's what you want.'

'It's what I want. Not what I'd wish for, but it'll do. As far as I'm concerned, you're in charge here now. Hold the manse and wait for me. Feygor can get his when we get back. I'll see to it personally. For now, let's just worry about getting the job done and not fething up.'

Caffran nodded.

Mkvenner took his hand and gripped it tight. 'I'm relying on you.'

'Signal when you can.'

'Not a lot of range on these micro-beads. No more than a league or two in these woods.'

'Do it anyway. If it's bad news… make the signal "come-uppance".'

Mkvenner smiled. Caffran hadn't seen him do that very often.

'Okay. Send Jajjo up. I'll see you in a day and a night.'

Caffran stood and watched Mkvenner stride away through the rain until he had vanished into the edge of the wood.

Thunder boomed.

'WHERE'S JAJJO?' ASKED Muril, wandering into the kitchen. The storm had worsened and the light was bad. From the drawing room, they could hear sounds of laughter and drunken antics.

'He's gone with Ven,' said Caffran.

Muril sat down on the window bench. 'Oh, that's just typical!' she said venomously.

'Calm down,' said Rerval.

'Bite me, Tanith! This whole tour's turning into crap,' she complained.

There was a particularly loud roar from the drawing room. A crash. Laughter.

'What are they doing?' asked Caffran.

'Using that stuffed thing as a battering ram,' said Rerval. 'I think the game is to see how long one of them can stay on its back with the others running it around the room.'

'Children,' Muril said, acidly.

'Listen,' said Caffran. 'I spoke to Ven. He thinks there's no point going up against Feygor. But he wants us to hold this place, in case.'

'In case of what?' asked Rerval.

'In case he and Jajjo find something out there. Okay? Where's Larkin?'

Rerval shrugged.

'Muril, you seen Larks recently?'

'No,' she said, preoccupied. 'Why the gak does Jajjo get to scout? Why the gak does that happen?'

'Just forget it,' said Caffran. 'We have to focus. We'll take watches. Two hours on. You handle the first one, Muril?'

'Sure,' she said.

'Rerval. Sweep the perimeter and then start building cover for us. Anything you can find.'

Rerval nodded. 'What'll you be doing, Caff?'

'I'm going to find Larks,' he said.

NIGHT FELL. THE rainstorm continued to hammer the forest and drench the manse. In one of the outbuildings, an old greenhouse at the edge of the rear yard, facing north, Muril cowered and shivered, watching the tree-line. It was just a dark expanse of trunks half-screened by the sheeting rain.

Rerval brought her a cup of hot caffeine and a plate of sliced salt beef.

'Been busy?' she asked him.

'There's not a lot to use, but I managed to raise a barricade across the yard at the back of the kitchen. And I boarded up some of the ground floor windows at the back.

'Where's Caffran?'

'Doing the rounds,' he said.

* * *

CAFFRAN WAS ACTUALLY emptying pots. No one had bothered to tip out the pots and pans that had been standing under the drips, and now some of them were overflowing. He opened the front door and slung each one empty into the downpour.

Light bled into the hallway from the drawing room, along with raucous noise and the smell of a decent fire. Caffran could hear Brostin telling a coarse story, and Cuu and Gutes exploding into laughter. A bottle broke. There was another, stranger sound that Caffran realised was Feygor laughing too, choking the noise in and out of his augmetic throat.

Caffran shuddered.

He closed the front door. He hadn't been able to find Larkin anywhere.

He looked at the coatstand. The raincoat had gone.

The drawing room door burst open and Gutes tumbled out. Light and heat and laughter spilled out around him.

'More wine!' he exclaimed.

'Haven't you had enough?' Caffran asked.

'Don't be so fething uptight, Caff!' Gutes replied. 'Why don't you join us. We're having a fine time.'

'So I heard.'

'Makes a change from the fething war!' Gutes slurred.

'The war's still going on,' smiled Caffran.

Gutes looked sad. He pulled the door shut, cutting out the sounds of merrymaking. He leaned against the hall wall and slid down until he was sitting.

'I know. I know. It never lets up, does it? War. There's only war. It's the only future we've got. Dark? Yes! Grim? Oh, yes, sir! There's only ever war!'

'Don't worry about it, Piet,' Caffran reassured.

'I don't, Caff, I don't,' Gutes mumbled. 'I'm just so tired, you know? Just so very fething tired of it all. I'm worn out. I've had enough.'

Caffran crouched down beside the intoxicated trooper.

'Get off to bed, Piet. Things'll seem better in the morning.'

Gutes struggled up to his feet. Caffran had to help him.

'Things seem better now, Caff! They really do. I gotta get more bottles.' He lurched away towards the cellar door.

Caffran thought about trying to stop him, but decided not to. Gutes was too far gone.

He heard a creak on the stairs above him, and quickly brought round his lasrifle, switching on the lamp pack under the barrel.

Halfway down the stairs, a little old woman flinched at the sudden, fierce beam of light. She was wearing a raincoat, and it was dripping wet.

Caffran's light illuminated Larkin beside her. He was smiling as he steadied the old woman's arm.

'Hey, Caff,' he said. 'Look who I found...'

TEN
SANTREBAR MILL

'Blood for land: the commerce of war.'
  – Satacus, 'Of the Great Sezars'

THE REPUBLIC SUBJECTED sectors 57 and 58 of the Peinforq Line to a sustained gas attack during the morning. The wind, a brisk westerly, favoured their enterprise, and carried the gas swiftly into the Alliance fire trenches: so swiftly, in fact, Alliance respirator drill was found wanting. Men died in dreadful numbers. Three hundred and forty-eight in one five-kilometre stretch alone. Hundreds more were brought out of the reeking amber mist, frothing and blistering, screaming and crying.

A fitful barrage responded to the gas attack. Less modest artillery quaked the earth for over an hour to the north, in 59th sector.

The gas took a long time to dissipate, and the Shadik had undoubtedly been planning on that. At a few minutes before 15.00, a considerable portion of the 57th sector fire trench was assaulted by a brigade of raiders who had advanced under cover of the chemical fog. For a period of about twenty-five minutes, savage, blind fighting occurred at the 57th, and there seemed a genuine danger that the line would be penetrated. The timely arrival of a detachment of the Bande Sezari, as well as a company of elite Kottsmark chemtroops, tipped the scales. Then the wind turned, and the poison smog began to drift east off the Peinforq defences. The Shadik raiders beat their retreat.

By then, this possible opportunity had been anticipated, and Alliance Staff Command 57th/58th opted to press. Cavalry and light foot elements were pushed through to overtake the raiders then continue on for a counter-attack. They were supplemented by armour.

Alliance armour was in the main ponderous, primitive, rhomboidal tanks with heavy roof or sponson guns. These sluggish giants rumbled their way out into the Pocket. They were menacing, but had not achieved much success in anything but psychological terms since their first employment twelve years earlier. However, on this day, five Imperial Guard Thunderers, spared from the action at Gibsgatte, led them out. By evening, they had made a memorable dent in the Shadik lines. It was the first demonstration of modern armour superiority witnessed on Aexe Cardinal.

At the time of the first toxin shelling, the First was laid up in a secondary line, awaiting the evening advance to the fire trench. They had decent warning time on their side, but their respirator drill was excellent anyway. They sat tight, until word started to come in of the raid on the 57th sector. Daur went to see Gaunt immediately.

'We can reinforce,' he suggested. 'We're close enough to do some good.'

Gaunt refused the idea. He'd worked hard to secure a legitimate role in the Alliance for both arms of the First, and he wasn't about to upset that stability with a show of unilateral bravado. However much he wanted to.

'Stand three platoons to,' he conceded to Daur finally. 'If command requests us, we'll move at once.'

They waited, tense, for an hour or so. When the wind turned and the counter-assault pushed through, Gaunt and Golke moved down to an observation post on the hem of the secondary line.

Borrowing Gaunt's magnoculars, Golke watched the steady advance of the tanks, his gaze lingering over the heavy-set, trundling shapes of the Guard armour pieces. The Thunderers were painted mustard drab, and moved forward with their siege-dozers lowered, ripping through piquet lines and thorny barricades of wire. Sprays of liquid mud kicked up from their churning treads.

Golke was seriously impressed. He spoke for a while about armour clashes he'd witnessed, though he was so preoccupied with what he was seeing there was no real thread to his talk. Gaunt understood that Golke had received his injuries during one of these clashes, but he didn't want to press the count for details. Golke mentioned 'dreadnoughts', yet the word did not seem to mean the same thing for him as it did for Gaunt. To an Aexegarian, 'dreadnought' was a catch-all word for any armoured war machine.

Whistles were blowing all along the trench system to sound all-clear. The gas had washed out of the line. Gaunt took off his respirator and wiped his sweat-damp face. The afternoon light was good and clear, grey and bright, except for the roiling yellow fume of the departing gas that blanketed no-man's land.

'Nightfall's at 19.40,' Golke remarked. He produced a dataslate. 'I have a schedule for tonight's barrages. When do you want to move out?'

It was a legitimate question. Provided he informed Allied GSC, the timing of the Ghosts' next raid was down to him.

Gaunt looked at the Aexegarian. 'Now,' he said.

THE MAIN FIELD infirmary of 58th sector was a large system of bunkers situated amidst the reserve and tiring trenches at the back of the line, west of the main gun-pits and artillery dens. Set well underground, beneath a roof of rockcrete and flaksacks, it was said to have its own shield umbrella too, but Dorden didn't believe that.

However, the facilities were decent. Curth had made strenuous efforts, since they'd moved north, to secure fresh supplies from the Munitorium fleet, and Mkoll had taken his own platoon back to escort the supplies and make sure they arrived unmolested. Many of the First, Dorden included, had been surprised that Mkoll had not been part of the regiment's eastward deployment to the Montorq.

'Scouts are needed here too,' Mkoll had told Dorden when the subject came up. 'I'm not about to head for the forest and expect the lads I leave here to do something I wouldn't do myself.'

There was an implication in the master-scout's remark, Dorden felt. Whatever happened out in the Montorq, good or bad, only bad was going to happen here. The Pocket was going to see action, no matter what. Mkoll's selfless sense of duty wasn't going to let him shirk.

When the First had been moved up to the 58th sector, Dorden had packed up his field hospital at Rhonforq and brought it with him, wounded and all, so he could maintain personal care for them and be on hand for the new fighting. That afternoon, gas-attack victims poured into the infirmary's triage hall. None of them were Ghosts, but Dorden and his medicae staff didn't hesitate. They sprang up to support the Alliance surgeons, bathing eyes, treating burns, washing poisons out of cloth and bubbling flesh. The respiratory damage was the worst. There was little they could do for the victims with fluid-filled, drowning lungs except try to stabilise them.

Dorden worked urgently. He dearly missed Foskin and Doctor Mtane, who had both gone west with the Montorq mission. He wanted to trust the ministrations of the Alliance surgeons, many of whom were devoted, good men, but their medical practices seemed so terribly outmoded. He took careful note of the treatment deficiencies he saw, and hoped there would be an opportunity for him to advise the sector's chief of medicine on better, less barbarous techniques. At least three troopers he saved that afternoon were dying as a direct result of treatment rather than gas.

A terrible stench of chemical burns and corrupted blood filled the infirmary. Frothy, discoloured waste matter wept in lakes across the stone floor. Corpsmen turned on the roof vents and hosed with disinfectant, but it didn't do much good.

'Feth!' muttered Rawne. 'The smell is going to choke me to death!'

'Will it make you stop talking?' asked Banda. He looked across the aisle at her cot with a withering stare, but she just grinned. She was pale, and a cut above her right eye was black with stitches. Her mending lungs were having a hard time coping with the wretched air. Still, she found the breath to taunt him.

Rawne got up off his cot, and sat carefully. The ward hall was full of Ghosts, as well as a few Krassians, casualties from that first trench fight at the 55th sector. Many, like Rawne, were healing well, but it would be a long time before they could be pronounced fit for active duty. Rawne wondered how many more Ghosts would come through these halls before the present occupants made their way out.

The days since he had been wounded had passed at a dishearteningly slow crawl. Rawne felt detached and very much out of the loop, even though he'd been brought regular reports. He wanted to get up and out, but not because he was such a dutiful soldier he needed to get back to play his part.

He was distressed at the prospect of what feth-heads like Daur might be doing in his absence.

'What are you doing?' asked Banda.

He didn't reply. He grabbed hold of the back of a wooden chair and slowly dragged himself to his feet. The pain in his stomach, which had been a dormant ache for the last thirty hours, started to throb again.

'What are you doing?' Banda repeated. 'Doc Dorden'll have your guts.'

'Feels like he already has,' Rawne snapped.

He took a deep breath, and let go of the chair back.

God-Emperor, it was hard. It felt like his legs had atrophied. It felt like someone had upturned a live brazier in his belly. It felt like someone was stabbing a bayonet into his spine.

'What are you doing?' Banda repeated for the third time. Then added, 'Major?'

That did it. Rawne hadn't been addressed by rank for what seemed like an age. Especially by Jessi Banda. If he but admitted it, that had been the best part of this enforced stay in the ward. Jammed together by the proximity of their beds, the comatose nature of their immediate neighbours, and their shared suffering at station 293, they had provided conversational company for one another. It wasn't a friendship, exactly. Rawne certainly wouldn't acknowledge anything like that, but they'd talked, and played boredom-defeating word games, and joked occasionally. After the first few hours of them being cooped up together involuntarily, she had stopped calling him major and he'd stopped calling her trooper. They had formed a cordial, sparring companionship as a reaction to their situation.

'I'm going for a breath of fresh air,' Rawne said, panting.

'Oh, what? And leave me here? And I thought we were mates.'

It was too much effort to shoot her another withering stare. It was almost too much effort to remain standing. 'Just...' he said. 'Just...'

'What?' Banda asked.

He sighed. 'Can you get up?'

'Can I gak.'

'Oh, for feth's sake...' Slowly, very slowly, he plodded round the end of his cot and grabbed hold of a wheelchair that had been folded up against the foot of the next bunk. It took him a moment to force the spring-shot seat back into place, and he almost fell doing it.

'Careful!' she said.

'Like you care...'

He got the chair stable and shuffled it across to her bedside, leaning hard on the handles.

'Come on,' he said.

She looked up at him. 'Gakking well help, then.'

Setting the chair's brake, he got her by the wrists, and levered her forward to the edge of the cot. He could hear the wheeze in her lungs.

'Maybe we shouldn't-'

'You started this, Rawne,' she said.

'On three. You'll have to help me. One, two...'

She almost missed the seat completely. As it was, she had to wriggle around once she'd got her breath back. Rawne leaned over, doubled up, dizzy from the pain in his gut.

'Okay?' she said.

'Oh, sure...'

He grabbed the handles of the chair, kicked off the brake after a couple of feeble tries, and trundled her up the aisle towards the exit. Pushing really hurt his fethed-up gut.

But at least now he had something to lean on.

BANDA WAS CHUCKLING to herself. Despite the real and growing pain in his stomach, Rawne realised he was smiling too. There was a genuine sense of escape. A comradely feel of fellow prisoners sticking together and making a break for freedom.

And there was an agreeable sensation of flaunting the system that Rawne hadn't felt since he'd been coining it as part of Tanith Attica's black market.

The two invalids edged up the infirmary's exit ramp and out into the firing trench. It was their first sight of daylight in a while. He wheeled Banda along the duckboards as far as a waystation, pausing every few metres to rest, and then got an arm around her and manhandled her up into a vacant obs post. By then, they were both exhausted, and they flopped down onto the sandbags, leaning their backs to the parapet face.

Yet they were both sniggering too.

The pain in Rawne's belly flared for a while, but slowly it subsided now he was no longer exerting himself. They both took deep breaths, enjoying the fresh air. It wasn't fresh, exactly. There was a reek of mud, general sweat, wet sacking, fyceline, promethium, fungus, sour food, latrines. But it was light years better than the gas-corrupted waste-stink that permeated the infirmary.

'We ought to do this more often,' she quipped, clearly in pain but relishing the escape.

'Now I know what Corbec meant,' he replied.

'What?'

Rawne looked at her. 'He's had a tough run, this last while. Wounded, bedridden. He told me the thing he missed worst, what hurt him worst, was missing stuff. The physical pain of injuries didn't matter so much. It was losing his place in things.'

She nodded.

'I didn't appreciate what he meant, really. I thought getting wounded was a vacation. And that you'd be too taken up with your injury to worry about anything else. But he was right. It feels like I've been buried and left for dead and the galaxy has moved on without me.'

There was a long pause. A detachment of Fichuan Infantry tramped past along the reserve trench below them. Somewhere, muffled, a field-vox jangled.

'Why did you order me not to die?' she asked.

'What?'

'In the trench. I heard you. I couldn't answer, but I heard you. You ordered me not to die.'

He thought about it. 'Because I didn't want the bother of finding a new platoon sniper,' he said.

The trace of a smile crossed her lips and she nodded sagely. 'That's what I thought,' she said.

Rawne got up and looked down over the sandbag wall into the reserve trench. Troops were coming and going. A dirty, black ATV grumbled past, laden with shells for the feldkannones and hessian-bagged rockets for the shargen-launchers.

'Something's up,' he commented.

'What?'

'Beltayn just came running up and went into the infirmary.'

'Ah,' Banda said, knowingly. 'You mean something's awry...'

'I'M A LITTLE occupied, Adjutant Beltayn,' Dorden remarked as he made yet another attempt to rinse the eyes of a screaming, thrashing Aexe trooper.

'I can see that, doctor,' Beltayn said.

'So it'll have to wait.'

'With respect, doctor, the colonel-commissar said you'd say that. He said to tell you that the infiltration unit is moving out in fifteen minutes and—'

'And?'

'And you should move your fething arse. His words.'

'Really?' said Dorden. 'I thought he wasn't mobilising until tonight?'

Beltayn said something that was drowned out by a particularly curdled shriek from the man on the gurney.

'I said... change of plan, doctor. We've got daylight cover. The gas, you see? And a whole bundle of distractions. There's a counter-push going on. Tanks and everything.'

'I just can't leave this, Beltayn,' Dorden said. He'd promised Gaunt he'd move out with the next patrol in the hope they'd find some of Raglon's platoon, but he hadn't counted on a triage hall full of chem-burned men.

'Go, Tolin. I can handle it,' said Curth, appearing from nowhere, her apron stained with bile and foam.

'You sure, Ana?'

'Yes. Just go.' She started to apply herself to the thrashing victim.

'Hold him!' she snarled at the stretcher bearers standing nearby. They jumped to help.

Dorden yanked off his smeared gloves and scrub-top and tossed them into a soil-bin. He took a fresh apron from the laundered rack, and started to fill his medicae kit from the supply shelves.

'We haven't got much time,' Beltayn urged.

'Then be a good man and get my jacket and camo-cape from the side office. They're on the peg.'

Dorden buttoned up his kit and slung it over his shoulder. 'Attention!' he yelled above the tumult of the ward. 'Be advised that Surgeon Curth is now in operational control here. No excuses, no exceptions. Go through her.'

Beltayn returned, and helped Dorden into his black, First-issue field jacket.

'Good luck!' called Curth.

'Keep it,' he replied. 'You'll need it more.'

PULLING HIS CAPE around his shoulders, Dorden hurried up the entrance ramp of the infirmary behind Beltayn.

'You say he's decided to go in daylight?' he asked.

'Yes, doctor. I heard him telling Count Golke that stealth works even when it's not quiet. He wants to make use of the noise and gas and confusion to get back to where the teams were last night.'

'I see. We have to go back. I've left my respirator behind.'

Beltayn turned and winked. 'I brought that too,' he said.

'You think of everything,' Dorden mocked.

'That's my job,' said Beltayn, without a hint of irony.

They ran out into the reserve trench and hurried along north towards the first communications spur running east.

Dorden suddenly stopped and looked back. Beltayn skidded to a halt.

'What the feth are you doing up there?' Dorden yelled at a nearby obs tower.

'Feeling better already!' Rawne shouted back, giving a little wave. 'Good hunting, doctor!'

'Just… just take your medicine!' Dorden yelled at Rawne in frustration, then followed Beltayn up the trench.

RAWNE SAT BACK down and produced a hip-flask from his pocket. He unscrewed the cap and offered it to Banda.

'What is it?' she asked.

'Sacra. The best. The very last of Bragg's legendary brew.'

'Don't know if I should,' she said.

'You heard our venerable medic,' Rawne said. 'Take your medicine.'

Laughing as hard as their painful wounds permitted, they drank to one another's health.

THE INFILTRATORS WENT over the top and into the dead lands of the Pocket at a minute before five in the afternoon. Four platoons – Criid's, Domor's, Mkoll's and Arcuda's – along with a command team of Gaunt, Dorden, Zweil, Beltayn, Count Golke and four elite troopers from the Bande Sezari.

Respirator masks clamped on, they extended into the soupy veil of the drifting gas, which wrapped the landscape with a tobacco-yellow stain. Visibility was down to twenty metres, though the overall light was good. A bland glow of daylight bathed them through the toxin clouds, white and flat.

Scout Hwlan, from Criid's platoon, took point, along with Mkoll himself and 'Lucky' Bonin from Domor's mob. Hwlan had found the mill the night before, and they were trusting his instincts to lead them in.

To Hwlan, an experienced scout with many years as a tracker in the nalwoods of Tanith in his past, it was a strange experience. Many said the Tanith could never get lost, and claimed they had the most unerring sense of direction. The constantly shifting trees of Tanith had bred that into them.

That was the theory, anyway.

The chemical attack had changed the ground, baking the mud so dry it had begun to crack. Underneath it was wet and soft, and the feet of the troopers cracked the surface as they advanced, spilling up mud as fluid and yellow as custard.

Vague landmarks from the previous night – a broken tree, a fence of wire, a dead tank – had solidified and become permanent, but they'd also been changed by the action of gas. The Pocket had become a dead space of embalmed features, desiccated, fused, chemically transmuted.

The point men reached a wire barricade that collapsed into rust as they touched it. The liquid chemicals accreted in some crater holes were burning.

And there were so many corpses. Dorden was shocked. Fresh corpses, hooked in wire or lying on the ground, so florid they looked like they were still alive. Others, older, hunched and flattened into the postures of submission only dead men can afford. Others, older still, cadaverous and dry, opening their bones to the sky.

It was also grimly silent. There was no wind, and the gas clouds stifled all noise. A bright, dry desert of war, lethal to the touch and the merest breath.

Gaunt placed Milo and Nehn from Domor's platoon with Zweil. The old ayatani was a newcomer to gas gear and was clearly uncomfortable with the mask and the thick gloves. He'd cinched up the skirts of his long coat so that they wouldn't drag in the mire, revealing an incongruous, borrowed pair of heavy Aexegarian army boots. Gaunt could hear a mumbling over the vox. Zweil was quietly reciting a prayer of protection. Gaunt signalled Milo to show the priest how to turn off his micro-bead.

'I appreciate your blessings, father,' he said, 'but perhaps for now you could keep them to yourself inside your hood. We need the link quiet.'

The riven landscape curled up over a long ridge where the mud was covered in a mosaic of bones, human and hippine. They saw the occasional rusting scrap of a respirator valve, a saddle buckle, the bent barrel of a carbine. On the far side of the ridge, the ground shelved away into a wide basin where a brackish crescent of water shone in the flat light. Old piquets marched in a line down the slope and disappeared into the pool. Along the eastern shore of the water, the mud was crinkled into strange patches that reminded Gaunt of rose blooms. Shards of ashy glass clung to the folds of each patch. He realised they were the impact marks of gas bottles from a previous attack. The mud had baked and puckered with the intensity of the leaking toxins.

An Alliance trooper stood on the far side of the pool, headless. His rotting body was held up by the metal stake he'd fallen against.

The trio of scouts led them round the side of the basin, and out over its lowest lip. They entered a flat area covered in shell craters some large enough to swallow a man, others just pock-marks the size of a fist. The craters overlapped each other, small inside large, large intersecting with larger. The pattern was so dense and seemed so deliberate, it was surreal. To their north, on a bank of mud, lay the burnt-black carcass of a Shadik tank.

Mkoll indicated they should turn south a little, but Golke consulted his chart and advised against it. A row of crossed timbers suggested to him the edge of a mined area. Old munitions, but it was stupid to risk it, and they weren't set for sweeping work. In order to move light, landmine experts like Domor had left their sweeper sets at the line.

They moved north-east instead, following a mangled ridge, plodding through murky strands of water and oil. To their left was a series of waterlogged pits absolutely choked with bodies, as if the dead had all decided to congregate in one place. Zweil realised he was glad of his mask.

Since they'd set out, they'd been able to hear the roaring of the counter-assault pushing ahead of them, a little to the south. Now they heard a deeper, more booming noise. Boxed in by the gas-clouded air, they could see nothing, but Gaunt was sure it was the Shadik super-siege weapons opening up at the Peinforq Line in response to the push.

'Any way we can fix a source at all?' Gaunt asked Mkoll without much hope. Mkoll gestured at the hood he was wearing.

'Not really,' he replied. He thought about it and listened to the thumps. 'Best guess is that way,' he pointed. 'But it's vague.'

Gaunt turned to Hwlan. 'How far to this mill?'

'Another half kilometre. We're approaching from a slightly different angle to last night. There's a creek, with a fence nearby, and then the mill itself in a wide hollow.'

'It's more like three-quarters of a kilometre,' said Golke over the link, wiping specks of mud off his chart's plastic cover. 'And slightly more to the south.'

Gaunt looked back at Hwlan. Through the lens-plates of his bulky hood, he could see Hwlan shake his head slightly.

'With respect, sir,' Gaunt told Golke, 'I have to trust my scout.'

Golke didn't seem abashed. He was quickly coming to admire the First's field skills.

They moved on. In less than fifteen minutes, they were drawing in on the south-eastern side of the ruined mill, just a vague shape in the fog of gas.

Hwlan had been spot on.

It looked quiet, empty. Perhaps the Shadik had been unable to resecure it since the previous night. No sense taking chances, though.

The Ghosts advanced, low. Gaunt spread Criid's platoon in a semi-circle to his right, and Mkoll's and Domor's wider to the left, with Arcuda's in place to the rear, ready to support.

The troop got to within fifty metres of the shattered mill.

'Hold,' Gaunt signalled. Down, hidden under their capes, the Ghosts lined up their weapons, studying the ruin for movement. Gaunt gestured to Mkoll.

The master scout began to slide forward under his cape. To Golke, he seemed to all but vanish. Bonin and Hwlan quickly followed Mkoll, along with Oflyn, the scout from Arcuda's platoon.

After ten seconds, Mkoll voxed. 'Clear. We're at the outside wall. Two big rockcrete beams fallen in a V-shape. See them?'

Gaunt acknowledged. Golke tried to see the beams. Even when he found them, he couldn't see the Tanith.

'Move up the assault squad,' Mkoll linked.

The squad came up, and Gaunt advanced with them. Six men: Domor, Luhan, Vril and Harjeon, with Dremmond and Lubba and their flamers. Gaunt left fire command with Criid.

They reached Mkoll's position. The scouts were ready to go in. Dremmond and Lubba prepped their flames.

'On three—' said Gaunt.

'Wait!' Bonin voxed. 'Movement. Up, to the left. The rafters over the far window.'

Before Gaunt had time to take a look, a shot zipped out of the mill and went over their heads, followed by another that smacked off a tie-beam Luhan was using for cover.

'Wait!' Gaunt yelled, just before his men started to return fire and hose the south face of the mill.

The shots had been las-rounds.

Gaunt adjusted the setting of his micro-bead. 'One, who's up there?'

A pause. Faint static on the link.

'One,' Gaunt repeated. 'Identify.'

'Two-oh-three, one,' came the response.

It was Raglon.

ELEVEN
THE DUTIFUL

'Cuu's a fething maniac, Larks…'
— Trooper Bragg (deceased), on Phantine

SHE WOULDN'T TALK. She wouldn't even take off her raincoat.
She allowed Larkin and Caffran to lead her into the gloomy
kitchen and sit her at one of the chairs by the table.

She flinched as Rerval suddenly came in from outside. He
looked at the old woman in confusion.

'She was hiding upstairs,' Larkin told him. 'I was…
patrolling and I heard a noise and I found her. She's our
ghost.'

Caffran poured a hot drink from the stove and set it on the
table beside her.

'Drink up,' he said. 'You look hungry. And cold.'

She looked up at Caffran slowly, her old eyes not blinking.
There was something far away in her gaze that suggested she
didn't really see him.

'Drink up, ma'am,' said Caffran again, encouragingly. She
didn't. Her gaze returned to the glow of the stove plate.

'What do you mean she's our ghost?' Rerval asked Larkin.

226

'Moving things, you know. Putting the plates away. She's been here all the time, hiding from us.'

'How do you know?'

Larkin shrugged.

'Hey, do you think she took the circuit out of my vox?' Rerval said suddenly. 'Did you mess with my vox-caster, mother?' he asked.

The sudden voice made her flinch again.

Larkin took Rerval by the arm and tugged him back. 'Have a heart, lad. She's scared witless. I promised her we wouldn't hurt her.'

'Of course we won't hurt her,' said Caffran. 'We won't, ma'am.'

'Besides,' Larkin added, 'I don't see an old girl like this having the knack to disable a piece of Guard kit. Smash it, maybe. Lift the primary transmission circuit? I don't think so.'

'Who the feth is she?' Rerval whispered. 'Apart from being our ghost, I mean. Do you think she just came here to shelter?'

'Doesn't feel like that to me,' said Larkin. 'The way she cares about the place. Tidies stuff away, hangs up her coat. I think this house is hers. Her home.'

'But this whole area was evacuated years ago,' said Rerval. 'That's what the colonel told us. Why would she still be here?'

'Sometimes people don't want to leave,' said Larkin. 'Old, set in her ways, tied by memories to this place. Maybe she chose not to.'

'Then she could have been here for ages. Years.'

'Waiting for the invaders to come. Hoping they wouldn't,' Larkin murmured.

Caffran looked at the frail old woman. She was still immobile, placid. Her hair was silver, almost white, pinned back tightly with small metal clips. Her clothes were clean, but old and faded, and her little leather buckle-on shoes were worn. He could see the sole was coming away from one of them. The only reaction she made, every once in a while, was to wince and look round at any loud noise emanating from the drawing room. The crash of a glass breaking. A thump. Brostin's booming laugh.

We're invaders, he thought, invaders in her home.

'Why's her coat wet?' he asked suddenly.

'What?'

'If she's been hiding from us here, why's she been going outside? In the rain? And if she's been hiding, why hang her coat up where we can see it?'

Larkin frowned. 'I don't know. Maybe we should check around outside again when it gets light. The outhouse Ven mentioned. He said he thought someone had been sleeping out there.'

'Someone else?' asked Caffran.

'Maybe.'

'Should we tell Feygor about her?' Rerval asked.

'Feth, no! Not tonight. Not the state he's in. Do you want to scare her even more?'

Rerval considered Caffran's words. 'No,' he said. 'There must be some clue as to who she is. I'll nose around.'

'Okay,' said Caffran. 'Stay with her, Larks. I'll go tell Muril about her and advise her to keep her eyes peeled for any other houseguests.'

RERVAL AND CAFFRAN had both been gone for ten minutes, and Larkin had simply sat there in the kitchen with the old woman, listening to the rain and the spit of the stove. The wind was getting up again, and the thunder was rumbling closer.

Cuu was suddenly just standing there in the kitchen doorway. The old woman started, and Larkin looked up sharply.

'Hey, Tanith. Who's your girlfriend?' Cuu said. His eyes were hooded and he swayed slightly.

'Go back to your drinking, Cuu,' said Larkin softly.

'We got hungry. I came for some food. Where'd you get this old witch from?'

'She was hiding,' said Larkin.

'Hiding? In the house? Gak. What's she got to say for herself?'

'Nothing. Just go away.'

Cuu drunkenly flapped a hand at Larkin, his attention on the old woman. He leaned down, putting his leering face close to hers. She pulled away, avoiding eye contact.

'Stop it,' said Larkin.

'Who are you, witch? Eh? Speak up, I can't gakking hear you? Where the gak were you hiding? Eh?'

She drew back as far as the chair would allow.

'Back off, Cuu,' Larkin warned.

'Shut up, Tanith. Come on, you old witch! Who are you?' Cuu reached out and grabbed her roughly by one thin shoulder. She let out a little gasp of fear. 'Who the hell are you?'

Larkin leaned forward and grasped Cuu tightly by the wrist. He yanked Cuu's arm back, tearing his grip from the old woman's shoulder, and slowly rose to his feet, pushing the drunken Verghastite backwards.

'Get the hell off,' snapped Cuu, his attention switching entirely to Larkin. He fell back unsteadily, drink slowing his reactions, but quickly locked and pushed back. Larkin wasn't giving.

'Get your hand off me, Tanith,' Cuu growled.

'If you leave her alone.'

'Oooh, that's it. You've done it now, sure as sure.'

Intoxication made him telegraph the punch. Larkin dodged it easily, and pushed Cuu right back across the kitchen. He fell heavily against the dresser and several plates and pots fell off with a crash.

'You piece of shit,' Cuu said, reaching instinctively for his blade. But his kit was lying back in the drawing room. In the instant it took him to realise the dagger he was groping for wasn't there, Larkin had thrown a left hook that twisted Cuu's head round and dropped him to the floor. Cuu lay there, moaned, and spat bloody saliva onto the red-glazed tiles.

Larkin paused. He could do it now. He'd even have a cover story. He could fething well–

But the old woman was staring at him. Her hands were up over her head, protectively, though she was still sitting in the chair. He could see the glint of her eyes staring out between her gnarled fingers.

'Feth, it's okay!' said Larkin. 'He won't hurt you. I swear he won't!' He crossed to her and bent down, trying to calm her.

'Please, it's okay. It's really okay. I–'

He blacked out. There was a dull thump, like a muffled peal of thunder, and he blacked out.

He came to, sprawled face down across the table. The back of his head hurt really badly. His vision swam.

He tried to rise, but lost his balance and fell off the side of the table onto the floor.

The fall saved him. Cuu brought the iron skillet pan down for a second blow and hit the table where Larkin had just been crumpled. The pan exploded the cup and sprayed porcelain shards and tepid caffeine across the polished wood.

Larkin tried to crawl backwards away from Cuu, but the Verghastite came for him, swinging the pan again. It caught Larkin on the shoulder. He kicked out at Cuu's legs.

Cuu reached down and grabbed Larkin by the throat. With a snarl that flecked spittle out between his clenched teeth, Cuu hauled Larkin up and threw him against the side counter. He pinned Larkin with the flat of his forearm, and hit him with the pan again. Larkin squealed as he felt a rib go. Another savage blow and pain flared through his left elbow. But for that raised arm, the heavy pan would have mashed his face.

'You Tanith gak! You little shit! You stupid bastard!' Cuu rained down slurs and blows alike in a berserk fury.

Suddenly, Cuu shrieked and collapsed off Larkin, dropping the pan with a clang. The metal frame stock of a Mark III lasrifle had just smashed up between his legs from behind.

Cuu hit the floor, convulsing and choking, tears washing down his screwed up face. He fell in a foetal position, clutched at his groin and threw up.

Dripping with storm water, Muril turned her lasrifle round so that the muzzle was pointing at Cuu's temple.

'Any more from you, Cuu, any more, and I use this end on you instead.'

'What the feth's going on?' demanded Caffran pulling down his cape hood as he came in through the kitchen door behind Muril. The old woman made a sudden dash for the open door, but Caffran intercepted her gently and sat her back down. She didn't protest.

Muril helped Larkin up. He was shaking. One cheek was swelling and turning blue, and blood streamed from his nose. The back of his head had left more blood on the countertop.

Muril dragged out a chair and helped Larkin sit down.

'Cuu... Cuu was gonna hurt her–' he stammered.

Muril looked round at Caffran. 'Little bastard nearly beat Larkin to death. If we hadn't come back...'

Caffran looked down at Cuu, who was still curled up and weeping out jagged groans. Every few breaths, he retched again and added to the expanding pool of liquid vomit around his head.

'Feth,' Caffran murmured. He was reaching down to grab hold of Cuu when Feygor and Brostin stormed in. They were both very drunk, more obviously drunk than Cuu had been. Feygor was having trouble walking. They reeled to a halt and blinked repeatedly, trying to take in the scene before them and understand it.

'Where's the fething food, Lijah?' Feygor said.

'You want some food?' asked Caffran. 'I'll bring you some. Go back to the drawing room and I'll bring you some.'

His head swaying back and forth like his neck was rubber, Feygor frowned and made several vague pointing gestures around the room.

'What the feth?' he barked, his augmetic voice box coarse and indistinct as it tried to cope with his inebriated sounds. He looked at the old woman and tried to focus his eyes. 'Who the feth is this?'

'It's likely we're all guests of hers here, so show some respect,' Caffran said. 'She's old and she's scared.'

Feygor snorted. 'What's with Larks? And why's Cuu down?'

'Cuu was making trouble for the old lady,' Muril said. 'Larks tried to stop him and he went wild with a skillet.'

'We had to subdue him,' Caffran added, hoping to take a little heat off Muril if necessary.

'Cuu was hurting the old lady?' slurred Brostin. The idea seemed to offend him.

'He's drunk,' said Muril.

'No excuse,' said Brostin with great certainty.

'Who the feth is she?' Feygor wanted to know. He took a step forward, approaching her. Caffran stepped in and carefully steadied Feygor.

'She's the owner of the house,' he said. He didn't know that for sure, but it had a certain weight Feygor's addled brain might take in.

'Where'd she come from?'

'She was here all the time. Hiding.'

'Fething spy!' Feygor said, clapping his hands. The old woman jumped.

'No, sir.'

'I fething say so. Sneaking and hiding.'

'She was scared of us. Does she look like a Shadik agent?'

'Fethed if I know!' Feygor said. He stood straight and waggled a finger. 'Lock her up somewhere. Lock her up. I'll question her in the morning.'

'We can't lock her up,' Muril began.

'Lock her the feth up!' Feygor spluttered. 'Who's in charge here, bitch?'

Good question, Caffran thought.

Brostin tugged at Feygor's arm. 'You can't lock her up, Murt. Wouldn't be right. Not an old lady.'

"Kay, what then?'

'I'll look after her. I'll stay with her,' said Caffran. 'You can talk to her tomorrow.'

'All right,' Feygor said, satisfied. He wheeled around, unsteadily, and wandered into the pantry. They could hear the smash of breaking jars as he foraged for food.

Brostin stood for a moment, and then followed Feygor out.

'Feth,' murmured Caffran. He looked over at Muril, who shook her head. Caffran bent down and hauled Cuu towards the door. He threw the coughing Verghastite out into the rain.

'Sober up, you little swine!' he snarled after him. Cuu lay in the yard, whining like a canine in the beating rain.

When Caffran came back into the kitchen, he saw that the old lady was carefully picking up the objects that had fallen during the fight. Pans went back onto the dresser. Shards of china were picked up one by one.

'She just started doing that,' Muril said, dabbing disinfectant pads from her field kit to the back of Larkin's head.

Caffran watched. The old lady threw the broken cups into the kitchen waste, and then swept up the bits she couldn't pick up with a dustpan and brush. She took the skillet Cuu had used to beat Larkin and hung it back on its hook over the stove. Then she shuffled into the wash house and re-emerged with a mop.

Caffran stepped forward and took it from her. She gave it up without resistance. 'Let me do that,' he said, and started to clean Cuu's spew off the tiles.

He wouldn't watch her do that.

IT WAS WELL past midnight. The electrical storm had returned with a show of force even greater than the previous night. Rerval gave up his search of the upstairs. There was no sign of anything personal apart from the old furniture and bed-clothes. Wardrobes were mostly empty except for a few dry pomanders rolling about their floors. Just about every upstairs room was damp, some saturated, from the leaking roof. Trickles of water streamed down. The air stank of mildew and rotting linen.

He played his flashlight around the halls and the walls of the rooms. There were few pictures, but in places his light revealed the pale oblongs where pictures had once hung. There was an ormolu clock on the mantle of one bedroom. It had stopped at half past four. The gilt decoration showed two soldiers in plumed hats, standing either side of the face and supporting it with their hands.

He found a linen closet where the old, piled sheets were generally dry. There were a few items of kit and some hot-shot clips stacked in the corners. This was evidently where Larkin had chosen to make his lair.

Rerval left it alone.

He saw the attic hatch, and got a chair. Pushing up through the hatch, he shone his light around. The attic was swimming. Many tiles had gone. His beam picked out black, mouldering rafters, streams of rainwater and stacks of rotting junk. He decided not to waste his time.

He wandered back to the stairs. How had she lived here for so long? Alone? Had the isolation snapped her mind? Was that why she wouldn't speak?

He went down the stairs, avoiding the plinking pots and water catchers. Lightning flashed.

Lamp light was shining from the half-open drawing room door, and he could hear voices and the clink of glasses.

A paler light was coming from under the dining room door.

Rerval switched off his flashlight and drew his laspistol. He put his hand on the door knob and carefully opened the door.

A single candle was guttering in the middle of the long dining table, its twisting flame reflecting off the dark, varnished top.

Piet Gutes sat on his own halfway down, his head in his hands. There was a half-finished bottle of red wine next to him, and some pieces of paper spread out on the tabletop.

'Gutes?'

Gutes looked up. He was drunk, but that didn't completely explain the redness of his eyes.

'You all right, Piet?'

Gutes shrugged. 'Doesn't matter where you go,' he said, 'it always finds you.'

'What does?'

'The war. You think you're so far away it can't touch you, but it finds you anyway.'

Rerval sat down beside him. 'War's our life, you know that. First-and-Only.'

Gutes smiled bitterly. 'I'm tired,' he said.

'Get some sleep. We—'

'No, not like that. Tired. Tired of it all. When we got sent out here—'

'Aexe Cardinal?'

'No, Rerval. The woods. This mission. When we got sent out here, I was thankful. We might get a few days, leave the war behind. Get out from its embrace. And when Ven and Jajjo found this place... feth, it seemed like a little paradise. A little paradise, just for a day or two. I'm not greedy.'

'Sure.'

Gutes drummed his fingers on the table top and then took a swig of the wine. He offered the bottle to Rerval, and Rerval knocked back a sip himself.

'Everything's okay from far away,' Gutes said. 'I mean, when you get back far enough, nothing matters.'

'I suppose,' said Rerval, handing the bottle back to Gutes.

'I was far away when Finra died. And little Foona too.'

'Finra? Your wife?'

'No,' Gutes chuckled. 'My daughter. My wife died eighteen... no, nineteen years back. I raised Finra on my own, you know? Did a good job, I think. She was a beautiful girl. And Foona. A little darling, my first grandchild.'

Rerval hesitated. He didn't know what to say. It was ironic, he thought. I'm signals, a vox-officer. Communication is my speciality. But I have no idea what to say to this man.

'I wish I had pictures of them,' Gutes said. 'There was no time, when I signed up. It was last minute. We agreed she'd send some on via the Munitorium. She promised me a care package. Letters.'

'They didn't suffer, Piet,' Rerval said.

'No, I know that. Just a little flash and Tanith was dead. Bang, goodnight. Like I said, nothing matters if you're far enough away. You know that song? "Far away, up in the mountains"? Brin Milo plays it sometimes.'

'I know it.'

The candle flame fluttered and almost went out. Then it flared again, as wax dribbled from the lip. Thunder slammed above the percussion of rain outside.

'I always thought,' Gutes said, 'that she'd be the one getting the letter. My daughter, I mean. The one that comes in the vellum envelope. The one that says blah blah blah regret to inform you that your father, etc.'

'That letter,' Rerval nodded, taking another sip from the bottle.

'Turns out, it was the other way round. Except I didn't get any letter. Just saw a little flash from far away.'

'You should get some sleep,' Rerval said.

'I know. I know, Rerval.'

'Come on then.'

'Far away. That's what this place is. So I thought. A chance to be far away at last, just for a few days. But it doesn't matter where you go. It always finds you.'

He fumbled with the old papers in front of him and pushed them over towards Rerval. A letter sheet, brown with age, and its envelope. The letter was embossed with the crest of the Aexe Alliance.

Rerval read it.

'Feth, where did you find this?'

'In the rack, in the hall. It was there when we came in. I didn't pay it much heed before.'

The letterhead date told Rerval it had been sent nearly seventeen years before. It began: 'Dear Madam Pridny, on behalf of the General Staff Command of the Aexe Alliance, I regret to inform you that your son, Masim Pridny, corporal, was reported missing during action at Loncort earlier this week...'

'RAIN'S STOPPED,' MURIL said. A pre-dawn glow was spreading in through the kitchen windows.

The old woman was asleep, curled up on the bench seat. Larkin was sitting hunched at the table, nursing a glass of sacra. The bruises on his face were almost black, and Muril was worried about the wound on the back of his head.

Everyone else was long since asleep, except Caffran and Rerval, who were standing guard.

Muril got up and used a cloth to open the stove plate. She tossed some more logs in, and raked them around with the poker.

'You okay?' she asked.

'Yeah,' said Larkin. He was still studying the letter Rerval had shown them. 'Poor old girl, waiting all this time... seventeen years... waiting for her son...'

'You suppose that's why she didn't leave this place?'

'Yeah, I suppose. Waiting at home for a son who's never actually coming back.'

'Poor woman,' Muril said, looking over at the sleeping figure. She sat down opposite Larkin.

'Tell me about Cuu.'

'Cuu?'

'Lijah gakking Cuu. He nearly killed you, Larks. That wasn't about some old lady, was it?'

'He was drunk. He was hurting her.'

'Still... there's more to it than that, isn't there.'

Larkin shrugged. The gesture was painful. Muril wished they had Dorden around, or Curth, or even a corpsman, to check Larkin's ribs and elbow.

And his head.

'Don't know what you mean,' he said.

'What I mean,' she said, 'is that you and Cuu have a thing. Everyone knows it. Don't know when and why it started, but you have a thing.'

'A thing?'

'A feud.'

'Maybe.'

'For gak's sake, Larks! I could help you!'

'Help me? No, Muril, you don't want to help me. No one would want to get dragged into what I'm doing.'

'What are you doing? I mean, why the gak did you volunteer for this detail when you knew Cuu was part of it?'

Larkin smiled. He sipped his drink. Muril could see the blood blossoming in the clear liquor as he lowered the glass from his mouth.

'I mean… the two of you have a famous feud that everyone knows about. He treats you like crap. And here you are, signing up to join a squad that you know he's in too. You usually do your best to stay away from him, but now it's like you wanted to be close, you wanted to… oh gak!'

'Now you're getting it,' Larkin smiled.

Muril blanched. 'What the gak are you planning?'

'Nothing you need to know about. Forget it.'

'I will not, Hlaine! What is this about?'

'Payback,' he said.

'Payback? For what?'

'Doesn't matter. I should go relieve Caff.' He knocked back the drink and stood up.

'With your head? Are you sure?'

He sat back down, blinking, and felt the back of his skull with cautious fingers.

'Maybe not.'

'So tell me about payback.'

'You wouldn't understand.'

'Try me.'

Larkin smiled. 'You're a good girl, Muril.'

'So they say. Don't change the subject. Payback.'

'What can I tell you? What if I said I want to get even for the way Cuu has persecuted me since the day we first met? Would that be okay? He's made my life a misery, leant on me, beaten me down. Would that be enough?'

She shrugged. 'Probably. Cuu's a bastard. A predator. He bullies anyone he can. Caff hates him, you know? After that thing on Phantine. I know Gaunt got Cuu off, but Caff believes Cuu killed that woman. And Caff nearly went to the wall for it.'

'I got Caff off,' Larkin said. 'Me and Try. We got Caff's case dismissed and got Cuu sent up in his place. Bragg ratted on him. Then Gaunt got Cuu off on a technicality. Got him the lash rather than a firing squad. That's why he hates me. He blames me for the lashes. Me and Try.'

'So his hate is focused on you now Bragg is gone?'

'Kind of,' Larkin said, with a smile Muril didn't like the look of.

'So that's why you want–'

Larkin raised a finger. 'I never said that. What if I want payback on Cuu because I'm crazy? Everyone knows I'm crazy. Mad Larkin, you know the form.'

'Yeah, but–'

'I'm not right in the head. Everyone knows that. Maybe I want Cuu because I'm insane.'

'You're not insane.'

'Thanks, but the jury is still out. I don't care. Maybe I am crazy. Look out, Lijah Cuu.'

'What's the real reason?' she asked.

Larkin hesitated. He wanted to tell her, but he knew how the others treated him. Mad Larkin. Untrustworthy. Crazy. His head hurt.

'He killed Bragg,' he said simply.

'He what?'

'I can't prove it. Not even slightly. But from what he's said to me, he killed Bragg. For ratting on him. And now he wants me too. So I thought I'd cut to the chase and get in first.'

She stared at him. 'Really?'

'I believe it. I don't expect you to. In fact, I've probably just proved to you that I'm crazy after all.'

'No,' she said. She leaned forward towards him.

'Larks… tell Gaunt about it. Gaunt or Corbec or Daur. They'll help you. Don't do something you'll regret.'

'Like killing Cuu before he kills me? Too late. And it doesn't matter what Gaunt and Corbec and Daur believe. With what little I've got, their hands would be tied. Don't you think I've thought of that? It goes as it goes.'

He got up unsteadily and hefted his long-las. 'Thanks for smacking Cuu off me,' he said, 'but do me a favour. Forget this whole conversation. It'll be better that way.'

STARK DAWN LIGHT spread across the back lawns of the manse. Mist wisped up from the wet grass.

He caught the movement out of the corner of his eye. Not much, just a flicker of something. The vaguest flicker.

Caffran left his sentry post in the greenhouse and ran up the main back lawn. Daybreak birdsong rang around him. He reached one of the most distant sheds, and yanked open the door.

'Out! Now!' he barked, his lasrifle aimed inside.

The Aexegarian trooper was young and matted with filth. He had a dirty twist of beard. He came out into the open, blinking, his hands over his head.

'Don't hurt her,' he said. 'It wasn't her fault.'

'Shut up and get your hands on the wall!' Caffran snapped.

The trooper turned and spread against the side of the shed.

Caffran reached forward to pat him down. He kept his lasrifle at the man's back.

His vox crackled suddenly.

He backed off and adjusted his micro-bead's setting.

'Say again? Say again?' he called.

The vox buzzed again, and he heard a single word.

'Comeuppance.'

TWELVE
ANYWHERE BUT HERE

'So I'm a plucky soldier boy,
My country I hold dear,
Find me somewhere to fight for, sir,
Anywhere but here.'

– refrain of popular Aexegarian song

NINE MEN DEAD. Six injured. Three more sick with gas-related injuries caused by tears in their kit. Seventeen platoon was a mess. And Raglon knew it. Gaunt could tell the novice sergeant was badly shaken and terribly ashamed of himself. His first field office, and he'd ended up with less then fifty per cent of his platoon alive or able-bodied.

Gaunt's infiltration force moved up to occupy the ghastly ruins of the Santrebar Mill, and as the four platoons took station at windows and likely firepoints, Dorden co-opted half a dozen of them to help him deal with Raglon's wounded.

Two were close to death. Sicre and Mkwyl; there was no hope for them. Dorden called for Zweil.

It was getting on for 19.00 hours, and the day was beginning to fade. The dull bluster of the counter-push still rolled

240

across the wasteland towards them from the south, and the deep booming of the super-siege guns continued. Everything was still closed in and swaddled by the yellow gas vapour.

Just after the hour, it began to rain. The light changed, a soft blush across the low yellow sky. It reminded Golke of the way a brush wash could alter a watercolour. Painting had been his hobby, years before. He stood, looking out from one of the mill's low windows, almost admiring the view. It was stark and unlovely, but there was a quality to it. The dark, rusty ground, the off-white sky slowly saturating with blue-grey.

Weighed down with his battlefield mail, heavy coat and respirator, he felt distanced. This was the land he was fighting for, the land he had spent his adult life fighting for. As far as his eyes could see, there was nothing but the scarring of warfare. This wasn't the site of a battle, this was landscape transformed by the brute sorcery of relentless fighting. Stripped, burned, poisoned, malformed, killed.

He wondered why, then, he admired its eerie beauty. Surely it wasn't just the amateur painter in him making a trite aesthetic response. This was the Pocket, he told himself. The Seiberq Pocket. That murderous slab of country that had robbed him of his friends, his men and his health.

He'd emerged from this place a wreck, so dismayed by its horrors that he'd been receiving counselling from his physician ever since. The memories still lacerated his mind.

He tried to picture it living again. Ten, fifty years in the future, a hundred... whatever it might take. He tried to imagine the war over, and peace slowly restoring the rule of nature. Trees. Fields. Life of any kind.

Golke could imagine it, but the vision was not convincing. This, the ravaged vista before him, was the only truth.

He knew why it was important to him. The Pocket had haunted him for years, lurking in his nightmares and daydreams. And now he'd come back to face it. That's really why he had volunteered to assist Gaunt's mission. This was aversion therapy. He'd come back to face his daemons and deny them, exorcise them, banish them. He'd come back to recover something lost by his younger self. The Pocket was a hellhole, an unfeasibly ugly ruin. But already he could see some beauty in it.

He'd taken the first step. He'd looked upon the landscape of his nightmares and hadn't frozen in terror.

He could do this. He could break the Pocket just like it had once broken him.

Two months earlier, his aides had dragged him out for a night at the musical hall in Ongche. A popular touring show was in town, and they'd insisted he'd enjoy it. The gaudily-painted theatre had been packed with rowdy soldiers on furlough, but Golke had enjoyed the performance from one of the balcony-boxes. It had all been amusing enough, though the common troopers loved it as if it was the best thing ever. A conjuror, an acrobat troupe, a virtuoso viol player, a clown act with trained canines, singers, bandsmen, a rather feeble soprano. A famous comedian in a too-small hat who strutted the stage and made off-colour remarks about Shadik sexuality and hygiene to furious approval.

Then had come the girl, the little girl from Fichua, the top of the bill. This, his senior aide told him excitedly, was what the boys were all waiting for.

She didn't seem much, just a child in a hoop skirt and bodice. But her voice...

She sang three songs. They were funny and saucy and patriotic. The last was a ditty Golke had heard the men singing from time to time. An ironic piece about doing your bit in which the soldier assured his superiors he was willing to fight, but expressed the wish to do so somewhere safe. The chorus went something like 'I want to find a place to fight, anywhere but here.'

The crowd had gone mad. The little Fichuan girl had repeated the song as an encore. Flowers had been tossed onto the stage.

It had stayed with him. Golke had found himself humming it. 'Anywhere but here, your lordships, anywhere but here.' Three curtain calls and goodnight.

It was in his head now. The refrain went round and round. Anywhere but here.

He understood why the men, sentimental fools the lot of them, like all soldiers off-duty, loved it so. It was catchy and bright and funny. It voiced their secret desires. It let them laugh away their dearest and most hidden wishes.

The tune died away in his head. Staring out at the misery of the Pocket, it simply faded away. Golke could see through its reassuring lie.

This was where he wanted to be. This was where he needed to be.

Not anywhere but here.

Right here. And right now.

THE RAIN FELL harder, sizzling on the poisoned ground, gushing through the crippled drainage of the mill. It was so intense that within fifteen minutes the air had cleared and the sky had become greyer and bigger.

Dorden used his atmosphere sniffer and declared that the gas-level had dropped under advised limits.

Gratefully, the troopers began to unbuckle their hoods.

The open air was cold and damp, and retained the metallic scent of the gas, muddled with rot and soaked earth. Some of the men were so relieved to be out of their hoods, they started laughing and chatting. Gaunt got Beltayn to circuit the mill and relay orders for them to hold it down.

Zweil, his head bared again, said a blessing to the sky, and then went back to Sicre and Mkwyl. Both were dead, and he'd said last rites over both of them already. Now he repeated the duty. 'So they can hear me,' he told Dorden.

It was getting darker. Apart from drifting streams of artillery smoke, they could see for several kilometres. The sky was turning black, and the lights of the lines, both friend and foe, were visible. Over in the east, the false dawn of a flare barrage lit the landscape white. From the south came the flashes and glows of the counter-push. Beyond the eastern horizon, the great blinks of light from the super-siege guns backlit the land.

Overhead, in the dark, muddy blue, Gaunt could see stars, for the first time since he'd set foot on Aexe Cardinal. They were twinkling and blurred by the thinning smoke in the upper atmosphere, but he could make them out. Every now and then, a red or orange line scored the sky as rockets flew over. Part of the Peinforq Line – Sector 56, Gaunt guessed – began to strobe as it started off the night's barrage. They could hear the whine and squeal of shells in flight. Fires began to burn along the reciprocal edge of the Shadik lines.

Mortars pounded from somewhere. Feldkannone crumped.

Another night on the Front began.

'WHAT HAPPENED?' GAUNT asked. He led Raglon to a quieter corner of the mill ruin and sat him down. Raglon was strung out and shaking.

'I'm sorry, sir,' he said.

'What for?'

'For fething up so badly.'

'Skip it, sergeant. What happened last night?'

'We got pounced on. We were following a dead trench and we ran smack into enemy raiders. The fight didn't last long. But it was furious. Back and forth, almost single file. We gave a decent account, I think. They fell back and we moved north, dragging the wounded with us, hoping to join up with ten. We'd heard Criid had taken the mill.'

'And?'

Raglon sighed. 'I don't know how much we missed them by, but they'd already fallen back. The enemy had begun to shell. So we stayed put. It seemed like the right choice. I thought I could feasibly hold the mill, even cut to half strength.'

'Any contact in the night?'

'None, sir.'

Gaunt nodded. 'Did you leave any men behind, Raglon?'

'No, sir!'

'Then I think you did all right. You should stop beating yourself up.'

Raglon looked at Gaunt. 'I thought you'd take my pins right away, sir.'

'For what, Rags?'

'For fething up. For losing so many men.'

'One of my earliest actions, Rags. One of my first real command actions, you understand, I led a ten-man unit of Hyrkans into a forest ward on Folion. We had been told it had been cleared. It had not. I lost seven men. Seventy per cent losses. I hated myself for it, but I retained my rank. Oktar knew I'd just got myself into a bad place. It happens. It happens to all Guards, sooner or later. When you're in a position of authority, it seems to matter all the more. You did all right. You were just unlucky.'

Raglon nodded, but he still seemed unsettled. 'I just hate the responsibility—'

'Of the deaths?'

'And the mistake…'

Gaunt paused. 'Raglon, this is your first real test of command. Not the fight, not the actions afterwards. Truth is the test. If it all went off the way you say it did, fine. If you're covering for someone, then it's not. If you want to be an officer in my regiment, then you have to deal in the truth, right from the start. So… is there anything else you want to tell me?'

'I was in command, sir.'

'Yes, you were. So who fethed up?'

'I did. I was in command.'

'Sergeant, the mark of a good squad leader is that he or she recognises weaknesses and brings them to the attention of his commanding officer. Take it on the chin by all means. Feth knows, you'll have to live with the pain. But if there's a loose link, tell me now.'

Raglon sighed. 'I think we'd have run into the raiders anyway, although I'm told Scout Suth had advance warning. I had allowed myself to be spaced too far back in the file. As I understand it, Trooper Costin blew our cover.'

'How?'

'He was drinking on duty, sir. He gave away our position by failing to observe proper stealth discipline.'

Gaunt nodded and got to his feet.

'For the God-Emperor's sake, sir!' Raglon moaned. 'Don't!'

'Sergeant Adare, may the Emperor rest him, advised me of Costin's unguarded drinking last year. Adare should have come down on it. I should have come down on it. At the very least, I should have warned you about it when you took over seventeen. This is my fault, primarily, and then Adare's, long before it's yours. First and foremost, it's Costin's.'

'Sir…'

'Speak?'

'I only got half my platoon out of that trench. Please don't reduce the number of survivors.'

Gaunt put a hand on Raglon's shoulder. 'See to your duty and regret nothing. I'll see to mine. You'll make a first class platoon leader, Raglon.'

Gaunt walked through the mill. Mkoll hurried up to him.

'Sir?'

'In a moment, Mkoll.'

Gaunt reached the dingy alcove of rockcrete where Costin was lying. Dorden was changing the dressings of the trooper's shattered hand.

The doctor looked up, and recognised the grim set of Gaunt's face.

'No,' he said, rising. 'No. No way, Gaunt. Not now. He's half bled to death and I've spent the last twenty minutes saving his hand.'

'I'm sorry,' said Gaunt.

'Fething no! No, I said! I will not stand by and let you do this! Where the feth is your humanity? I respected you, Gaunt! I'd have followed you to the ends of the worlds, because you weren't like the others! That shit at the triage station… that I understood! I hated you for it, but I forgave you! But not this.'

'He confessed to you, then?'

'It all came out,' Dorden looked down at Costin. 'He told me about it. He's traumatised. Remorseful. Suicidal, probably.'

'Suicide is no option. His laxity caused the death of several Ghosts.'

'So what? You'll shoot him for it?'

'Yes,' said Ibram Gaunt.

Dorden stood in front of Costin. 'Through me, then. Go on, you bastard. Do it.'

Gaunt slid his bolt pistol from its holster. 'Stand aside, Doctor.'

'I will not. I fething well will not.'

'Stand aside, doctor, or I will have you stood aside.'

Dorden leaned in, standing on tip-toe so his eyes were level with Gaunt's. 'Shoot me,' he snarled. 'Go on. I'm defying your orders. If Costin deserves the bullet for breaking your orders, so do I. So, shoot me. Or have everyone know you as an inconstent leader… one rule for one, another for another.'

Gaunt didn't blink. He slowly raised the bolt pistol until the muzzle was pressing at Dorden's adam's apple.

'You're forcing an issue that shouldn't be forced, doctor. You are the backbone of the First, depended on by everyone. You are loved by the men. I consider myself lucky to count you as a friend. But if you choose to take a stand on this, I will shoot you. It is my duty. My duty to the Guard, to the Warmaster and to the God-Emperor of Mankind. I cannot make exceptions. Not Costin. Not you. Please, doctor… stand aside.'

'I will not.'

Gaunt raised the bolter a little so that Dorden was forced to tilt his head back.

'Please, doctor. Stand aside.'

'I will not.'

'We are mirrors, Tolin, you and me. Mirrors of war. I break them. You put them back together. For every gramme of your soul that wishes war would end, mine matches it tenfold. But until the killing ends, I won't back down from my duty. Don't make the next round I fire be the one that kills Tolin Dorden.'

'You really would shoot me,' Dorden marvelled softly, 'wouldn't you?'

'Yes.'

'Holy feth… then that just makes me want to stand here all the more.'

Gaunt's finger tightened on the trigger.

Tighter.

Tighter.

He turned away and lowered the weapon, clicking on the safety.

'Tolin,' he said quietly. 'You've just undermined me in front of my men. You've just weakened my authority. I'm glad to the bottom of my heart that I couldn't shoot you, because of our friendship. But I hope you're ready to cope with the consequences.'

'There won't be any consequences, Ibram,' Dorden said.

'Oh yes, there will,' said Gaunt. 'Oh, most certainly there will.'

* * *

MKOLL STOOD NEARBY, alarmed by the confrontation. For a minute, he'd thought Gaunt was going to ask him to step in and bundle Dorden away.

He should have known better. Gaunt would never involve another man in a personal fight.

But it was bad. There wasn't a trooper in the First who'd take a gun to Doc Dorden. The idea was criminal. Time would tell what Gaunt's loss of face would lead to.

The stand-off had shown Gaunt was human. Ironically, that wasn't necessarily a good thing. Even more ironically, most of the First probably knew it already.

GAUNT STOOD ALONE for a few minutes. Around the mill, troopers whispered to each other. The Colonel-Commissar suddenly turned and walked back towards Costin. A hush fell. Dorden looked up from treating another man and saw where Gaunt was heading. He rose, but Milo stopped him.

'Don't,' whispered Milo. 'Not all over again.'

'But–'

'Milo's right,' said Mkoll, stepping closer to the pair. 'Don't.'

Gaunt crouched down by Costin and took off his cap. He smoothed out the brim.

Costin lay against the pock-marked wall, fear overlaying the pain in his face.

'This is a regiment to be proud of, Costin,' Gaunt said finally.

'Yes, sir.'

'We stick up for one another. Look out for one another. That's the way we've always done it. It's the way I like it.'

'Yes, sir.'

'The doctor is my friend. We don't see eye to eye on some things, but that's the mark of friendship, isn't it? I think you deserve to be executed. Right here and now, because of your neglect. The doctor believes otherwise. I'm not about to shoot him. It turns out, in fact, I couldn't even if I thought it was the correct thing to do. So that puts me in a hard place. I have to be fair. Even-handed. If I don't shoot him for breaking orders, I can't very well shoot you for the same, can I? So you should consider yourself lucky.'

'I do, sir.'

'You should also know I hold you in the deepest contempt for what you did. I can never trust you. Your comrades can never trust you. Many, in fact, may hate you for this. You better watch your back.'

'Yes, sir.'

Gaunt put his cap back on. 'Consider this your first and only chance. Clean up your act. From this moment onwards. Become the model of the perfect trooper. Prove Dorden right. If I see you take another drink, *ever*, or if I learn from others that you have, on duty or off, I will come down on you with the fury of a righteous god. It's all up to you.'

'Sir?'

'What?'

'I'm... I'm sorry. Truly sorry.'

Gaunt got to his feet. 'Words, Costin. Just words. Actions speak louder. Don't tell me you're sorry. *Be* sorry.'

GOOD ADVICE, GAUNT mused to himself as he rejoined Mkoll. Deeds not words. Time was getting on and they were in danger of losing the lead they'd gained earlier. Either they moved on the Shadik lines now, or packed it in.

Gaunt called Golke, Beltayn and the platoon leaders to join them.

'I estimate from the light flashes the target guns are about seven kilometres away, sir,' Mkoll said. 'North-east. It could be more, given their range, but their firing lights are brighter than the last time I saw them so they've like as not moved up.'

'They're heavy. Rail-mounted. Do the Shadik have tracks in that area, count?'

Golke shrugged. 'There was a rail line up the east side of the Naeme Valley, years ago, but these days? No one from the Alliance has seen past the Shadik front in decades. Even our aerial obs is limited. Of course, they may well have purpose-built something.'

'So how do we get there?' Gaunt said, inviting opinions.

'It's straight across no-man's-land,' said Domor. 'About a kilometre and a half from here. There's some decent cover apart from the last few hundred metres. We'd have to go slow, the Ghost way.'

'What about this dugout, Criid?' Gaunt asked.

She walked them to the back of the mill and showed them the pile of blast-collapsed rubble that marked the tunnel mouth. 'I've every reason to think this runs right back to their lines,' she said. 'A covered arterial route for getting obs patrols back and forth from the mill. I'd have checked it if there'd been time last night, but there wasn't, so I sealed it.'

'Something Raglon and his boys are grateful for, no doubt. You used a single tube?'

'Yes sir.'

'So, if we clear this opening, the rest of the run should be sound?'

'They'll have it guarded,' Golke said. 'They may well even be trying to clear it now.'

Mkoll shook his head. 'I can't hear anything. No sounds of picks or shovels. I think they've just assumed we hold the mill now. Either that, or they haven't had time to detail sappers in.'

'If we go that way, we can be on them a lot quicker,' Gaunt mused. 'It's going to get nasty at the far end, whichever way we go. I think I'd rather come up through a guarded tunnel and take my chances. The alternative, as Domor said, is a run at the lines, and that could get messy.'

'We'd still have to clear it,' said Golke.

Gaunt smiled. 'An opportunity for the Verghastite element of the First to shine. Arcuda... round up every man you can find who used to be a miner or an ore worker. We need six or seven. Any more and they'll be getting in each other's way. Move Dremmond and Lubba in to cover them. We'll flame the hole the moment anything moves.'

Arcuda nodded and hurried off.

Gaunt looked at the rest of them. 'Once we go, we'll have to work to fluid plans. This is going to be hit and run. Opportunistic. We're going to need everyone ready to improvise. Best case, we find these weapons and throw a rod in their spokes. Worst case, we simply find them and relay their precise location back to the Alliance. Everyone clear on that? Minimum result is locate. Any questions?'

'What about the wounded?' asked Mkoll. There were seven men from seventeen unfit to move.

'They stay here. Zweil stays with them, along with a backstop team. I'll select it. Anything else?'

'One thing that might be useful, sir,' said Beltayn. 'I've been monitoring vox traffic. About five minutes ago, the Alliance distributed the signal "rogue behj".'

'By which they mean?'

'There's another assault due,' said Golke. 'The counter-push must have produced results in the 57th. GSC must have decided to capitalise on that, and send out a second wave. What was the qualifying code, Beltayn?'

'Eleven one decimal two, sir.'

Golke nodded, impressed. 'They're coming on force. Right across 57th and 58th. We can expect a serious bombardment to start with, and then skirmishers followed by main assault. This part of the front is going to be lively tonight.'

'Works in our favour,' said Gaunt. 'Confusion, line assault. We couldn't want for better distractions. And being underground during the bombardment can't hurt either.'

'Unless a stray shell brings the roof down,' muttered Criid. Her pessimism made Gaunt laugh.

'Let's get set,' he told them. 'The clock's running. I want to be coming up on the Shadik lines during or after the first assault. Then we play it as it comes.'

ARCUDA HAD ROUNDED up six Verghastites with mine experience: Trillo, Ezlan, Gunsfeld, Subeno, Pozetine and, of course, Kolea. Stripped down, they got to work with their nine-seventies and their bare hands. Other troops were brought in to form chains and clear the rubble the Verghastites were digging out. Lubba and Dremmond, their flamers ready, stood by to hose the opening if anything stirred.

Gaunt stood and watched the work for a while. He was fascinated by Gol Kolea. Criid had had to explain to Kolea what was needed, because his mind lacked even the most basic memories of his long years as a miner in Number Seventeen Deep Working, Vervunhive. But his body had not forgotten the skills. He set to work, relentless, inexhaustible, clearing the rubble and dirt with expert efficiency. He wasn't just a powerful man mucking in, he knew what he was doing. He was able to advise on clearance and support measures. He set up the work chain so it moved effectively.

Except he didn't know what he was doing. It was all automatic. The physical memory of mining practices informed his limbs. His eyes were vacant.

Gaunt considered that of all the men the First had lost, Kolea was the one to be most dearly mourned. A superb soldier. A fine leader. If it hadn't been for Ouranberg, Kolea might have made serious rank in the Ghosts.

Most of all, Gaunt missed Kolea's quiet, insightful character.

When men died, you simply mourned their absence. The lack of them. You missed their presence. He could think of many like that: Baffels, Adare, Doyl, Cluggan, Maroy, Cocoer, Rilke, Lerod, Hasker, Baru, Blane, Bragg...

God-Emperor! That was just scratching the surface.

But with Kolea it was worse. He was still there, in body, in voice. A constant reminder of the warrior they'd lost.

Gaunt walked back from the tunnel mouth and found Milo.

'Got a duty for you,' he said.

'Ready and willing, sir,' said Milo.

'I want you to hold this mill. Zweil's staying, and the wounded need looking after. I also want a team here in case we come back in a hurry. You and four men. You've the command, so you pick.'

Milo looked crestfallen. He was clearly disappointed not to be advancing with the main mission.

'Isn't there someone better suited for the job, sir?' he asked. 'Like?'

'Arcuda? Raglon? They've both got rank. And they're–'

'They're what, Milo?'

Inexperienced, Milo wanted to say. 'Good choices,' he said, uncertainly.

Gaunt sighed and nodded. Milo had turned out to be a first class soldier, with a real promise of leadership qualities, despite his age. Either of the suggestions – Arcuda, green and nervous, and Raglon, shaken and tired – would make more sense. Indeed, Gaunt knew he'd rather have Milo in his fireteam than either of the sergeants.

There was another reason for his choice, one that had been nagging at him for days. He wanted to tell Milo about the old

Sororitas woman in the forgotten woodland chapel, but every time he turned it over in his mind, it sounded stupid. He didn't really even believe it himself.

She'd said Milo was important. Not here, important elsewhere. Then again, she'd been barking mad.

If, he acknowledged to himself, she'd even been there at all. That whole incident had taken on a very dreamlike quality in his head.

But Ibram Gaunt had been alive long enough to know that the galaxy moved in ways far stranger than he could ever divine. His whole life had been bisected and intercut with mysterious truths and consequences. Coincidences. Destinies. Truths that didn't seem to be truths until years afterwards.

He could not risk it. He could not risk Milo.

'I want you to do it,' he said. 'I trust you. Think of it as a test.'

'A test, sir?'

'Maroy's dead, Milo. Sixteen platoon needs a new sergeant. I'm considering you for that. Get on with your duty, and I'll consider you more seriously. Pick your four.'

Milo shrugged. He was quite taken aback by the prospect of a promotion and a command. At Vervunhive, it had been a toss up between Milo and Baffels, and Gaunt had given the command to Baffels on the basis of age and experience. Milo was so very young. But war had aged him since then. So had experience. Gaunt knew that if he offered the rank to Milo now, it wouldn't be turned down. He wasn't a boy any more. Vervunhive, Hagia, Phantine and Aexe Cardinal had turned him into a soldier.

'So?' said Gaunt. 'Your four?'

'I'll need a sniper, Nessa.' That made sense. Milo and Nessa had formed a good bond during the Ouranberg raid. 'A flamer to cover the tunnel. Dremmond. Beyond that… I dunno. Mosark? Mkillian?'

'You've got them. Do me proud. If we're not back by dawn, retreat towards the line if you can. Identifier from me is "piper", challenge is "boy". Failing that, one long tap and two short ones. Make sure it's not us before you get Dremmond to roast the tunnel.'

Milo nodded.

'Watch Zweil. He can be a handful. Consider yourself in receipt of the brevet rank of sergeant.'

'Thank you, sir.'

Gaunt smiled and saluted Milo. Milo returned the gesture.

'You've come a long way from Tanith Magna, Brin. Be proud of yourself.'

'I am, sir.'

THE HOLE WAS a dark, sinister space.

'Clear?' hissed Gaunt.

Two micro-bead taps from Mkoll said yes.

'Advance,' Gaunt said.

The infiltration team filed quickly into the dugout run. Mkoll and Domor had the lead, followed by Lubba and Hwlan. Gaunt was right behind them with Bonin.

INITIALLY, THE EARTH-DUG tunnel dropped away rather sharply. The floor was a congealed mass of soil-waste. But after about ten metres, it levelled out and its nature changed. Rather than earth-cut walls, the tunnel was made of mouldering stone, old, but well-laid. It reminded Gaunt of a storm-drain or a sewer.

It was far too elaborate and significant to have been built to cover Republican troops out to the forward observation point at the mill. This was ancient. Gaunt realised it was most likely some part of the mill's old water-system, a drain or possibly a feeder sluice. The Shadik had unearthed it and put it to use.

It was quite narrow and low, and the wet, slime-covered stones were treacherous, especially in the near-pitch darkness. They dared not use lamp packs for fear of advertising their approach. That was why he'd put Sergeant Domor in the lead. 'Shoggy' Domor had been blinded on Menazoid Epsilon, and his eyes had been replaced with bulky augmetic optics, which made him resemble a certain bug-eyed amphibean and thus earned him his nickname. Domor adjusted his optics to night-vision mode.

After a further twenty metres, the tunnel dropped again, this time suddenly, and they had to wade through knee-deep water. There was greater damage to the stone work – evidently this part of the tunnel had subsided or dropped badly.

Gaunt looked back down the file. His eyes had adjusted to the gloom, as much as they were going to, anyway. He could see grey-black shapes moving against the darkness, and hear the occasional splash or clink of rock. It was hard effort, and the men were trying to keep their breathing quiet. It was also hot and airless, and everyone was sweating freely.

About three hundred metres along, Mkoll called a stop. A secondary tunnel opened up to the left, also stone-built, and water gurgled out of it. They waited while the master scout checked it. A minute. Two. Three.

Then a double-tap on the micro-bead link.

Gaunt risked vocals, keeping his voice low. 'One, four?'

'Four, one,' Mkoll responded, barely audible. 'A side chute. Dead-end. It's collapsed.'

They moved on. In the space of the next two hundred metres, three more side chutes opened. The party waited as Mkoll checked each one scrupulously.

A few minutes more, and Gaunt felt cool air moving past his face. He could smell water. In another step or two, he could hear it. A torrent, fast moving.

The tunnel opened out. Gaunt couldn't see enough, but he could feel the space in front of him.

'Some kind of vault,' Domor reported over the link. There was a sudden scrabbling noise and a low curse.

'Report!' Gaunt said.

'Lubba nearly slipped over. Sir, I think we're going to have to risk lamps.'

'How clear is the way ahead?'

'No sign of contact. Wait.'

They heard soft boot-steps on stone, a wooden creak, and then it fell silent for a few seconds.

'Domor?'

'It's clear. I think we should use lamps. Someone's gonna fall, otherwise.'

'Your call, Domor, you're in the best position to decide.'

'Do it, sir.'

'Two lamps only. Hwlan. Bonin.'

The scouts switched on their packs. The pools of light they cast seemed alarmingly bright. They illuminated the chamber, and Gaunt realised at once that Domor had been correct.

The tunnel they had been following came out halfway up the stone walls of a deep cistern area. It dropped away below them. Narrow, rail-less stone steps led down from the tunnel to a stone buttress where lengths of duckboards had been placed as a bridge across the gap over onto a matching buttress. From there, another flight of steps led up to the resumption of the tunnel. Domor was on the far side, crouched at the top of the opposite steps, watching the way ahead.

There was nothing to hold on to, and every surface was dripping with slime. Without the light, a good many of them would have lost their footing on either set of steps, and the narrow duckboard bridge would have been impossible to negotiate.

Far below them, water thundered through the bottom of the stone vault.

Holding his lamp, Hwlan went across the bridge. He stood at the foot of the opposite steps to light the way. Bonin waited with his own lamp at the bottom of the near flight.

Gaunt and Mkoll went across with Lubba. Gaunt turned back and signalled the troop to follow, single file. He wanted Bonin and Hwlan free to move up at the front. He instructed every third man to stop and take over the job of holding the lamps. The last man through would collect in the lamps and turn them off.

THEY'D BEEN UNDERGROUND for about fifty minutes, and had advanced what Mkoll reckoned was about two-thirds of a kilometre, when the barrage began.

It sounded like a distant hammering at first, then rose in volume and tempo until they could actually feel the earth around them vibrating. Gaunt calculated there was between eight and twelve metres of solid earth above their heads, but still everything jarred. Spoil and water squirted and dribbled out of the roof, shaken loose or forced out through ground distortions. Every once in a while, a whole stone block popped out of the wall and fell on the floor.

Agitation rose. Gaunt could feel it. It wasn't hard to imagine what would happen if a heavy shell scored a direct hit above them. Crushed, suffocated, buried alive. The tunnel could cave or collapse. They'd already seen it had done that further back.

Even the most confident Ghosts wanted to be out of this potential grave. They wanted to be taking their chances in the open. It didn't matter that they were probably at less risk from the shelling and the shrapnel down in the drain.

Indeed, Gaunt felt his own pulse rate rising steeply. Claustrophobia had never been a private fear of his, but down here, like this…

The earth shook with an especially violent jar. Someone back in the line moaned in fear.

'Quiet!' Gaunt hissed.

Then he realised how stupid the comment had been. If it was loud down here, it would be deafening above ground. The shelling would cover their noise. They could advance now at double time, not worrying about stealth.

He issued the order and they started to move, almost fleeing down the line of the tunnel. The deluge of explosives continued to roar above them.

'Hold it!' Mkoll cried.

They skidded up. 'What is it?' Gaunt asked.

'You hear that?'

Gaunt couldn't hear anything above the shell blasts and the panting of the men. 'What?'

'A scratching noise. A rattling…'

'Sacred feth!' Domor suddenly cried out. He could see further than any of them. He could see what was coming.

'Vermin!' he said in horror. 'A swarm of vermin, coming this way! Oh God-Emperor!'

'Sir?' urged Lubba, slightly frantic. He had his flamer ready.

'No,' said Gaunt. The shelling might be covering their advance, but sustained flamer-bursts would be an insane risk to take. 'Stand your ground!' Gaunt said. 'They're fleeing the shelling. Just grin and bear it. That's an order.'

The rats hit them.

A river of squealing, matted bodies, surging in a tide back along the tunnel, filling the floor space to shin-depth, some scampering along the walls. Gaunt felt them collide with his legs, rocking him back, and then pouring around and under him. Men cried out. The noise and stench of the living river was atrocious. The writhing pressure of the rats' bodies was even worse.

Frantic, seeking cover in the deeper drains, the rats clawed and bit as they swept past. Gaunt had to steady his hands against the tunnel wall to prevent himself being knocked over. He felt sharp needle-bites on his shins and calves.

There was a scream, and frantic activity behind him. Harjeon had been carried over, and had virtually disappeared into the streaming mass of black bodies.

Criid and Livara struggled and swore, trying to get him up again.

We're probably all dead, Gaunt thought to himself. All of us infected with the multitude of filthy plagues and infections these vile things carry. Golden throne! Of all the things that I imagined might end my service to the Imperium, it was never rats.

As suddenly as it had begun, the vermin tide stopped. A last few squeaking things scuttled by in the gloom. Gaunt heard men stamping at them.

'Report!' he said.

There were general moans and comments of loathing. Not a single member of the mission had avoided bites or tears. Harjeon was covered in them, and started shaking and vomiting in loathing.

'They got on my face... in my mouth–' he wailed.

'Shut him up, Criid.'

'Yes, sir.'

'Let's move.'

THE SOUNDS OF the shelling grew louder, but not because they were closer. There was a faint, cold light ahead, and the noise of the barrage was being carried back along to them from the tunnel mouth.

Just a hundred metres to go.

Gaunt ordered Mkoll, Bonin and Hwlan forward.

'Ready order,' he said to the rest. 'Straight silver. Let's keep the surprise on our side as long as possible.'

Two taps.

'Forward,' he said.

UP AHEAD, THE three scouts emerged into the open air. It was cold and foggy from the shelling, and the shock-flashes of blasts backlit the misted air. The sound of the barrage was deafening: whooping shell-falls, some high-pitched, some low and basso, others still oddly melodic and expressive. Most detonations were huge and so loud they shook the diaphragm. Others made hotter, flatter sounds. Some made no sound at all, just a flash and a quake of the ground. After every single one there was a surging, pattering hush, like breakers on a shingle beach, as soil and shrapnel rained down.

Finding their way by the strobing flicker of the impacts, Mkoll, Bonin and Hwlan scurried out of the tunnel mouth, heads down. There was a sandbagged revetment and a guard point at the Shadik end of the tunnel, but it was unmanned. The guards had fled for cover.

The scouts found themselves in a deep bay off the main fire trench. They fanned out to the exit, and then ducked back as three Shadik troopers ran past, boots clumping the duck-boards. These disappeared, and then two more came by, carrying a screaming man on a stretcher. They too vanished into the glowing smoke.

Mkoll signalled the other two up with him. They emerged into the fire trench proper. It was deeper and better laid than the Alliance trenches, with a wider firestep and a back-slanted parapet of rockcrete blocks. The trench, as far as they could see, which was to the next traverse, was empty.

'Move up,' Mkoll said.

A moment later, five Shadik troopers, running hell for leather, appeared round the traverse to their left. They didn't seem to register the Tanith until the last moment.

The scouts didn't give them a chance to react. Mkoll brought down the first one, sliding his silver knife through gas-mask and windpipe. Hwlan skewered another in the sternum and then propelled himself and the corpse into a third.

Bonin crashed his rifle-butt into the belly of the enemy soldier nearest him, and sent him tumbling away, winded, then put his weight into a stinging sidekick that snapped the fifth trooper's neck and dropped him abruptly onto the duckboards. Bonin leapt over him, and quickly killed the winded man with his bare hands.

Hwlan tried to make a clean kill of the last trooper, but the fether was struggling hard. The Tanith man got his lasrifle braced across the man's neck and wrenched it around, twisting the helmeted skull down hard against the trench floor.

Five men dealt with in just a few seconds.

They were dragging the bodies into cover behind the camonets of a funk hole as Gaunt led the first of the main party into the fire trench.

'Which way?' Gaunt asked.

Mkoll pointed left.

'Lead off with Hwlan,' Gaunt told him. He turned to Bonin. 'Set here with Oflyn, and take up the rear of the file. Stay in close contact.'

'Sir,' nodded Bonin.

The party moved off quickly behind Mkoll and Hwlan. Two scouts at the head and two at the rear was the best insurance Gaunt could muster.

Beyond the second traverse they came to, a Shadik fireteam was trying to set up a pair of autocannons at the parapet. Nine men, all told.

Mkoll and Hwlan came at them from behind, knives out. Gaunt followed them, drawing his power sword, along with Criid, Ezlan and LaSalle. Brutal killing followed. One of the Shadik got a shot off, but Gaunt hoped its sound would be drowned by the barrage. He decapitated a man with his sword, and then impaled another. Nothing stopped his ancient blade, not mail-armour, not battle-plate, not leather and certainly not flesh.

Criid finished off the last man, and looked up at Gaunt.

The shelling had just suddenly ceased.

That meant the ground attack was coming. And it also meant that the Shadik would be streaming back out of their bunkers and shelters to man the step and repel.

THIRTEEN
CORPSE LIGHT

*'Sometimes, y'know, I really miss my slum.
Times like this, for instance.'*

– Flame-Trooper Lubba

FIFTEEN REGIMENTS OF Alliance troops assaulted the line in the wake of the barrage. A wave attack, welling up from the smoke-skeined darkness of no-man's-land. The twenty-kilometre stretch of line had been lit up for half an hour by the salvos of the bombardment. After a moment's eerie silence, it lit up again. Small-arms. Machine guns. Grenades. Flamers. From the air, the wide band of massive light bursts reduced to a thinner, fizzling line of fire.

It was the most significant attack mounted on the Shadik line in eighteen months. An offensive, the officers of the GSC were calling it back in the safety of the rear-line bunkers. Lyntor-Sewq and Martane had been prepping for it since Lyntor-Sewq's promotion to supreme commander. Lyntor-Sewq had dearly wanted to make his mark early, and prove to the high sezar how lax his predecessor, Count Golke, had been in his accomplishments. It was all part of a

greater strategy that incorporated the northern push through
Gibsgatte, where the supreme commander had invested the
bulk of his Imperial Guard armour. The idea was to sucker
punch Shadik by a northern thrust and then take him hard
in the belly at the Pocket and Bassin-on-Naeme. Lyntor-
Sewq's overall scheme was to divert the enemy's strengths to
the north and retake the river valley, establishing a new front
he called the Frergarten Line before winter set in. If successful, the Peinforq Line would become obsolete for the first
time in twenty-six years.

Over winter, the new line could be reinforced using
Alliance troops, and be ready by spring not only to hold
against the inevitable counter-push, but also to launch an
invasion of the Southern Republic, in concerted effort with
the Kottmark armies on the Ostlund Line.

It was an over-ambitious scheme, typical of a new commander trying to be emphatic and break the deadlock
apparently imposed by his predecessor. If Golke had been
privy to the planning meetings, he'd have been able to tell
Lyntor-Sewq frankly that the same thing had been tried
before, three times, in point of fact. The 'Oust-and-Out' strategy was an old one, and it had never worked.

If Ibram Gaunt had been privy to the planning meetings,
his comments would have been earthier still. Lyntor-Sewq
was playing the war like a game of regicide. The first thing a
commander learns that's of any use at all is that army groups
do not behave like playing pieces. They don't obey set rules,
they don't have preset 'moves'. Often a strong group signally
fails to do what was expected of it. Often, too, a 'weak' piece
can win the game by being used cleverly.

Unfortunately, neither officer was present at the meetings.
By the time it was getting too late to advise Lyntor-Sewq dif-
ferently, both Gaunt and Golke, the latter by choice, were at
the sharp end of things.

Van Voytz was at the meetings, most of them anyway. His
counselling efforts were completely eclipsed by the determi-
nation of the new supreme commander. When, months later,
Van Voytz finally withdrew from Aexe Cardinal, he would
come to regard his time there as the most frustrating and
impotent of his career.

Most GSC staffers believed that this particular night had been chosen to launch the offensive because of the opening the counter-strike at 57th had provided. Its success had jibed in a timely way with the frontal press at Gibsgatte. This was only partially true.

Though Gaunt never learned the truth, the offensive had been launched because of Redjacq Ankre. Discovering, from logged notes, that the First was infiltrating that night, he'd persuaded Martane to put the call in. Ankre was a proud man. His pride would eventually cost him his life, many years later. He hated the idea that the Tanith could have found an opening, and he used that hate to fuel his persuasive powers. If the stealthers of the First could break the Shadik line, then so could the Alliance ground forces. Ankre was actually afraid that the off-worlders of the Guard might actually achieve something that the Alliance had failed to do. He could not stomach the idea.

He personified the emotion-led failing of the Alliance top brass, a failing that had prolonged this war by decades. As with all efforts of such scale, his failing went unnoticed in the general scheme of things.

Almost three thousand Alliance troops fell casualty on the line assault that night. No figure, not even an estimation, was made for the Shadik forces. At one stretch of the line, one hundred and seventy-eight men of the Genswick Foot, including Lieutenant Fevrierson, became encumbered in lines of wire and were slaughtered by machine guns. At another section, no more than fifty metres long, three hundred Fichuan infantrymen died in the storm charge. The trench filled up, level with the surrounding terrain, packed with bodies so deeply the Shadik were forced to fall back and hold a reserve trench. Trench mortars killed sixty men of the Meuport Fifth as they came towards the parapet and were illuminated by starshells sent up by a nearby Brunsgatte unit who had become disoriented. The surviving men of the Meuport Fifth later took the fire trench, held it for an hour, lost it again and then retook it before dawn. The action entered their regimental legend.

At the northern tip of the assault, a detachment of struthid cavalry overran the held position under cover of autocannons, and stormed the main reserve trench. Then a counter-strike of gas shells and nail grenades broke their sturdy advance and left them dead and dying. Hussars, individually untouched, lay twitching and screaming in the foggy dark, sharing through the mind-links the death-throes of their wounded mounts. Alliance troopers advancing through the area started to mercy kill the birds, and then found themselves, in tearful desperation, mercy killing the hussars too.

They could not bear the screams.

The Kottstadt Wyverns, under Major Benedice, assaulted, took and held a kilometre stretch of fire trench, and then storm-fought their way back down the communication alleys to secure a line of gun-pits. South of them, a brigade of Mittel Aexe dragoons, the Seventh Ghrennes or 'Steeplers', did likewise, and then tried to spike the guns and destroy their munitions. Ninety-three men were incinerated when a high explosive dump was enthusiastically flamed, blowing a hole in the earth two hundred metres in diameter. The rest of them, along with a fair number of Wyverns, subsequently died in the clouds of toxic gas that spewed from storage pits ruptured by the main blast.

All the while, set far back, the Shadik super-siege guns continued to bombard. Their immense shells broke shield umbrellas on the Peinforq Line, and obliterated an ammunition dump, a command bunker, nineteen artillery stations – including five heavy howitzer mounts – a sector infirmary and a reserve trench full of young, conscripted Fichuans who thought they'd managed to skip the war for a night.

Some of the massive shells even struck Peinforq itself. The Manorial House was destroyed, and the abattoir, along with the burial chapel, two cafés, and a street of billet-housing full of Krassian troopers.

Despite the monumental losses, the Alliance offensive didn't lose momentum that night, or the day after. Lyntor-Sewq, determined to press for the victory he saw beckoning, deployed greater and greater numbers into the push until it ran out of steam on the fourth day and he conceded defeat.

But for Gaunt's mission, that was in the unknowable future. By midnight on that first night of offensive, they were a kilometre inside the Shadik lines, following a supply trench.

All hell was breaking loose behind them at the Shadik front, lighting up the sky and filling the valley with smoke fumes.

But they were pushing forward, silent, relentless, into the depths of the enemy fortifications.

CORPSE LIGHT BROKE above them, white and pale. More flares. The roar of the battle was distant and muffled. They'd just slaughtered twelve Shadik infantrymen in their fifth skirmish of the night. The First had suffered no losses so far, but Gaunt wondered how much longer they would be able to work with blades alone.

The sound of the siege guns was deafening now, even though they were still several kilometres away. The ground vibrated, not from impacts but from firing.

'I'd say there were six guns at least,' Mkoll told Gaunt. 'I've been counting the flashes and the rhythm.'

'Seven,' said Bonin. 'Definitely seven.'

'If Bonin says seven, seven it is,' said Mkoll. 'He's got an ear for these things.'

'How far?' asked Gaunt.

'Well, it's not like we can't find them,' said Mkoll, pointing to the superheated flashes of discharge lighting up the north-eastern sky.

'Yes,' said Gaunt, 'But there's no sense of scale. How far?'

'Two, maybe three kilometres.'

Gaunt sighed and looked around. The supply trench system they were in was dark and quiet. Everything had been pushed towards the front.

Once in a while, Shadik personnel appeared, and were knifed to silence by the Ghosts.

But Gaunt knew they'd been lucky. All it would take was for them to meet an advancing brigade head on.

Then it would come down to firepower. Firepower and numbers.

If only they had a decent fix on the guns. Something concrete to take back with them. He'd told them all that locate was the minimum requirement of the mission.

Two or three kilometres to the north-east wasn't precise enough.

Round the next traverse of the supply trench, they found themselves in a deep ammunition corridor laid with track. It was twice the width of the infantry burrows, and ran north-east, dead straight.

The feeder roads for the big guns. Wide enough to take the girth of the shells on munition trains.

They were closing on it.

'Fan out and follow,' Gaunt ordered, and dropped his team into the bottom of the wide, man-made gulley.

A rifle cracked, twice. Trooper Sekko convulsed and fell.

Gaunt looked back and saw Shadik elements emerging from the gloom, weapons blazing. The Ghosts returned fire, lasguns cracking. Lubba spat fire down the wide space of the ammunition corridor.

The game was up. They'd been rumbled.

FOURTEEN
THE FIRST STAND

'This one's for Try.'

– Hlaine Larkin

'WHAT DOES IT mean?' Feygor asked, angry.

'It means trouble,' said Caffran.

'What sort of trouble?' Feygor snapped.

'I don't know! I agreed the word with Ven before he left. If he found trouble, that was the signal: "Comeuppance". I don't even know if it was him who sent it or Jajjo.'

'Anything else? Anything more?' Feygor asked. Rerval looked up from the micro-bead set he'd been playing with. 'Nothing. Not enough gain. Now, if my main set was working–'

'Feth take your main set,' Feygor replied. He sat down at the kitchen table and drummed his fingers in agitation. 'Define trouble,' he said, looking at Caffran.

'Ven wasn't specific. It could mean they've run into enemy scouts, a patrol… maybe brigands… maybe Jajjo's fallen and broken a leg… or it could be there's an entire army group moving this way.'

'Next time you agree on a code word, you fether, make sure you know what it means!'

Caffran looked Feygor in the eyes. 'At least I bothered to check with him before he left. You just let him walk out of here.'

'Shut your damn mouth,' Feygor growled. He looked round at the others. They were all watching the exchange. 'Pack your kits. We're leaving.'

'What?' cried Caffran.

'You heard me! We've no idea what's coming. There's eight of us here. What good are we going to do holding a place like this?'

Brostin and Cuu began to head for the door.

'I'm not going,' said Caffran. They stopped in their tracks.

'I gave you a fething order,' said Feygor, slowly rising to his feet.

'And you can stick it. Mkvenner asked me to secure this place until he got back. So that's what I'm doing. A strong-point. We've been building cover around the back area.'

'Who's we?' asked Gutes.

'Me, Muril, Rerval and Larks. You lot can split if you want. I'm not going to let Ven and Jajjo down. If they sent the signal, they meant it. And given the range on the beads, they can't be more than a few kilometres away. So... go if you want to.'

'I gave you an order,' Feygor repeated, malevolently.

'Any notion that you're actually in charge vanished when you decided to take a holiday here. You've hardly been following orders since we arrived, so don't give me that. We're staying, at least until Ven gets here or we hear more from him.'

Feygor's glare moved across their faces. 'You all feel this way?'

'Yes,' said Rerval.

'I'm staying,' said Muril.

Larkin just nodded.

'I'm staying too,' said Gutes suddenly. He looked at the old woman huddled in the corner. 'I don't think she's going anywhere, not if she's stayed here this long. I ain't leaving her for the wolves.'

'Feth it!' said Feygor. He looked at Brostin and Cuu.

'I'm with you, Murt, sure as sure,' said Cuu. 'Just say the word.'

Brostin shrugged. He looked uncomfortable.

Feygor scratched his neck. The idea of running clearly appealed to him but he was considering the consequences. If trouble was that close, they'd stand a better chance of survival here as a group than alone and moving through the forest.

'Okay,' said Feygor, 'okay, we stay. For now. Prepare for contact. Caffran, get everyone deployed.'

The Ghosts began to ready themselves, Brostin and Cuu hurrying out of the kitchen to gather kit. Feygor turned and faced the Aexe trooper Caffran had found.

'Of course, we haven't even started with you,' he said. 'Get talking.'

The dishevelled young man refused to make eye contact. Feygor hit him and knocked him onto the floor. He was about to hit him again when Caffran grabbed his arm.

'He's a deserter. That much is obvious, isn't it? He ran into these woods and he's been hiding here, probably because it was out of the way and the old lady fed him.'

'Why?'

'Gak it, Feygor,' said Muril, 'how dense do you have to be? She must think it's her son, come home again after all this time.'

'This sounding like the truth to you?' Feygor asked the young man, who was picking himself up.

'Don't hurt her. Please,' he whispered.

'And don't hit him again in front of her,' Caffran advised. 'If she does think he's her son, you might find yourself with a bread knife stuck in your back.'

'What's your name?' Muril asked the young man.

'Private First Class Rufo Peterik, Sixteenth Brunsgatters.'

'How long ago did you... run?' Caffran asked gently.

'Six months,' said Peterik.

'You been here ever since?'

'Couple of months living rough, then here.'

'Did you disable my vox-caster?' Rerval asked from across the kitchen. It was a blunt but obvious question. It was just the sort of thing a desperate deserter might have done.

'No, sir,' said Peterik straight away. 'I did not.'

'We haven't got time for this,' said Feygor. 'Lock him up or tie him to a chair. Or something.'

There was no point objecting. None of them could predict what the youth might do, though Caffran had a hunch they didn't have to worry about him. Caffran tied him to a chair anyway.

'Piet, Larks… sweep the ground,' said Feygor. His manner was calmer now. Having made the decision to stay, he was eager to reimpose his leadership.

Both Larkin and Gutes looked at Caffran first and only left the kitchen when he nodded.

OUTSIDE, THE MIST had grown heavier, gauzing out the rising sun. There was no wind, but the air had a tang of rain. They still hadn't quite shaken off that storm.

Larkin and Gutes hurried up the back lawn, following the line of the garden wall, their boots and trouser legs becoming soaked with dew from the wet undergrowth.

It was terribly still, terribly quiet. Birds called intermittently from the woodlands beyond. They reached the tumbledown, overgrown sheds at the edge of the property and crouched down, watching the trees. The softly billowing mists created brief shapes occasionally that made them tense up, but it was just mist.

'You took the circuit, didn't you?' Gutes said at length.

'What?' Larkin's tone was short. His skull felt like it was splitting from the blow Cuu had given it, and he could taste one of his migraines creeping in.

'The circuit from Rerval's vox. You took it, didn't you? I've seen the way you mess with tech-kit. You're the only person apart from Rerval who's got the skills.'

'Piet, considering how dumb you like to play, you're a smart man.'

Gutes grinned. He scanned the woods again.

'Why'd you do it, Larks?' he said after a pause.

'I…' Larkin hesitated. 'I wanted to make sure we were left alone for a while.'

'Oh,' said Gutes.

Then, 'I think maybe we need that vox again now. I think maybe we've been alone long enough.'

'Yeah,' said Larkin.

'You'll give it back?'

'Yeah.'

'I won't say nothing, Larks.'

'Thanks, Piet.'

AN HOUR PASSED, slow and taut. It began to rain, lightly at first and then with greater force. Despite the rain, the mist refused to budge. The light ebbed as it became overcast, and the early morning seemed like wet twilight.

There was no signal on the beads. Caffran began to wonder if he'd imagined it.

All fully kitted and prepped, the members of the detail took station to cover the back of the manse. Caffran was set up in the greenhouse, one of the western most outhouses running off the back yard, with a good angle across the rear lawn, and a decent view left into the patch of kitchen garden behind the pantry. He and Rerval had strengthened the defences in the greenhouse with packing crates, earth-filled sacking and part of an old iron bedstead they'd found on a bonfire heap. They'd carefully knocked out the last of the glass panels.

East of him, across the mouth of the yard area, Cuu was crouching in place at the end of a long barricade Muril and Larkin had built from fence timbers and corrugated iron sheets. They'd had to dismantle several of the lean-tos to cannibalize for material.

Rerval was positioned further along the same barricade, hunched in the corner it made with the stone wall of the old coal bunker.

Brostin was sitting on a chair just inside the half-open kitchen door, his flamer broom across his lap, his tanks beside him. He checked the power cells of the two laspistols – his and Feygor's – that he carried as small-arms. Feygor, his rifle primed, was a few metres away at the main kitchen window. A thick wall separated him from Gutes, who was in the dining room, dug-in at the rear window overlooking the coal house and the hedges of the side ditch. Larkin was on station on the first floor above them all, using a bedroom window as his fire point.

Muril, insisting she was the closest thing they had to a scout, was up at the top of the rear lawn in the derelict sheds at the end of the garden wall. She knelt, perfectly still, watching the trees.

About twenty minutes earlier, as they'd run final checks before taking up station, Rerval had found the missing transmission circuit on the kitchen table. Assuming that it was Feygor, or one of Feygor's cronies, who'd left it there for him to find, Rerval made little fuss. They were all in this together now and there was no point racking up the tension any more.

He'd fitted it back into the caster and, after consulting with Feygor, sent a message back to Ins Arbor. Position, situation, the prospect of enemy contact.

Ironically, there had been no reply, apart from a few strangulated whines of static. Rerval didn't know if it was atmospherics or some slip-up he'd made repairing the vox. There was no time to strip it out and start again. He prayed company command had heard him. He prayed there'd be help coming. Failing help, he hoped that a warning had got through.

IN THE DAMP, mouldering back bedroom, Larkin settled himself on the pungent mattress he'd pulled up to lie on, and rested his long-las on the paint-flaked sill. He shook out his neck, tried to ignore the pain clawing into his brain from the top of the spine and across the back of his head, and scoped up.

His swollen face ached as he pushed it against the eyepiece. His cracked rib stung and he had to alter his stance.

He had a good sweep of the entire back lawn. He panned the rifle around, taking distance readings off the various features: the end sheds, the sundial at the centre of the lawn, the coal bunker, Caff's greenhouse.

Down below him, in the yard, he saw Cuu crouching at the barricade with his back to him.

Larkin turned the rifle down and took aim on Cuu. No more than fifteen metres. Clear. An easy shot. Target-fix. Larkin's fingers twitched on the trigger.

Not yet. But maybe soon. If there was shooting, if there was a fight, he'd take Cuu and damn the consequences. He'd take

Cuu Cuu's way: in battle, when no one would know. What was it that little bastard had said? War's a messy thing, Tanith. Confused and all shit like that. Middle of combat, all crap flying this way and that. Who's gonna notice if I get my payback? You'd just be another body in the count.

Good advice, Lijah Cuu. Good advice.

RAINWATER DRIPPED FROM the shed roof and hit Muril's cheek with a plick. She wiped it away, and then realised it wasn't the drip that had made the noise.

Her micro-bead had tapped.

'Who goes there?' she said into the mic.

Silence.

She waited. Something moved in the trees, but it seemed likely it was just a bird.

She was about to ask if any of the Ghosts at the house had signalled when a figure tore out of the trees, running towards her position, leaping fallen logs and ripping through undergrowth. Her rifle came up and she had a clear shot.

She froze.

It was Jajjo. Filthy, covered in mud, his uniform ripped, Jajjo was running almost blindly towards her.

'Jajjo!' She called. He skidded to a halt, looking around.

'The wall, man, the wall! Get in here!'

He started forward again and vaulted the low stone wall, then came crawling round on his hands and knees into her shed.

'M-Muril?'

'Gak! Look at you. What happened?'

'En-enemy p-patrol,' Jajjo stammered, so exhausted and out of breath he could barely speak.

'I've got Jajjo here,' Muril voxed to the manse. 'Stand by.'

She dragged Jajjo over against the shed wall. He was in a bad way, thin, pale and dehydrated.

'Report!' she hissed.

'W-where's Ven?' he asked.

She shrugged. 'Haven't seen him.'

'He should be here already! He was ahead of me!'

'Slow down! Slow down! Tell me about your contact. What did you find out there?'

'Shit, Muril,' he said, and clambered over the window slit. He peered out.

'Twenty, maybe thirty of them. They're right behind me. Didn't you get my call?'

'Just the signal. Comeuppance.'

'Gak, I knew the link was bad! I–'

He shut up and ducked down.

'They're here!' he hissed.

She wasn't about to cower with him. She got up to the shed's window and looked out.

Figures, three or four of them, were approaching through the mist and the trees. Big men, in battledress.

Carrying lasrifles.

She recognized their blood-red tunics and their leering iron face masks at once.

Not Shadik. Not Shadik at all.

Blood Pact.

As if they had smelled her sudden fear, three of the Chaos infantry swung round and opened fire on the outhouses. Laser rounds chopped into the roof tiles and shattered old brick and chafstone. Support fire – three or four more lasrifles and then what felt like an autocannon – whickered out of the trees.

Muril yelped and covered Jajjo's head with her arms as lasrounds punched in through the woodwork of the window and tore apart the leading edge of the roof.

'Contact!' she yelled into her bead. 'Contact!

'GOLDEN THRONE!' said Feygor, peering out of the window. 'That's las-fire! Eight, maybe nine shooters.'

Brostin was on his feet. He took a glance round at Peterik, who was shielding the old woman in the corner of the pantry.

'Shadik don't have las weapons,' he said, in gruff confusion. 'Murt? How come they have las weapons?'

'I don't know!' snapped Feygor. 'Muril! Muril! Report!'

The bead-link crackled. '–od Pact! I say again, contact is Blood Pact!'

'Oh, sacred feth!' Feygor said.

* * *

CAFFRAN HEARD THE signal too and his blood ran cold. They'd met the Blood Pact before, on Phantine. The Pact was the devoted vanguard of the arch-enemy. Not cultists, not rebels. Drilled and trained infantry, highly motivated, highly skilled and well equipped. If they were here, fighting for the Republic... well, that meant a forty year old war had just changed as radically as it had done when the Guard arrived in support of the Alliance. This had ceased to be a global matter. Now it was well and truly part of the Crusade.

From his position, all he could see was the back of the outhouse and the sprays of tile and stone smashing off it under the heavy fire. He yearned for a target.

'Keep it close! Wait until they commit!' Feygor urged over the link. The hell with that! Muril and Jajjo were dead meat if no one took up the fight. Feygor clearly didn't want to give away the fact that a unit was dug-in here. Not until he had to.

A slightly different noise now rose from the beleaguered outhouse. The whine-crack, higher-pitched, of first one Imperial lasrifle, then another. Muril and Jajjo were returning fire.

That was play, as far as Caffran was concerned.

'Larkin!' he voxed. 'You got a target?'

'Yes, Caff. At least two.'

'I've got an angle on one too,' reported Gutes.

'I think it's time for us to go to work,' Caffran said.

'Hold fire!' Feygor snarled over the link. 'They don't know we're here yet! Hold fire!'

'Feth that,' said Larkin and took his first shot.

The overcharged sniper-round zapped off up the length of the garden and blew out the head of one Blood Pact trooper in a sideways spray of blood, tissue and metal. His almost headless body toppled over into the ferns. The others started running for cover. From the dining room, Gutes took one out with hits to the hip and the side of the neck.

'Holy Feth!' Feygor was screaming. 'I didn't give the fire order! Who's firing? Who the feth is firing?'

'I am,' said Larkin and did it again. Target-fix. Seventy-three metres.

Another head shot. The Blood Pact trooper flew off his feet, his legs kicking slackly up into the air as he cartwheeled.

'I think we're in this now,' said Rerval and started to clip las-shots up over the lawn.

'Sure as sure,' agreed Cuu, opening fire alongside him.

'Holy Feth! Won't any of you take a fething order?' Feygor shouted over the vox, almost apoplectic.

In the perimeter outhouse, Muril and Jajjo were blasting away and rejoiced as first one Pacter dropped, then two more thanks to fire from the house. Muril recognised and admired the work of a long-las.

She tracked another one into the trees as he sought cover, and sprayed the area on full auto, kicking up a fuss of torn leaves and stalks.

Jajjo was firing on single shot. His gun followed a Blood Pact trooper who was dashing back into the misty shadows of the pines. Jajjo squeezed the trigger.

The dazzling round hit the figure in the spine and tumbled him over.

Autocannon fire continued to strafe the sheds where Jajjo and Muril hid. After a couple more fierce bursts, the side wall came down in a tumble of dislodged chafstone, and the two Ghosts had to crawl out from under the slumped roof and move in a rapid crouch back along the garden wall.

'Can't someone tag that fething cannon?' Muril barked.

'Negative, can't see it,' Caffran voxed, his opinion swiftly agreed with by Gutes.

'Larks? You see it?' Muril called.

'Too deep in the woods,' Larkin replied. 'Can't even see a snout flash.'

'Gak that!' said Muril. She and Jajjo were pinned down behind the narrow stone wall, and cannon fire was gradually creeping their way. They needed a break, enough time to run back down the lawn to the main house.

It didn't look like they were going to get it.

'Hold tight and wait for my word,' said Larkin over the link. 'Wait for it…'

He couldn't see the cannon crew, even from his raised vantage, and he couldn't see any muzzle flash. But he watched the dipping line of the cannon's tracer rounds as they tore out of the woodland. The high calibre shots punished the garden wall and made sappy steam out of the undergrowth.

Another few seconds and it would be punching through the wall where Muril and Jajjo were sheltering.

Larkin rolled his aim back, following the line of tracers until it vanished at its mysterious source. He made an educated adjustment to his aim, and fired into the woods.

The cannon fire stopped abruptly.

'Go! Muril! Go!' he cried, as he reloaded and fired another shot exactly where he'd placed the first.

Muril and Jajjo fled down the garden towards the barricade. A few loose las-rounds from rifles chased them, chewing up the turf.

The cannon started up again, but it was lacking confidence now, as if someone else had taken over. Its shots bombarded the back wall of the garden or shot clear over it, smacking into the rear face of the house. A window smashed.

By then, Muril and Jajjo had reached the barricade and had hurled themselves over it.

The cannon continued to spray.

'First thing you learn,' Larkin said to himself, 'is move if someone knows where you are.'

He fired another shot, aiming exactly at the point he'd placed the last two. For the second time in thirty seconds, the cannon fell suddenly silent.

'Nice bit of shooting that, Larks,' voxed Gutes.

Now Caffran felt exposed. With Muril and Jajjo dropping back, he now occupied point position in the defence.

He kept scanning the end of the garden, the wall, the chokes of undergrowth leading into the trees.

He didn't have to wait long.

At least two dozen Blood Pact troopers came out of the treeline and assaulted the rear wall, sheeting fire at the manse. All of the Ghosts, even Larkin, had to drop down to avoid the ferocity. The attackers were now using the rear garden wall and the ruined sheds abandoned by Muril and Jajjo as cover.

Caffran was the first to begin return fire. He lanced shots along the back of the wall that hit at least one attacker and caused several more to duck. This interruption in firing gave Cuu and Larkin an opening. Cuu sprayed the back of the outhouses with fire, and Larkin fired another hot-shot that took a Blood Pact trooper in the chest.

To the east, from the dining room window, Gutes took up the slack, firing his trademark way: slow, methodical, jaggedly. Two Blood Pact troopers tried to flank by sprinting down the side wall of the property, following the hedges into the ditch. Gutes got them both. Then a third that he didn't kill outright. Then a fourth who emerged, trying to drag the injured man back into cover.

As an afterthought, Gutes picked off the wounded bastard too.

A flurry of fire was hitting down at the manse and the barricade from the central portion of the rear wall. Cuu and Rerval replied, supplemented by Jajjo and Muril, who were now up the barricade with them. Feygor added his own support from the kitchen window, and Brostin suddenly broke from the kitchen doorway and ran up the yard to the side of Caffran's station, leaving his flamer behind. The big thug wriggled in beside Caffran and started to fire his pistols, one in each meaty hand.

'What I wouldn't give for a tread-fether right now,' Brostin grumbled.

'I hear that!' said Caffran.

A shot spat across them from the left. Blood Pacters moving west to flank them from the other side. Brostin rolled to his feet and slid out of Caffran's greenhouse, swung round behind it and came up over the low wall to meet the three Pacters rushing them across the kitchen garden. His laspistols chattered as he raked them back and forth. He killed two and winged a third.

Down at the barricade, Cuu deselected rapid fire and switched his Mark III to single shot. He hunted the garden wall, waiting for Blood Pacters to pop up for a shot. Every time they did, he shot them in the face. Three in a row. Four. The fifth one was smacked over by one of Larkin's shots before Cuu could fire.

Ducking round the kitchen doorway for cover, Feygor dared the yard and ran for the barricade as a welter of shots rained down, exploding plaster, brick, gutters, tiles.

He ducked in beside Muril.

'Get up with Larkin!' he said. 'I know you don't have a long-las any more, but you'll do more good up there.'

She nodded and ran back for the kitchen door.

Feygor got up and started firing. He looked over at Jajjo. 'Where's Ven?'

Jajjo shook his head.

Beside Jajjo, Rerval fired and scored a killshot. He distinctly saw the Blood Pact trooper fall.

He turned to grin triumphantly at Feygor and a las-round hit the side of his head.

Jajjo ducked down to help him, but Rerval was getting up without assistance. 'I'm okay,' he said, but it didn't sound like that. From the corner of his mouth back to his jaw-line, his cheek was flopped open and blood was streaming out down his neck. Rerval fired one more shot, then reached up and felt the rip in his face.

'Feth–' he slurred and fell over.

Jajjo dragged him back into the kitchen. The amount of blood pouring out of Rerval's torn face was extraordinary. 'Help me!' Jajjo shouted to the old woman and the young boy he saw cowering in the corner. He had no idea who they were.

Las-fire smacked and punched through the kitchen window and covered the tiles with glass shards. Several more shots exploded fibres from the kitchen door. Jajjo tried to hold Rerval's face together.

The old woman ran across the kitchen, her head down, and took over. She pinched the wound tight and started to wrap it with her shawl.

'Let me free! Let me free, for god's sake! I can help!' bellowed the young man. Jajjo realised the youth was tied to his chair.

Jajjo got up, went across to the boy, and cut his bonds with his dagger. 'I don't know why you're tied up,' he said, 'but don't gak with me.'

The young man – Jajjo realised how dirty and unshaven he was – darted across to the field dressing kit Gutes had left on the bench seat. He recovered it and ran over to join the old woman cradling Rerval. An astonishingly wide pool of blood had spread out under her.

'Do you know what you're doing?' Jajjo asked.

'I was a corpsman. I know field aid,' replied the boy.

'Don't let him bleed out,' said Jajjo, and ran out into the fight again.

LAS-FIRE FLICKERED UP and down the lawn, fierce and heavy. Caffran thought he'd scored another hit but it was hard to tell. There were at least a dozen shooters up there.

Muril arrived on the first floor, and tried to find the window with the best sweep.

She could hear the hot-shot whine of Larkin's weapon from nearby.

Larkin reloaded again and took aim. He'd switched bedrooms three times since the fight had begun so his shots didn't come from the same place each time. In the far end bedroom, he knelt and sighted.

A steel helmet over a grotesque iron mask.

Bang!

The Blood Pact trooper fell. Larkin reloaded.

He hunted for targets. The back of his skull hurt worse than ever, and he could taste blood. Every now and then, his vision faltered. The blizzard of las-fire coming down at them was almost overwhelming. Middle of combat, all crap flying this way and that...

Larkin stroked his long-las and tilted the aim down. Lijah Cuu was below him in the yard, firing away up hill.

The scope's crosshairs made a luminous frame around the back of Cuu's head.

Larkin paused. He breathed carefully. His head was really aching now, that terrible stabbing migraine that had haunted him all his life.

He blinked away sweat. He would fething do this.

Cuu, right in his sights. Lijah Cuu. His nemesis. The embodiment of his fear. The man who had killed Try Again Bragg.

One shot.

Pop.

Easy.

Larkin's finger tightened on the trigger.

Target-fix. Cuu. Nine point seven metres.

Larkin whined aloud, a pitiful sound. He wanted to do it, yet he couldn't. He was a sniper, a marksman, a killer. But not a murderer. He couldn't shoot one of their own in the back, even if it was Lijah fething Cuu.

He wanted to. He had to. It was the only way. It was why he'd come.

But…

Cuu would have done it without hesitation, Larkin thought. That thought and that thought alone convinced him to take his finger off the trigger.

'Larks! What the gak are you doing?'

Larkin looked up from his carefully laid gun. Muril stood behind him, appalled.

'Don't do it,' she said. 'Please. I know you want to. I know he deserves it. But don't…'

'Sehra,' he said quietly. 'I can't anyway.'

'That's good,' she said. 'Really, Larks. Don't descend to that animal's level.'

'Oh, feth,' sighed Larkin. His head was truly spinning now. His vision was closing in with flashes and lumps of colour. She was right. He was so fething glad he hadn't stained his soul the way Cuu had stained his. There was honour. There was morality. There was sleeping at night without waking up screaming. Bragg would understand. Wherever he was, Bragg would understand.

Larkin turned and took a last look out of his scope. Cuu was looking right back at them.

Lijah Cuu saw the aimed rifle.

And smiled.

BROSTIN AND CAFFRAN finally drove the last of the Pacters back from the left hand flank of the house. Feygor and Gutes smacked shots against the rear wall, and Feygor hit another body.

Then the Blood Pact fell silent.

The Ghosts waited. No contact. No sound. The rain got heavier and washed the traces of Rerval's blood out of the yard.

'Stand down,' said Feygor, at last.

'They'll be back,' said Caffran.

* * *

'LIE DOWN,' MURIL advised him.

'My head really hurts.'

'Cuu smacked you a good one with that skillet, Larks. I've been worried.'

Larkin lay back on the dirty mattress in the upstairs room. 'It's not that. I get headaches. Really bad ones. I've always had them.'

'Whatever,' said Muril. 'I think it's that headwound. Cuu really hurt you. I don't want to worry you, Hlaine, but it needs to be looked at. I wish for gak's sake Curth or Dorden was here.'

Larkin had already passed out on the mattress. Watery blood wept into the padding behind his head.

'Gak,' said Muril. 'You really need a doc fast…'

She froze. Down below, she could hear Feygor and the others repairing defences and reloading for the next wave.

She'd heard a sound from the front of the house.

She took up her lasgun and went out onto the landing. Another tiny sound, a movement at the porch.

She went down the staircase slowly, gun raised.

At the foot of the stairs, she wheeled round, and found herself aiming at Cuu. He winked at her.

'Careful, girl.'

'What are you doing here?'

'I heard something out the front,' he said.

She covered him with her weapon. 'Check it out,' she said.

'Why the hostility?' he asked.

'You know why, you bastard. Now… check it out.'

Cuu went down to the front door, Muril watching him every centimetre of the way. He drew his blade.

Cuu threw open the door.

The dagger flew from his hand as a tall figure took him in a choke hold.

'Do you realise how easy it was to get round the front of this place?' asked Mkvenner.

FIFTEEN
THE MONSTERS

*'In the long run, a man with a brain is more dangerous
than a man with brawn.'*

– Warmaster Slaydo,
from *A Treatise on the Nature of Warfare*

FIREBREATHING, LIKE THE giant creatures of old myth, the monsters lay before them.

When the monsters roared, the ground shook and the air came past, hot and acrid, in a pressurised shockwave. The light flashes were painful and immense, like grounded stars being switched on and off in the night. The sound shook teeth and bone and marrow.

The battle in the ammunition corridor had taken seven minutes to conclude in the Ghosts' favour. Squaring off against a Shadik battalion of slightly greater size, Gaunt's infiltration group had lost five men – four Ghosts and one of Golke's Bande Sezari troopers. But their superior weaponry and, in Gaunt's opinion, far superior battlecraft had left nearly thirty Shadik troopers dead. Broken, the rest had fallen back.

Undoubtedly, the Shadik commanders knew they had intruders now. Despite the open invitation to the siege guns' location offered by the corridor, Gaunt and Mkoll had pulled the mission team off east into a muddy, trackless wasteland beyond.

The area was lightless and cold, rambling with old lines of wire and jumbles of wreckage. Weeds and thorny scrub grew in clumps and thickets, sprouting around the split rockcrete of old pill boxes and between the axles of rusted trucks. This was an old battlefield, years old, that the war had passed over and left behind. Now it was just dead ground in the hinterland of the Republican line.

The Ghosts advanced silently through the dark terrain, heading north, towards the titanic blasts of the guns. They kept the ammunition corridor just in sight to their left, and moved parallel to its course.

There would be troops out searching for them. Gaunt was sure of that. Even with the huge offensive going on, drawing on Shadik manpower, the enemy commanders would not allow a suspected infiltration so close to their super-guns to go unchecked.

On three occasions, the Ghosts dropped down into cover when the scouts alerted them to Shadik patrols in the corridor. Gaunt didn't need another stand-up fight at this stage. Better to hide and wait and move on once the jeopardy had passed.

The night sky was amber, tinged by the vast doughnut of smoke drifting out from the guns. On occasions, they glimpsed the moon, an orange semi-circle dancing in and out of the bars of cloudy exhaust.

Nearly three hours after they had first emerged from the mill tunnel, they came up to a ridge that overlooked the guns.

The monsters.

It was physically hard to observe them directly. For the last forty minutes the Imperials had been trudging through a wasteland made spectral by the almighty flashes going off beyond the black horizon. They had almost become acclimatised to the noise and the light and the trembling soil.

But looking on the guns was virtually impossible. The flashes seared eyesight, leaving idiot repeats glowing on the back of the eyelids. The shockwaves came like slaps. The discharge blasts felt like they were exploding eardrums. Beltayn reported that the pulse shock had killed all vox-links.

Lying on his side on the earth near the top of the ridge, with the men spread out below him, Gaunt pondered his next move. He felt frustration gnawing at him. They'd got so close, against all expectations except his own, and now they couldn't go the last distance.

It was like one of the myths he'd read as a child in the scholam progenium. Monsters so ghastly that the very breath or sight of them blinded men and turned them to stone.

He adjusted his data-slate and took a compass bearing. At least now he had accomplished something. The precise location of the siege guns was known to them. Without other options to hand, their imperative now was to get that information back to GSC. And that meant physically, with the vox dead.

Gaunt turned to Mkoll and the sergeants and used Verghast scratch-company sign language to communicate his intention to pull back and break out. Halfway through, a chillingly eerie thing happened. Darkness and silence fell.

It wasn't complete silence. The distant, frenzied commotion of the offensive was now audible, and it wasn't true darkness either because of the ambient background firelight.

But the guns had stopped firing.

Gaunt crawled back to the top of the ridge. What he had only vaguely glimpsed before was now laid out below him. The monster guns, each one set on a huge rail cart, their massive barrels, the size of manufactory chimneys, elevated to the sky. There were seven of them, just like Bonin had insisted. Smoke lay thick like ground fog around them, blurring their shapes and distorting the bare white glow of the chemical lanterns strung up around the area. Gaunt saw figures moving around, gun-crew dwarfed by the huge railway cannons. Electric hoists and flatbed loading carts, which had been occupied serving shells into the automatic arming mechanisms, were now busy clearing unused shells and propellant-mix cartridges clear of the firing site. Some laden carts were being attached to a greasy shunting engine that began puffing them away down the ammunition corridor.

'Why d'you think they've stopped?' whispered Golke.

'They've been firing all night,' Gaunt replied. 'I imagine there comes a point when the barrels get so hot, you have to let them cool. God-Emperor! Now we've found them, what do we do?'

Golke shrugged. Even dormant, the massive guns and their rivetted steel cars looked invincible. Oil and condensation dripped from their huge shock-absorber pylons and clung in glittering droplets to the taut wires of the warping winches. The shells alone were taller than a man.

The Ghosts had proved their bravery, tenacity and ability to Golke without doubt, but what could they, with lasrifles or even tube-charges, do against such juggernauts?

'I don't think there's much chance of us spiking them,' Mkoll said to Gaunt, as if reading Golke's thoughts. 'I reckon I could feth up a field gun or a howitzer fairly permanently, but I wouldn't know where to begin with one of these. Let alone seven.'

'What about the munitions?' Domor suggested.

Gaunt thought about it. None of them were demolitions experts. Domor's landmine skills were as close as that got. Although a big explosion was the basic result he was looking for, he didn't want to go fiddling around with the shells or the cartridges.

They didn't even know what mixes and forces the Shadik were using, or what type of explosives or propellants. They might get a big explosion all right, but one that incinerated them and left the guns standing. Besides, the Shadik were shipping the spare munitions away even as they watched. They knew the risks.

'I think we have to cut our losses,' said Gaunt. 'Getting these co-ordinates back to the GSC is going to be a job in itself, and I think we're going to have to settle for being content with that.'

'If we can't screw with the guns themselves,' said Dorden suddenly, 'why don't we screw up their use?'

'What, doctor?'

'Their mobility. They're too big for us to deal with, so we use their size against them. You fancy moving one of those without rails?'

Gaunt chuckled to himself. Obvious, elegant, simple. The Republic had constructed a major system of wide-gauge tracks along their front line, connected with service lines, sidings and ammunition corridors, so that the siege guns could be shunted from one firing position to the next. At locations like the one they overlooked, the double line fanned out into reinforced spurs so that the guns could sit alongside each other. But that main double line was their only way of moving.

'What are we carrying in the way of tube-charges?' Gaunt asked Mkoll.

'Enough to blow the main line here and on the far side for a good distance.'

'They'll repair them,' said Golke.

'Of course, but how long will that take, sir?' asked Gaunt. 'A day? Two days? Besides, struggling back with this location setting will be a pointless effort if by the time we've got an airstrike or an armour push lined up the guns have been moved again. I don't think we've got a choice, realistically. We have to blow the line. If we take out the ammo corridor too, they won't even be able to fire the guns let alone shift them until the repairs are done.'

Golke nodded. 'How do we do this?' he asked.

THEY BROKE INTO four groups roughly along platoon lines. Mkoll's unit would move up, skirting the firing site, and wire the track sections north of the guns. Gaunt allowed him ten minutes' head start to get into position. Domor's squad went east, to rig the ammunition corridor's line. Arcuda's dropped back west and right of the ridge to set their charges along the southern stretch. Gaunt stayed with Criid's platoon and the elements of Raglon's on the ridge, ready to provide fire support if things woke up.

Ideally, the blasts should happen pretty much simultaneously. Co-ordination was hard without the vox. Gaunt had them synchronise their timepieces. The deadline was at 04.00 hours. Charges should be laid by then. At 04.00, each team leader would fire a red starshell to signal readiness, then Gaunt would fire a white shell to order detonation. If any reds hadn't fired by that time, then

Gaunt would wait two minutes. After that, it was white flare anyway and pull out. They agreed a rendezvous back in the deadlands.

'Remember,' Gaunt told them, 'if it comes to a choice between sticking to the deadline and blowing the tracks, blow the tracks. We can always improvise if we have to. The Emperor protects, so serve him well.'

IT WAS TWO minutes to four. The sounds of battle were still rolling in from the front line. The cover team left on the ridge waited nervously. They felt vulnerable and alone now there were so few of them.

Beltayn snapped a white signal pellet into his flare pistol and handed it to Gaunt. 'Safety's off, sir,' he said.

'Problem!' Criid hissed urgently. Gaunt looked where she was pointing. A detachment of Shadik troopers was filing out into the siege gun firing area from a trench head to their west. Gaunt counted at least sixty men. Clad in long coats and helmets, their weapons ready and lowered in their hands, they were searching between the gun cars and the loading hoists.

Looking for us, Gaunt thought. Looking for the infiltrators.

'Ready your weapons,' he called down the line. 'Wait for my word.'

Some of the Shadik had lanterns. Two had teams of snarling canines.

Gaunt tucked the flare pistol into his pocket and took out his boltgun. Full clip. He drew his power sword and laid it on the earth beside him.

Down the line, the Ghosts in Criid and Raglon's squads fitted new clips to their Mark III's and fixed their blades to the barrels, each trooper stabbing the warknife into the ridge soil first to dull its shine.

Golke and the Bande Sezari soldiers got their solid-round weapons ready.

One more minute.

Be on time, all of you, Gaunt willed. Be on time.

Alarm whistles suddenly blew. The enemy detachment abruptly began running, moving in a flood to the east. Gaunt saw muzzle flashes and heard the crack of rifles.

They were heading into the ammunition corridor. Domor's team had been spotted.

'On them!' Gaunt yelled. 'First-and-Only!' The cover team broke from the ridge and came down the slope, guns blazing. The Shadik unit faltered, suddenly under fire from their left. The Ghosts ripped into them.

Gaunt was right in the middle of it. His boltgun howled and blew an enemy infantryman apart. His majestic blade, the power sword of Heironymo Sondar, gifted to him in gratitude by the people of Vervunhive, flickered with blue lightning. Beside him, Beltayn was firing from the shoulder as he ran, thumping bright las-bolts into the greatcoated enemy.

Beyond Beltayn, Criid was urging her Ghosts on, deploying them in tight groups even in the mêlée of an impromptu charge.

I made a good choice in Tona, Gaunt thought.

A second later, a Shadik battletrooper was in his face, lunging with a serrated bayonet. Gaunt deflected with the sword, shearing off the front half of the man's gun and an arm with it. A bolt-round settled the man right behind him.

Lubba's flamer roared and lit up the night. Gaunt saw two Shadik lurching away, burning from head to toe. Hwlan, Vulli and Kolea laid in side by side. Kolea seemed to have forgotten how a lasrifle worked. He was scything into the enemy with his bayonet fixed, reaping them down like corn stalks, hacking like a miner at an ore-face.

It was a blur of frantic, face-to-face killing. Golke blasted with his revolver until it was empty, and then grabbed up a Shadik submachine-gun that had fallen on the gravel of the track bed.

One of the Bande Sezari men beside him convulsed as rifle rounds tore through him. Golke swung round and cracked away with the compact weapon, knocking three of the enemy troopers off their feet.

'More of them!' Raglon yelled above the din of combat. Gaunt could see another company of Shadik troopers streaming out of the eastern trench-head to reinforce the first. Grenades blared and flashed in the night.

Domor's squad had been pinned down and then driven off by the first fusillades. They had taken cover around a parked munitions truck about two hundred metres down the corridor.

'Sir!' Beltayn yelled. Gaunt looked up and saw two red starshells fading away. In the frenzy of it all, he'd almost missed the signals from Mkoll and Arcuda.

Two out of three. Good enough. It would have to do.

'Break off and retreat!' he bellowed, and fired the white flare.

As soon as the corpse light of the white signal bloomed above them, a hot yellow burst exploded to the north, and then another, seconds later, to the west.

The cover team, firing behind them as they went, battled up the ridge and back into the darkness of the wasteland. They left the sidings and track beds littered with Shadik dead.

GAUNT CHECKED HIS bearings by the luminous dial of his compass. They were right on the rendezvous point. 'Head count!' he ordered to Beltayn.

Behind them, yellow light flickered the night. The main line was severed both north and south of the gun sidings.

Two minutes passed, and Arcuda's team emerged out of the gloom. Then Domor's squad struggled in, breathlessly.

'I'm sorry, sir,' Domor panted. 'We were almost set when they hit us. I tried to go back and finish the job, but they had the area bracketed.'

'Don't worry, Domor. You did your best. We hit the main transit line, that's the important thing. Those guns aren't going anywhere.'

'But they'll still be able to fire with the corridor open to supply them.' Domor looked forlorn with disappointment.

Gaunt gripped him by the shoulders. 'You did all right, Shoggy. Really. You did your best, that's all I ever ask for. We sit tight here now until Mkoll's mob rejoins us and then we have fun and games getting out of here. All right?'

Domor nodded.

Beltayn reappeared. 'We left a few dead behind us, sir, but everyone's accounted for. Except–'

'Except?'
'Count Golke, sir.'

SHADIK TROOPERS WERE milling around the firing site, and spreading out down the lines, surveying the damage with lanterns. Two huge craters marred the tracks, one on each side of the siege gun emplacement. More troopers, muffled in their heavy, drab coats and trench armour, shambled south down the corridor line, picking over the bodies. One called for an officer as he found the half-laid tube-charges between the sleepers.

Count Golke crouched behind the bogies of the munition cart, barely twenty metres from the nearest enemy soldier. He watched as they grouped around and cut apart the wires connecting the tube-bombs, pulling them off the tracks. The officer waved a hand and barked orders, sending a squad of about ten down to check the cart.

The troopers approached, rifles ready, the lamplight glinting off their helmets and bayonets.

Golke limped round the back end of the cart. It was actually a linked line of three, laden with propellant cartridges, waiting for the next shunting engine to move in and pull it down to the armoured magazines.

Golke climbed up onto the middle cart. It was hard work with his hip. He winced and grunted.

The bullet wound in his chest made it harder still.

He got onto the top, and sat down between the canister hoppers. He smiled. He'd come back into the Pocket, faced his demons, and come through it. Now he was going to his victory too. It was due him.

What he'd failed to achieve as a commander, he would do as a trooper.

The enemy soldiers were around the carts now. He could hear their voices. One called out. He'd found the trail of Golke's blood.

Golke heard more voices, and boots clunking on rungs of the cart's metal side ladder.

Those Shadik voices. The voices of the enemy.

Golke wished the whole war could have been as simple as this.

He coughed, and blood welled out of his mouth and down his chin. A Shadik called out, he'd heard the cough. Golke caught the sound of bolt-actions cranking.

He lifted up the tube-charge. It was the only one he'd been able to tear free from the tangle Domor's team had wired to the tracks. There'd been no time for more.

He wasn't sure how it worked, but there was a paper tab on the top that looked like an igniter strip.

He felt footsteps on the body of the truck. A Shadik trooper appeared around the side of the right hand hopper and called out as he saw Golke lying there.

The trooper raised his rifle.

'For the Emperor,' Golke said, and tore the det-tape away.

THE TUBE FIRED. Canisters around ruptured. Propellant cartridges ignited. The blast lit up the valley for a moment. One hundred metres of ammunition corridor and the land around it vanished in a geyser of flame.

SIXTEEN
COMEUPPANCE

'I hate last stands. You never get an opportunity
to practise for them.'

– Piet Gutes

THE SKY WAS full of stars. They were pink, and vaguely oblong. On the horizon, sheaves of white fireworks danced and burst, like the firecrackers of a victory parade. The air was pulsing with a strange humming sound, like a moaning human voice swimming in and out of hearing. A dark shadow suddenly eclipsed the stars. A big shadow that filled the sky.

'Wake up,' said a voice.

He obeyed, moving. The strange sky, with its ghastly, wrong stars, drained away. He smelled cold air and heard the patter of heavy rain close by.

'Larks,' said Bragg, 'it's time to wake up.'

'Try?'

Try Again Bragg smiled his big, genial smile. 'Time to wake up,' he said.

Larkin blinked and sat up quickly. The movement made him dizzy and he felt nausea rise through him. The hind part of his brain felt like someone was repeatedly clubbing it with a nine-seventy, spike first. At the edges of his vision, obscure lights danced and fire crackers burst.

He was on the dirty mattress in a damp bedroom of the Manse. Rain sheeted down outside, accompanied by lightning. It was late afternoon.

Bragg wasn't there any more.

'See you later,' said Larkin.

APART FROM THE rainstorm, things had been quiet since they'd driven the assault back first thing. They'd repaired the defences, and added a few more at Mkvenner's suggestion.

The scout explained how he and Jajjo had run across the Blood Pact unit late the previous night. A fair-sized patrol force, which Mkvenner was certain was just the spearhead of a larger advance. Shadik had been reinforced from off-world by the elite infantry of the arch-enemy, and the first action of that elite had been to pave the way for an invasion through the Montorq Forest.

Ironic, Caffran thought, that both Chaos and Imperial elements had brought the same advice to the warring nations of Aexe Cardinal.

Rerval was stable, thanks to the deserter's field aid, though weak from loss of blood. They put him in the drawing room out of the way, and Caffran asked Peterik to look after him. No one complained that Peterik wasn't tied up any more. The old woman sat with them and banked up the drawing room fire.

With Rerval out of commission, Mkvenner operated the vox-caster, and sent a more detailed repeat of the original message. Again, there was no reply. There was still no way of telling if anyone had heard either warning.

'We're done here now, anyway,' announced Feygor. 'I mean, now Ven and Jajjo are back. We know the situation. So we can get out of here now. Just get up and go.'

'And how far would we get?' asked Mkvenner. 'With an old lady and a man who can't walk?'

Feygor shrugged. 'Then we fething well leave them! I know, tough. I don't like it. But aren't we obliged to carry a warning back now? I mean, the vox is probably down. We'd be failing in our duty if we didn't get off our arses and try to get word back to company command.'

Mkvenner frowned. He didn't want to get into his thoughts on the subject of Murtan Feygor and failure of duty.

'He's right,' he said instead, surprising them all, including Feygor. 'Up to a point, anyway. We have to assume the vox is dead. We have to get a warning through to Ins Arbor, or this could turn into a first class feth-up. But even without the old lady and Rerval, even moving as fast as we can, I don't think we'd outrun them. They're swift, they're good and they're right on us.'

'So?' asked Cuu.

'So, we maintain the defence of this place. For as long as we can. We keep the Blood Pact busy right here.'

'Because?'

'Because we'll be buying time for someone to get word back. Someone fast might have a chance if the enemy push was delayed here.'

Caffran, Muril and Jajjo looked solemn. Feygor shook his head. Gutes sat down, tutting. Brostin growled an unhappy curse.

Cuu asked the obvious question. 'Who goes?'

'Who's fast?' Mkvenner replied.

'You,' said Feygor.

'I'll be staying here,' said Mkvenner. He'd suggested the plan. He wouldn't leave the hard part to them.

'Then Muril or Jajjo,' said Feygor. 'Maybe Cuu. He's light on his toes.'

'Who's going to decide?' asked Caffran.

'I am,' said Mkvenner, and no one argued. 'Jajjo. You're up. Take the bare minimum so you move light. Don't stop for anything.'

The young Vervunhiver nodded. He was swallowing hard. The weight of responsibility scared him. So did Mkvenner's trust. Worst of all was the idea he was leaving them behind. They were going to die to buy him time.

'Come on,' said Mkvenner. 'Get going. There's no time to waste.'

They all said their goodbyes to Jajjo in turn. Caffran and Gutes helped him pare down his kit and wished him well.

Feygor tried to say something and then just nodded, lost for words. Brostin slapped him on the back and told him not to feth up. Muril filled a pair of water canteens for Jajjo to take with him. 'Good luck,' she said.

'I wish he'd picked you,' Jajjo told her.

'Me too,' she smiled, 'but not for the reason you think.'

'You can do it, Jaj,' Cuu said, winking at the cadet scout. 'Sure as sure, you can.'

Jajjo left by the front door, into the rain and the bad light. He turned back once, to look at Mkvenner. 'Sir, I–'

'Go,' said Mkvenner.

And Jajjo was gone.

MKVENNER SHUT AND bolted the front door. Feygor was already deploying the remaining members of the detail to fire positions. He sent Muril to the first floor, to check what shape Larkin was in and take up a sniping position. 'Use Larkin's long-las if he's out of it,' Feygor instructed.

In the hallway, she passed Mkvenner heading back from the front door.

'Sir,' she said.

'Trooper?'

'I know things have gone… bad,' she began. 'But for the record… for what that's worth… I wish you'd taken me more seriously during this patrol.'

'You don't think I've taken you seriously?'

'I want to be a scout, sir. All the way along, you've given the opportunities to Jajjo, brought him along. Even now, even this. He gets trusted with the break out run.'

'You know why I chose him over you?'

'No sir.'

'You're a better shot, Muril. We need you here. When we… if we get back, I'll be making a recommendation to Mkoll. Scout advancement.'

'For Jajjo?'

'For both of you. I've been impressed with your work from the moment you signed up. Jajjo needed a bit of extra coaching to make the grade.'

She opened her mouth, then closed it again. She wasn't quite sure what to say.

Then the opportunity was gone anyway. They both started as they heard a flurry of explosions from the back of the house.

NINETEEN DETAIL HAD set half their tube-charges in the undergrowth and outbuildings along the back of the rear plot. Brostin had found some bales of fence twine in the cellar and they'd rigged tripwires.

The first intruders into the garden, moving clumsily in the heavy rain, found the wires with their boots. A whole cluster of charges had gone off along the ragged rear wall and demolished it completely. Two more had been triggered at the top of the ditch on the east side of the garden. The Blood Pact troopers, so far invisible in the downpour, began shooting at the house. The defenders at the manse fired back a few discouraging blasts. After a minute or so there was another flash and boom from the left side of the property line as another set of charges was tripped.

The firing stopped. The Blood Pact had fallen back again.

MURIL WENT TO fetch Larkin's long-las, but found it in his hands. He was crouched by one of the bedroom windows, scanning the rain outside.

'You all right?' she asked.

'Yeah,' he said. He didn't look it. He looked dreadful. His thin face was almost white except for the livid bruising, and his eyes were dark hollows.

'I feel better,' he said. 'Really. I feel better for not… taking that shot.'

'Good,' she said. 'We'll get Cuu, Larks. We'll get out of this and get him. I saw him try to kill you, remember? We'll talk to Corbec. Tell him everything.'

'Okay,' said Larkin.

'I mean… Cuu, Feygor, Brostin… Gutes too, I guess. They're going to be up on charges for what they did here. Feygor as good as deserted for a few days. I can't believe Ven won't make a full report. And we'll make a full report of our own about Cuu.'

'Good,' he said.

'So… you fit to do some hunting?'

'I'm fit,' he nodded, settling his long-las.

'I'll be down the landing in the end bedroom.'

'Okay.'

She disappeared. He turned back to his scope. For a moment, he couldn't see the garden or the fringe of woods at all. Just oblong pink stars and firecrackers.

He blinked, then blinked again, until his vision cleared.

HALF AN HOUR later, the Blood Pact returned. In the makeshift pillbox of the greenhouse, Caffran thought he saw movement in the rain, and craned his head up over the edge of the old bedstead and the sacking.

He heard a noise. A hollow puff followed by a whine. Then another. Then yet another.

He knew that sound.

'Incoming!' he yelled.

The first mortar shell blew a hole in the middle of the lawn and threw clods of torn earth into the air. Another made a fireball halfway down the garden's east wall and stone chips rattled down with the rain. A third hit the roofless coal bunker.

The shells kept coming, pounding the rear lawn with fierce explosions. Then autocannons opened up in the tree-line, stitching the back of the house.

Mkvenner was down at the barricade with Cuu. Any moment now, and a mortar round would flatten the greenhouse and Caffran with it.

'Fall back! Caff, fall back!' he shouted. The heavy structure of the house itself at least offered some protection.

Caffran was curled up protectively, trying to keep an eye out. A shell went off right outside, shaking the greenhouse and spraying him with dirt.

'Caffran!'

'Wait!' he shouted back.

Under cover of the furious mortar and cannon fire, the troopers began their assault. Caffran glimpsed red-clad figures pouring in through the rubble at the back of the lawn, some crawling along the side ditches or below what was left of the back wall. Now small-arms fire came their way too.

He waited as long as he dared, until enemy shapes had almost reached the sundial half-way down the lawn.

He yanked the twine in his hand. The cord was tied off to the det-tapes of their remaining tubes, buried in the lawn itself. They went off in rapid series, hurling two or three bodies into the air.

Satisfied, Caffran leapt up, and scrambled out through the back of the greenhouse into the yard. Las-rounds flew past him. A mortar bomb exploded in the kitchen garden off to his left, and then another hit the greenhouse squarely.

The blast threw him onto his face. Mkvenner dashed across to him and dragged him back towards the kitchen doorway where Brostin was covering them. Cuu had already run inside out of the deluge.

Mkvenner got Caffran into the kitchen as two more mortar shells hit the barricade and the remains of the coal bunker. Stone fragments peppered the back wall of the manse. Everyone firing from a window ducked. A further shell hit the west side of the wall and brought the roof down into the pantry with a terrible crash.

'Okay?' Mkvenner snapped at Caffran. Caffran was dazed, and his shoulders and the backs of his legs were covered in shrapnel cuts.

'Fine!' he gasped, and got up to join Brostin at the door.

'Get that flamer up!' Mkvenner said. 'They'll be in range soon!'

The house shook as another mortar struck it. Broken tiles avalanched down into the yard. There were Blood Pact troopers all over the rear lawn now, coming in low on the far side of the barricade and the shredded greenhouse. Thick smoke and the flash of explosions fogged most of the view. The Ghosts fired at every target they could make out. From the first floor, Muril and Larkin were making the best of the kills.

'Somebody else get upstairs!' Feygor bellowed, blasting from the main kitchen window. Cuu leapt up and ran.

'The right! They're getting round from the fething right!' Gutes yelled over the link from the dining room. Mkvenner moved to the kitchen door and peered out east. Over the burning vestiges of the coal bunker, he could see Gutes's las-fire hammering at the hedge-veiled ditch running up the side of the manse.

'Keep that up, Gutes!' he snarled. 'Keep them ducking! I'll come around the front and set up a crossfire!'

'Read that!' Gutes sang back.

Mkvenner ran back along the hall from the kitchen, and unbolted the front door. The house vibrated with the rattle of gunfire and the batter of the mortars. The pots and pans on the stairs were quivering and spilling their contents as the whole manse shook. He felt a particularly loud bang that sounded like a mortar had taken the roof in. Mkvenner realised it was simply the thunder splitting right overhead.

He got the door open and edged out into the rain, weapon up, moving round the eastern side of the building. The roar of battle floated round from the rear.

The Blood Pact was already tearing through the ditch hedge into the front lawn area. One spotted Mkvenner, but the scout shot him dead before he could raise either weapon or cry. He fired again. Two more toppled backwards into the hedge, arms flailing.

Three more opened fire, and Mkvenner was forced to dodge back into the cover of the porch. Las-rounds whirred off the stone porch posts. From cover, he managed to hit two of the attackers and then made a dash for the hedge, hoping to cut off the ditch with an enfilade.

A grenade tumbled through the rain. Mkvenner threw himself out of the way, but still the blast lifted him and slammed him into the long, wet grass of the lawn.

He came round again moments later to see an iron mask leering at him, and a blade striking at his throat.

Mkvenner rolled and kicked his legs round, smashing the Blood Pact trooper over. Another one lunged at the Tanith with his bayonet, but Mkvenner grabbed the barrel, wrenched it out of the enemy's hands, and killed him with a savage blow using the stock. A las-round cracked at him from point-blank range, but Mkvenner had crouched low, and came up, scything the bayonet of the captured weapon through the belly of the third attacker. Without looking, he planted a kick backwards, breaking the neck of the first man, who was now trying to get up from the grass.

But there were more of them, so many more. Almost a dozen, rushing him, some firing. He sidestepped another bayonet, and a las-round ripped through his right thigh. Fuelled with pain, he rammed the blade of his borrowed rifle through the neck of the closest invader.

Full auto las-fire tore across the lawn, making trails of steam in the downpour. Three Blood Pacters fell immediately, then a fourth. Mkvenner opened fire with his lasrifle and took out two more before turning and sprinting for the porch.

In the porch doorway, Peterik stood, blasting furiously with Rerval's lasgun. Full auto.

The remaining Blood Pact exposed on the lawn either died or fled.

Mkvenner tumbled in beside him.

'Thank you,' he said.

'You need to get that leg wound treated,' said Peterik.

'I'll do it later, if there's a later,' said Mkvenner. 'Right now, we have to hold the front of the house. You up to that?'

Peterik nodded. 'Yes, sir. I am.'

AT THE REAR, a series of mortar rounds had struck the yard and blown paving slabs through the kitchen wall. Another two shells had slammed into the pantry, already a ruin. Caffran and Feygor were down behind the cast-iron bulk of the stove, firing through the shattered hole that had once been the main window. The kitchen door had been blown off its hinges, but Brostin was in the doorway, revving his flamer.

A trio of Blood Pact troops leapt the barricade and charged the kitchen. Brostin hosed them and they torched in their tracks, the grenades they carried blowing out and showering the fractured yard with metal chips, pieces of gristle and burning scraps of fabric. Brostin nursed the flamer, and sent a second flare right over the barricade, sizzling in the rain. They could hear screams. An enemy trooper, burning across his back and legs, ran hopelessly towards the greenhouse and fell when Feygor shot him.

Brostin had an infamous affinity with fire. Now the enemy was in range, he started bursting sprays of liquid flame up over the barricade and the wall of the kitchen garden, sliding it round angles that las-rounds couldn't touch. He washed the jumbled wood of the felled green house with a blanket of warm, orange fire, blistering the old paint and cooking the wood, and then ignited the toasted kindling with a spear of blue, super-hot fire. Another enemy voice rose up in a scream. A blizzard of touched-off grenades added to the raging fire.

The mortar rounds still thumped in. Caffran flinched as he heard one go through the roof. Cannon fire raked the back wall, splitting exposed brickwork and stone. The manse's original lime wash render had long since been shot away.

Feygor looked across at Caffran as they ducked another salvo.

'This what you wanted to stay here for?' he asked, sarcastically. Feygor always sounded sarcastic, but this was the real thing.

'No,' said Caffran. He pointed to the Tanith regimental badge on his jacket. 'I wanted to stay for this.'

Brostin's flamer spluttered and whooshed again. The stink of burning promethium filled the kitchen.

'They're rushing us!' Brostin yelled. 'They're rushing us!'

IT WAS OVER, Larkin knew. The manse was falling apart under the mortar rounds, and the back of the house was under assault from a battalion-strength enemy unit. The Blood Pact was in the side ditch too, he could hear that, and round the front.

He made what shots he could, knocking down scarlet shapes on the lawn and behind the barricade. But one thing was for sure. There were more enemy troopers outside than he had hot-shots left in his satchel.

He wondered if they'd bought enough time. He wondered where Jajjo was. He wondered if anyone would ever know what a thing they'd done there this day. That handful of them, against an army.

His vision was going again. The lights were dancing. He blinked hard and shook his head, trying to clear his eyes. Shaking his head made it feel like he was sloshing his brains around.

He wondered if the pain would overcome him before the Blood Pact reached him. Which would be quicker? Which would hurt less?

He took another shot, but missed. He fired again, and missed a second time. His eyes were so foggy and the pain so almighty. Pink, oblong stars. Firecrackers. Firecrackers...

A hand grabbed him by the back of the neck and slammed his face into the window sill. Larkin squealed in pain and passed out briefly.

Lijah Cuu held him by the back of his head, fingers pressing like iron tongs into the damaged region of the sniper's skull.

Larkin writhed, tears of pain rushing down his ashen cheeks.

'What...? What...?' he mumbled.

'We're dead now, Tanith, sure as sure. They're in at the doors and windows. We're finished. Except I'm not finished. I'm not going anywhere, even all the way to hell, without settling my business.'

'Feth!' screamed Larkin, trying to struggle free. Cuu's hands twisted at the fracture in the back of his skull and he gagged and howled. Blood spurted from Larkin's nostrils. 'You crazy bastard!' he spluttered. 'This isn't–'

'What? What, you little Tanith gak-face? The right time? That's funny, sure as sure. You have to pay, and if this isn't the time, there'll never be another.'

Cuu wrenched at Larkin's head again, and the sniper threw up. Cuu shoved him off onto the mattress.

Larkin tried to move, but the oblong pink stars filled his vision, merged into one huge firecracker that blasted through his mind.

He went into spasms. His back arched and his eyes rolled back until they were just bloodshot whites. Blood spattered as he bit his tongue. As the seizure smashed through his stringy body and limbs, he made an unearthly groan.

Cuu stepped back for a second in disgust. He drew his blade. Tanith straight silver, thirty centimetres long.

'You animal,' he growled, avoiding Larkin's thrashing limbs. 'Looks like I'll be doing you a favour, you freak.'

He raised the knife.

'Get off him, you bastard!' Muril spat. She stood in the doorway of the bedroom, her lasrifle aimed at Cuu's scar-split face.

She edged towards him. 'You shit. You little shit.'

Cuu rose, grinned his grin. 'I was just trying to help him, girly. Look at him. He's spazzing out. Let's help him before he bites through his gakking tongue.'

'Leave him alone! I saw you, Cuu. I saw what you were doing.'

'I wasn't doing nothing.'

'You were going to kill him. Like you killed Bragg. And God-Emperor knows who else. You piece of shit.'

'So what are you going to do, eh? Eh, girly? You gonna shoot me?'

'I might.'

'We're all dead anyway. Listen to the crap out there. They must be into the kitchen by now. Go ahead, shoot. It won't matter.'

'It'll matter to me, Cuu. I'll die happy.'

There was a stunning flash and a noise that sounded like thunder but wasn't. The bedroom wall exploded in, strewing bricks and plaster across the room. Another mortar shell came in through the attic overhead and blew out the landing behind them.

Muril tried to get up in the choking dust and smoke. There was no sign of her weapon in the debris, so she drew her warknife. Covered in shreds of plaster and curls of wallpaper, Larkin was still alive, and still convulsing and groaning on the mattress by the window.

Muril stumbled towards him, searching for Cuu's body in the rubble.

He was behind her, his blade in his hand.

With a cry, she swept round, as fast as any Tanith scout had ever moved, before or since.

Straight silver punched through flesh and bone and didn't stop until it had impaled the beating heart.

PART OF THE roof collapsed. Piet Gutes ducked as falling rafters tore through the ceiling of the dining room, crushing the long, polished table. The vases and precious porcelain tumbled off the shelves and smashed. The oil paintings had caught fire.

Gutes got up, spitting out dust. The ceiling was open right to the sky and rain drizzled down. He took a look up through the smashed window hole he had been defending. A red-painted light tank was rolling down the back lawn from the trees, enemy troops surging around it. It raked up the over-grown grass and knocked over the sundial. When it fired again, Gutes felt the manse shake. One of the pictures fell off the wall.

For the first time, he wondered who they were. Those solemn faces, dark with age, looking out from the frames. Staring at him from so far away.

The pictures burned, despite the rain.

Gutes saw movement at the window and fired. An iron mask lurched back. Shots came in, ripping into the floor. Gutes backed down the dining room, rainwater pattering off him, avoiding the smashed furniture and firing at the gap. Multiple points of gunfire tore through in reply.

A single dining chair had survived the collapse of the rafters. Gutes sat down on it and continued to fire at the window until his cell ran dry.

Half a dozen Blood Pact troopers scrambled in through the window, aiming their weapons at the lone figure sitting on a chair at the end of the room.

They started to shoot.

Gutes wondered if the old woman would make it. He hoped so, though he doubted it.

But it didn't matter any more.

Nothing matters if you're far enough away. That's what Piet Gutes had always told himself.

And now, at last, he was as far away as he could possibly be.

SEVENTEEN
FIRST AND LAST

*'There can be honour in life, and honour in courage,
and honour in action, but the most certain honour of all,
to man's regret, is the honour in death.'*

– Iaco Bousar Fep Golke, from his diaries

SMOKE WEPT OUT of the forest like blood from a wound. The storm had passed, heading out at last across the peaks of the Massif, but the air was still damp and the sky still black.

The sound of warfare continued to drift back through the pine stands of the Montorq. Small-arms, vehicle-mounted cannon, grenades.

Colm Corbec jumped down from the eight-wheeler APC he'd been riding in and called out to the unit groups ahead.

'Are we clear?' he yelled.

'Clear!' Varl shouted back.

'Go get me a sit-rep!' Corbec hollered.

'Sir,' said Jajjo, rising from his seat in the APC. 'I'd like to–'

'I know you would, son,' said Corbec. 'But I think maybe you should stay here for now.'

'I–'

'That's an order, lad.'

Corbec wandered up through the trees towards the smoking shell of the old, lonely house. 'The manse', Jajjo had called it.

To his left, light tanks and clanking sentinels of the Krassian Armoured ploughed up the valley through the trees, lending fire support to the First fire-teams Corbec had sent in ahead of him. A fairly serious firefight was occurring in the woods behind the house.

Commissar Hark trudged back to meet him. He was swinging a helmet in his hand.

'Trooper Jajjo was right,' Hark said, showing Corbec the helmet's iron mask. 'Blood Pact.'

'I never doubted Jajjo's word for a moment,' said Corbec quietly. 'The vox messages were plain enough.'

Hark nodded. 'Just so, Corbec. I'm just glad we mustered up and got here in time.'

'Did we, but?' Corbec said wearily.

'We've driven the Blood Pact force right back into the woods. Major Vikkers of the Krassian armour says they're in retreat, falling back up the valley to the high pass. Looks like the Krassian tanks scored a good few kills against enemy armour pieces and–'

'We've won, for today. I know that, Hark. I meant… did we get here in time for our own?' Corbec fell silent, looking at the smoking ruin of the manse.

'Nine platoon's checking it now. We–'

'Round up the rearguard and send them through,' Corbec told him abruptly. 'I'm going to see for myself.'

VARL WAS WAITING for him at the battered porch of the manse. Enemy dead littered the lawn. An old woman – Corbec had no idea who the feth she was – was kneeling on the gravel path and weeping over the body of a young Alliance soldier. On the steps of the porch, a Krassian corpsman was treating a Tanith trooper for multiple injuries. He was shouting out for a medic as he worked. The Tanith man was so covered in blood he was unrecognisable at first. A bad leg wound, a gut shot, a scalp wound, something messy through the left shoulder.

Corbec ignored Varl and knelt down beside the man. Only then did he realise it was Mkvenner.

'Feth, Ven! It was only meant to be a patrol!'

'That's all it was,' said Mkvenner, weakly blinking blood out of his eyes.

'You'll be okay,' Corbec said. 'Make him okay, feth it!' he said, looking up at the frantic corpsman.

'You got our signal then?' Mkvenner whispered.

'If you're going to waste talk, don't state the fething obvious. We got it, Ven, we came. We kicked their arses back into the woods. You did a fine job, you and the rest.'

'Commendations,' Mkvenner sighed.

'Just shut up now,' said Corbec.

Mkvenner shook his head. 'I may not get another chance to say this, Colm. I commend them all. All of them. They were true to the last. First and last. If Jajjo made it, then he deserves scout rank. Muril too, no question. Make sure she knows I commended her. And I want a special mention put in to Alliance GSC. Will you do that for me, sir?'

'Of course I will.'

'Private First Class Rufo Peterik, Sixteenth Brunsgatters. For valour. Can you remember that name, Colm?'

'I will, but I won't have to, Ven. 'Cause you're fething well not going to die.'

Krassian medicae ran up the front lawn to assist the corpsman. Corbec rose and turned to Varl.

'Tell me. How bad?'

'Piet Gutes is dead in that room there. Looks like he gave a good account of himself. Rerval's alive. Took a hit to the face in an earlier phase of action. Docs are with him now.'

'That's something,' Corbec sighed. He'd missed his vox man these last few days.

'Brostin, Feygor and Caffran made it too, though Brostin and Caff are hurt bad. Somehow Feygor came out without a scratch.'

'Luck of the devil,' Corbec said. 'What about the rest?'

'Larkin's touch and go. Doc Mtane's with him. Head wound. The doc doesn't know if he'll make it. Says we have to get Larks back to Ins Arbor for surgery.'

'Feth,' said Corbec.

'I–' Varl began.

'What?'

'I found Muril upstairs with Larks. The bastards had bayonetted her.'

Corbec closed his eyes. He felt a pain worse than any injury he'd ever received. 'I want to go see her,' he said.

'Chief–' Varl tried to stop him. 'You don't want to see that.'

'I need to, Varl. I need to.' Corbec pushed past the sergeant and walked up the steps into the house.

In the doorway, he paused and glanced back at Varl.

'What about Cuu?'

'Oh, he made it,' Varl said.

THERE WAS A lot of commotion around the house. Not the same sort of commotion that had all but demolished it, but still. Troop carriers were gliding up. Krassian tanks were churning up over the lawns and into the woods.

There was a gak of a fight going on up there in the trees.

Not his problem any more.

Lijah Cuu sat on an old bench at the side of the front lawn and watched it all.

He licked the blood from the straight silver of his warknife and slid it away into its scabbard.

EIGHTEEN
ENDING IN THE MIDDLE

'When I speak of a body in this way, I mean the body as a
figure for an armed force. To the leader, that force becomes
his body. He must care for it and drive it and feed it and see
to its well-being and its ills. It thuswise becomes his limbs,
and organs of life and sense, the body militant. Thus the
scale magnifies. All commanders and their men are bodies in
war, fighting and falling in the way of things as sole men
fight and fall and shew their woundings.'

– DeMarchese, *On The Use of Armies*

A WEEK LATER, in the dismal streets of Gibsgatte, more rain
fell.

Colonel-Commissar Ibram Gaunt, still limping slightly
from the rifle-round that had scraped him during the six-
hour break-out from the Shadik lines, came up the steps of
the Sezaria, a gold-domed building that dominated the skyline of the dirty northern city.

Bande Sezari sentries at the door checked his papers and
then bowed to admit him, the struthid plumes in their caps
touching the floor.

Gaunt nodded to them with genuine respect. He knew who the Bande Sezari were now. He'd seen several of them fight to the last.

An Alliance adjutant escorted him up three flights and along a splendid corridor of gilt-framed paintings. The adjutant knocked at a set of painted doors and announced him.

'Colonel-Commissar Gaunt, sir.'

Gaunt stepped in, the doors closing behind him, and saluted.

Supreme Commander Lyntor-Sewq rose, and came round his desk to greet Gaunt.

'Good to see you, Gaunt.'

'Sir.'

Lyntor-Sewq was a thin, bald man with a plucked moustache and limpid eyes. 'How are you, sir?' he asked.

'Well enough.'

'Leg troubling you?'

'Not so much, thank you for asking.'

'Rough ride you must have had, getting out from the enemy lines that night.'

'Indeed, sir. It took us a day and a half, all told, laying low, moving when it was clear.'

'Your stealthing arts. Why, they're the talk of the General Staff! You ran into trouble, though?'

'Yes, sir. Twice. The last time when we were almost clear. I lost a few good soldiers there.'

'A terrible shame, Gaunt. Drink?'

'I'll take a small amasec, sir.'

Lyntor-Sewq poured two drinks into priceless crystal glasses. He handed one to Gaunt.

'Here's to your efforts, sir,' said the supreme commander.

'And my dead,' returned Gaunt.

'Quite so.

They sipped.

Lyntor-Sewq led him over to a chart table on which the full expanse of the Aexe Cardinal war was laid out.

'Many doubted you, Gaunt. You and the Imperials. Of course, we were grateful for your intervention. But still… I won't ever mention your name to Redjacq Ankre.'

'If I never see him again, sir, I will not be forlorn.'

Lyntor-Sewq chuckled. 'We got the guns. The siege-guns. I'm sure you've been told. They were stuck right where you'd stranded them. A flight of marauder aircraft destroyed them the following night. Those marauders. Fine vessels. I'd dearly like a few to bolster the Alliance Air Corps.'

'I'm sure General Van Voytz will oblige. Actually, I expected to see him here today.'

Lyntor-Sewq smiled. 'He's gone south. To Frergarten. We're pushing up through the Montorq now, you know. And that's where I must thank you again. Your scout units, stemming the tide, calling a warning. Alerting us to the presence of the arch-enemy elite on Aexegarian soil. My plans have changed, of course. Radically. But I'm focusing on the new initiative, and I think we may have turned a corner. The war will be over by Candlemas.'

Gaunt finished his drink. 'I hope so, sir,' he said. 'Either that, or this war will last forever.'

Lyntor-Sewq looked down into his glass grimly. 'It takes as long as it takes,' he said.

Gaunt nodded. He'd been reviewing battle reports for the last week. They'd killed the super-guns and fronted the invasion through the Montorq and even so both actions seemed like tiny pieces of a whole.

Sarvo had been lost. The Meiseq Box punctured. The lower Naeme Valley overrun. The Ostlund Shield broken in two places. For every victory, a loss. For every metre taken, a death. The war simply ground on, like a furnace fed by manpower.

'I presume you'll be deploying my units to new locations?'

'Actually, no.' The supreme commander handed Gaunt a data-slate. 'New orders. From the Warmaster, relayed by the Astropathicus. Your regiment is being retasked. Navy transports are moving in system to collect you.'

Gaunt looked at the slate.

He felt a peculiar sense of shock. He'd never been pulled out of a warzone before the fighting was done. In his opinion, there was still a year or more of bloodshed to go on Aexe Cardinal before the Imperium could claim victory. Macaroth was pulling the Tanith First out. It was like ending in the middle of things. According to the slate, elements of the Second

Crusade Army were moving in to replace them and finish the job.

And his heart skipped when he saw the destination the Ghosts were heading to.

'The Emperor protect you, where you're going,' Lyntor-Sewq said.

'Thank you, sir.'

'I only asked you here today to give you this.'

He reached into his desk and produced a slim, oblong box covered in gold-flecked blue satin. Lyntor-Sewq opened it.

A Gold Aquila, pinned to a white silk ribbon, lay in the cushioned interior.

'This is to acknowledge your devoted service to Aexe Cardinal. The Order of the Eagle. The greatest honour it is in the high sezar's gift to bestow.'

Gaunt had seen one before, pinned proudly to Iaco Fep Golke's coat. He dearly wanted to take the medal and stuff it into Lyntor-Sewq's throat until he choked. Or at least refuse it. But he knew the trouble that would follow if he did either.

He allowed the supreme commander to pin it on him, and saluted. He'd wear it now, and never again.

As GAUNT STRODE out through the echoing hallway of the Sezaria, an officer of the Bande Sezari raced up to him with a package wrapped in brown paper.

'Sir,' he said. 'Tactician Biota said to expect you and give this to you with his compliments.'

Gaunt took the package with a vague nod.

BELTAYN WAS WAITING outside, sitting behind the wheel of a huge black staff car. His thumb was better. He could do gears now.

Gaunt got in the back.

'Sir?'

'Take us back to Rhonforq, Beltayn,' Gaunt said.

The motor car roared off from the long steps and turned into Gibsgatte's cross-town traffic, heading south.

In the back of the car, Gaunt stripped the brown paper off the parcel. Inside was an old edition of a book. He checked the spine: DeMarchese, *'On The Use of Armies'*.

Gaunt smiled, despite the deep misgivings aching through his heart.

There was a handwritten note from Biota tucked inside the cover.

'Colonel-commissar,' it began, 'I hope you find this instructive. I salvaged it from the lord general's library and I'm sure he won't miss it. As to the question you asked me...'

AT GAUNT'S URGING, they drove through the woodlands around Shonsamarl on their way back to Rhonforq. The sunlight played through the trees, dappling the car as it switched back and forth down the narrow, meandering lanes.

Beltayn pulled the car to a halt.

'We're lost, aren't we?' Gaunt said.

'No, sir,' said Beltayn. 'I'm Tanith. I don't get lost.'

'You got lost on the way through here.'

Beltayn shrugged. 'All I know is, sir, this is the place. Don't ask me why it's not here anymore.'

Gaunt got out of the car. The woodland looked familiar, very familiar. He was sure Beltayn was right.

There just wasn't a chapel there any more. There was no trace of the Chapel of the Holy Light Abundant, Veniq. Nothing, except the lingering perfume of a particular flower.

Beltayn stepped over to join him. 'Where did it go, sir?' he asked.

Gaunt handed Beltayn Biota's note so he could read it.

'As to the question you asked me, I have researched the Imperial records and found a mention of an Adeptus Sororitas warrior named Elinor Zaker. She was a key member of Saint Sabbat's retinue during the original crusade, and died on Herodor six thousand years ago.'

Beltayn shivered. 'Something's awry, sir,' he said.

'I think so,' said Ibram Gaunt.

ALL ALONG THE 58th sector of the Peinforq Line, the word was spreading. The Ghosts were being pulled out. Enervated, Daur went down the line, distributing marshalling orders to the platoons. They were to pull back the following night to the cathedral city of Ghrennes and await Navy collection.

The orders didn't say where they were heading, but all the troops were excited. It sounded significant. And most of them were just desperate to get out of the trench horror of Aexe.

Daur was torn. He wanted to see the First out of the murderous front line, but he was going to miss the XO role. Ana Curth had told him that Rawne was almost fit. In a day or two, the major would return to duty.

Daur conveyed the orders dutifully, getting the regiment to prep for off-lift.

He got Haller's platoon roused up, then Obel's.

Then he walked down the zagging trench to Soric's command post.

Daur looked in through the gas curtain. 'Chief? Get your men ready,' he said. 'We're shipping out tomorrow night.'

Soric was seated at the table in his gloomy dugout. He held a twist of blue paper in his fingers.

'Right you are, captain,' he said. 'I know.'

Daur shrugged and left.

Soric looked down at the paper in his hands. 'Ghosts leaving. Tomorrow night,' it read.

Soric balled it up and threw it aside.

Vivvo suddenly peered in through the curtain. 'Word is we're moving on, chief. Any idea where to?'

'No,' snapped Soric.

'Okay,' said Vivvo warily, backing out and leaving him alone.

Soric sat back. The gleaming brass message shell sat on the camp table in front of him. He waited, hoping, wishing. Then he reached forward and grabbed the shell.

Agun Soric unscrewed the cap and shook out the spill of blue paper.

He unfolded it and read what was written there, written in his own hand.

One word.

'Herodor.'

ABOUT THE AUTHOR

Dan Abnett lives and works in Maidstone,
Kent, in England. Well known for his comics
work, he has written everything from Mr
Men to the X-Men in the last decade, and
currently scripts *Legion of Superheroes* for DC
Comics and *Sinister Dexter* and *Durham Red*
for 2000 AD.
His work for the Black Library includes the
popular strips *Lone Wolves* and *Darkblade,* the
best-selling Gaunt's Ghosts novels, the
acclaimed Inquisitor Eisenhorn trilogy and
his fantasy novel *Riders of the Dead.*

More Warhammer 40,000 from the Black Library

THE EISENHORN TRILOGY
by Dan Abnett

IN THE 41ST MILLENNIUM, *the Inquisition hunts the shadows for humanity's most terrible foes – rogue psykers, xenos and daemons. Few Inquisitors can match the notoriety of Gregor Eisenhorn, whose struggle against the forces of evil stretches across the centuries.*

XENOS

THE ELIMINATION OF the dangerous recidivist Murdon Eyclone is just the beginning of a new case for Gregor Eisenhorn. A trail of clues leads the Inquisitor and his retinue to the very edge of human-controlled space in the hunt for a lethal alien artefact – the dread Necroteuch.

MALLEUS

A GREAT IMPERIAL triumph to celebrate the success of the Ophidian Campaign ends in disaster when thirty-three rogue psykers escape and wreak havoc. Eisenhorn's hunt for the sinister power behind this atrocity becomes a desperate race against time as he himself is declared hereticus by the Ordo Malleus.

HERETICUS

WHEN A BATTLE with an ancient foe turns deadly, Inquisitor Eisenhorn is forced to take terrible measures to save the lives of himself and his companions. But how much can any man deal with Chaos before turning into the very thing he is sworn to destroy?

More Warhammer 40,000 from the Black Library

THE GAUNT'S GHOSTS SERIES
by Dan Abnett

In the nightmare future of Warhammer 40,000, mankind is beset by relentless foes. Commissar Ibram Gaunt and his regiment the Tanith First-and-Only must fight as much against the inhuman enemies of mankind as survive the bitter internal rivalries of the Imperial Guard.

The Founding

FIRST AND ONLY

GAUNT AND HIS men find themselves at the forefront of a fight to win back control of a vital Imperial forge world from the forces of Chaos, but find far more than they expected in the heart of the Chaos-infested manufactories.

GHOSTMAKER

NICKNAMED THE GHOSTS, Commissar Gaunt's regiment of stealth troops move from world from world, playing a vital part in the crusade to liberate the Sabbat Worlds from Chaos.

NECROPOLIS

ON THE SHATTERED world of Verghast, Gaunt and his Ghosts find themselves embroiled in a deadly civil war as a mighty hive-city is besieged by an unrelenting foe. When treachery from within brings the defences crashing down, rivalry and corruption threaten to bring the Ghosts to the brink of defeat.

The Saint

HONOUR GUARD

As a mighty Chaos fleet approaches the shrineworld Hagia, Gaunt and his men are sent on a desperate mission to safeguard some of the Imperium's most holy relics: the remains of the ancient saint who first led humanity to these stars.

THE GUNS OF TANITH

Colonel-Commissar Gaunt and the Tanith First-and-Only must recapture Phantine, a world rich in promethium but so ruined by pollution that the only way to attack is via a dangerous – and untried – aerial assault. Pitted against deadly opposition and a lethal environment, how can Gaunt and his men possibly survive?

STRAIGHT SILVER

On the battlefields of Aexe Cardinal, the struggling forces of the Imperial Guard are locked in a deadly stalemate with the dark armies of Chaos. Commissar Ibram Gaunt and his regiment, the Tanith First-and-Only, are thrown headlong into this living hell of trench warfare, where death from lethal artillery is always just a moment away.

SABBAT MARTYR

A new wave of hope is unleashed in the Sabbat system when a girl claiming to be the reincarnation of Saint Sabbat is revealed. But the dark forces of Chaos are not oblivious to this new threat and when they order their most lethal assassins to kill her, it falls to Commissar Gaunt and his men to form the last line of defence!